The Roof Above

gail dwyer

Black Rose Writing | Texas

ISBN: 978-1-68513-370-2
LIBRARY OF CONGRESS CONTROL NUMBER: 2023944464
PUBLISHED BY BLACK ROSE WRITING
www.blackrosewriting.com

Printed in the United States of America
Suggested Retail Price (SRP) $22.95

The Roof Above is printed in Book Antiqua

*As a planet-friendly publisher, Black Rose Writing does its best to eliminate unnecessary waste to reduce paper usage and energy costs, while never compromising the reading experience. As a result, the final word count vs. page count may not meet common expectations.

The Roof Above

part one

before

chapter 1

May 2003
West Point, New York
I sat on the bleachers above the fifty-yard line, fanning myself with my program, as the Vice-President droned on about the Bush Doctrine and precision technology and the War on Terror. I knew I should be listening, but it was too hot, and I couldn't stop thinking about road-tripping with Matt to Georgia, finding a high-speed job at an accounting firm, and buying duvet covers. I couldn't stop wondering why Matt's parents didn't like me.

My best friend, Sara, sat next to me, and when they called Matt's name, we both stood and hooted and hollered as he walked across the stage, saluted with one hand, and received his diploma with the other. Then we sat back down and continued to fan ourselves through another few hundred cadets until they finally called Sara's fiancé's name. We stood again and cheered with Jake's parents, who sat in their very large pools of sweat on Sara's other side. By the time they reached the *Y*s, I sat perched on the edge of the bleacher, ready to bolt onto the field. I wanted to be the first to greet Matt.

Sara shooed me, her long, curly red hair bouncing up and down. "Kelly, go! Don't wait. It'll take us a while." She whispered so her future in-laws couldn't hear. An offensive lineman, Jake's size came from both sides of the family tree. His parents were gentle giants, so sweet, each of them as big as a house. They wouldn't be setting any land speed records making it down the crowded bleachers.

As the last cadet crossed the stage, Sara elbowed me. "Get a head start on his parents. They'll stick around to schmooze with the beautiful people. And when you see them, flash that ring. Maybe they forgot he proposed."

"Funny." I grinned at her sarcasm. "You're right about the schmoozing, though. They probably will. I should be able to beat them down there."

Matt's father was a general officer, West Point Class of '74, and he and his wife had been invited to sit in the distinguished visitor section with the bigwigs. When I met them for the first time the night before, they'd treated me like I had leprosy. They'd told Matt where they'd be sitting, but hadn't invited me to join them.

I scooted past the family sitting next to us and started down the wide concrete steps, crammed with others who had the same idea. After West Point's class of 2003 was officially released, and 873 brand-new second lieutenants tossed their white caps in the air, I was in the first throng of families and friends to amass on the field.

But it was crazy. Too many people. I searched for the twenty-yard line, where I was supposed to meet Matt and his family, but the white yard lines were already hidden under the feet of a thousand cadets and their families and friends. I squeezed in and out of uniformed cadets hugging each other, holding white tubes containing their diplomas high in the air. Their happiness poured out of them, like an eruption of pure elation, and it was hard to keep walking, to not stop and watch and smile at the scenes of joy. Mothers and fathers were crying, girlfriends were hugging and kissing, and I was panicking. My head was on a swivel and my heart beat too fast. I'd never find Matt.

In the middle of the chaos, I heard a loud, excited "KELLY!"

Alex, Matt's roommate and best friend, ran into me with his arms out and pulled me into his chest. When he finally released me, he took both my hands and held them in front of him. I was five feet ten, a hurdler in college, and Alex, a lanky blond, stood a few inches taller than me. When our eyes met, we laughed, and I felt the stress of the past four years tumble out of him.

A short-haired blonde woman in her forties, with a Kleenex in one hand and a water bottle in the other, bounced up and down on her toes next to us, smiling ear to ear. She wore the same flowered, no-sleeve A-line dress that I did. TJ Maxx. When we saw each other, we burst out laughing.

"I'm Alex's mother, and I'm a hugger," she said with a distinct drawl, and swooped in for a hug. "It's nice to finally meet you, Kelly. Love your dress."

Alex rolled his eyes, grinning, and introduced me to his father, younger brother, and sister.

"I'd love to stay and chat, but I've got to find the Carpenters," I said, peering through the crowd. "I don't see the twenty-yard line. With all these people."

Glancing left and right to get my bearings on the field, I noticed Alex and his mother staring with their mouths open. I followed their gaze, trying to see what they were looking at. A crush of happy people mobbed their cadets. *How would I ever find Matt in this chaos?* Two little boys jumped up and down, hanging on the arm of a new graduate; an elderly man with a cane solemnly shook the hands of another; a girlfriend kissed a third. There were too many people milling around: parents and siblings and grandparents and aunts and uncles, and even what I assumed was an older sister holding a baby. Amid the bedlam, I finally spotted Matt, taller by a head than most, standing with his parents.

Alex saw him when I did. "Follow me," he said. "I'll run interference through the crowd to get you to him."

I stayed close to Alex until we walked into General Carpenter talking to another man in uniform. Mrs. Carpenter hugged Alex, dabbing her eyes with a tissue. I ran up to Matt, but his embrace seemed less dramatic, less emotional than the one I'd shared with Alex. My timing was off. His parents had gotten to him first and hugged the enthusiasm out of him.

•　　　•　　　•

June 7, 2003

It was a million degrees outside, and the Catholic chapel had no air-conditioning, but when I saw Sara standing at the end of the aisle, I got goose bumps. My best friend, her red curls frizzing in the heat, her face shining pink with perspiration, was beaming. I felt her joy. It gave me the chills.

She adjusted her train and took her father's arm, and together they began the walk toward the altar. I squeezed my lips shut, willing the tears that were filling my eyes to stay put. My father sat in the back of the church, and as she approached his pew, I watched her turn toward him and smile. Sara. Only she would notice him sitting there alone on her big day.

When I first saw my father outside the church before the ceremony, I almost didn't recognize him. I'd seen him three weeks earlier at my graduation, but he'd cut his hair, and his thick brown curls barely extended over the collar of a suit I didn't know he owned. He was a history teacher and hockey coach at Forkton Middle School, and I'd never seen him wear anything other than Bruins sweatshirts and jeans. Months earlier, when he received the invitation from Sara, he told me he didn't want to miss her big day, and the opportunity to see me one more time before I drove to Georgia with Matt.

Sara told me my mother had RSVPed no, including a handwritten note saying that she had to work. The wedding was on the first Saturday in June, and it's not as if my mother was a brain surgeon on call. She was a middle school principal, but after four years as my roommate, Sara understood. My mother always had to work.

I stood on the altar in my maid of honor position, to the left of Jake, who leaned toward his approaching bride as if he wanted to run down the aisle and take her in his arms. Alex, the best man, stood on Jake's other side and wiped his hands on his pants. He rocked on his toes and smiled so wide, I could have put quarters in his dimples. It made me happy to see everyone so happy.

Sara's bridesmaids, two cousins and a friend from high school, stood in the first pew in front of her parents. Across the aisle, the groomsmen were arranged by height, a band of brothers from his past four years at West Point. Redheaded Tyler, the shortest, stood closest to the aisle, directly in front of his high school sweetheart, Heather, in the second pew. Turning to watch Sara walk down the aisle, Tyler's left hand rested on the top of the back of his pew, enclosing Heather's hand. They were too cute.

Dark-haired Sean stood next to Tyler. Sean scanned the church, looking for his latest girlfriend. I wasn't sure who this plus-one was, but most of his dates were pink or purple-haired, heavily pierced, and tatted with a lot of ink. I had met all three of them—Sean, Tyler, and Heather—on the same spring break trip to the Bahamas our junior year of college. Sara had talked me into going because Jake was going with a bunch of cadets. Sean seemed different to me, less of the All-American athlete-scholar type than the other cadets, but when I asked Matt about it, he'd said, "We're all brothers," and shrugged. I didn't bring it up again.

Matt, broad-shouldered and thick-necked, hovered a half foot above Sean on his other side. I stared at him, hoping to connect, but he was somewhere else, staring into space. Since graduation a week earlier, he'd been zoning out, either preoccupied or pensive. I wasn't sure which. After four years of living in the barracks, his life had changed drastically. I figured this was an adjustment period and would pass.

I fixed my eyes on him, hoping he'd feel me staring, and he finally did as Sara passed his aisle. He tilted his head toward me and smiled. I melted. My heart fluttered, as it always did when his deep brown eyes met mine. Matt looked like he stepped off a recruiting poster, high cheekbones, perfect lips, a chiseled chin. He hadn't shed a tear. *When we get married, he'll be the rock,* I told myself as I wiped my eyes, watching Sara's father kiss her on the cheek before giving her away.

I stood a few feet away from the bride and groom, but their love was so intimate, I felt like I was infringing on their privacy. I smiled when I saw Matt inspecting the stained-glass window behind the altar. I was confident we'd grow this type of love once we drove away from West Point. I never connected the serious speeches from the podium at graduation with my future. I never connected the War on Terror, or Afghanistan, or Iraq, to my life.

I couldn't have been more clueless.

chapter 2

June 7, 2003
West Point, New York
The reception was held near the barracks at the West Point Club, a faded beige brick building with tall windows overlooking the Hudson River. Matt and I walked inside and found my father gazing out the window at a freighter plowing up the river. I wanted to talk to my father before we sat down to eat. He was driving back to New Hampshire after the wedding, and I had the feeling that he wanted to tell me something. I wasn't sure what, but I'd convinced myself that's why he drove to this wedding.

"Want a beer, Mr. McGowan?"

"Sure, Matt, thanks," my father said. "But please. Call me Bill."

"Um, yes, sir," Matt said awkwardly. He looked at me. "Wine? Beer?"

"White wine, thanks." I smiled to suppress a sigh. I appreciated Matt's consideration, but I liked where his hand was, resting on my lower back. I put my arm around his waist, clinging, not excited about him leaving me for the open bar. Since his graduation, we'd stayed with friends of his parents who lived on West Point. Mrs. Carpenter had arranged it so we could "save money," but I was convinced it was because she wanted me on the bottom bunk in the eight-year-old's room, and Matt two floors below me in the basement. Earlier that morning, I happily said goodbye to my pigtailed roommate and checked into a hotel in Highland Falls, the town outside West Point's gates. I hoped to make up for lost time as soon as we got to the hotel room.

While people drifted into the ballroom, I stood with my dad and watched Matt work his way toward the crowded bar, stopping every two feet to talk to someone. I saw him point me out to Heather and Tyler, and behind them, I saw Alex with his arm around Kate. *What's that all about? And no one told me?*

Kate was a cadet in their company, one of thirty members of the same class who'd lived together for the past four years. I'd only seen her in uniform or jeans. I barely recognized her in the snug, low-cut silver dress and silver sandals with four-inch spike heels. She looked amazing, and she looked like she knew it. That worried me. Before I'd met them, Alex and Kate had been together — until she broke his heart. Alex was such a good guy; I didn't want to see anyone hurt him.

When I'd first met Alex, no one else was there. We'd checked into the hotel and Sara had immediately taken off with Jake, so I'd wandered down alone to a bonfire at the beach. Alex saw me and we sat and talked for an hour, until a bimbo in a bright pink string bikini pranced over, dragging another cadet behind her. She'd grabbed Alex's arm possessively and led him away, leaving me with the other cadet — Matt. Months later, after Matt and I were a couple, I learned Alex had dated Ashleigh, the blonde, in high school, but they hadn't been a couple for years. Also, she was bonkers. Matt had laughed, telling me Alex was a chick-magnet for women who were bonkers.

"What are you thinking?" One problem with having a father who read your mind was that your father could read your mind.

"Nothing, Dad," I answered too quickly. "Hey, there's Heather and Tyler." I waved and Heather waved back. They were flagged down by Jake's father on their way toward us.

"I think I remember meeting them," my father said. "At that hockey game?"

"Yeah, the Holy Cross game we went to. They got married by the justice of the peace, the day after graduation," I explained.

Not that I thought he'd say something inappropriate, but I never knew with the McGowans. They're not known for their filters.

"They have a baby, Caleb," I rushed. "Six months old now. We're going to their real wedding next week in North Carolina."

He nodded as they approached. I wasn't sure if he remembered Heather got pregnant when we were in the Bahamas, but cadets aren't allowed to be married or legally responsible for anyone, so she had the baby and lived with her parents. When Matt called to tell me Heather had the baby, it was December of our senior year. That was our first real argument.

"Tyler should quit, go home, and marry her," my straight-arrow-black-and-white-go-by-the-rules fiancé had said matter-of-factly. This was the same guy who wouldn't hold my hand walking around West Point because of the rules about PDA, public displays of affection. Also, he stopped at yellow lights. Where I came from, yellow meant speed up.

I disagreed and told him so. "It makes more sense for him to graduate."

"No," he'd argued impatiently. "West Point is founded on discipline and rules. You're not allowed to be married. You're not supposed to be responsible for others."

I didn't cave. "So, because there's some dumb rule, he should toss his future away? Because if you ask me, it makes no sense for him to quit his senior year, when they could wait five months and get married then."

"It's not an option. Those are the rules. He's the father and should be with his family."

"Agree to disagree." I let it go. I had a test in advanced auditing the next day, and the phone call had become too annoying.

Tyler and Heather had finally disengaged from Jake's father and walked up to my father and me. Tyler's arm draped comfortably over Heather's shoulder, and they looked so right together. I was glad that he'd stayed and graduated.

Tyler walked right up to my father and embraced him like he'd known him since birth. My father stepped out of the hug awkwardly, wobbling a bit on his feet, grinning. Heather winked at me, understanding that New Englanders typically aren't big on public displays of affection. I laughed out loud.

"Dad, you remember Tyler and Heather. You met them at that Holy Cross hockey game."

"Sure." My father smiled. "It's good to see you again."

"We love your daughter," Heather told my father. "We first met her at the airport in Atlanta on the way to Nassau. Matt's a lucky guy."

"Oh, he out kicked his coverage, for sure," Tyler agreed.

"Who are y'all talking about?" Alex asked, walking up with Kate. "Who out kicked his coverage?"

He turned to Tyler, then me, and my reddening cheeks answered his question.

"Ah, yes, my roommate. He sure as hell did. Excuse my language, Mr. McGowan."

My father laughed. "Good to see you again, Alex. Hey, I know Matt and Kelly are going to Fort Benning in Georgia," he said. "Where are the rest of you going?"

"I'm going to Fort Sill, Oklahoma, sir," Tyler responded. "We get married next week, back home in Raleigh, take some leave, and then we'll drive out to Oklahoma. My school starts in

September and lasts four months. After I graduate, we'll move to Fort Stewart in Georgia."

"What about you, Kate?" I asked. "Dad, have you met Kate? She was in the same company as Matt, Alex, and Jake."

"It's nice to meet you, Mr. McGowan." Kate smiled her perfect I-should-be-on-the-cover-of-Cosmo smile. "I'm going to Fort Lee, Virginia, for quartermaster school—that's logistics. Then Germany. Not sure where I'll land in country until I get there."

"That's great," my father said. "We'll have someone to visit when we travel to Europe."

I laughed. "If you leave New Hampshire to see Gram in Dorchester, it's a big day. Who are you kidding?"

"Where's Dorchester?" Kate asked politely.

"Boston," I told her, shaking my head, smiling. "About forty-five minutes from where we live in the boondocks in New Hampshire. My dad grew up there. My grandmother and his brothers never left."

"Well, Mr. McGowan," Alex said, "if you ever get the travel itch to visit Lower Alabama, you're always welcome. I'll be in flight school at Fort Rucker with Jake and Sara, and it's only two hours from Fort Benning, so when you visit Georgia, drive on over to the Home of Army Aviation in Alabama. Bring your daughter to come visit us, and," — seeing Matt walk up to us, carrying two beers and a glass of wine, Alex grinned—"I guess you'll have to bring my roommate, too."

"I'd hit you if I had a free hand." Matt said. "Hey, Sara's mother told me to tell everyone to go sit down. They're getting started soon."

Tyler nodded and led Heather to their table. Kate whispered something to Alex before she followed them. Matt handed me my wine and my father his beer and walked toward the head table with Alex.

"That's my cue, Kel," my father said. "I'll walk you to your seat and then hit the road. Before I go, I want to talk to you."

"Wait. What? You can't go now," I said, surprised. I stopped in place and stared at him.

"We haven't eaten yet!"

"Oh, I didn't RSVP for the meal. I've got a four-hour drive tonight."

My heart sank. It hit me then that he was leaving, and I didn't know when I'd see him again. My shoulders slumped and my eyes watered.

"You can't stay? We barely talked."

He shook his head and put his beer down on a table next to the wall. "Sorry, Kel."

I wanted to argue, but he meant it. He was leaving. I felt my body stiffen. "What do you have to tell me?"

"It's not a big deal," he said, watching the crowd mosey toward their tables. "But I wanted you to know. Megan's on her way home. To New Hampshire. Moving back in with your mother. I wasn't sure when the last time you'd talked to them. Or if they told you."

I'd seen my mother at my graduation three weeks earlier. I didn't remember the last time I talked to Megan. She never picked up when I called, and I'd stopped trying. I hadn't seen her in over six months, and the only reason I saw her then was because Matt's mother had decided the day before Thanksgiving to *unin*vite me to their house.

When I'd walked into our living room the night before Thanksgiving, I'd been surprised to see Megan. Two years younger than me, she'd moved to Maine with a boyfriend shortly after she barely graduated from high school. I was surprised she was home, but mostly I'd been completely caught off guard at her appearance. While I was brunette, brown-eyed, tall, and wiry, Megan had always been blond and blue-eyed, shorter than me, and curvy, with huge breasts. But last

November, her pale skin hung off her bones. Her blond hair was dyed jet black. Seemingly out of it, she barely acknowledged my parents telling her they'd found a rehab in Rhode Island that would take her.

"I haven't talked to either of them. What happened?" I asked my father. "I thought she got out of rehab. Didn't she move back in with her boyfriend in Maine?"

He frowned. "I'm not sure what happened with that boyfriend. But she called and told your mother she was coming back home."

My mother treated Megan like she walked on water, which meant my father could never find the balance between disciplining her and keeping my mother happy. When I left for New Hampshire State, Megan was a junior at Forkton High. She fell in with the wrong crowd and stayed there. When I came home, she snapped and scowled at me, angry at me for not being with her, there all the time, upset that I'd escaped the house. I gave up trying to be friendly to her. It was easier to ignore her.

"She'll be in your old room. But if you come home, there's always room at my place."

I sighed. Before my senior year of college, my parents, after twenty miserable years together, finally divorced. My mother, who in a previous life must have been a prison warden, stayed in the three-bedroom house we grew up in. My father moved into a studio apartment the size of a refrigerator. Which meant I had no place to stay long term for free in New Hampshire. *Good thing I was moving with Matt.*

"Aunt Patty told me to tell you she lives four hours from where you'll be in Georgia. She hopes you'll visit." He smiled, his attempt to end the conversation on a happier note. "But I gotta go. Before everyone sits down and it's obvious that I'm leaving."

My voice stuck in my throat. When I left for college, I rarely returned home. It was not fun living in a house with two parents who only talked to each other if one needed the other to pass the salt at the table. But my father drove to every track meet and visited me every few weeks to take me to lunch or dinner and catch up. I kept in touch with some friends from high school, had a few close friends from the track team at New Hampshire State, and Sara was like a sister to me. It was unusual, but my father had always been one of my closest friends.

And I was moving to Georgia. Away from all of them. Where I knew no one but Matt, and where I had no job. I was leaving my father, the only normal family member I had. I couldn't talk, or I'd cry.

"Hey, I'll visit," he said. "I'll call after you get settled in. No tears. No goodbye. Just see you soon."

Before I could respond, he turned and walked out of the ballroom. I hated the McGowan Irish goodbyes, and I thought about following him, but Sara and Jake had sat down, and the DJ was telling everyone to please fill your glasses. Plus, if I followed my father out to the car and said goodbye, it would only make me teary. So I walked to my seat and sat down, picked up the peach napkin under my silverware, and wiped my eyes. I looked for Matt, but his seat was empty. I saw him at the bar. *Did the bartender just slide two shots in front of him?*

Alex, sitting on the other side of Jake, tilted back in his chair. He mouthed, "Are you okay?"

I sighed and shook my head. No. When he started to get up to walk over to me, I waved my hands in front of me, and mouthed back, "I'm okay, really."

Matt turned from the bar, holding a bottle of beer, and walked toward his seat, searching for me as he zigzagged between tables. When he saw me, he smiled, and I forced a half smile back. *I'm okay. Really.*

chapter 3

June 7, 2003
Three hours later
West Point, New York

I was not okay when Matt threw up all over my dress. At least we were outside. I'd dragged him off the dance floor, thinking a good dose of fresh air would help sober him up. Instead, it brought a tsunami of barf that caught me off guard, splashing the front of my dress before I scrambled out of the way. After he slurred apologies and stumbled away, I yanked off my sandals, pulled my dress away from my skin, and stormed off to sit on the steps of the building next door, away from everyone, away from him. Matt sat in the grass on the side of the West Point Club. I watched him, not sure if I should cry or scream. My throat felt too thick to do either.

Tired of looking at him, I slumped forward, put my head in my hands, and moped. I lifted my head when I heard someone approach.

"I helped him get to his truck," Alex said, handing me a towel to wipe up the barf. "I saw you drag him out of there and followed y'all. I didn't want an MP to find him sitting out there. His truck was unlocked. Do you have the keys?"

I looked over to where Matt had been sitting, and sure enough, he was gone. "Thanks, yeah," I mumbled. "The keys are in my purse."

"Come on, let's get out of here." He offered me his hand. "I'll drive you to the hotel. Where's your purse? I'll get it. You can go wait by the truck."

I didn't argue. "Under my seat. Thanks."

I walked barefoot to the parking lot, holding my sandals in my hand, and when I saw Matt passed out in the back seat of his F-250, my anger consumed my self-pity. I wanted to scream. When Alex arrived with my purse, I tasted blood. I'd bit open my bottom lip.

"I can drive," I fumed, trying to control my voice. Opening my purse, I took out a crumpled, used Kleenex and held it to my lip. "You go back in there. Thanks, though."

He shook his head, opened the passenger door, and helped me step up into the truck. "He's too heavy. There's no way you can carry him. I wasn't drinking. Well, some beers, but I can drive."

I couldn't talk. Handing Alex the keys, I stared straight ahead, furious at Matt for ruining my best friend's wedding.

When we got to the hotel, Alex helped me step out of the truck before he pulled Matt's arm over his shoulder and dragged him into the room. Walking straight to the bathroom, he turned on the cold water in the shower. Matt leaned on the wall outside the bathroom door, staring at the rust carpeting on the floor. He didn't make eye contact with me. He knew better. Or maybe he figured keeping his head down would reduce the probability of repeat barfing. I grabbed a pair of boxers from his bag on the floor and threw them in the bathroom for him to change into after he showered. Glancing at my dress, Alex handed me a towel before he closed the bathroom door.

As soon as the door closed, I stepped out of the dress, thought about throwing it in the trash can, remembered how much it cost, and gingerly stuffed it in the hotel laundry bag. Wrapped in the towel, I waited for them to finish in the bathroom.

As he stepped through the door, Matt glanced at me once. Water dripped off his massive frame, his brown eyes watery and sad. I wondered if Alex dousing him with cold water for fifteen minutes had sobered him up a bit, but he immediately cast his eyes down after seeing my glare. It figured. Our first night alone together since he graduated. No way in hell would I get into that bed with him. I'd sleep on the floor.

Alex pulled a light blanket over Matt and turned his head to the side. Matt's eyes closed before they hit the pillow, and Alex turned to me. He looked at the ratty hotel towel wrapped around me and grimaced, but his eyes shone with empathy. "The shower's gross."

"Ugh." I flipped the fan on as I walked into the bathroom, then poked my head out to see Matt already asleep on the bed. Turning to Alex, I said, "Thanks, Alex. I ..." I choked up and couldn't finish.

"Take a shower. You'll feel better," he said.

I let the hot water soak over me, as if it could wash away my anger at Matt, my sadness about leaving my father, my anxiety about moving to Georgia. I thought about my friends from high school who were sharing an apartment in Boston and thought I was nuts for moving to Georgia with a guy I'd dated long distance. I thought about my friends from college who'd wanted me to move to New York City with them so I could live in a room the size of a shoebox and party before I settled down. Could they be right? Was I making a mistake?

Finally, I ran out of hot water. Naked, I opened the bathroom door and stepped out into the room. I jumped when I saw Alex sitting on the end of the bed.

"What the hell? Shit!" I turned and ran back into the bathroom. "I didn't know you—you were s-still here," I stammered, my face peering through the door. "What are you doing?"

"I'm sorry! Damn! I should have told you I was still here! I'm so sorry, Kelly. Damn. I'm sorry. Do you need me to get you something? Want your bag?"

He stood with his hand on his forehead, his eyes darting anywhere but at me.

"Um, yeah, that blue suitcase in the corner. Some sleep pants and a T-shirt. But you don't have to stay. Go back to the reception." I wondered if Kate was waiting for him, but I didn't have the energy to ask.

"I will," he said, handing my clothes through the partially opened door. He looked away, as if that would erase what he'd already seen. "I wanted to make sure he only had one barf in him tonight. I'm going to borrow a pair of his gym shorts and a T-shirt and get out of this uniform."

He'd left his dress coat in the truck, but he still had his uniform shirt and pants on.

When I finished changing and stepped out into the room, Alex was sitting on the floor at the foot of the bed, wearing Matt's shorts and a T-shirt, watching ESPN on mute. I sat next to him and we listened to Matt snore lightly behind us.

I stretched my arms out in front of me, my fingers connected, then released them, crossing them in front of my chest, hoping it would relax some of the tightness in my neck and shoulders. It didn't. "I'm so pissed off," I snapped. "What's the matter with him? What was he thinking?"

"I'm not sure he WAS thinking." Alex leaned back against the end of the mattress.

"Seriously, Alex. What's going on?"

He waited a few seconds, thinking. "He messed up, Kel. But he's a good guy. I've never seen him this drunk—this is a fluke thing for him. I think it's the pressure. He's got a lot going on."

"Like what? I thought this was the fun time—you guys graduated. No more school and rules. Free and easy. Out in the big world. What's he got going on?"

Alex opened his mouth and then closed it again. He heaved himself up off the floor, peered down at me, his eyes full of compassion.

"Are you okay?" he asked.

"No. I'm not. I'm thinking, 'Oh my God. What did I do?' I blew it, turning down that job offer in Boston. I could be living with my old friends. Could have a real job. What am I doing?"

"I've never seen him drink like this before." He stood over me, considered Matt asleep on the bed, then sat back down next to me on the floor.

I bit my lip, trying not to look or sound insecure, but I still asked. "Never? You've never seen him this hammered?"

Alex stared at the TV, oblivious to the baseball game on mute. "He was always with Eve. She wasn't much of a drinker."

I sighed, dropped my head, and stared at my arms, still crossed on my chest.

The headlights of a car flashed by the window. Alex watched the lights fade away and turned to me slowly. "He loves you. He does. It was those shots. He never does shots. He only drinks beer. He's going to feel awful about this."

"Yeah. Sure. Take the truck back," I told him, tired of the excuses. I stood and got the key from my purse. "Leave it on the back wheel well. We'll get it tomorrow. I've got my car here. Thanks. For all this."

I wanted to hug Alex, to make sure he knew how grateful I was, but he'd just seen me naked, and something told me a hug would be awkward. I stood looking pitiful, and he lifted his hand in a half-assed wave before he opened the door to leave. If I'd known it would be so long before I saw him again, despite the nudity bit, I'd have gone for the hug.

chapter 4

June into July 2003
Fort Belvoir, Virginia
Raleigh, North Carolina
Fort Benning, Georgia

The morning after Sara's wedding, Matt woke up enormously remorseful and embarrassed. He begged my forgiveness repeatedly and tried to convince me it would never happen again. Matt wasn't the type of guy who showed emotion. When his eyes watered as he promised me he'd never drink like that again, I agreed to open the door to forgiveness. He tiptoed through it and piled on so much kindness, I almost quit worrying about our next stop: his family's house in Virginia.

The first and only time I'd met Matt's parents was the night before his graduation and they'd made it crystal clear they weren't enamored with me. I'd never met his younger brother, Tim, a senior in high school, who adored his big brother and hung out with us nonstop. Tim helped make me feel comfortable, but didn't ease the awkwardness of being in that house. We spent two overnights in separate bedrooms, because his very Catholic parents didn't believe in sex before marriage. Plus, they didn't like me. That baffled me. Most people liked me. It bugged me they didn't, and it bugged me that Matt didn't try very hard to convince them I was going to be around for a while.

"What's up with them?" I asked Matt. "They act like I'm a stray puppy you brought home from the pound."

He laughed, stopping mid chuckle when he saw my eyes narrow and lips close.

"You told them we're engaged. Right? I mean, my car's in your driveway with everything I own crammed into it."

We were in the guest room; the walls covered with décor from Germany and Korea and other places Matt had lived as a kid. The Army was like a foreign country to me, one I'd never visited or read the travel guide about. I'd lived in the same house in New Hampshire my entire life.

Matt stood near his father's framed West Point diploma on the wall between assorted awards and medals. He turned and walked toward me, sitting on the bed. "Yeah, they know we're engaged."

"They don't seem too happy about it," I whined.

He shrugged. "They'll get used to it." He plopped down on the bed and pulled me on top of him, his hands on my bottom. Suddenly he heard his mother in the hallway and, with one sudden jerk, rolled me off him and sat straight up on the bed.

"You're afraid of her!" I teased, sitting up next to him.

He nodded and half-kiddingly said, "You bet your ass I am! Don't talk about living together at Fort Benning," he whispered. "They haven't asked and I'm not bringing it up."

I was beginning to realize his family wrote the book on conflict avoidance.

We drove from his house to Heather and Tyler's wedding in Raleigh and it was fun, but I missed Sara and Jake, who were on their honeymoon in Hawaii, and Alex, who was at his brother's high school graduation. Kate was there, though, dancing her tight butt off. I wasn't sure what was going on with her and Alex. Matt told me he didn't care. He was like that.

•　　•　　•

The day after Heather and Tyler's wedding, on the last leg of our trip to Fort Benning, Georgia, I followed Matt's black pickup truck down a single-lane road bordered on both sides by endless pine trees. My eyes widened at the barrenness; my heart sank at the sad desolation. The tree line was dotted with rusted worn trailers or wheelless corroded cars hoisted on cinder blocks. My stomach felt like I swallowed a brick. *You're not in Kansas anymore, Dorothy.*

A thin, crinkled old man wearing overalls sold boiled peanuts from a makeshift stand. At the other end of the driveway, a Confederate flag, that looked like it had been painted shortly after the Emancipation Act, peeled off one side of a ramshackle wood barn. But the oversized white wooden sign in a vast empty field in the middle of nowhere put me over the edge. A six-foot devil with pointy ears, a thin mustache, evil squinty eyes, and a tall, flaming pitchfork stared back at me. Next to him, big black letters read: IF YOU DON'T GO TO CHURCH, THE DEVIL WILL GETCHA.

Oh my God. What did I do?

Every possible alternate scenario flashed through my mind. I could sleep on a cot in Kim and Sharon's apartment in Boston and find a job waitressing while I looked for an accounting job. I could squeeze into Linda's apartment in New York City and work at a fast-food place. I sighed. If Matt hadn't redeemed himself after Sara's wedding, I'd have turned around at the next exit and headed north at the sight of that devil.

The blinker on Matt's truck flashed. I used my shoulder to wipe my devil-induced tears and followed him into an old country gas station, a faded white shingled building with two rusty pumps out front. Jumping out of his truck, he signaled to me he'd go in and pay, and I turned off my car. When he came back out, I hadn't moved. Since he walked into that gas station, the only thing I'd done was roll down my window to prevent my immediate death from heatstroke. He jogged over to me, and when he saw my face, blotchy and red, he leaned forward, touching my cheek. "Hey, what's the matter? Are you okay?"

Nodding, I mumbled, "I might have had a little meltdown. This place is different, Matt."

He motioned me to get out of the car and pulled me into a sweaty embrace. "Yeah, it's pretty rural. But Columbus isn't like this, really. It's a city. It'll be great."

I exhaled into his chest. I hoped he was right. I hoped the accounting firms in Columbus weren't in barns with Confederate flags painted on them.

After I filled my tank, I hustled inside the gas station to get a bottle of water. Matt was still filling his ginormous gas tank when I returned.

"Oh my God," I said, my eyes wide.

He cocked his head and looked at me as I smoothed the frizz out of my hair. This humidity was going to kill me.

"I don't know what that old man just said to me!" I handed Matt the water bottle.

He laughed and took a sip. "I'm betting he didn't understand a thing you said to him, either." He handed me the water. "We're only about an hour out. Are you all right?"

"Yeah, but I feel like I landed on a different planet."

"I'm glad you're with me," he said, leaning over to kiss me on my forehead, before climbing back into his truck.

I turned on the radio, moved the dial to find something not country, settled on a classic rock station, and kept driving, thinking about Matt. He'd been so sweet, but every few days, he lost focus and our conversations shifted off-balance. I brought it up after it happened and he said he didn't know what I was talking about, then apologized for whatever it was he did that bothered me. His apologies became a blanket response to forgive him and move on.

He was jittery, maybe because he was worried about doing well in the Army or performing to his father's standards. Or maybe he'd always been this way, and I didn't know because I wasn't around him twenty-four/seven.

We finally emerged from the land of pine trees and entered the city of Columbus, where there were Country BBQs and Popeyes and Piggly Wiggly grocery stores. I followed Matt's truck into a Burger King parking lot. I parked next to him and watched him get out, walk around to the passenger door, and toss a box that had been on the front seat back behind the seat, beside a cooler and lacrosse stick.

"You'll have to drive with me when we go on post," he explained, pointing to the space he had cleared on the seat. "You don't have an ID card, so you won't be able to drive onto Fort Benning without me. We'll leave your car here and get it later tonight."

I grabbed my purse, locked my car, and jumped up into his truck. "Post is Fort Benning, right? Is that what you mean? Why do you need an ID card? I didn't need one at West Point, right?"

"Yeah, post is Fort Benning. They have a gate, like they did at West Point, with military police manning the gate. You had to show your license at West Point," he said. "Now you have to get a visitor's pass, even with the license. Security stuff," he told me, starting the truck, and driving out of the parking lot.

"Oh, so I guess we won't live on post? Heather said they were going to live on post at Fort Sill."

"No." He shrugged. "We can't, since you don't have an ID card, but I'd rather not, anyway. I'll want to get away from the place after work."

"Oh," I said, and then I remembered something. "That's why Heather and Tyler got married right after graduation. To get the benefits. The ID card, medical insurance, that stuff?"

He beeped his horn at a rusted pickup truck loaded with old furniture that cut him off, then replied quickly, "Yeah. They wanted to get Caleb on Tricare as soon as they could."

"Should we do that?" I blurted. The minute the words came out of my mouth, I wished I could take them back. Sometimes I did that. Words that were supposed to stay in my head spouted out of my mouth before I could stop them. I looked out the window at a series of tattoo parlors and nail salons. I wasn't sure

I wanted to get married so soon. I wanted to live together first, to make sure our relationship was really what I thought it was. We'd dated long-distance and living together made sense. If I was honest with myself, Matt's zoning out scared me a little. But the health benefits through Tricare and on-post privileges were worth considering.

Matt exhaled, tapping a finger on the wheel. "My parents asked that. They don't think it's a good idea. Not that you'd ever do this, but they've seen soldiers' wives clear out their husbands' accounts when the guy was in the field and then take off with the money."

I flushed with irritation. "I can't believe they'd even think that."

"They didn't say you'd do it. They said they didn't think it was smart. To get married for the paperwork," he said apologetically.

"Well, it gets me mad they'd think that about me." Truthfully, I was equal parts mad and relieved.

Matt didn't respond. Focused on the road, he peered out the windshield, looking for signs for the gate to Fort Benning.

"I don't know." I conceded. "I guess when we get married, it shouldn't just be for legal benefits. When we find the perfect date, the wait will be worth it."

He turned and smiled, then reached for my hand.

"Are you nervous?" I asked, squeezing his hand. "Signing in here? I feel like you're stressed about something."

He turned to me, grinning. That one grin made my worries dissipate. "Nah," he said. "I'm good. Sorry. I guess I've been focused on getting us settled in."

•　　•　　•

Two days later, we moved into a one-bedroom furnished apartment with a one-car garage located close to the Fort Benning gate in a maze of gray brick buildings and interlaced stairwells. It was infested with roaches the size of small cats. The air conditioner burped out warm air and it was hotter than Hades outside. I only knew Matt, who left the apartment before the sun came up, and was the last lieutenant to pull into the parking lot every night.

Once I'd moved everything we owned into the apartment—this took a day—I bought the local newspaper and scoured the Help Wanted ads. Unless I wanted to sell used cars, inhale nail fumes, or drive a semitrailer, I was out of luck. So, the next morning, I put on a dress and makeup, drove downtown, and knocked on business doors, trying to look confident and not too desperate. I'd worked since I was thirteen—babysitting, answering the phone at a tax firm, tutoring, counseling at summer camps, and waitressing. I had a tireless work ethic. I had an accounting degree, and I ran track for four years in college. Who wouldn't want to hire me?

Everyone.

I refused to give up. I smiled at four different secretaries, in four different businesses, along the main street. When I trudged into the fifth company, my cheeks hurt from my forced cheerfulness. I handed my resume to an older woman with a towering gray beehive hairdo, who took it and smiled at me kindly, revealing huge yellowed teeth. She offered me a hard candy from a glass bowl on her desk. The melted candy wrappers reminded me of the butterscotches in a glass bowl on my gram's coffee table that had been there since the turn of the century. I declined politely.

The beehive lady barely glanced at my resume, then stood up and walked around from behind her desk toward me, leaning in close. Her cigarette breath and hair spray odor made me blink. She put her arm in mine, like we were old pals, and walked me toward the door. "Honey," she said in a hoarse voice, "no one's going to hire you for only five months. Y'all go down to the school admin building. Do the paperwork to be a substitute teacher. That's what all the Army wives do."

I thanked her and managed to hold it together until I got back in my car. I held my eyelids open with my fingers, willing my tears to stay put. The blazing heat had probably dried up my tear ducts, anyway.

I drove to the admin building and completed the substitute teacher paperwork.

"We'll call you, honey," the woman behind the counter told me. She must have gone to the same hairdresser as the other lady, although her beehive was jet black. "School starts in a month. Y'all be subbing five days a week if you want."

I forced another smile and thanked her. *Whoopee.* I drove back to our apartment, past the pawnshops and nail salons and barbeque restaurants, and tried not to think about the job I'd turned down in Boston.

chapter 5

July into October 2003
Fort Benning, Georgia

We got into a routine. Matt trudged in the front door about 5 p.m., and I tried not to bowl him over with enthusiasm, but I was so lonely. It was hard to hold back. We ate whatever salad and vegetables I'd prepared for dinner, then Matt got up and searched the fridge. Until we lived together, I had no idea Matt never ate anything green. Never. After he inhaled leftover pizza or some variety of red meat, we fooled around on the couch and watched TV until he fell asleep. Then I stayed awake for another hour or two, wallowing in self-pity and watching re-runs of Dawson's Creek.

I wanted to whine to Sara, but I hadn't talked to her since her wedding, and I didn't want to trample on her bed-of-roses-everything-is-peachy-keen life with my bellyaching. I wanted to whine to Alex. But what could I do? Call him and say, "Hey, my life sucks! I see Matt two hours a day. I can't find a job. I don't know anybody. What was I thinking?" I wanted to call my friends in Boston and New York, but what could I say? "You were right! I should've listened to you." I wanted to vent to my father, but he'd only worry. So I didn't call anyone, and I let my unhappiness fester inside me until it felt like it might rip me apart.

The first week, I shopped, but I had no money. I needed to find another hobby. The following week, I fell into a schedule. I ran in the morning, changed into my bathing suit, and took my CPA exam study books, sunscreen, towel, and a bottle of water to the apartment complex pool.

During my third week living in Columbus, Georgia, I sat with the thick study book on my lap and my legs hanging over the edge of the pool into the water because it was about 150 degrees outside. A short, muscular woman, about my age, with multiple piercings in both ears, and a bracelet tattooed on her wrist, plopped down on the lounge chair behind me.

"Hey, I'm Tess," she said, lowering her sunglasses to see what I was reading. "That looks boring."

"Oh, it is," I smiled. "Nice to meet you. I'm Kelly." I closed the book, stood up, and walked to the lounge chair next to her.

She grinned. She had green eyes and full lips painted pink. "You're new, right?"

I nodded, sitting down beside her.

"Me, too. Isn't it lovely here?" she asked sarcastically, sweeping her colorful nails and ring-adorned hand across the pool patio. "The humidity wasn't in the welcome information."

"Was there welcome information?"

She laughed. "If there was, they didn't send it to my husband."

Her husband, Tony, she told me, was in the Infantry Basic Officers' Course, the same course as Matt. They'd arrived the week before us.

"Registered dietician jobs open up as frequently as astronaut positions in this town, but I'm still looking." She shrugged good-naturedly. "I'm keeping busy. I found a pretty good yoga class. Wanna come with me tomorrow morning?"

I smiled hesitantly. Tess wasn't the preppy, practical type of friend I was used to, but I was desperate. So I went. After yoga, we browsed an antiques store, and the day after that, we met for coffee at a shop downtown. *Loneliness forces strange friendships*, I thought. Tess brightened up the dreary room I'd locked myself in.

The following week, after a late yoga class, we stopped for lunch at a Mexican restaurant, where Tess told the waiter it was my birthday. I sent her a puzzled look, and she kicked me under the table, whispering, "Go with it."

A few minutes later, the waiter reappeared with a birthday cake complete with lit candles and a sombrero, which he put on my head. Tess asked the waiter to take our photo, and we leaned over our sweet tea and nachos and made goofy faces. The minute the camera flashed, I decided I'd send the photo to my mother.

From as early as I could remember, my mother was, as my gram once phrased it when she thought I was out of earshot, "a guest in our hotel." She worked and graced us with her presence only at the dinner table, where she critiqued me from the minute she sat down to the minute she excused herself, leaving the dinner cleanup for my father, sister, and me. She found fault with everything I wore. "Did you wear that to school today, Kelly? It makes you look even longer and skinnier than you are!" She found fault with everything I did. It didn't matter that I lettered in three sports in high school and was class salutatorian. If I hadn't played as many sports, I would have been valedictorian. She never called or visited me at college. Not once. She left that, and all other nurturing duties, to my father.

As an adult, I found one of my favorite hobbies was to unsettle my mother. Which is why I sent the photo of Tess and me with the sombrero. Sure enough, the day she got the photo in the mail, she called. "Who's the tattooed, pierced girl?"

"Tess. My friend," I explained. "Don't worry, Mom. I insisted we pay for the cake. As you may recall, it wasn't actually my birthday. Tess thought I was nuts for my paying, but . . . Oh, and guess what? I got a job there!"

"What?" she asked, confused.

I smiled and wished I could see her face through the phone.

"The chicken nachos are so good," I began. "The best I've ever had. Tess and I were talking. There's no way she'll find a job as a registered dietician—that's what she does. She told me she needed a plan. I told her I was going to substitute teach, and she asked what I thought about working at Effie's. That's the name of the restaurant. So I'll sub when the school year starts, and work part-time at Effie's. I'll have plenty of time to study for the exam."

My mother stumbled over her words. "Wait. What? A waitress? How can you be a waitress? You're a CPA!!"

"No, Mom. I'm not. I'm a college graduate with a degree in accounting and I can't find a job. I won't even take the CPA exam until we move to Tennessee. I need to *do something* here."

My father and Matt thought it was great. Or they didn't care. Matt had never complained that I wasn't contributing toward paying the bills, but I was pretty sure he assumed, like I did, that I'd be pitching in. It's not as if second lieutenants raked in the big bucks, and since we weren't married, he didn't get paid more for having "dependents". When I moved in with him, I never intended to be reliant on him. The fact that I was bothered me.

•　　•　　•

"What about this weekend?" I asked, watching Matt fork a piece of chicken off his plate. We sat at the kitchen table I was so proud of, one of the few pieces of furniture we owned. It was the first piece I refinished myself and it fit perfectly in our tiny kitchen.

Tess had found the round oak table, hidden beneath the clutter of vases and lamps, in a store downtown, and talked me into buying it along with four chairs. The other two chairs were stacked against the wall in the garage, next to footlockers filled with Matt's field gear, waiting for me to get to them. There was no rush. I'd asked Matt about having Tess and her husband over for dinner, but he'd pleaded exhaustion, grumbling that he was too tired after a long day sitting in a boring classroom to entertain.

"Well? I really want to show you Seabury. And see my aunt. We can leave early Saturday morning and be back here Sunday night," I insisted. "You'd be home by nine. It's four hours away."

He chewed, thinking, and I continued to speak. "We've been here three months and you always have an excuse." I sounded more pitiful than I'd intended. But it was true, he was so full of excuses. Whenever I asked about driving to see my aunt in Seabury, he had homework or a test or a field gear display.

"We leave for the field on Friday, for a week, Kel." And then, like he'd been doing since graduation, he left me. Physically, he sat across from me at the table. Emotionally, he was somewhere else. He stared out the window, his mind on something other than me and my request to visit my aunt.

"Earth to Matt." I tapped his arm. "Are you there?"

He blinked and reentered my world.

"What's going on with you?" I asked, pushing him. "You do that. You fade off like you're thinking about something else. Are you all right?"

"Yeah, I'm fine," he snapped defensively.

"You've got to be kidding me." I stood abruptly and brought my plate to the sink. My festering unhappiness boiled over and I pointed at his untouched plate. "You don't like that?"

He took a long sip of his sweet tea. "Not really."

"I bought, washed, and grilled those vegetables when you were at work." My heart raced.

"Okay," he mumbled, as if he suddenly realizing that he messed up. "Uh, thanks?"

I exhaled, long and slow, to calm myself.

"Jesus, Kelly," he said. "You asked me if I liked the vegetables. I said, 'Not really.' Do you want me to lie?"

He finished his drink, stood up, and brought his plate over to the sink.

"I'm sorry," he said, dumping his vegetables into the trash. "I didn't write this training schedule. If I did, I wouldn't make us go to the field for ten days over two weekends." He yanked the door on the dishwasher open and put his plate inside it, then walked to the fridge. He took out a bottle of Gatorade, walked into the living room, and turned on the TV.

I had a flashback of being at West Point with Heather, standing in front of the mirrors in the ladies' room at Grant Hall, a restaurant with dining tables and couches next to the cadet barracks. It was April, and the hills were budding with green. We'd touched up our makeup and fixed our hair, antsy with anticipation, waiting for our boyfriends to be released for the weekend. Heather, applying fresh mascara, had told me that every time we saw our cadets, it was a mini honeymoon. "It's not real life," she'd said. "I just hope we can make this dating magic last after they graduate."

I'd looked at her sympathetically, like she was nuts. I was absolutely certain that I'd always be excited to see Matt. *Ha!* He didn't even try my grilled zucchini! That dating magic faded fast.

Matt looked over at me from the couch, his brow wrinkled. He wore his oblivious look, the one that told me he wasn't sure how he got into this conversation.

With no warning, my tears started, and I couldn't stop them. I stood at the edge of the living room, crying. I'd bawled more since his graduation than I had in the first twenty-two years of my life.

His eyes widened, and he turned off the TV. "What's the matter? Come here." He patted the seat next to him on the couch.

I shuffled over and sat down beside him. I bent forward and put my head in my hands, my elbows resting on my thighs.

"What's going on?" he asked, softly, breathing down my neck. He stroked my back, his fingers tracing lines up and down my spine.

I mumbled, addressing my sandals. "I want you to come to Aunt Patty's. I understand you can't, but I want you to. But it's more than that. I have one friend here. I have an accounting degree. I'm a waitress serving nachos, with an accounting degree." I sniffled. "And you're distant. There's something going on with you." I took my hands away from my face and gazed into his eyes. "What is it? Are you sorry you asked me to move in with you?"

He put his arm around me and pulled me in close. I couldn't see his face anymore, but I smelled his fruit punch Gatorade breath and body odor. "God, no, Kelly. I'm not sorry you're here at all. I'm glad you're here with me."

I moved in tighter and let him pull me in and I nuzzled against his neck. We sat like that for a few minutes before he said, "Listen, call Sara. They're only two hours from Seabury. Maybe she and Jake and Alex can drive down and meet you there."

"I want you to come," I pleaded, sounding like a spoiled brat.

"And I want to. We'll go for Thanksgiving. Or . . . no . . . we'll go before then. We'll go the weekend after I get back from the field. We'll drive down late Friday night and come back Sunday. Even if we're only there Saturday."

I nodded, still stuck to his side. He leaned down and kissed my forehead. I didn't move. Finally, I whispered, "Do you still want to get married?"

He pulled me away from him, his eyes looking into mine, confused. "Damn, Kelly, really? Why would you say that? Yeah, I do. Don't you?"

I leaned in and kissed him softly. When we separated, I said, "We never talk about a date."

He took both my hands and nodded. "I know. But I don't know when we could set a date. I graduate in December and go to ranger school in January. I don't know when I'll be done with ranger school. It's usually three months, but it can be longer if I have to recycle—that means if I have to do any of the phases again. If I graduate—and I say *if*, because that's not a given— we'll move to Fort Campbell right away. That could be anytime in April or May or June or July. It depends on how long I take to get through ranger school. Then we'll be at Fort Campbell for three years, but right away, sometime right after we get there . . . I'm not sure when . . . I'll probably deploy. I don't know how we can set a date when I'm not sure when I'll graduate from ranger school or deploy."

His voice was so genuine, so contrite. When we were together romantically, we were as close as we were when we were dating. When he drifted away, it was as if he had walked into a dark cloud, a place I wasn't allowed. Clinging closely to him on the couch, feeling his heartbeat through his T-shirt, I thought maybe that was okay. Maybe because he was usually so extroverted, he hid in himself for some quiet time. Maybe he'd done it for years. Alex would know. I'd have to ask him. I'd call him and Sara and see if they could meet me in Seabury.

chapter 6

October 2003
Seabury, Florida

It had been ten years since I'd driven on the only road into Seabury. For the first thirteen summers of my life, my father, sister, and I loaded our Dodge Caravan with boxes of Cheerios and macaroni and cheese, and cans of SpaghettiOs—Were there no grocery stores in Florida?—and drove from Forkton, New Hampshire, to my aunt's house on the Gulf of Mexico. We spent two glorious months with my father's favorite sibling, and our favorite aunt. Patty was the second oldest of the six McGowan children, ten years older than my father, and she never had kids. She treated Megan and me like daughters.

My mother never came with us. She stayed home to work, and that was fine with us. She was my mother, so I loved her, but that didn't mean I wanted to spend time with her. Those summers at the beach—without her—were the happiest memories of my childhood. I had no idea why they stopped so abruptly the summer I turned thirteen.

Driving over the bridge into Seabury, I exhaled and smiled at the boats bobbing in the canal below, the pelicans perched on the poles, and the sun lowering toward the horizon against the blue canopy of sky. Happy memories of my youth, and I didn't have many, comforted me. I slowed down, hit my blinker, and shrugged off what felt like a tight woolen winter coat that I'd been suffocating in since I left West Point with Matt.

I turned right on the third street after the canal, Sand Dollar Lane, and passed the familiar houses, visibly unchanged over the past decade. Only the DelGreco's house, directly across the street from my aunt's, looked different from what I remembered. It had new white shutters, a blue metal roof, and a freshly stained deck. October was off season in Seabury, sometimes bathing-suit weather, sometimes sweatshirt weather, and I was surprised to see lights in DelGreco's house and a car parked out front. The family lived in Atlanta and never rented their house. I'd have to ask my aunt who was there.

The gravel crunched under my wheels as I pulled into the driveway and sat in my car inspecting my aunt's sky-blue house. A few years back, she'd replaced the wood pilings with concrete ones, a major undertaking that required a crane and many thousands of dollars. Aunt Patty owned a small art studio in the next town, teaching watercolors and making ceramic mugs with the tourists as they drank wine. She wasn't made of money, but she'd told my father the new concrete pilings helped her sleep at night and were worth every penny.

I stepped out of my car and stretched, staring at the blue-green waters of the gulf beyond the adjacent sandy lot between my aunt's house and the beach. From the deck above, I heard a familiar, cheery voice. "Well, look at you! Get up here. Give me a hug!"

My aunt, all five feet of her, leaned over the railing, smiling. I grabbed my bag from the back seat, and took the steps two at a time, then slowed down when I saw her. She had to weigh less than a hundred pounds. Since I'd last seen her at my graduation, she'd shrunk. The top of her little head fell below my shoulders and her twig arms wrapped around my waist.

"I like your hair." I followed her through the sliding glass doors from the deck into the house.

"Thanks, Kel. I cut it shorter," she said, running her tanned hand through the short, spiky gray hair. "You're back in your old room. Oh, and Sara called. I'm glad you gave her my number. She said she tried to reach you, but couldn't get through."

"I was surprised at all the dead spots," I told her. "I was talking to my dad, and the call was dropped three times before I gave up."

"You've gotta love Lower Alabama, right? There are still gaps in cell phone service there. Sara said to tell you she's sorry. Jake got out of class too late and they won't make it down tonight. They'll get an early start in the morning, and she'll bring donuts. She said your other friend—Alex?—should still be coming tonight."

"Thanks for letting them all come, Aunt Patty." I bit the inside of my cheek. I hadn't seen or talked to Alex since Sara's wedding and didn't want to go into that with my aunt. "Can't wait to see my old room," I said, walking down the hall to the bedroom I'd shared with Megan a decade earlier.

Nothing had changed, and that made me smile. The walls were painted a soft pastel blue. Two white spindle twin beds wrapped neatly in crisp white cotton sheets, under quilts of blue and white circles, were separated by a tall dresser painted white. I plopped down on my bed and picked up a small pillow, yellowed with age, a *K* embroidered on a background of seashells. I held it close to my chest and looked around the room.

The two large Mason jars, one filled with sand dollars, and the other with jingle shells, still sat on the dresser. Clutching my pillow, I stood and looked in the jar filled with the tiny translucent shells my aunt called jingle shells. I used to collect them, adding to the jar every summer. My aunt collected the rare, fragile sand dollars.

I put my suitcase on the bed that Megan had always slept in and returned to the kitchen to find my aunt pouring red wine into two glasses. "I can't believe I haven't been here for what? Ten years?"

She put the bottle down and handed me a glass of wine. "Let's *not* do that again. Oh, I should have asked. You want a beer, instead?"

"No, this is great. Thanks," I said, taking the wine. "And it's a deal. I won't let so much time pass again. I love it here. Just coming over the canal made me feel like I was home. I missed it. I missed you." I walked toward the door to the deck. "Can we sit out here and catch up? Do we need sweatshirts?"

"Not yet. Probably when the sun goes down."

We walked outside and sat on Adirondack chairs as the fading orange sun lowered itself toward the horizon. The wind chimes that hung from the pitch in the roof tinkled. The weight of the world flew off my shoulders with the breeze.

"October's my favorite month," Aunt Patty said, peering at the water. "The tourists are gone. The weather's perfect."

I nodded, following her gaze. The water under the fading sun was mesmerizing.

"Except for the hurricanes," Aunt Patty said.

"What do you do?" I crinkled my brow. "If there's one coming?"

"Evacuate," she said nonchalantly. "I've done it before, and I'll do it again. I'm sorry Matt couldn't come with you, Kel." She looked at me closely. "Everything all right with him?"

When I first called her to ask about visiting, I'd told her it would be the two of us, so I understood why she was asking. I paused, thinking about how to reply.

"I was so happy to meet him at your graduation," she continued. "What a surprise that he showed up, right?"

I smiled, remembering. "Yeah, big surprise. Matt broke the rules, and Matt *never* breaks the rules. He had a final that morning at West Point and it's a four-hour drive from there to New Hampshire State. He couldn't have made the ceremony.

And he couldn't take a pass that weekend. So he wasn't allowed to leave the campus." I took a sip of my wine and grinned.

My aunt laughed. "Well, I'm glad he did. I was happy to meet him. He looked smitten with you—as he should be."

As soon as Matt finished his exam, he'd hurried to his truck, somehow changing out of his uniform while he was driving. When I walked out of the auditorium with my diploma in hand, and into the parking lot with my parents and aunt, I stared in disbelief at the tall guy in a dress shirt and khakis, drenched in sweat, jogging to meet us. He drove back to West Point after dinner to be back in his room before taps. That night, when he called to tell me he got back safely, I couldn't have loved him more.

"Yeah, that was a good day. It was too nice of you to come, Aunt Patty."

"Pshaw, my favorite niece graduating magna cum laude? Of course, I'd be there. Hell, even if you weren't any cum laudes, I'd be there." She waved her hand in front of her. *No big deal.*

"But your fiancé showed his true love for you that day. What a man," she said, watching my reaction.

I nodded, thinking about that dating magic, wondering where it went, and if it was my fault it went there. "Yeah," I explained. "It's a bummer he couldn't come this weekend, but they're going to the field. He's busy in this course."

My aunt nodded and changed the subject. "I talked to your father about Megan. Sounds like everything's the same with her," she said.

I exhaled before lifting my shoulders and dropping them slowly. "I haven't talked to her," I confessed. "I feel terrible about it, but she never picks up when I call her. I haven't talked to her in months."

My aunt regarded me with deep-set brown eyes, her eyelids creased like accordion blinds over them. Her bronzed leathery skin formed pucker lines as she pursed her lips before stating,

"You can't do a thing to change her, Kelly. All those summers you were here, I watched you take care of her. You brushed her hair; you told her to eat her salad; you taught her how to write her name. I told your father—more often than he wanted to hear—that you did too much. That Megan needed to do things on her own—that her own damn mother should be the mother."

My eyes bulged, and she explained: "I'm not going to bad-mouth your mother. Even though she was never good enough for my little brother." She grinned, before taking on a more serious tone. "She shouldn't have left you playing mother to her youngest daughter. That was her role, not yours."

She leaned toward my chair and rested her veiny hand on my forearm. "I know you feel bad about not doing more for your sister. About not being able to fix her problems. Megan knows you love her and are there for her. She needs to get back into rehab. But until your mother makes her, until she kicks her out of her house, until Megan gets the help she needs—Megan will keep relying on those who enable her. That boyfriend or your mother." She removed her hand from my arm and turned her head to the horizon.

I sat still, not sure what to say. My aunt had never come right out and said she didn't think much of my mother. But that had nothing to do with my relationship with my sister, and my stomach hurt, like I'd eaten bad eggs, when I thought about me and Megan.

"You were both always so different." My aunt turned back toward me, then took a long sip of wine.

"Why?" I asked softly. "How can two people who come out of the same womb be so different?"

"That's—" She stopped short.

I pressed her. "What do you think?"

"Oh, that's just the way it is sometimes. Look at me and my sister, Clare. She's an ex-nun living in Montana, with an ex-priest and their six kids, right out of Little House on the Prairie. And two years later, they had me, the hippie artist living at the beach." She shrugged, then changed the subject. "Have you kept up with the DelGrecos?"

"I was going to ask you." I shook my head no. "Is someone over there?"

"You haven't met Kyle," Aunt Patty said, out of left field.

I looked confused. There were four DelGreco children: Mary Ann was my age; Johnny was Megan's age; and Joey and Mary Martha were younger. No Kyles.

"Ohhh. Mary Ann's boy. She had a baby—almost two years ago."

"Huh? What? Is she married?" Before my aunt could answer, I added, "We were so close as kids. After we stopped coming down, we wrote letters back and forth for a couple of years, but then that faded."

I didn't tell her that when I was a kid, I wanted to be a DelGreco. Mrs. DelGreco was a bighearted, big-boned, boisterous woman who played Monopoly with us and gave us ice-cream sandwiches. She was the mother I wanted. Mary Ann's father worked during the week in Atlanta and drove to Seabury every weekend.

"No. Not married," my aunt responded. "No father in the picture, I don't think."

Interesting. The Mary Ann I remembered was shy and insecure, a people pleaser.

"She started at Boston College—like her parents," my aunt said. "You know, Joe and Mary were both originally from Weymouth, south of Boston, and moved to Atlanta after college. I don't think Mary Ann was happy there, so far away from home. Her parents seemed to forget that she wasn't from Boston. She was from Atlanta and didn't know a soul up there. But sweet Mary Ann. She tried to please everyone. God bless her." She paused, shaking her head.

"Anyway, she got pregnant. I don't know the details—and I'm not sure what her parents think. It's none of my business, but they all love that little boy. He's precious and Mary Ann's a wonderful mom."

"I didn't know any of this," I said. "I'd like to catch up with her."

"She'd love to see you if you have time. And what about Johnny being in the Army?"

"What's that about?"

"He's at Georgia Military College. He won't graduate until next May, but he's in a program where he got commissioned early. He's a second lieutenant!"

"I can't believe we're this old. And Mary Ann has a baby."

"Well, look at you, a college graduate living in Georgia," my aunt said. "I don't think you'll find Mary Ann any different from the girl you used to share Nancy Drew books with, just older. She's a preschool aide, going back to school nights to be a teacher. She's a good kid. Comes down most weekends and keeps the house up for her parents. Joe and Mary don't get down much. I was surprised Mary came down this weekend. I didn't tell her you were coming—I swear that woman bugs my phone. She always knows what's going on."

I laughed and sipped my wine, watching the sun dissipate below the horizon and the pinks and purples of the sky fade into darkness. I noticed the Smith's house, perched on the dunes between the DelGreco's and the gulf. "Wow. The Smith's house looks great."

The yard was meticulously manicured, with sand, rocks, shrubbery, and palm trees. The wraparound porch, metal roof, and hurricane shutters were painted a deep red.

"It always does. You know they got divorced, right?"

"Dad told me." I nodded. "I always thought the Smiths were perfect. Beautiful and rich. And I thought the DelGrecos were perfect, too. They always had fun. They did everything together."

"Things aren't always what they seem," my aunt said.

•   •   •

Headlights turned the corner, illuminating the quiet street. I jumped up and walked anxiously to the railing overlooking the street. *It has to be Alex.*

"Okay, so tell me about Alex?" My aunt stood and joined me watching the headlights approach.

"He's stationed at Fort Rucker with Jake and Sara. He and Jake are going to flight school there. Alex was Matt's roommate all four years at West Point. They're closer than brothers. He's become like a brother to me, too. He's a good guy, from Georgia."

He parked his jeep next to my car and stepped out, lit by the glow of the streetlight. He smiled up at us, waved, and reached into the back seat. After he grabbed his bag, he bounded up the stairs to the deck, his black backpack slung over his shoulder. He hugged me first and then moved to my aunt.

"For you." He handed my aunt a brown paper bag and a bottle of wine he pulled out of his backpack. "Thanks for having me this weekend, ma'am. I've heard so much about you."

"What's in the bag?" I asked.

My aunt opened it, revealing the soft, slimy nuts inside.

"Ugh." I laughed. "Those boiled peanuts are gross."

"I expected y'all might not have gained an appreciation for our bald peanuts yet." He smiled and pulled a box of fudge out of the backpack. "I brought fudge just in case."

"Good move." I grinned. "'Bald'? You mean *boiled*?"

He laughed. "You Northerners say 'boiled.' We Southerners say 'bald.'"

"They're an acquired taste, for sure," my aunt agreed. "My house is your house, Alex. Don't ever feel like you have to bring a thing. Although the wine and fudge will be gone before the morning."

Alex settled in my father's old bedroom, and I grabbed a sweatshirt and joined both of them on the deck, where we eased into small talk. I asked Alex if he lived near Jake and Sara. He told us he lived in a house on Fort Rucker, and Jake and Sara lived in an apartment outside the gate in Enterprise. He shared a house with Will, another guy from West Point. They hadn't known one another, but they signed in at the same time. Will turned around in line, and asked Alex if he wanted to live together to save money.

My aunt chuckled. "You didn't know him, and you agreed to be his roommate?"

"Um, yeah," Alex explained. "Classmates are like brothers you've never met. Although some of them are odd. Will's a good guy. He was roommates with Eric at West Point."

His head snapped toward me, as if expecting a reaction, but I didn't remember meeting an Eric.

"Should I know Eric?" I asked.

Alex's face relaxed. "Nah, I guess not. He went to high school with Matt in Virginia. And some grammar school years, too, when their fathers were stationed together. Sometimes they shared rides together back and forth to school, but I guess that was mostly plebe and yearling years, before Matt met you."

My aunt interrupted. "Plebe and yearling years? What's that mean? Secret Army language?"

I suddenly remembered Eric. I'd never met him, but after Matt and I had been dating for a few months, Jake told Sara, and Sara told me. Eric's father and Matt's father were West Point classmates, and their families were old friends. But more importantly, Eric was the twin brother of Eve. And Matt had dated Eve throughout high school, and during the first two and a half years of West Point. Eve was the girl who broke Matt's heart, dumping him with no warning over Christmas his junior year. Three months later, I met Matt on spring break.

"A plebe's a freshman," Alex explained before I could chime in with my sudden recollection of who Eric was. "A yearling's a sophomore. Don't ask me why."

I listened, thinking it was a good thing that I hadn't blurted out what I'd remembered. It was too complicated to explain to Aunt Patty.

Alex told my aunt that juniors were called "cows," an expression I'd never understand, and my aunt asked him about flight school, his family, where he was from in Georgia. The sky brightened with stars, and I leaned my neck back and stared upward, until my aunt yawned and told us she was going in for the night. As soon as she closed the sliding glass door behind her, Alex sprang up from his chair without saying a word and ran down the deck stairs.

chapter 7

October 2003
Seabury, Florida

Before I could jump up after him, he reappeared carrying two blankets. I recognized the "green girls" that cadets used on their beds in the barracks.

"What the —?" I tilted my head, puzzled. "I didn't know where you were going. I thought you were taking off."

Handing me a blanket, he shook his head. "Nope. I don't scare off that easy. You look freezing. Here, take the new one. I bought it before graduation. I'll use the ratty one that was on my bed for four years. It really needs to be washed."

I laughed and huddled under the blanket.

"I don't want you to go in because you're cold." He sat in the chair next to me. "We have a lot to catch up on."

"Yeah, the last time I saw you..." I looked away from him, toward the dark gulf.

"Yep. I remember. I still have Matt's shorts and T-shirt. I meant to bring them to give you. How've you been?"

"Oh, boy," I answered weakly. "Super. Great. Waitressing. One friend, Tess. She's a hoot."

"Wait. Waitressing?"

"Yeah. Hard to find a job when you're only going to be there for six months. Go figure. I get a discount at Effie's. It's a win-win." I forced a chuckle.

"Effie's? We have one in Enterprise! They've got the best chicken nachos, right?"

I laughed. "They're amazing."

Out of nowhere, my eyes watered, and I dabbed them with the sleeve of my sweatshirt.

Alex leaned over my armrest, his eyebrows raised. "What's going on?"

I shrugged. "I don't know. Matt works all the time. I never see him."

"Yeah," Alex said. "I called him and gave him a hard time about not coming down this weekend. But it sounds like he really couldn't. He went to the field today, right?"

"Yeah, I know. He had no choice. But, God, Alex. He's so crazy. All the other lieutenants in our building come home after school and hang out at the pool. Not Matt. He's studying or working out or sleeping. Was he this bad at West Point?"

"He's intense." He shrugged. "You know that. He spent nights at the library before tests and doing papers, but he had no aspirations of being high in the class. He wanted to be high enough to get Infantry and Fort Campbell, but that was it."

"I don't get it," I whined. "I mean, this is supposed to be fun, right? Being at an Army school?"

"Yeah, if he didn't put so much pressure on himself. His father was honor grad in the Infantry Basic Course in 1974. I think he puts pressure on Matt, like wouldn't it be nice if his son was honor grad, too. And Matt can't stand to disappoint anyone."

"He didn't tell me about his father." In a meager attempt to be positive, I added, "At least he's not drinking anymore. Right after graduation, he drank too much. When we stayed on West Point with those friends of his mother's, he tried to hide it by avoiding them. But after they went to bed, he was down in their basement pounding beers. Until Sara's wedding. After that, you were right. He felt bad. So embarrassed. He's barely drunk anything since."

"That's good," Alex said. "Right?"

"Yeah, but," I started, "let me ask you something. He zones out sometimes. He'll be sitting right next to me, and a random commercial comes on the TV, and I lose him. Emotionally. He fades away, like he's thinking about something else. He'll be gone for a few minutes, and then when I elbow him and say, 'Hey, are you okay?' He nods and comes back to me. It's the weirdest thing."

Alex bit his bottom lip. "Have you talked to him about it? Asked him what he was thinking about?"

"He denies anything's wrong. Did he ever do that when you guys were roommates? Like, go into his own little world?"

He paused. "He liked his space. We both did."

"Have you talked to him since the wedding?"

"A couple of times. I was pissed. He knows it. He tries to please everyone . . ." He tipped his head back and stared up at the stars. "He loves you. Y'all will figure this out."

I inhaled deeply and exhaled. *He's right. I need to give Matt his space.* We sat in silence for a few minutes before I blurted out, "Hey, I remember Eric. Or the story, anyway. I never met him. Where's Eric stationed?"

Alex lowered his gaze to the gulf. "He went FA. Field artillery, like Tyler. He's at Fort Sill. I think he's going to Bragg after his basic course. In North Carolina. I didn't know him well at school. We had a few classes together, but that was it. Will keeps up with him, but I don't think Matt does anymore."

I nodded, not sure why I asked, not sure why it mattered.

"What about you?" I asked, ripping off the rest of my filter. "Are you still with Kate?" He hesitated long enough for me to add, "Not that it's any of my business. Just wondering."

He leaned back over my armrest, grinned and cocked his head to the side. "My business is your business, Kelly McGowan. That's the way friends work. Nah, I'm not with Kate. Flight school's way harder than I thought it would be. I'm studying a lot."

We listened wordlessly to the night. The half-moon was bright, a spotlight on the tide as it crashed, the heartbeat of the ocean, thumping rhythmically against the shore. My eyelids fluttered, and I pulled the green girl up under my neck. The waves lulled me to sleep, and I woke with a start, hearing Alex snoring lightly in his chair next to me. I thought briefly about waking him, but didn't have the energy, and didn't want to leave the sounds of the shore. I pulled the green girl up higher, felt warmth spread through my body, and closed my eyes.

•   •   •

"Well, good morning," my aunt said as I entered the kitchen. She glanced at me, then continued to unload the dishwasher. "You two were out late last night."

I opened the cabinet and pulled out a chipped ceramic mug with bright yellow bees buzzing above the motto BEE KIND. "We fell asleep." I filled the cup with coffee. "Alex woke up about two and woke me. It was getting chilly out there."

I put the creamer back in the fridge and looked out the window as Jake's truck turned the corner. "They're here!" I yelled like a kid watching Santa's sleigh land on the roof next door. Behind me, I heard Alex's bedroom door open, but I didn't wait for him. Closing the refrigerator door, I ran out onto the deck and down the steps as Jake's truck pulled in. Before Sara had two feet on the ground, I hugged her like I hadn't seen her in years. She laughed, and I ran over to Jake's side, pat him quickly on the back, and raced back to Sara.

"Call me chopped liver," he shouted. "Where'd you learn to give that hug? Your fiancé? Mr. Touchy-Feely?"

I laughed as Sara reached behind her seat and handed me two boxes of donuts to carry up to the house.

•   •   •

I leaned forward over the kitchen table. "Okay, start with the honeymoon." That was my first mistake. She launched into massages and sunset cruises in Oahu and rambled on, in excruciating detail, about the amazing professional opportunities in Alabama, the magical and talented friends she'd made, and the rainbows that followed her wherever she walked. Oh, and she landed her dream job teaching English at a high school outside Fort Rucker. I didn't ask if she rode a unicorn to work.

After thirty minutes of preaching the "Beautiful Life of Sara Morgan" sermon, she stopped short. "Oh, I've been doing all the talking. Your turn. Tell me about Fort Benning!"

Thankfully, my aunt, who'd occasionally rolled her eyes behind Sara during the "Beautiful Life" documentary, interrupted. "Oh, Kelly, I don't want to interrupt, but when Sara unpacks, perhaps you can walk across the street and say a quick hello to Mary Ann." She looked sympathetically at Sara. "She hasn't seen her in over a decade!"

"Oh, sure! I remember you talking about her. Please! Yes! Go see her! I have to call my mother and tell her how pretty it is here, anyway. I'll put on some sweats. Let's walk on the beach when you get back. And you can tell me about Fort Benning, then?"

I smiled and tried to hide my jealousy. *What a selfish brat I am.* As we got up from the table, I looked at my sweet friend bringing the empty box of donuts to the counter and her coffee cup to the dishwasher. *Stop. Be happy for her. She's your best friend! Stop wallowing in your own self-pity!*

I looked down at my feet, embarrassed that I was allowing my own unhappiness to turn me into a bitch.

·   ·   ·

I jogged across the street and knocked on the DelGreco's front door like I was ten years old again. When Mary Ann opened the door and smiled shyly at me, I laughed out loud. Her brown eyes were as big and kind as they were when we were kids. Her tight, curly hair hung to her shoulders. She wore snug gray yoga pants with a mauve V-neck T-shirt that showed cleavage and arm definition.

"You look great," I said honestly, stepping in the door as she opened it.

"So do you! I'm glad you came over. Your aunt said you were coming down this weekend."

Flooded with memories, I followed her down the hall into the kitchen, past the framed family photos plastered on the walls. A toddler with dark curly hair sat on the floor playing with Tupperware containers and lids. He looked up at us and smiled impishly.

"Lots to catch up on." Mary Ann lifted her shoulders, then dropped them. "Kyle. Come say hi to Mommy's friend. This is Miss Kelly."

He glanced at me, revealing his mother's chocolate-colored eyes, before turning his attention back to stacking the plastic bowls. I bent down next to him. "Hey, Kyle. Nice bowls."

He handed me a lid.

"Aw, thanks, Kyle." I stood up and smiled at Mary Ann. "He's adorable."

Mary Ann's eyes met mine. "Thanks. Long story. I'll tell you some time you have a few hours."

"I'd like that. I've got some friends down this weekend, but I'll be back down to visit my aunt again soon. You'll have to tell me everything. Everything that's happened in your life since we were thirteen."

A rumpus thumped down the stairs, and Mrs. DelGreco, wearing a tent-sized, bright-colored housecoat, plod into the hall. "Oh. My. Goodness! Is that my Kelly McGowan?"

I laughed. Mary Ann rolled her eyes. Mrs. DelGreco's girth, wide a decade ago, had expanded, and she enveloped me with the same smothering embrace I remembered. Her round face remained clear, but for a few lines near her eyes and chin hairs. She cornered me and peppered me with a thousand questions, until I apologized, and told her I had to get back to my friends. As I hugged Mary Ann goodbye, I whispered, "We'll talk again."

She nodded, smiling, and I swung my arms happily as I walked back across the street, bolstered by an old friendship that I hadn't realized I'd missed so much.

•　　•　　•

The high sun contrasted with the cool air. Sara and I wore sweatshirts as we walked along the packed sand. Before we'd walked a hundred yards, Sara asked pointedly, "What's going on with you?" Her eyes crinkled with concern. "We roomed together for four years. I know you. Something's going on."

I sighed and stared out at the horizon as we walked.

"You don't have to tell me. But if you want to vent or unload, I'm here."

I crossed my arms across my chest. "I'm okay," I said, trying to convince the both of us.

"It's just harder than I thought it would be. I can't find a job. Matt's at work all the time. I have a friend, but she's not you." I stopped to bend down and pick up a shell, avoiding eye contact with her.

"I'm sorry, Kel. I get what you mean about friends. Mine aren't you, either. But they're all I have. I mean, they're fine, but not sisterlike, like you are."

I smiled and scraped the sand off the shell in my hand. "You always say the right thing."

"What about you and Matt? How are you dealing with no health insurance? Have you guys thought about doing what Heather and Tyler did? Why don't you do that?"

I waited to respond. "I don't think so."

She stopped walking and turned to look at me. "Why not?"

I'm not ready to get married until we live together longer and I'm confident this is right. That's what I thought, but I couldn't say it out loud. For the first time with my best friend, I withheld the truth. Instead, I said, "I think we should wait and do it once, right." I bent to pick up an oyster shell, worn white and hard as ice.

My explanation seemed to appease her. She started to walk again. "Do you have a date yet? Have you guys talked more about that?"

Off in the blue waters, a pelican dove into the water before crashing the surface again and flying low toward the canal. I watched it and waited. "No. No date. Matt goes to ranger school after Christmas—that's three months or it could be longer. After that, he'll report to Fort Campbell—in Kentucky. Well, on the Kentucky/Tennessee border, I guess. His father thinks Matt will deploy right after we get there. We're not sure when there's a good time. To get married."

She stopped walking again and looked at me, her eyebrows squeezed together. "Wait. If he's going to be deployed, and you don't get married, would you stay in Tennessee? You'd have no health benefits. You'd have no ID card."

I swallowed. "There's a lot up in the air."

"That's a long time to be with him not married, no benefits."

I nodded to end this conversation. I understood it was a risk not to have health insurance, and not to be his wife. My parents were a wreck about me getting strep, or worse, in a car accident. *But it's an even greater risk to rush into a marriage that might not be right.*

"Whatever you decide will be the right decision." She put her arm around my waist and squeezed me, before letting go.

I bent down and picked up one of the tiny, translucent yellow shells that I collected as a kid. My aunt always told me the jingle shells reminded her of me. Unlike the sand dollars, the jingle shells were beautiful and sturdy and resilient. They never broke. I stuck it in my shorts pocket to take back with me to Georgia.

chapter 8

October 2003
Seabury, Florida
The next morning, Alex popped his head into the kitchen. "Be right back. I told your aunt I'd change a light bulb in the storage room." He opened the sliding glass door and turned toward me. "Jake and Sara are packing up. I'll be done in a minute."

I finished unloading the dishwasher and walked down to see if he needed help. When I opened the door to the storage room, the new bulb shone bright. Alex stood with the old bulb in his hand, reading the plaque that had hung on that wall for as long as I could remember.

"I like this." He pointed to the words etched on the metal plaque:

May the roof above you never fall in
And the friends beneath it never fall out.
  — Irish Toast

I nodded. "Me too. It hung in my dad's kitchen in Dorchester, where he grew up. When my aunt moved here after college — that's another whole story — she inherited this house from her husband who died."

"What?" Alex jerked his head back, surprised.

"It's so sad," I explained. "She dated a guy she met at the University of Tampa. An art teacher she had in high school in Dorchester knew someone who taught art at the University of Tampa and worked a scholarship deal for her. Her high school art teacher understood my aunt needed to get out of the house. Her father, my grandfather, was apparently a real piece of work. Anyway, this was the late sixties, and my aunt dated this guy, Aaron, in college, but she broke up with him because she was so mad at him for dropping out of college to become a poet. She knew if he dropped out, he'd get drafted. She told us this story the last summer I was here, when I was thirteen. I'll never forget it. She went to college during the Vietnam War, and sure enough, after he dropped out, Aaron's number got called up. Did you know they did that then? They had a draft where they printed numbers in the paper and that's how you knew if you got drafted?"

He nodded. "Yeah, that's how it worked. What happened? Didn't you say they broke up?"

"Yeah, but before he had to report, he came to see her. Fall semester, her senior year. He told her he had a bad feeling. He told her he loved her and wanted to marry her."

Alex pulled his head back, stiffened his neck, and frowned.

"I know, right? I couldn't believe this, either, when my aunt first told us." I brought my hands up, palms to the ceiling, then dropped them. "She didn't love him. She knew he wasn't the one for her. But she was so worried about his morale and how devastated he was about going off to war, she would have felt terrible if she broke his heart, and then something happened to him over there. So she married him legally, but didn't tell anyone, and kept her last name. She figured when Aaron got back safe and sound, she could divorce him."

Alex listened quietly.

"She wrote him letters—as a friend—and she said it was as if he understood. He expected nothing more from her. But then, four months after he got to Vietnam, she got a telegram. Can you imagine? That's how they told her."

We both sighed at the same time.

"She was a senior in college when she opened that telegram. I can't imagine. Anyway, she had no clue he owned this house. She found out a few months after he died, when his mother called her and told her he'd inherited a cottage from his grandparents and he'd put it in my aunt's name when he enlisted. After she graduated from college, Aunt Patty drove through this way, on the way back home to Dorchester. She figured it was a shack in the middle of nowhere, and she'd put it on the market and unload it. But then she saw it. It needed a lot of work, but it was nowhere as bad as she thought it would be. And the location? Right? So beautiful! She had to stay. Here. In Seabury. She loved it. Her parents thought she was nuts. But when Gram realized she was serious, she sent a box to my aunt with a note. Here. Let me see if it's still there."

I reached up and removed the plaque from the wall. A yellowed piece of paper with Gram's penmanship was taped on the back: *Hang this and let your house become your home.*

"My aunt stuck this note here. It's hung here since she moved in."

"Wow." Alex smiled. "The Irish toast is neat, but the story. . . that's special."

It was hard not to notice his perfect teeth. His parents would be happy to learn that the cost of orthodontics was worth it.

Jake yelled from the deck above us. "Hey, you guys coming up? We have to get going."

I hung the plaque back up and followed Alex out to where Jake and Sara were standing with my aunt next to his truck. I held Sara tight, wishing Matt had gone to flight school, missing our times together. Neither Jake nor Alex knew where they'd be stationed after the year-long flight school course. Though I harbored hope it would be Fort Campbell, Jake's first choice was

Fort Drum, New York, to be closer to their families. I tried not to think about it.

When we stepped apart, Sara looked at me. "I'll call more. I will."

I tightened my lips and smiled, wondering if she'd get too busy with her new life to think about me.

She stepped up into the passenger seat of Jake's truck, rolled down her window, and waved to my aunt. "Thank you so much, Mrs. McGowan."

"Oh, pshaw, come back now, Sara." My aunt stuck her thin arm up and waved.

"And take it easy on your students," I said as they pulled out of the driveway. "Shakespeare's boring!"

As their truck rolled down Sand Dollar Lane, Alex threw his bag into the back of his jeep and walked toward us to say goodbye.

"Come back anytime, Alex." My aunt smiled and wagged her pointer finger at him.

"I'll be back to change those exterior lights. Call me when they're in."

My aunt looked at me and lifted her shoulders to her ears before dropping them. "He insisted."

I laughed.

"I'll let you know when the lights are in, as long as you promise not to bring any boiled peanuts with you next time. Be safe driving back." She waved and walked up the stairs into the house.

I leaned up against the back of his jeep and looked at the gulf. "Do we have to go back? Can't we live here forever?"

Alex smiled. "I get why you love this place so much. You should come down more often. Your aunt would love it." He paused. "Maybe it'd be good for you to get down here more."

I scrunched my face. Matt would be in the field when I got back to Georgia. I had nothing back in Columbus, except for an empty apartment and a job that left my jeans stained with queso.

Alex misread my expression. He looked at me, his brow creased. "He loves you, Kelly."

My eyes watered, and I nodded. "I know. Thanks, Alex. You're right. It's just new. I've got to let him take his quiet moments and let him be. I'll try to be more understanding about that parental pressure on him."

"Call me anytime. I'm glad to listen."

I hugged him again and mumbled my thanks into his shoulder.

Reluctantly, he opened his door and stepped into his jeep, rolling down the window as he pulled out of the driveway. "Thanks for inviting me. I love this place!"

I smiled and waved, watching the rear of his jeep diminish as he drove away. *We're all grown up now. I moved to Georgia, and I need to figure it out. Change is hard.* I put my hand in my pocket and felt my shell, determined to make it work.

chapter 9

October to November 2003
Fort Benning, Georgia

On the four-hour drive back to Columbus, I ate a bag of Chex Mix and did a lot of thinking. I thought about country music. It was growing on me. That was mind-boggling. I thought about dating long-distance. It seemed like centuries ago when I ran to the phone to hear his voice; when I got my hair highlighted and my nails done before I saw him. I thought about living together. He drank milk out of the carton and farted out loud; he didn't even try to hold them in. On the radio, someone crooned about fighting for her man. I tried to remember the last time I had anything on my body waxed.

Before I knew it, I pulled into the gas station near our apartment, behind a white Subaru Forester with a peace sticker on the rear bumper. I laughed out loud. *Tess.* She'd finished pumping and had opened her car door, but when she saw me, she marched toward me, her face tight. She wore paint-splattered jeans, a stained T-shirt, and stood with her hands on her hips.

"Am I ever glad to see you!" she barked. "Can you talk me out of killing my husband?"

My eyes popped open and my hands froze in front of the gas pump. "Um. Are you okay?"

"No, he's a dick. I married a dick. I was in the garage painting that chair I bought. Remember the cherry armchair with the nice trim?"

I nodded, wondering where this story was going.

"And Dickweed comes out and tells me I'm spending too much money. That we need to budget better if I'm not working. Like it's my fault that I can't find a decent paying job here?" She looked at my hand resting on the pump handle, suddenly realizing I needed gas. "Oh, go pump. I'm not going to really kill him. I'm only venting."

More interested than worried, I hesitated. "Are you sure? Cause if I should be preventing a murder, my gas can wait . . ."

She walked to her car and popped the trunk, pointing to white plastic bags from TJ Maxx and HomeGoods. "Instead of killing him, I went shopping. Yeah. Yeah. Money's the problem. But I do the bills. He'll never know."

I laughed.

"I shouldn't have. But I was pulled like a magnet to therapy shopping." She opened the bags to show me a new dress, some bath towels, a wicker basket, and a pair of sandals. "Don't you guys ever fight?"

"Yeah, we fight," I admitted, hoisting the pump into my gas tank. "Honestly, it's nice to hear you guys do, too. I thought we were the only ones."

"Ha." She closed her trunk. "If anyone in a relationship tells you they don't fight, they're either married to Jesus or lying."

Before she walked back to her car, she turned to face me. "I totally forgot. How was your weekend?"

"Good. It was nice to see my aunt and old friends. I'd ask how yours was, but . . ."

She laughed. "It was great! I love my new dress! Hey, we're both on the same shift tomorrow. Drive together? I'll pick you up?"

"Sounds good." I smiled.

Tess got in her car, stuck her arm out the window, and waved goodbye as she drove away.

I finished pumping my gas. *I'm relieved that Tess's marriage wasn't perfect. I was jealous of Sara for being happy. What a terrible friend I've become! Have I always been such a bitch? Or is this a new me?* Whoever it was, I didn't like it.

•   •   •

I unlocked the door to our apartment and flipped on the light switch, clicking the dead bolt behind me. Dropping my suitcase on the floor next to the couch, I walked into the kitchen and picked up the phone to call my aunt. She was a worrier, and since I'd invited three friends to her house for the weekend, the least I could do was tell her I'd made it home safe and sound.

"Kelly," she said, after listening to my profuse thanks. "You said Matt's going away after Christmas to some sort of school?"

"Ranger school." I opened the refrigerator door and took out a bottle of water. That bag of Chex Mix sat heavy in my gut, and my mouth screamed with thirst. "It's a three-month course, where they live in the woods and eat berries. They say it's a real suck. He's in this Infantry Basic Course now, here at Benning, and graduates right before Christmas, and then he'll go to ranger school after Christmas. After that, we move to Fort Campbell."

"Well, I was thinking," my aunt said, "if you wanted to save some rent money, why don't you move out of your apartment when Matt leaves and come live with me while he's at the course? I'm sure you could find a job here. I could ask Betty. From bunko. She's the secretary in the accounting firm in Yarmouth. Her office is ten minutes from my house and I bet they could use temp help. You could save some money and I'd enjoy the company."

I thought about it for less than half a millisecond. "I'd love it! Are you sure?"

"I don't offer things I don't want to offer. That's not the way I roll, missy. Think about it. Talk to Matt. Let me know whenever."

I hung up the phone and danced around the kitchen like a disco queen. Tess and most of the other wives would leave Fort Benning after graduation in December. I'd been dreading Matt being gone for three or more months and me serving nachos alone. Live at the beach? Twist my arm. I couldn't wait to tell Matt.

•   •   •

"You have to keep busy," Tess told me in the parking lot after work the next night. "That's the only way you can make it in this life." Her husband had been prior enlisted, which meant they'd lived at other Army posts before Fort Benning.

"Especially in a place like this." She spread her long, toned arm across the parking lot. "One thing I've learned in my four years of marriage, your happiness can't depend on him. Sure, he makes your life fuller, more complete. All that lovey shit. But don't depend on him to make you happy. You've got to do that yourself. So, tomorrow night, come to dinner with us. A BBQ place in Phenix City. A bunch of the wives are going."

"I'm not a wife." It came out snippier than I intended.

"Who cares? No one. You need to carve a life out for yourself, Kelly. He's making his own life, right?"

I'd never complained to Tess, but she seemed to understand what I was going through. She told me she'd pick me up the next day at 5:30 p.m.

•   •   •

Smokey's BBQ was a log cabin, with red-and-white–checkered curtains peeking through the windows in the front, and its gravel parking lot was so crowded, we had to park in the feed store's lot next door. Tess and I entered the restaurant and canvassed the room, looking for a familiar face. A tall redhead saw Tess, stood up, and waved. I was surprised to see about fifteen women sitting with the redhead at a long table in the back.

Tess looked at me when the woman offered her the empty seat next to her. I motioned for Tess to sit, and I turned to a tanned brunette woman next to another empty seat near the center of the table. After I asked the brunette if the seat was taken, she pulled it out, excitedly, which should have been a red flag. I picked up on the warning sign too late. Before I'd hung my purse on the back of the chair, she'd yanked a folder out from under her seat.

"Hi, I'm Lynnette," she babbled cheerfully, as my butt fell hesitantly on the seat. "I'm a Twenty-One consultant! Are you familiar with our products?"

My eyes bulged as she handed me the pamphlet. "Oh, thanks so much," I mumbled. Twenty-One consultants, I'd learned in my time at Fort Benning, sold bags. "Until I find a job that pays more than I'm making now, we're on a pretty strict budget. I'll be using my old purse for a while, I'm afraid." I held up my worn brown leather purse before hanging it over the back of my chair.

Lynnette's face puckered into a pout. "Are you sure? At least look. I'm hosting a party next week and will send you an invitation. If you decide on one now, I'll put in the order tonight and you can take it home after the party!"

I drew my lips together and forced a smile. "I wish I could. But I can't right now. Not until I find a better job."

"Well, consider being a consultant. We're hiring!" She handed me her card from the folder. I had to admire her moxie, but I took the card like it had cooties, hoping she'd give up on me. She did. She rotated her folder to face the woman on her other side. She began her spiel: "Hi! I'm Lynnette!"

Strike one for my first attempt to make new friends. I shifted to the purple-haired woman on my other side. She introduced herself as Margaret, and I tried not to stare at her face that hung so low, she looked like she hadn't slept in five years. Everything drooped, from her eyelids to her chin, and it drooped miserably, like she was not only tired, but bitterly unhappy.

"Hi," she whispered so softly I had to lean into her. "I don't eat meat. I'm not sure what I'll order. I think I'll have a tea. Do you think they have green tea? I don't consume sugar. Or I could just have water."

I nodded politely.

"Do you eat sugar? Or meat?" She waved a long, thin, tired finger in my face.

"Both. In large quantities." I smiled.

You'd think I'd told her I married Hitler.

"I have to use the ladies' room. It was nice meeting you, Margaret." I stood up, took my purse off the back of my chair, and looked for the restroom.

When I returned, Tess pulled a chair up next to her to make room for me. I fell into it, muttering, "Thanks. This is an eclectic group of women."

Tess laughed, rolling her eyes. "We're a cross section of America, for sure. Hey, Maria." She reached across the table to get the attention of a bubbly blonde sipping a margarita. "This is Kelly. Don't you do yoga? We've been going to a class occasionally together."

Within minutes, Maria from Nevada talked Tess and me into signing up for her yoga class at the Y. To Maria's left sat Ginny, a financial advisor from New Jersey, who volunteered with the Red Cross and walked every morning in the park near our apartment. "Want to meet there and walk this week?" she asked.

Over BBQ and pitchers of beer, these women talked about where to get the best pedicure, what books they were reading and shows they were watching, and how to decipher the Army acronyms Matt always used. None of them could find a decent job in their field; none of them made more than minimum wage doing whatever they could to keep busy and make a little extra money. The only thing we shared in common was that we lived outside an Army post in Georgia with the men we loved. But somehow, these women—even the ones at the bottom of pyramid schemes selling bags, and the ones who were surprised that a BBQ restaurant in Georgia wouldn't have a vegan menu—made me feel like I wasn't alone.

chapter 10

November 2003
Fort Benning, Georgia
One afternoon, in the first week of November, Tess picked me up for work. When I got in her car, she handed me a clipboard. "Friendsgiving. Sign up for what you want. Do you cook?"

I laughed. "Depends on who you ask. No, I take that back. I don't. I come from a long line of lousy cooks. My mother froze meals every Sunday for the week, then zapped them before dinner. They always contained condensed soups and Ritz crackers, and sometimes green beans. You could eat them with a spork. You know. A spoon and a fork combined. We spent most of the meal picking pieces of saran wrap out of our teeth."

"Okay, you win paper products. How about plates, cups, and flatware for twenty? And maybe a case of beer. Maria's parents are coming from Nevada, and she wants to do the turkey. She said they'll do two, a breast and a whole bird. And Tony wants to deep-fry a turkey in a barrel. The first year he tried it, he almost blew up the turkey, but I think he's figured it out. Ginny and the others will do sides."

"This is such a great idea," I said. "I'm pitiful, I know, but this is my first Thanksgiving away from home. As dysfunctional as my family is, I wasn't looking forward to being away. This will be fun."

I couldn't wait to tell Matt. Later that night, when I heard his truck pull in, I greeted him before he could get through the door. "Hey! Guess what! Friendsgiving in the community room here! With Tess and Ginny and Maria and the others! We don't have to eat my dried-out turkey alone!"

I forgot he had land navigation that day and had spent the past twelve hours in the woods running around looking for points, or that's how he'd explained it to me, anyway, when he told me he'd be late getting home. His face was covered in sweaty streaks of green-and-black camouflage. But even the camo couldn't hide his reaction to my enthusiasm. His eyes narrowed; his lips squeezed shut. He didn't look happy.

He bent down to untie his boots, which were caked up past the ankle in red clay. He placed them outside the door. "I'll clean them later. I'm spent." He walked past me to the refrigerator, opened the door, and took out a bottle of water.

"There are enchiladas on the bottom shelf. Isn't it great about Friendsgiving?"

He took a long swig of the water, put the bottle on the counter, and turned to the fridge to get the enchiladas.

"Hey? Did you hear me? Are you ignoring me?"

He kept his eyes on his plate as he placed it in the microwave, pressed the time, and watched it rotate. He swallowed before he glanced at me. "Sorry. I forgot to tell you my parents are coming."

"You've gotta be shitting me." It came out. One of those thoughts that skipped the filter. I crossed my arms over my chest.

Matt laughed. "I wish I was."

"Why didn't you tell me?" My surprise morphed into anger in record time. He should have told me. His parents! Last Thanksgiving, when we were dating, he'd invited me to meet his family and spend the holiday with them in Virginia. The day before I was planning to drive down — *the day before!* — his mother dis-invited me. Change of plans, she'd told Matt. They were going to a neighbor's house, and she couldn't very well invite "your little friend" to someone else's house for dinner. I was angry and hurt, but Matt drove to my house in New Hampshire the day after Thanksgiving to surprise me, so it worked out. But still. His mother and Thanksgiving left a very sour taste in my mouth.

Matt took his plate out of the microwave and brought it to the table. "I'm sorry, Kel. I should have told you. They called over the weekend, when you were at yoga. They told me they were coming down. My father wants to eat in the mess hall. So we'll do that with them."

He inhaled the enchiladas like a Tyson vacuum cleaner, his face about an inch away from his plate. He didn't see the explosive speed at which my blood boiled.

"WE WILL WHAT? WE WILL DO WHAT WITH THEM?"

That got his attention. His head popped up and away from his plate. His eyes opened wide. Cheese dripped off his lip as he asked, "What? What did I say? I'm sorry. I figured it'd be all right."

"God! You can be so clueless!"

I continued with my angry rant, decreasing the decibels, only so the neighbors didn't hear. "Did you think at all about me? About last Thanksgiving? About how your mother dumped me the day before? Did you think I might not want to spend Thanksgiving with them? And in a mess hall? Who eats in a mess hall on Thanksgiving?"

He put his fork down, his shoulders slumped. "I should have thought about last year. I forgot. Soldiers eat in the mess hall. Officers usually serve them, and my dad knows the CG here, so he talked to him about serving."

"Like I know or care what a CG is. Like I want to go to a mess hall on Thanksgiving. Like you even care. Did you even think to ask me?"

When I got mad as a kid, it came on like an earthquake. It was a rumble that erupted and found no place to hide. It happened sporadically, and usually when my mother did or said something to me. My solution was to storm off; I used to walk around the block. I hadn't done that in years, but I felt a walk coming on.

"You're right. I should have asked you. I was watching the game when they called, and then I fell asleep on the couch, and I forgot all about it until you brought it up tonight." He waited a second before adding, "CG is the commanding general. He's in charge of Fort Benning."

"La-di-da," I said with an attitude. "I bet they love the CG. But they never ask about me, do they?" When I got angry, I brought up topics that weren't related to the issue at hand. My anger earthquake had no boundaries.

Matt moved a piece of chicken around on his plate and stared at it like it had the answer to all the world's problems. In the year and a half that I'd known Matt, he never lied. He was incapable. Where I grew up, it was okay to lie if you didn't want to hurt someone's feelings. Matt didn't play that game. It was never okay for him to lie. He might withhold information, but he never lied.

"Well? Do they?" I pressed him.

He sighed, then looked at me, and said simply, "I'm sorry, Kel."

In an instant, I fell apart. I was a waitress. I had one good friend. I hardly saw Matt. And we were going to spend my first Thanksgiving away from my father at a mess hall with Matt's parents, who didn't like me. I hated my life. Abruptly, I turned and stormed out of the house, slamming the door behind me.

It wasn't a well-planned exit. It was dark and cold, and I wore a T-shirt and shorts and didn't bring my car keys or purse. I walked around the block three times, before I got too tired and too cold, and sat in the dark outside our front door, my head in my hands.

The front door opened behind me, and I looked up to see Matt. His forehead was cut, dried blood smeared with dirt above his tired eyes. His camouflage uniform pants were dirty, and his T-shirt was sweat stained. His black socks hung loose at his ankles; a bloody toe stuck out of a hole in one sock. He sat down next to me on the step and put his arm around my shoulders tenderly. "We'll do Friendsgiving. I'll tell my parents we have plans."

I peeked through my hands to look at him. "Really? You'd do that?"

He squeezed me tight into him. "Yeah, Kel, I'll do that. I love you, remember?"

Someone turned on my waterworks. I sobbed into his smelly T-shirt and pulled it out of his pants to wipe my snot on the bottom.

"Oh, nice," he said. "Come on, let's go in. I gotta take this shirt off. And it's cold out here."

Inside, he led me into the bedroom. Slowly undressing each other, we moved from the shower to the bed, where the distance between us was never far. Until my outburst, it seemed like we were getting used to each other, growing more familiar with each other. Sometimes, I lashed out, tired of my life, sick of nachos. Sometimes, Matt got preoccupied, introspective, aloof. But that night, he chose me over his parents, and it made everything better.

chapter 11

January 2004
Fort Benning, Georgia
Seabury, Florida

I sprayed a blast of Windex on the kitchen window at the same time my phone buzzed on the counter. When I saw the number, I dropped the paper towels and picked up the phone fast.

"Miss me?" I asked, pulling a fleece jacket off the coatrack, and walking out the door to the back patio. I hadn't talked to Tess since she and Tony drove away after the Infantry Basic Course graduation, the week before Christmas.

"It's good to hear your voice. Yeah, I do miss you, and believe it or not, I miss the damn humidity."

I laughed. "How are you? Are you settled in? Is it freezing?"

"It passed freezing about thirty degrees ago. I'm not kidding. It's beautiful, but *sooo* cold. I'm not sure what we were thinking."

"I wondered why anyone would want to move to Alaska. Too late now. Tell me about your road trip, where you're living, everything."

"Not until you tell me about Christmas with the General and his high-and-mighty wife. Oh, wait." She stopped short. "Is Matt around? I don't want to interrupt your last days together. When are you driving to Florida?"

"It's been crazy." I stared at the bare trees beyond the apartment complex fence. "The movers came yesterday and took everything to Fort Campbell, except what Matt needs for ranger school and what I've packed in the back of my car to bring to my aunt's. The apartment's empty except for Matt's gear. He's counting and cleaning it for the millionth time in the garage now."

Tess laughed. She'd been through this drill three years earlier when Tony had gone to ranger school. "And now you're cleaning the empty apartment so you get the security deposit back. I get it. We had to pay for the hole Tony put in the drywall when he moved the bureau into the guest room via that wall. But that's all they gigged us for. When does Matt report?"

"Sunday. But he's going to Ben and Maria's on post tomorrow morning. They're in the same class. Maria will drop them off on Sunday." I wiped a cobweb off the corner of the deck railing. *Do they inspect for cobwebs?* "I'll drive to Florida after we say goodbye tomorrow. We'll stay at a hotel tonight. Hey, give me a quick update on you guys. Then call me back next week when I'm in Florida at my aunt's and we'll catch up more."

"Sounds good. Yeah, so, we're in quarters on post."

I wasn't sure why Army families called post housing "quarters."

"I never liked living on post, but I told Tony, I needed to be near people up here. These quarters aren't bad. He'll be gone a lot. His unit deploys this summer, and, apparently, before they deploy, they pretend to deploy by going to the field all the time. I told him we're buying a snowmobile. I'm making the most of this."

"If you could bottle your attitude, you'd be rich."

"Nah, believe me, I'm not always so positive. You saw me at that gas station, remember?"

I laughed.

"But we've got to carve out our own lives, right?" She paused. "You need to go spend today with Matt, but first, in ten words or less, tell me about Christmas with his family. Were they over you ditching them at Thanksgiving?"

"Oh, that's a story that's a lot more than ten words and requires alcohol. Bottom line? I think the General was mad he had to tell the CG their plans changed, and he wouldn't be serving in the mess hall, but Matt's mother mumbled something about not liking the CG's wife, anyway. I think she was okay not coming. But, yeah, Christmas. Three long days in that house. I can't figure his mother out. I almost think she might like me. But she keeps her distance. His father ignored me, but I think he's that way to everyone. Matt was good, understanding—but spent a lot of time working out, so we were mostly at the gym. It got us both out of the house."

I didn't tell her about Mrs. Carpenter pulling Matt aside, and away from me, our first afternoon there. She took him into her bedroom and talked to him for over an hour. When he walked back into the guest room to find me after, he was close to tears. I was sure that his explanation—"She wanted to catch up with me alone and make sure I was happy"—didn't fully cover whatever she talked to him about. I'd pushed him and bugged him and asked him if it was about me, and he held me tight and told me no, it wasn't about me. He'd told me he loved me, and his mother didn't understand him. "You have nothing to worry about," he'd whispered, sitting next to me on the bed, "and my parents will come around and realize what a gift you are to me." Blah, blah, blah. He'd been so tender, so loving, so hurt by that witch. I fell into his arms, and I got up and closed the bedroom door. I tried to convince us both that we didn't need her blessing.

That story would have taken more than a quick phone call and it wasn't something I wanted to share with Matt nearby. I didn't bring it up.

"Sounds like it was fun," Tess said, sarcasm dripping in her tone. "Go hang out with Matt. I'll call you next week."

I smiled. "Thanks, Tess. Stay warm."

We hung up, and I walked into the garage, empty except for two packed green duffel bags and two bulging rucksacks. Matt, wearing shorts and a T-shirt stained with sweat, leaned over one of the rucksacks, too preoccupied to notice me. I walked toward him, my arms opened wide.

He looked up and smiled, and I watched his internal struggle: stop what he was doing and embrace me, or ignore me and keep counting widgets. I kept my arms open, and, after a few seconds, he walked toward me, the skin on his face stretched taut as he enveloped me tensely. I felt anxiety in every chest muscle. I'd be glad when this course was over.

·   ·   ·

The next morning, I followed his truck through the streets of Fort Benning, identical houses, distinguishable only by the lawn chairs and bikes on the front grass. As we pulled up in front of Ben and Maria's duplex, I opened the console next to me and grabbed some napkins to wipe the tears that wouldn't stop. We said goodbye on the sidewalk in front of their house. Matt, typically hard to read, was rattled, his brow wrinkled, his lips sealed. He held my hands in front of us, then pulled me in tight.

"Hey, I'll be fine," he whispered in my ear. "It's not dangerous."

"I kn-know," I stuttered, getting a grip. "You'll be fine. You'll do great."

I didn't tell him it wasn't *him* I was worried about. If anyone was cut out for this survival stuff, it was Matt. It was *us* I was worried about. He still had those mood swings. On our drive back from his parent's house, they happened a lot. His mother made sure I realized that he'd have no time to write to me, and he'd only have three, at the most, phone calls in the next three months. It made my head ache when I thought about it. *He drifts away when we're together. How far will he drift when we're apart?*

After he graduated from ranger school, assuming he graduated—and I dreaded thinking about him *not* graduating—we were supposed to move together for his first real Army assignment. At Fort Campbell, he'd be out of the school environment. He'd be stationed with an infantry company for three years before the Army assigned him somewhere else. I wondered if he'd miss me when he was at ranger school. I wondered if I'd miss him. If I'd want to stay in Seabury and not move to Fort Campbell with him.

The only thing I knew for certain: ranger school would make or break us.

•   •   •

"Ohhh," I said breathlessly. "I couldn't find my phone! I thought you might be Matt."

It was my first Saturday in Seabury, a crisp, cloudy January day, with the temperature in the fifties. Outside, foamy white waves crashed continuously in the wind.

"No, ma'am, he can't call now. Not during the first phase." Alex was still at flight school at Fort Rucker, but kept up with some guys in Matt's ranger class and was familiar with the schedule. Matt had asked him to check in with me, to keep me updated.

"Andy and Vinny were sent home the first day," Alex continued. "Push-ups. I couldn't believe it. They're studs. Vinny called me, mad at himself. He said Matt looked good—although he wasn't there long enough to see much of him."

I exhaled. "I don't remember Andy and Vinny. I think they were at Tyler's wedding?" I didn't give him time to respond. "So it's good I haven't heard from Matt?"

"Yeah. It's good. You don't want to hear from him until after this Benning phase. That's another three weeks. They can lose a third of the class during this phase. If he makes it through, he'll get an eight-hour pass."

"I could see him then? On the pass?"

"Yeah, you could, but he's not sure when he'll get it. If I hear anything, I'll call you, but I wouldn't worry about it. He'll eat a lot and shower. Then they go right back out for the next phase. Maria will probably pick them up and bring them to their house over the break. She's got your number, right?"

"Yeah, she told me she'd call." I twisted a strand of my hair in my fingers and stared at the waves.

"How are you doing?" Alex knew me well.

"Oh, I'm great. I'm at the beach, eating and showering. I feel guilty when I think about Matt in the woods starving."

"Don't feel guilty. No one forced him to do this. He loves this stuff. It's a dream come true for him."

"Something I'll never understand," I said.

"You and me both." He laughed.

I asked about flight school and his voice picked up, enthusiastically telling me he got the Blackhawk, a type of helicopter, he explained, his first choice. "It's hard," he admitted. "I've never had to study so much."

"Didn't you have to study at West Point?"

"Ha!" He laughed again. "Yeah, but not like my life depended on it. I did what I had to do to pass. Plus, where you end up in your class here makes a big difference in where you get assigned after graduation. We put in requests for the posts we want. Although I sometimes think Big Army tosses a bunch of slips of paper in the air and you get whatever one lands near your name."

From the little I'd seen of the Army, that sounded about right to me. "What are you asking for? Where do you want to go?"

"I'm thinking Fort Campbell, to be near my old roomie, and it's a big aviation post."

I wondered which meant more to him—his personal friendships or his career ambitions. For Matt, it was all about his career. He wanted to go to Fort Campbell because his father told him the unit there would most likely deploy right after Matt arrived. I didn't think Alex was as "hooah"—the term the cadets used to describe someone who was all about the military stuff.

"I have to study. Or I'll end up at Polk."

One of the fun Army facts I'd picked up in the past year was that Fort Polk in Louisiana was like living at a dump on Uranus.

"I hope you get Campbell. That'd be awesome. Hey, you should come down to see us some weekend. My aunt loves you. I told Sara to come."

"Thanks, Kel. Maybe it'll work out."

Hmm. He sounded vague. Noncommittal. I wondered if he had a girlfriend, and I didn't hold back. "Might you have a distraction keeping you in the Fort Rucker area? A Southern belle looking for a man in uniform?"

"Ha, right," he said, avoiding my question. "Tell me about your job. Do you like it?"

I could take a hint. I'd have to ask Sara about the possible girlfriend. I told him about running on the beach in the morning, showering, driving to work wearing jeans and a sweater. I didn't tell him about Joel, a coworker with long, curly blond hair, who kept asking me to go to lunch with him. I'd assumed he was being nice to me because I was the new girl in the office. But Betty, the receptionist and heavyset, matronly bunko buddy of my aunt's, pulled me aside on my second day in the office. "Watch yourself, Kelly. There aren't many cute young women your age in Yarmouth, sweetie."

I'd flashed my ring, surprised.

She'd shrugged as if that didn't matter one bit.

I sighed and answered Alex. "This doesn't suck. I could live here. I need some friends my age, but other than that, I love it."

"Would it get boring?"

"I'm not sure," I admitted. "I'll keep you posted."

When we hung up, I looked out the window at the waves, confident I'd never tire of this view. But I got lonely. My aunt was amazing, but almost forty years older than me. Most of the full-time residents in Seabury drove sedans with FOLLOW ME TO BINGO bumper stickers. It had only been a week. I missed Matt. I missed Tess. I missed having friends.

chapter 12

February into March 2004
Seabury, Florida
Fort Benning, Georgia

Late one Saturday morning, three weeks after that conversation with Alex, I sat on my bed studying for the CPA exam, when my phone rang with a call from a 706-area code—Fort Benning. I grabbed it before the second ring. Matt was on his eight-hour break. Relieved that he'd made it through the Benning phase in his first attempt, his voice tensed when he talked about the next phase in the mountains.

"It's good to hear you, Kel." Background noises drowned out his voice. "Oh, yeah, pepperoni, great. I'll take a Coke, too. And water, thanks," he said to someone. Conversations droned in the background, plates clattered, an ESPN announcer jabbered above the din.

"Getting food?" I asked lamely, feeling far away.

"Uh, yeah, it's crazy here. Steve, Rob, and Mo are here. I don't think you know them. They're classmates, but were in a different platoon at the basic course. We're eating and I think Chris is asleep on the couch. There's not enough time. Yeah, ice, thanks!"

"Oh." I shrank inside. He had things to do that were more important than talking to me. "Go eat and get a shower."

He didn't argue.

"I'm proud of you. I love you," I added, subdued.

"I love you, too, Kel," he said hastily. "Thanks. I'll call after mountains, I hope."

He didn't ask about my job. He didn't ask how I was doing. *He's tired.*

Later that day, Alex called to tell me he'd talked to him, too.

"I barely got anything out of him," I told Alex, trying not to sound petty.

"Yeah, I don't think he'll really relax until this course is over. It's a real suck. He was pissed and starving. But he asked about you. I think he only called me to get my take on how you're doing."

I wasn't sure how true that was, but I appreciated Alex saying it.

Maria called me after she dropped them back off after their break. "They're worried about the mountain phase. The weather's supposed to be rainy and cold next week. They're dreading it and just want to get mountains behind them. You didn't miss anything, Kelly. All they did was eat and sleep."

But I still felt like I missed something.

•   •   •

The next weekend, Sara and Jake visited. We spent the afternoon wandering the cute shops and breweries in Brewster, a nearby fishing village. Jake told me about flight school, and Sara told me about her students and how she got roped into being the sponsor for the junior prom. She couldn't stop smiling when she talked about her job.

Sara and I stood outside a dress shop window, pointing out what we'd buy if we had a million dollars, when I asked, out of the blue, "Do you see Alex much?"

She pointed to a red silk dress. "Oh, that's you."

I laughed. "It's probably only five hundred dollars. I haven't worn dresses in months. Here it's all flip-flops and jeans."

We turned and followed Jake, who ambled ahead of us.

"This beach life suits you. Five-hundred-dollar dresses are overrated, anyway. And no, we hardly ever see Alex. I told Jake on the drive down. We need to have him over for dinner. He only lives about ten miles away, but by the time I get home from school, that seems so far. Plus, he's got the girlfriend now."

I stopped in place. "Excuse me. What?"

Jake turned and gave Sara a face that said, *"I told you not to say anything."*

"What? What's the big deal? Why can't you tell me Alex has a girlfriend?"

Sara looked down at her feet. "We're not sure if it's a thing. His roommate told Jake that Alex was dating his sister. Will's family visited from Texas and he met her then. The sister's back in Texas now, so we don't know what's going on."

"I don't get why you couldn't tell me." Out of the corner of my eye, I saw Sara and Jake exchange glances. "What's the problem?"

Sara shook her head. "Nothing. Well, okay, something. You're sort of a mother hen about Alex. No one's good enough for him."

I laughed out loud. "Jesus, you're right. I guess my standards are high. But he's such a good guy. All right, point taken. I'll lighten up. But you guys need to include me in this stuff. I have no life here. I need to keep up!"

"Roger." Jake nodded. "We'll keep you in the loop from now on."

"Well," Sara said, "what about Kate?"

Jake shot her another look that said, *"I'm out of this."*

"What about Kate?" I asked.

"Well, we heard through one of Kate's friends from the lacrosse team, who's at flight school, that Kate told Alex to request Germany for his first assignment after flight school — so they'd be close and could travel together."

I wasn't sure what to say, so I opened my eyes wide, looked at Sara, and said nothing, until I had a thought. "But wait. What about the girlfriend in Texas?"

Sara tilted her head and looked at Jake. "We're not sure what he'll do. He's in high demand." She shrugged, pulling the inside of her cheek to one side. "It makes sense, though, that he'd have Will's sister *and* Kate after him. Like you said, he's a good guy. And he's almost as good-looking as Jake." She leaned into her husband, who shook his head, grinning.

We'd stopped on the sidewalk outside a café. Jake focused on the menu posted on the sign out front. "Let's go in," he said, opening the door. He led us past a sign that read SEAT YOURSELF to a booth by the window. We sat and sipped our beers and watched people walk by.

I listened to them talk about going to a concert in Montgomery with some friends, and playing *Guitar Hero* with friends, and when their softball team would start practicing. I was happy for Sara. I was. I wanted her to be happy. Spending time with Sara made me realize how much I missed having friends.

·   ·   ·

Early Sunday evening, my aunt and I stood on her deck and waved goodbye as Jake backed his truck out of the driveway. The sky was painted with cotton balls soaked in pastels, sweeping above the gulf in blues, oranges, yellows, and reds.

"Wow. Are winter sunsets the best?"

"They're my favorite," my aunt said. "The cold seems to make the colors more vibrant."

We stood quietly until she broke the silence. "Why didn't Alex come down with Sara and Jake?"

"Not sure. I think he has a girlfriend. I'm not sure if he had plans with her this weekend."

"Oh, a girlfriend. What do you think about that?"

This woman didn't mess around.

"I think I need to lighten up about that. Sara and Jake told me that my standards are too high for Alex. I don't think anyone's good enough for him."

My aunt grinned. "I feel the same way and I just met him."

"I think I blew it when he was here in October. When we talked out there that first night, I told him stuff about Matt that I probably shouldn't have. Nothing major, but Matt can sort of go off into his own world sometimes. He gets distant, like he's thinking about something else, but he won't open up to me about it. It's not a big deal, and I'm used to it now, but I put Alex in the middle by asking him about it. I shouldn't have done that."

"Did he seem uncomfortable? When you talked to him in October?"

I sighed. "No, he was great. He said anything I told him stays with him. He's a good friend."

My aunt put her arm around me. "Let's go in. It's getting cold."

In the house, she opened the cabinet and took out a bottle of wine. I took out two glasses and the corkscrew. Carrying my glass into the living room, I stood in front of the large, detailed painting that hung behind the sofa. When I was young, I used to stare at it for hours on rainy days, inspecting the beach scene filled with tiny detailed bodies, loaded with activity and color. The gulf was blue green; the sky was bright blue. The faces weren't clear, but the bodies and towels, even the paddleboards, were tiny, intricate, perfect.

"I love this."

Aunt Patty smiled and nodded. "Thanks. That was a fun project. Took me months."

She carried her glass to the couch, and I followed her and sat on the recliner.

"Alex is a good person and a good friend," she said. "I wonder if he told Matt the same thing he told you. That Matt could tell him anything and it wouldn't go anywhere. Maybe he's afraid that if he spent time with you, he'd let something slip."

"Maybe," I agreed. But I wasn't sure if that was it.

Aunt Patty's milky eyes sparkled less than the brown eyes I remembered from when I was a kid, but they were still empathetic and kind.

"None of my business, but I'm going to ask you, anyway. Do you only want Alex to be your friend?"

"What do you mean?" I sucked my cheeks in and sat up straight.

She said nothing, so I filled in the silence. "Oh, come on, really? I'd never do anything with anyone when I was engaged. You know me better than that."

"Oh, I know, honey. I've heard about surfer Joel." She winked. "Like I said, it's none of my business. But . . . it's not always easy to have a platonic relationship with someone like Alex."

"What's that mean?" I drew my chin in.

"Oh, nothing." She shrugged. "Except he's kind and thoughtful and exceptionally good-looking. Oh, and he seems very interested in you."

"He's not," I said, forcing myself to remain calm.

She raised her eyebrows, keeping her eyes on mine.

"Okay, so Alex was the first cadet I met on spring break. I met him before Matt. As soon as Sara and I checked into the hotel, I put on my bathing suit and went down to the beach, and he was there. Sara went off with Jake—and I was alone with Alex for an hour or two, talking—but then I found out he wasn't available. There was this blonde, Ashleigh, and they dated in high school. She walked over to us and pulled Alex away, like she owned him."

I remembered every detail of that first night. I left out the part about Ashleigh bouncing over, all blond hair and big breasts, wearing a hot-pink bikini. My aunt sipped her wine, waiting for more of the story.

"So, when Ashleigh walked over, she was with Matt. And when Alex left with her, I was left with Matt. I assumed she and Alex were a couple. I didn't find out until later that they hadn't been together in years. The whole trip, we all hung out together, the whole gang of cadets—Jake, Sara, Matt, me, Alex, Tyler, Heather, the other guys—and Ashleigh wasn't around. I saw her a few times with guys from other colleges, but Sara didn't know the full story and I didn't ask. By then, Matt was always around me, and we started hanging out together. I found out the real Ashleigh story later. She had issues."

"What's her story?"

"Alex and Ashleigh dated, off and on, in high school, and on and off during his freshman year at West Point. They weren't dating before that spring break trip, but she saw him over Christmas vacation junior year and found out he was going, so she signed up to go. He figured, it's a free country. He couldn't make her not go. But then she got all crazy possessive and told him if he didn't pay attention to her, she'd hurt herself. Sara said it's not as if she wanted him, but she didn't want him to have anyone else, either. Real manipulative stuff."

"Oh, Kelly. That's such a burden on Alex. Has she received help?"

"Jake told Sara that Alex called Ashleigh's parents after the trip. He told them what she said, about hurting herself, and he told Ashleigh that he'd help her, but as a couple, they were done."

My aunt nodded.

"I didn't learn any of this until I'd been quasi-dating Matt for a few months. Whenever I was with Matt, we were always in a group, and Alex was always part of that group. We became really good friends. But we've never been anything more than friends." I paused. "I wish I'd never said anything to him in October about Matt, though."

"You tell good friends everything. But I see your concern. Since he's Matt's best friend, he's stuck in the middle."

We sat in silence and finished our wine, and I wondered how much damage I'd done to my relationship with Alex.

chapter 13

March into May 2004
Seabury, Florida
I wrote letters to Matt at least twice a week, filling pages with mundane comments about the weather, new tax regulations, and my yoga class. I wrote about the new pottery class my aunt was teaching, Mary Ann and Kyle, and Tess's new snowmobile. I knew he didn't have time to write back, but still, I wrote faithfully, like a good fiancée.

In mid-February, over a month after he had started the course, my heart leaped when I saw a white envelope addressed to me in his big, loopy, messy writing, sitting in the pile of my aunt's mail on the kitchen table. I ripped the envelope open. My first letter from Matt contained three sentences of barely decipherable cursive:

It's freezing up here. I started mountains, and I'm doing okay so far. There's no time to write. Love, Matt

I stared at the page, thinking, *Really? That's all you've got? Way to make me feel inconsequential to your life.*

But I kept writing to him. It was the right thing to do. I missed him. I wanted to stay close to him. If neither of us wrote, our relationship seemed doomed.

On my calendar, I circled the date he was supposed to complete the mountain phase. I didn't run that morning. I kept the phone on my desk at work. I took it into the bathroom with me. I didn't shower. I waited. At least fifteen times, I checked the volume on the phone to make sure it was up. I ate dinner with the phone next to me at the table.

An hour after dinner, Alex called. "Hey. I wanted to touch base with you. I heard from Matt."

"Huh?"

"He figured you were at work. He said to tell you he's okay. But, bad news. He has to redo mountains."

"Oh, no!" *Why didn't he call me?* "Is he really okay?"

"His pride's hurt, but he's all right. He got a no-go on patrols. He's mad as hell."

I was quiet. Upset for him, but mostly annoyed that he'd called Alex, and not me.

"At himself," Alex added.

"I sent him my work number in every letter. And I had my phone next to me all day and night." I regretted it the second it left my mouth. It wasn't Alex's fault.

"Yeah. I'm sorry. I know you wanted to talk to him. But it might have been a good call to miss. He was pissed."

"Yeah, I guess." I forced myself to pretend I understood. "I'm sorry I shot the messenger. I didn't mean to take it out on you."

"Don't worry about it."

"Did he ask you to call his parents?"

"Yes, ma'am. I don't mind. I'll call them next. I wanted to call you first."

"Thanks." I thought about it. "Hey, what's this mean for graduation? Probably not until the end of April now?"

"Yeah. I think so. If he's out for two weeks, then in mountains for three weeks, then he has the swamps for three weeks. I'd plan on the end of April, early May."

"He wants to get to Campbell before they deploy," I said.

"Yeah. That's why he wanted to go to the 101st."

I'd done some research and learned that Matt would be assigned to the 101st Airborne Division at Fort Campbell, Kentucky, after ranger school. It was on the state line between Kentucky and Tennessee, about an hour away from Nashville.

"Isn't that why you want to go?" Before he could answer, I remembered Sara telling me that Kate asked him to go to Germany. I'd never asked Alex about that, assuming he'd tell me if he wanted to tell me. "Oh, wait, are you still requesting Campbell?"

"Yeah. I think so. But I'm not trying to deploy right away. We'll all get over there, eventually. I'd like more flight time CONUS before deploying."

CONUS was continental United States, not overseas. I'd learned that at Smokey's BBQ, in between how to make brisket and where to buy the best produce.

It made sense. Alex wanted more time to train before going off to a war. I couldn't understand why Matt was in such a rush to deploy, but whenever I asked him, he told me this is what he spent four years at West Point training for. I thought he was trying to prove himself to his father, but if I brought that up, he shook his head a little too hard. I stopped asking.

I asked Alex about school, about his life.

"Nothing new. A lot of studying."

I stared at the calendar on my bedroom wall, trying not to look at the long months ahead until Matt's new graduation date.

Out of nowhere, Alex asked, "Hey, I was thinking I'd come down the first weekend in March?"

"Oh! Great!" I didn't even try to rein in my excitement or surprise.

When I told my aunt, she smiled as if she was not surprised at all.

•   •   •

"Oh, no, we're not together." I babbled self-consciously, glancing from the stocky gray-haired lady, with a black Lab puppy on a leash, to Alex, next to me, smirking. We'd been walking between the booths at the farmers' market in Yarmouth, a field filled with people selling everything from local corn to cypress tables. The lady's puppy had jumped on me and we'd stopped to pat it.

"Well, we're together, but not like that." I kept babbling.

The woman nodded at me, like I was simple, then pulled her puppy away from us, toward a booth selling homemade soap.

I looked at Alex. "Thanks for the help."

He shrugged and put his arm around me. "If some nice lady wants to think we're a couple, what's the big deal?"

He withdrew his arm as we walked away.

"I thought Mary Ann would come with us, but Kyle had soccer sign-ups." We walked across the street to an empty bench overlooking the bay.

"Did you honestly invite Mary Ann so we didn't look like a couple?" He sat on the bench, holding back a smile. He wore a snug long-sleeved T-shirt and jeans. With his dirty-blond hair and blue eyes, women looked twice at him when they walked by. Though I'd only ever admitted it to Sara, that was the way I'd looked at him the first night I met him.

"Okay, I confess, I thought about matching you up with her." I sat next to him. "But I hear you have a girlfriend?"

I glanced at him out of the corner of my eye, waiting for a reaction.

He smiled. "No, ma'am."

I nudged him. "Come on. I have connections. What about your roommate's sister?"

He turned and tilted his head toward the marshes across the bay. "Think there are alligators over there?"

"Think the pope's Catholic?" I shot back as I elbowed him. "You're stalling. None of my business?"

"Yeah, right." He elbowed me back. "I've told you before. My business is your business, Kelly McGowan. You know that."

"It better be."

"So, yeah, I met Will's sister on family day. We hit it off, did a little long-distance dating, saw her one weekend. We're done now." He seemed matter-of-fact about it.

"Um," I asked, not sure how to follow up with this. "Are you all right with it?"

"Yeah." He paused, then added, "So Kate . . ."

I turned to look at him, but he was staring at the marsh, as if searching for Waldo hiding in the reeds.

"Kate?" My chest tightened. I needed to be accepting or he wouldn't open up to me. I gave my filter a warning to kick in.

"Yeah. We talk." His eyes glanced at me, before he turned back to the marsh. "She thinks I should ask for Germany after flight school."

I bowed my head, examining my topsiders.

He turned to me with wide eyes. "No reaction? From you, that's something."

I waited, gathering my emotions in a meager attempt to sound nonjudgmental. I settled on, "I'd sort of heard something about this."

He grinned. "Nothing is sacred among classmates and their nosy spouses."

I stared at the tall reeds across the bay. Miles and miles of tan and green growing out of the bay. "So? What are you going to do?"

We gazed in the same direction, parallel lines of sight, avoiding eye contact with each other. A heron splashed into the bay before flying away toward the marsh.

Alex straightened his arms and leaned forward, his palms flat on the bench. His blue eyes met mine. "What do you think I should do?"

I felt my cheeks flush, and I blinked, then rubbed my eyes to buy some time. I decided to be honest. "I don't want you to get hurt. I'm not sure what you guys are — friends or more than friends, but either way, I don't want you to get hurt." Silence. I wasn't done, but I took a break to let us sit comfortably in quiet as rolling clouds dimmed the blue sky and a boat entered the canal and docked.

"Got it," he said finally.

"But," — I turned to look at him and waited until his eyes met mine again — "I'd be lying if I didn't tell you, I was hoping you'd be at Campbell with us. But that's selfish." I swallowed the lump in my throat. "You need to do what's right for you. I get that. I want you to be happy."

He put his arm around me and pulled me in tight, before releasing me and moving slightly away. "Thanks, Kel. I appreciate it."

•　　　•　　　•

The following weekend, Mary Ann and I sat on beach chairs, wearing sweatshirts in the cool sun, our bare feet dug into the sand for warmth. We watched Kyle build a castle, knowing he'd kick it over when it was big enough. The air was brisk, but there was no wind; the gulf was quiet and still.

"I have time for that long story now, if you have time to tell it."

She smiled. "If you're sure. I don't want to scare you away. I haven't always been as normal as you might think."

I threw my head back dramatically. "Right! Who said you were ever normal?"

She drew her lips together, grinning. Turning from me to Kyle, and back to me again, she said, "I guess it started when my parents talked me into applying to B.C. I didn't want to go. I mean, yeah, it's a good school, but I didn't know anyone in Boston, other than some cousins I hadn't seen in ten years. But my parents wanted me to go. *Especially* my mother. Legacy student, and all that. So I tried to convince myself that it'd be good for me to get away from her and move north. She drove me crazy."

I must have looked as surprised as I felt.

"I know. You never saw my mother as anything other than great. That's why I didn't want to—"

"Hey," I interrupted, holding one hand out in front of me like a stop sign. "Believe me, I get it. It's not always what it seems."

"Yeah, that's the truth. But she *was* great. She still *is*. When we were kids, she took you and Megan in, like you were hers, and y'all loved her. But y'all didn't see how controlling she was. It got bad in high school. She had to be involved in every aspect of our lives. She couldn't let us do anything without her. If I went to the mall, she was hiding in Abercrombie, stalking me."

"Wow!" I shook my head. "My mother's on the opposite end of the spectrum. She didn't care. She was done being a mom the minute we exited her womb."

Mary Ann raised her shoulders and dropped them. "There's probably a happy medium. For Kyle's sake, I hope I find it."

"You'll be perfect. You're a great mom."

As if on cue, Kyle ran toward us with a handful of shells. Mary Ann admired them and asked him to pick the most special ones and put them in the blue plastic bucket next to her chair. When he ran back to his sandcastle, she continued her story.

My heart sank as she told me how lonely she was in Boston; how her roommate had been a partier, a rich kid from Philadelphia with whom she had nothing in common. She told me how she lost interest in everything and spent days in her bed in her dorm room.

"Looking back, I was depressed," she said. "But I was too busy wallowing to think about it. I didn't care about anything. I quit before I lost my scholarship and got thrown out of school. I moved in with a guy I met. Kyle's father. It was stupid. I lived with him for four months, got a job bartending, and never talked to my parents."

"Were you happy?"

She shook her head. "No. I was being spiteful. At least, that's what my therapist told me. She said I felt like I had no control growing up. Not that I'm making excuses for my stupid behavior. When I got pregnant, Ian, Kyle's father—though he has nothing to do with either of us—told me to get an abortion. He couldn't afford a baby."

Her eyes watered as we both turned to watch Kyle digging in the sand. She shook her head. "He wasn't ready to be a father. He wasn't interested in having a baby."

"What did you do?"

"I called home."

I waited.

"My mother told me they loved me, and I could always move back home. They'd help."

I exhaled. "That had to have been hard. Going from being so independent. . ." I stopped myself from continuing.

She opened her eyes wide and grimaced. "You have no idea."

Kyle chased seagulls down the beach until they flew away and landed somewhere else; then he chased them again.

"On another note," —I sensed a change of conversation might be good—"I'm bummed you missed seeing Alex last weekend."

She looked at me, her head tilted, her lips pursed.

"What? I know that face."

She raised her eyebrows. "Nothing."

I waited for more. She cupped her mouth and yelled for Kyle to move back closer. He'd followed the gulls too far down the beach. Then she turned to me. "He's a good friend, right?"

I nodded. "Yeah. I never had such good guy friends until I met Matt. He came with a group of them."

She opened her mouth to say something, then closed it.

"Not you, too." I rolled my eyes. "We're *friends*. That's it. I love his best friend."

She barely nodded, then turned to watch Kyle, who'd given up trying to catch a seagull, and carried his shovel toward the water's edge.

"Being friends with a guy never works," she said simply.

I didn't respond.

She looked at me and raised her eyebrows. "Especially a guy that looks like Alex. I saw him that weekend he was down with Sara and Jake."

I had to smile. "I won't argue. He's not bad on the eyes. But I don't see it anymore. When I first met him, I admit I did. Yeah, he was really good-looking. Now, I just see him as a brother. And I'm marrying Matt." I held out my hand with the diamond to remind her.

She rolled her eyes so much, I felt like her head might roll off with them.

I watched Kyle throw shells into the gulf; then I heaved myself out of my beach chair to join him.

•   •   •

Over two months later, the phone rang as I stepped in the door after work. I'd been waiting for this call, the call after the swamp phase. I was packed and ready to go.

"I miss you." I fingered my engagement ring, hoping he'd say the same thing.

"I miss you, too." It sounded like he meant it, but sixty-plus days in the field—ninety-plus with the mountain recycle—he'd probably say the same thing to the cashier at the McDonald's drive-through window.

Since I left him at Fort Benning over three months earlier, we'd talked twice. Both calls were short: He'd been tired, hungry, and distracted.

I'd see him in two days. That's when I'd know what our future would hold.

*   *   *

I packed my bags, daydreaming of being together romantically, of capturing the dating magic we once had. Then my chest tightened, and I bit my nails down to nubs, thinking. What if this absence hadn't made his heart grow fonder? What if he were done with me? Then what would I do? Move in with my aunt? Move to New Hampshire? My second-grade friend Sharon called the night before. "Kim and I have a sleeper sofa with your name on it. If you move up here, we'll find a three-bedroom apartment when our lease is up."

I'd laughed, grateful for the offer to room with my friends in Boston. But I loved Matt. I wanted to make this work. I loaded my last bag in the back seat and turned to hug my aunt.

"This is your home and you're always welcome here." She wrapped her bony arms around my waist. "I hope you know that."

I wiped my eyes with the bottom of my long-sleeved T-shirt and held her tight. My stomach hurt as I drove down Sand Dollar Lane, my body revolting from my departure from the place I found so comforting. As I passed the tall pines on the road out of Seabury, I realized that the house in New Hampshire where I grew up was full of memories, some good, some bad, but Seabury would always be home.

chapter 14

May 2004
Outside Fort Rucker, Alabama
Fort Benning, Georgia

Sara took a handful of napkins and wiped the crumbs off the outside table before we sat down. I was glad I'd looked at the map before I left my aunt's house for Fort Benning. When I saw that I'd pass through a town thirty minutes away from where Sara lived, I called her and asked if she could meet for lunch. It was a school day, so we settled for coffee. She assured me she could tell her principal she had an appointment, show up late, and not get fired.

As soon as we sat, she babbled on about the prom, the decorations, the music, the kids making out in the bathroom. I nodded and smiled until she looked at her watch and realized she'd monopolized the conversation.

"Enough about me." She leaned across the table. "Are you nervous about moving to Fort Campbell?"

I put my mocha down and picked up a napkin, folding it into tiny pieces. I wasn't sure how honest I wanted to be. Anything I said, she'd tell Jake, and Jake would tell Alex, and Alex would tell Matt. Cadets gossiped more than seventh-grade girls. But it had been a year since their West Point graduation, and I sensed they were all too consumed with their new careers to gossip.

When my napkin couldn't be folded any smaller, I put it down and picked at my blueberry muffin.

"Yeah, I am," I admitted. "Nervous. I mean, getting used to life in Georgia took some attitude adjustment, right?"

She laughed. "Oh, my God. It's so different down here. So slow! But everyone's so nice!"

"I know. After I got to know some people and made some friends, Fort Benning was okay. Except for not finding a job. I need to find a job in Tennessee—a real job."

Sara put her coffee down, brought her elbow onto the table, and rested her chin in her palm.

I exhaled. "I don't know. Matt's been different—before he went to ranger school, anyway—different from when we were dating. He's great most of the time. Thoughtful, kind, still a hunk." I grinned. "But every so often, he gets distant. There's something off. And now, I haven't seen him for over three months, and I'm not sure if he'll be there—with me—when I see him."

Sara's eyes opened wide. "I'm sorry," she said.

"I didn't say anything. I mean, what could you do? I want to make this work."

She put her top lip over her bottom, then brought her hand up to her mouth. We both glanced at the traffic. A banana-yellow sports car beeped long and hard at an eighteen-wheeler, passing it on the right.

Sara moved her hand away from her mouth. "Do you think it's the living-together thing? How different that is from dating, when they're there *all the time*?" She emphasized their constant omnipresence by opening her eyes wide and bobbing her head.

I stared down at my muffin. "I'm not sure. Is it hard for you? The truth. Is it hard living with Jake? Twenty-four/seven?"

She shook her head imperceptibly, as if to answer both yes and no. "It's different. He snores, and he's a slob, and for such a big guy, he's a fussy eater." Her shoulders sagged. "But he's my best friend. I'm happy. I'm lucky."

I smiled. *Yes, you really are.*

We hugged goodbye, and she made me promise to call her either way, to talk to her always about anything, and I drove away, feeling lighter, relieved that I'd been honest with her. I turned on the radio station, searched for a '90s station, and belted "Bye Bye Bye" with NSYNC, one hand on the wheel, the other out the open window, until the humidity forced me to close the window and turn on the air in the car.

•　　•　　•

I stopped to ask directions from three different soldiers, on three different streets as I drove aimlessly through the back roads of Fort Benning, buckets of sweat pouring down my arms and chest, my heart racing. I looked up and there it stood, a two-story vinyl-sided barracks in the middle of nowhere, not another building in sight. Camp Rogers. Matt told me on the phone that he had four hours to prepare his uniform for graduation the next morning, and if I could find this place, he'd be able to see me. I parked and got out of my car, uncertain what to do next.

The door of the barracks opened and a red-faced soldier in a camouflage uniform and shaved head walked out. He saw me standing next to my car, asked who I was there to see, then walked back inside the building and, in a deep, echoing voice, yelled something indecipherable. I wiped the sweat off my palms on the side of my shorts and reached in my purse to grab a brush to run through my hair. My hand shook. I breathed deeply, in and out, to steady myself.

The front door opened again, and a thin version of Matt walked outside. He wore his Army PT uniform, a gray T-shirt tucked into black shorts. When he saw me, he smiled and broke into a jog toward me. Opening his arms wide, he wrapped me in his tight embrace. When he released me, we stood inches apart and stared in each other's eyes, until his lips met mine. I trembled. He'd never kissed me in a public setting — never mind, on a military installation.

"You look so good, Kel," he whispered in my ear, pulling a strand of my hair behind my ear. "Your hair's longer."

I closed my eyes and leaned into him, tracing his back with my fingers. "Thanks. I missed you so much. You're so thin." I brought my hands around to the front and felt his ribs through his T-shirt. "Do you feel okay?"

"I do now." He pulled me closer to him. My heart pounded and my body felt warm as I leaned into his chest and exhaled with relief.

·   ·   ·

The next morning, Mrs. Carpenter, wearing creased navy khakis, a red-and-white–striped blouse, navy flats, and her ever-present pearls, stood across from the check-in counter in the guesthouse where we were staying. Only military ID card holders could use the guesthouse, and since I didn't have a military ID card, Matt had asked his parents to make my reservation. I hadn't seen them when they arrived the night before.

She greeted me with a very loose hug which almost indicated she didn't think I was contagious. Her husband sat in the car out front waiting for us.

They'd insisted on driving me to the graduation ceremony. "It's out in the middle of nowhere, Kelly," General Carpenter told me on the phone the night before. "We'll drive. See you in the lobby at zero seven-thirty. Dress casual."

He was right, of course. I got the feeling he usually was. We drove through a series of dirt roads, lined with pine trees, before pulling into a cleared gravel lot near bleachers that overlooked a lake. I never would have found this place.

Less than two seconds out of the car, Mrs. Carpenter saw someone she recognized. A petite woman in denim capris and sneakers walked past us. "Brenda? Is that you? Don't tell me little Mike's in this course?"

General Carpenter and the woman's tall, lean husband walked ahead toward the bleachers. Their wives fell into a conversation behind them, exchanging the typical remarks of "You haven't aged a bit!" and "Where are you now?"

It didn't look like Mrs. Carpenter planned to introduce me, or even pretend to know me. I stepped off to their side, behind the men, but the little woman turned toward me and extended her hand. Mrs. Carpenter had no choice but to introduce me. I admit, I felt smug.

"Oh, yes, Kelly, meet Brenda Foley, an old family friend."

I shook her tiny, soft hand, and she smiled as if thrilled to meet me. I liked her immediately.

Mrs. Carpenter dug down into her purse and pulled out a small bottle of bug spray, and handed it to her friend. Brenda sprayed her arms, then handed it to me. I was pretty sure Mrs. Carpenter hadn't planned to waste any of her spray on me, so I smiled gratefully at Mrs. Foley, who put her arm around me like we were old pals. "Let's go get a good seat. These demonstrations are something to see!"

We walked to the bleachers as I thought, *Why didn't I get a mother-in-law like Brenda Foley?*

●　　　●　　　●

The new rangers lined up between Victory Lake and the bleachers. Mrs. Carpenter was convinced she saw Matt—"Oh, look, there! There he is!"—but the bald soldiers in soft caps and camouflage uniforms standing in formation all looked the same to me. Mrs. Foley was right about the demonstrations; they kept us awake. Rangers rappelled and attacked objectives across the lake in small collapsible boats. There were explosions and detonating devices, all performed and timed to precision. It was impressive, and it was a lot.

The uniformed man with the deep voice at the microphone invited the families to pin the coveted tab on the new rangers. I followed the Carpenters to where Matt stood in the back row. When he saw us approach, he'd lost so much weight, his smile hit his cheekbones. I almost keeled over watching General Carpenter hold back tears as he embraced his son.

I was so touched by the General's emotions—something I'd never seen before—that I didn't realize until after the ceremony that Matt had hugged his mother before he hugged me. He wasn't thinking, I rationalized; it was the excitement of the moment. Not a big deal.

I walked with Matt and his parents to the car, waiting every few feet as they stopped to talk to someone. They ran into another couple and their son, who looked like he'd lost even more weight than Matt. As they congratulated each other and compared notes, Mrs. Foley walked up to me, interlocked her arm in mine, and asked, "Well, wasn't that something?"

I laughed and walked with her toward the car. The Carpenters trailed behind us, and her husband wandered off to talk to someone.

She didn't give me time to respond. She leaned into me and said in a hushed voice, "I'm so happy that Matt met you. He was so devastated after that breakup. I can't imagine what a mess you walked into after that. Those two mothers had been planning that wedding since Matt and Eve were in second grade together at Fort Drum. Everyone was stunned when she broke up with him so suddenly, but my heart went out to Matt. He's always been such a good kid. He deserves to be happy."

My eyes had to have been as big as saucers, but she was too busy trying not to trip in the gravel to notice. She squeezed her arm into mine and released it, walking beside me until her husband turned and waved at her to hurry.

"Oh, I'd better run. It was so nice to meet you, Kelly."

I smiled, my lips tight, and didn't move until Matt walked up behind me with his parents.

•   •   •

In the back seat, Matt put my hand on his thigh and answered his father's questions about the course as we drove to the guesthouse. It was probably good that we weren't alone, and I didn't have the chance to ask about Mrs. Foley's comments. The last thing I needed to do was sound insecure about an old girlfriend. But it explained why his mother didn't like me so much. Who knew she'd been planning his wedding to another girl for years?

When we walked into the guesthouse, Mrs. Carpenter told Matt to run up and change, and insisted I stay in the lobby and catch up. It didn't seem appropriate to tell my future mother-in-law that I'd prefer to spend the next ten minutes watching the fiancé I hadn't seen in almost four months undress, so I sat in the lobby and listened to her reminisce about living at Fort Benning.

After dinner with his parents, we were finally alone in my room at the guesthouse.

"I need a shower," Matt said. "I didn't take one earlier. I didn't want to leave you alone with my mother any longer than I had to."

"Thanks for that. That was weird, right?"

Ignoring my question, he pulled his shirt off over his head and unsnapped his jeans to strip. "Come in with me?"

I turned my back to him, pointed to the top of the zipper on the back of my dress, and waited as he unzipped my dress too quickly. Stepping aside coyly to take it off, I turned around and faced him. His ribs protruded, exposed from the weight he lost. I saw the bruises on his arms and legs, a rash on his calves. I moved closer and traced my pointer finger down his chest until he dismissed my concerns, assuring me that everyone lost weight. He'd gain it back, he promised. But my heart ached for him, and when he took my finger and put it over my lips, then moved it down on his body and kissed me so tenderly, I forgot all about Mrs. Foley's comments. I forgot all about him hugging his mother before me at the graduation ceremony. I forgot all about everything, except how content I felt being loved again.

part two
the army

chapter 15

June 2004

Fort Campbell, Kentucky

I yawned and stood up to stretch, accidentally dropping my thick, incredibly dull CPA review book on the laminate floor. The thump echoed through the empty house. The webbing on the lawn chair had streaked the back of my legs red and I rubbed them before I bent to pick up the book. *Where is that moving van?*

I walked to the window. At one end of the street, a woman with a pink visor over gray curly hair, with a poodle on a leash, shuffled along the sidewalk. In the other direction, I watched a thin blonde wearing Ray-Bans, her ponytail poking out the back of her ball cap, push a stroller. I peered toward the street entrance: no moving van.

Five days earlier, we'd driven around Clarksville, a city outside the gates of Fort Campbell, looking at houses, before we signed a one-year lease on a three-bedroom, two-bath rental in a newly developed neighborhood. Every house on our street was a cookie-cutter replica of the house two doors down. I told Matt I'd buy a wreath for the front door so I wouldn't walk into the wrong house. Matt was a second lieutenant, the lowest rank in the officer corps, and I was unemployed; this rental met our budget. It was new and clean and convenient, off the busy main drag they called 41A, close to his work, grocery stores, shops, and the interstate.

As soon as we signed the rental agreement, we called to connect the water, electricity, cable, and internet. Like little kids playing house, we wandered the aisles of Walmart and bought a queen-sized air mattress, two pillows, sheets, fifty paper plates, a package of Solo cups, and two lawn chairs.

Along with our clothes, Matt had packed two sets of flatware, two coffee cups, two bath towels, and a roll of toilet paper in his truck. After we unloaded my car and his truck, Matt humored my request to be carried across the threshold. He held me tight, and once inside the door, we kissed deeply, with the passion I'd missed so much. I was hopeful.

"We're lucky," Matt told me. "The movers can bring our stuff Monday. Sometimes it takes weeks."

So lucky. Sharing an air mattress with a guy who weighs over two hundred pounds was not fun. Monday morning at five o'clock, when Matt rolled off his side to get up for work, the shift in pressure tossed me off my side onto the floor. He rushed over, stifling laughter, to see if I was okay. I might have laughed with him, if he hadn't snored like a freight train and kept me up all night. We needed a real mattress. And curtains. The lights of every passing car had flashed on the wall all night, making me feel like I'd slept in the middle of the Vegas strip.

After Matt left for work, I drove to Dunkin' and ordered a muffin and a large coffee with a shot of espresso. I rushed back to the house well before 8 a.m., and stood by the door like a doofus, mistakenly believing that when the Army Transportation Office said the movers would be there after eight o'clock, they meant it. Matt called about 9 a.m. to check in with me, and I told him the movers were late. That's when he told me that "after eight a.m." means "anytime during the day," so I sat on the lawn chair and waited and tried to stay awake studying financial accounting and reporting.

A few minutes before noon, a truck rumbled by and I jumped up and looked out the window. A faded orange moving van cruised past our house. I ran outside, waving it down like a crazed woman, as it drove merrily past the curve in the road lined with houses that looked exactly like ours.

Brake lights. *Whoa! Did he see me? Is he going to reverse that big truck around the bend? Is he nuts?* Two men in their twenties, wearing T-shirts and jeans, leapt out the passenger door and jogged to the rear of the truck to ground-guide the driver around the curve in the street, back to our house. Silently, I cursed Matt for missing this.

• • •

Later that afternoon, the garage door whirred when I was unpacking a box of pots and pans in the kitchen. I left two stacked pots on the counter and ran to meet Matt at the door. "How can you lose one end table?"

He laughed. "I see this is your first military move, ma'am."

He dropped his rucksack on the floor and joined me for a tour of the house, where I pointed out the broken TV and the deep gouge in the back of the couch. "Do you think they were looking for hidden treasure?"

He shook his head. "Nah. They must have tried to squeeze it into a crate. There had to have been something sharp—a nail?— in the side of the crate. Who knows? I'll submit a claim. What a pain in the ass. It looks good, Kel. Thanks for doing all this."

"It looks like we have the bones of a bachelor pad. I'm glad Tess took me to all those yard sales. Didn't your mother say she was going to send you two boxes of plates?" I didn't wait for an answer. "It'll probably cost her more to mail them than it would for us to buy them new, but it's nice of her. I'm assuming that means she knows we live together?"

"In my family, 'don't ask, don't tell,' Kel." He grinned, peeling off his uniform top and walking toward the washing machine to toss it in. "Did they hook this up?"

"Only because I looked pathetic and insisted." I stood next to him, my hands on my hips.

He pulled me in close to his tan uniform T-shirt and breathed deep into my ear. "Thanks. I'm glad you made them put the bed together. Let's go try it out," he whispered in my ear.

I nuzzled in close, ignoring the smells of grass and oil and perspiration that seeped from his pores. He lifted me a few inches off the ground, keeping us connected, carrying me across the living area to our bedroom. *This is all we needed. New beginnings.*

•　　•　　•

I didn't know anyone in Clarksville, but Matt couldn't walk four feet without running into someone he knew from growing up on some Army post somewhere in the world, or from West Point, or from Fort Benning. Our first Saturday morning in the house, when Matt went out for a run, I sat at the table with the newspaper laid out in front of me, looking at the Help Wanted ads. This was a three-year assignment for Matt. I needed a job.

Sipping a warm second cup of coffee, I was circling anything that looked like a good fit, when Matt walked in the front door. A blond guy in gym shorts and an Army baseball T-shirt followed him.

"Hey, Kel, this is Jim." He wiped the sweat off his face with the bottom of his T-shirt, before opening the fridge. "He was a cow in my company. He lives down the street."

I smiled at the West Point terminology, remembering that a cow was a junior, so Jim was a junior when Matt was a freshman.

Jim smiled. "It's nice to meet you. I'll tell my wife, Allison, to come by with Erin. She's our one-year-old."

I nodded. "Great," I said, distracted by Matt holding two beers. *Beer? What's this all about?* Matt had started drinking again after ranger school, but had been moderate about it. Drinking before noon wasn't moderate to me.

Jim shook his head and reached for a bottle of water. Matt put the beer back and took a water, too. *Phew!* I already liked this guy. I hoped I'd like his wife, but didn't count on it. I'd learned at Fort Benning that couples with kids usually hung out with other couples with kids.

They sat on the couch and Matt turned the TV on and switched the channel to ESPN. I could hear them talking as I continued to scour the ads. Jim told Matt about his platoon, his platoon sergeant. "My right-hand man. He was a good guy, but his wife left him for the company motor sergeant. Talk about drama. And get this. My company commander was an asshole in 2nd Regiment and haze in my beast company."

Jim talked about "JRTC" and the "203 range" that he had to "OIC" the day he reported to his unit. I wondered what language they were speaking. I scribbled notes on the corner of the newspaper. *What's a platoon sergeant? What's a JRTC? A 203? What's an OIC?* I'd have to ask Matt after Jim left.

I folded the newspaper and carried it into the bedroom, hearing Tess in my head telling me to find my own life, to rely on no one for my happiness.

•   •   •

I registered for the CPA exam in October, figuring that gave me plenty of time to prepare. I applied for ten jobs, interviewed with six of them, and the end of June, two weeks after we moved in, I accepted a job at a medium-sized accounting firm in downtown Clarksville. My boss was a middle-aged woman, originally from New Jersey, not associated with the Army, but she assured me she understood the challenges I faced. I wasn't sure what she meant, but I nodded and thanked her. I had to breathe deep and use every bit of self-control not to dance out the door after I'd signed my offer letter. *No more nachos! Yay!*

I had to tell someone, but I'd have to wait until Matt got home from work. He'd told me only to call him at work if it was an emergency, and I didn't think this counted. I dialed my father, but he didn't pick up, so I left him a message trying not to sound like an excited five-year-old who found money from the tooth fairy under her pillow. *Hey, I got a job. Yay for me!*

Then I called Sara, and she didn't pick up, either, but I didn't want to sound too braggy, so I mumbled into the phone, "Hey, checking in. Hope you're doing okay! Miss you!"

When I called Tess, I was relieved she picked up. My enthusiasm had been sucked dry leaving messages. After I told her about the job, I vented. "Matt's hours are ridiculous. I can't believe I complained about Benning."

"Yeah, I'm with you. Tony's hours are bad, too. We won't see much of each other here. But I'm going to see as much of Alaska as I can. Did I tell you I'm volunteering at the hospital? I figure it will look good on my resume and hopefully I'll find out early about dietician jobs opening up if I'm already there."

"I need your attitude."

"Join a gym. You got your teaching certificate for yoga, right?"

"Yep. I finished it in Yarmouth. I practiced on my aunt." I grinned, remembering my aunt doing Warrior 2 poses with me on the beach.

"That's so cool. Go use it! Go teach yoga. Matt won't be home for dinner. So don't sit around and wait for him. It'll only make you fight."

Across the miles, I could see her pointing a finger with sparkly nail polish on it, and it made me smile. "You always say the right thing."

"Then you better keep calling me." She laughed, then told me she had to go. "Hey, before we hang up, what do you have this afternoon?"

I paused long enough for her to know I had nothing.

"All right, then. Go find a yoga studio right now."

I laughed, but when we got off the phone, I changed into leggings and drove to a studio in the strip mall near our house. After taking ten seconds to review the application I filled out, the manager hired me on the spot. I drove home with the window down, singing with Shania Twain on the radio. When the song ended, I grinned so wide, my cheeks hurt. *Oh my God. I think I might like country music.*

chapter 16

July into August 2004
Fort Campbell, Kentucky

Tess was right. I met people at yoga, and it was fun and just what I needed. Two nights a week, I drove home after work, changed, and hopped back in the car to teach a class at the studio. Sun salutations were better for me emotionally than watching pork chops crisp themselves to death in the oven, while waiting for Matt to get home from work.

On the days I didn't teach yoga, I ran with Jim's wife, Allison. The day after I'd met Jim, Allison had shown up at our front door, pushing a stroller that contained their curly blond-haired daughter, Erin, and a plate of brownies. I immediately recognized her as the thin blonde I'd seen out the window the day I was waiting for the moving van.

"I've got to figure dinner out," I told her on our first run together. "Matt gets home at eight. That's too late for me to eat with him."

"I get it. We eat by six p.m." She jerked her head toward one-year-old Erin in the stroller. "When we first moved here, I tried to wait until he got home. No way. We can't eat that late. I make him a plate that he can heat up when he gets in. He tries to get home before Erin goes to bed, but that rarely happens. It's crazy in this division."

Not the news I was hoping for, but I'd expected it. I'd begun to realize that even if his boss released him at noon, Matt would stay late to sweep the floors.

A few nights later, jogging down a hill past some kids playing basketball in front of their house, Allison confessed, "This was not the life I thought I'd have. I never wanted to date a cadet."

"Why not?"

She stopped, dug a box of raisins out of the pocket of the stroller, and handed them to Erin. "They're all so obnoxious."

I laughed. "You're right. How'd you end up here?"

She shook her head as we started jogging again. "I grew up in Stony Point, close to West Point. My best friend, Jeanine, went out with a cadet, and she begged me to visit with her one weekend, so she didn't have to go alone. Her cadet boyfriend was supposed to find another cadet for me to hang out with, so we'd double-date. We were walking by the barracks on the way to meet the cadet she was dating—he's now her husband, and they're stationed in Germany—and we saw one guy leaning out the window of the barracks, no shirt on, all muscles, blond hair, and I told her, 'That's the *only guy* I'd ever think about dating.'"

We turned around in the cul-de-sac and ran up the slight incline toward the playground. She paused, taking a breath. "You talk."

I nudged her off to the side, taking the stroller from her.

"No, you keep talking. This is a good story. I'll push."

"Okay, but slow down, will you? That guy—the one hanging out the barracks window—he was the guy Jeanine's boyfriend had talked into going out with me that day. Can you believe it?"

I grinned. "Wow. Meant to be."

"Yeah, right. I'm not sure about that. It's been an adventure."

"When Matt offered him a beer on a Saturday morning at eleven, and he said no, I decided I liked your Jim."

"Yeah, the drinking gets old." We reached level ground near the playground. "The West Point guys drink too much when they get out into the real Army. It takes a year or two before they settle down."

I raised my eyebrows, hopeful. In my gut, I didn't think Matt had a drinking problem. But we'd been getting along so well. The last thing we needed was another drunken episode like Sara's wedding.

"Downhill, finally." She panted as we reached the top of the next hill. "I'm glad you're pushing the stroller. Hey, you won't have to worry about the drinking, anyway. He won't be able to drink on the deployment. Forced rehab in the desert."

"I never thought about that. I'm not looking forward to this deployment."

She nodded. "Yeah. Me neither. I'll probably go home for some of it. It depends on when they go."

Holding on to the stroller with one hand, I shook my other arm out and jogged down the hill. I pushed thoughts about the drinking and about the deployment out of my mind. I wasn't sure what I could do about either of them, so I ignored them and kept running.

•   •   •

"It's been so long since I've seen you," I whined to my father on the phone. "When are you coming to visit?"

"I want to, Kel. I checked it out on the map. Fort Campbell's in Kentucky, but you live in Tennessee?"

"Yeah, the post's on the border between Tennessee and Kentucky. But we live in Clarksville, on the Tennessee side. We're about an hour from Nashville—that's the closest airport."

"Ah. Okay. I'll look into tickets and let you know. Tell me about the job," he said, changing the subject.

"It's good," I admitted honestly. "I love it. My boss is awesome. So professional but kind, really smart. I'm learning a lot. The other women in the office are older and married, so we don't hang out, but they're all sweet and help me if I have questions. I'm still studying whenever I can for the exam in October."

"What about after work? Have you and Matt done anything fun?"

I sighed long enough for him to interject.

"I shouldn't have asked?"

"Yeah. I mean, no. We haven't done anything fun. It's okay if you ask." I tried to sound like I meant it. "Matt's hours are long. Like fourteen hours a day long. When he gets home, he wants to veg on the couch. I get that."

It sounded like I didn't, though, and my father usually picked up on things like that, so I deflected. "What's up with Megan? I asked Mom, but she changed the subject. Fast."

He was quiet.

"Uh-oh. Dad?"

"Oh, there's nothing you can do. Your mother lets Megan stay in the house when she's in town. She enrolled at Forkton Junior, but dropped out before the end of the first semester. I don't know what she's doing now. She knows I'm here, if she needs me, but the ball's in her court. She's got to grow up."

"Drugs?"

"I don't think so. Pot, but nothing harder. She's got no goals and parties too much. That's the bottom line, really. Until your mother charges her rent or throws her out, she'll stay on this path, I'm afraid."

"I'm sorry, Dad."

"Yeah, me too. I hope she goes back to school, but she's got to want it." He paused. "What about Labor Day? Do you have plans?"

"No plans! Please come for Labor Day. Or come before that if you can."

"I'm teaching two night classes this summer, hon, on top of summer school. But Labor Day's open. I'll look at tickets."

We talked at least two or three times a week, but I hadn't seen my father in over a year. I'd never tell him, but I needed him. I missed him. I circled Labor Day weekend on the calendar and started to count down the days.

•   •   •

It had been almost three years since 9/11. Since that horrific attack, service members lived every day with the possibility of impending deployment. But not Matt. He'd been safe at school—at West Point and Fort Benning—until he landed at Fort Campbell, where deployment was a massive dark cloud hanging over our heads. We sat under that cloud without umbrellas, watching it get closer, waiting for it to open and mercilessly drench us. The rumors changed daily; no one knew what to believe.

In mid-July, a month after we moved in, Matt came home late—after 9 p.m., particularly late, even for him. I sensed something was up when I saw him walk in, his shoulders slumped, his face drawn. He didn't yell 'I'm home!' when the door slammed behind him. I muted the TV and looked at him as he trudged over and sat down next to me on the couch.

"We're going," he said apologetically.

Mid-August. Iraq. Nine months or longer. Not sure.

I knew it would happen, but when he said it out loud, it felt like someone whacked me in the gut with an iron rod.

•   •   •

FRG Meeting. Wednesday. Come Learn and Meet Others!!!

That's what the flyer said. It was stuck on the fridge under a BEAT NAVY magnet. Matt had been getting home later and later and had to have hung it the night before. I'd waken up when he dropped into bed, smelling like sweat and gasoline. I rolled over and opened my mouth to nag him to shower, but he was snoring before his head had hit the pillow.

I opened the refrigerator door, pulled out the cream for my coffee, and took the flyer down so I'd remember to ask him what an FRG was.

"Family Readiness Group," he explained after he came home from work and slid his plate into the microwave. I'd already eaten, showered, and put on my pajamas.

"My mother led FRG groups my whole life. When I was a kid, we always had women at the house for meetings. Back then, before 9/11, they were social events. They called them 'coffees.' The wives got together and drank—mostly wine, I think. Maybe some coffee? They ate good food, though—appetizers and desserts. Tim and I liked when we had them at our house because we'd have junk food and Coke in the house, and my mother never bugged us to do our homework."

"Hmm. I'm good," I said. "I've got yoga or running with Allison after work. That's social enough for me."

Shaking his head, he took the plate out of the microwave into the living room to sit on the couch. He kept telling me he wouldn't have ESPN over there, so he needed to watch it every available minute until he left. "They're not social anymore. They're informational. How to get in touch with us, deployment and redeployment information, things like that."

I'd followed him into the living room, but didn't respond.

He lifted a shoulder and looked at me. "They're mandatory now."

"Someone's making me go?" I asked, half kidding.

He turned to me from the couch and flashed me his intense look, the one where his jaw looked like it was chiseled out of granite. "No. No one can make you go. But they can make me. I have to go. I've got married soldiers in my platoon and I hope their spouses go, too. They'll give out information about the deployment, our mailing address, how to reach us if you have an emergency, that sort of thing."

"Married soldiers? I wonder what that's like." I grumbled that comment without thinking.

He sat with his plate on his lap and looked at me, his eyes narrow. "What's that mean?"

"I don't know." I snapped. "Everyone at work is asking if I'm staying here when you go. Like if you're engaged, you don't stay and wait. Are we ever going to get married?"

His eyes opened wide, and he moved his plate to the coffee table. I stood with my hands on my hips, not sure where I was going with this. I really needed to work on my filter.

He stood up and walked toward me, his voice quiet. "We can't do a big wedding now. Obviously. Before I go. There's no time."

He stood a few inches away from me. "Do you want to do a legal ceremony at the justice of the peace? Is that what you want to do?"

I moved into his chest, embracing him, playing back his question in my head, and wondering if I was being insecure or if he'd sounded hesitant. *Did he trail off at the end? Did he falter? Am I imagining that?*

He squeezed me tight, and I breathed him in, trying to be logical. When we separated, I said, "I have insurance from my job, so I don't need the benefits. I'd only want to marry you to make sure you know that you're my person."

"Kel, we don't talk about this stuff, and I'm not worried about it, but you're my beneficiary on my life insurance."

I straightened my arms and raised both hands in front of me. *Stop.* "No, don't talk about that."

"That paperwork is part of this pre-deployment stuff we've been doing. We do wills, insurance, all that. I put my parents down, too, but I've talked to them, and they know what I want. I want you to be taken care of."

"Matt, I mean it," I said, stunned. "Don't talk about this. It's bad luck. It's not good."

He nodded and walked back to the couch. "All right, change of subject. Will you come with me? To the FRG meeting? Monday night?"

"Sure," I said. This was important to him. "It's a date."

chapter 17

August through September 2004
Clarksville, Tennessee

The next day on our run, I asked Allison about FRG meetings.

"Yeah, I go to them." She slowed down to pull the cover over the top of the stroller. "Have you been to one yet?" She stopped short. "Oh, never mind. I'm sorry. I wasn't thinking. I always forget you guys aren't married. But you should get invited. We invite our significant others if the soldier wants them invited."

"Matt told me I should go to this next one."

"That makes sense. With the deployment coming up." She let go of the stroller with one hand and moved to the side, panting. "You got it on this hill."

I grinned and moved over to push Erin.

"Yeah, you should go to the meeting," she said, catching her breath. "It's good to get the information and know the people."

•   •   •

Matt stood in uniform on the sidewalk waiting for me when I pulled into the parking lot, looking for a space that wasn't already occupied by a pickup truck or minivan. We hugged hastily, more like a soft chest bump for less than two seconds, and walked toward the building. He waved or saluted the soldiers we passed. I didn't know anyone. Jim wasn't in this battalion, so Allison wouldn't be here. No one from my work was related to the military. Two ladies from yoga were affected by this deployment, but their husbands were in a different unit.

I followed Matt into a conference room lined with rows of white folding chairs and a podium up front, a large screen behind it on the far wall. A woman in her mid-forties, striking blond hair with dark roots, wearing a neon-purple blouse, greeted us at the door. She stood next to a small table with blank name tags and a sign-in roster. Wrinkles escaped through her made-up face when she announced in a blaring Northern accent, "Hi! How are yah?" She looked at Matt's name and rank on his uniform. "A Company?" Before Matt could respond, she corrected herself, "No, B Company."

Matt nodded.

"My husband's Lieutenant Colonel Mudd. I'm Diane. It's nice to meet you." She smiled.

I smiled back, and as I leaned over to sign in, she fired questions at me: "Where do you live?" "Do you work?" "Have you met any of the other wives?"

Soldiers and spouses and children surrounded us in a setting of chaos, but Diane looked at me, as if I were the only person in the room. She turned and saw a soldier in uniform standing nearby, waiting to talk to Matt, and she nudged him, shooing him away. "We're fine. You go."

As I picked up one of the black sharpies to write my name on the name tag, Diane waved down a woman who was coming in the door. The woman with unkempt hair all over the map, carried a toddler, had a massive purse slung over one shoulder, and another older toddler grabbing her leg. Diane laughed. "Sheila! Good to see you! The kids got so big!"

Sheila put down the child she was holding and stepped next to me to take a name tag, both kids grabbing her legs.

Diane shook her head, smiling at the kids, then stuck her arm up in the air to get the attention of the woman standing behind a table loaded with desserts. "Hey, Vicky!" she yelled loudly. "Have you met Kelly?"

Vicky waved me over, but I continued to marvel at Diane's social skills. Somehow she'd shooed both Matt and me off without making either of us feel shooed.

Vicky was younger than Diane, older than me; I guessed in her mid-thirties. Built like a runner, she had short brown hair cut in layers, and wore only a touch of lipstick, with jeans and a pullover.

"Hey, how are you? Glad you're here." She passed her arm over the table of desserts, like a magician over a top hat. "Hungry?"

I smiled. "No, thanks. Do you need help?"

She laughed. "You're a doll. Thanks for asking."

A girl about six, with crooked pigtails, wearing a faded gingham dress and mismatched socks with sneakers that had seen better days, skipped up to the table. No parent in sight. Her hands and face were smeared with chocolate. Before she could grab the plate of brownies, Vicky swooped in and moved them aside. "Where's your mommy, sweetie?"

The little girl looked up skittishly before disappearing into the crowd.

Vicky looked at me. "Not sure where her owner is. Do you have kids?"

I shook my head no.

"I would have told you we have babysitting down the hall." She tilted her head toward the door.

I smiled.

"Things should settle down around here soon. Let's talk more later."

Things did not settle down. Kids continued to run the perimeter of the room as Matt led me to a seat near the front and the meeting started. I looked back to see Vicky guarding the desserts. These kids did not need more sugar.

"We're here to provide you with information." An older man in uniform, with a large forehead and stern tone, explained from behind the podium.

Matt whispered to me that he was the battalion commander, married to the blond woman, Diane.

"We want to empower you to thrive when your spouse is gone. We want to make sure you can communicate with him and with each other. We want to do our best to help make this deployment as stress-free as possible."

Lieutenant Colonel Mudd introduced the chaplain, a slightly built man with jet-black hair, who spoke in clipped, accented tones. His tiny wife stood next to him in a brightly flowered dress and low pumps, listening to him adoringly. Put him in a tux and his wife in a white dress, and they could have stepped off the top of a wedding cake.

"This is the rear detachment commander," Matt whispered as an attractive blond soldier in a maternity uniform stepped to the microphone. "She doesn't deploy. She stays back in the rear."

After introducing herself as Captain Keller, she used her arm as a pointer and presented slides with mailing addresses and phone numbers. She asked if anyone had questions.

After the presentation, people separated into pockets and socialized. Matt introduced me to people as his fiancée, and I was proud to watch him in his element talking to soldiers and their spouses, attentively, interested. But soon my need for sleep out-ruled my pride for Matt. I looked at my watch, then leaned into his ear. "We better go. It's getting late."

We skated in and out of people on the way to the door. When we ran into Vicky, she put her hand on my arm. "Hey, this is your first deployment, right?"

I nodded.

"Call me if there's anything I can do. If you need anything at all." She handed me a folded piece of paper with her name and phone number written on it. "I mean it. Call me. Just to talk or whatever."

I smiled and nodded thanks.

When we left the building, I said to Matt, "Nice lady."

"Her husband's a good guy, too. He's the battalion XO, the right-hand man to the battalion commander, Lieutenant Colonel Mudd, the one who started the presentation."

I didn't care about the officer she was married to. I thought about how nice she was. I hoped I'd see her again.

•   •   •

This was why Matt wanted to go to Fort Campbell. His father thought this unit would deploy. When we were dating and Matt told me all this, it seemed like light-years away. I cringed thinking about how love had made me so stupid.

I couldn't dwell on it, or I'd get mad at him, and I didn't want to spend our last few weeks together fighting. But despite my best efforts not to—when Matt left for work even earlier, and came home from work even later—I was angry. I was lonely. This life was too hard. I didn't want to be alone in Clarksville without the only reason I'd moved there.

At least he wasn't drinking. I think he was too tired. When he fell into bed at night, he was out like a light in minutes.

•   •   •

Everyone, including those who had never been in my shoes, had advice for me.

"Move to New Hampshire, honey," my father said. "Stay with me. Find a job up here."

"Your room is empty," my mother said.

"You're welcome here," my aunt said.

"You're crazy to stay there," my friend Sharon said. "Move in with us. We'll have a blast. Find a job in town. Why would you stay there without Matt?"

"Come live with us in the city," Linda said. "We'll make room. You're too young to stay there alone waiting for a guy you're not even married to."

Matt told me we had a military clause in our lease that allowed us to break it with no penalty because he had orders to deploy. "Orders" are the official paperwork, he explained, that say he's going overseas. I could move out of the house without a financial penalty. Or I could stay. It was up to me.

"I don't know what to tell you, Kel. I want you to be happy. Do whatever you want. We can hire movers and move everything into storage if you want to leave here." His voice was so sincere. I knew he meant it.

I mumbled thanks. I didn't know what to do. I'd be lonely when he left, but I loved my job. Moving was a pain. Where would I go? Would I be able to find a job that I liked as much as the one I already had? If I thought about it, I felt like I ate a boulder. So I worked, taught yoga, ran with Allison, and avoided making a decision.

chapter 18

August into September 2004
Clarksville, Tennessee

"I'm going to stay here." I opened a bottle of wine on the back patio, where Matt was grilling. It was our last Saturday night together. "It makes sense. I have a job, and it's a good job. It'll look good on a resume. I take the exam in October. I'm settled in here. If I go, it won't be until after the exam. But I don't know. At that point, it would be dumb to go, for just a few months."

"Makes sense. I get it. I want you to do what you want to do." He spoke slowly, thinking; his eyes cast down at the burgers.

Allison told me that some soldiers were upset their spouses were going home to stay with their parents. The soldiers wanted them to stay around, to support each other. I was grateful Matt hadn't pushed me either way.

I walked toward him, and he put down the spatula to wrap both his arms around me. When he released me, he picked up the spatula and turned to the grill, bobbing back and forth on his heels. He bit his lip, then looked at me gravely. "Um, Kel?" He put the spatula down and fingered the dog tags that never left the chain around his neck. "Before I go. We should talk."

"Yeah? What?"

He wiped the sweat on his brow with the back of his hand, and he shuffled his feet. "Something I wanted to tell you. I've—

I've been wanting to tell you." He stammered. His phone buzzed on the small table next to the grill. He shook his head, frustrated.

"Get it," I said. "It's fine."

He picked up the phone. "Lieutenant Carpenter."

That's never a good sign. That's work. He held the phone with one hand, picked up the spatula and flipped the burgers onto a plate next to the grill.

I listened to his side of the conversation.

"Are you kidding?" He didn't sound happy. "Where?" He frowned and shook his head as he turned the grill off. "I'll be right there." When he hung up, his shoulders caved.

"What's the matter?" I picked up the plate of burgers and followed him into the house.

"Davies got arrested. He's in the platoon. A sergeant. Car accident, and his wife is pregnant and in the ER on post. I have to go."

"That's awful. I hope his wife's okay. Go. We'll talk when you get back."

He nodded, his eyes glazed, as if he were already thinking of something else.

"Wait," I blurted, remembering that he was going to tell me something. I put the plate on the counter. "Is everything okay? What were you going to say? Before the call?"

He rubbed his eyes, exhaled, and pulled me close to him. "Nothing important. We'll talk later." He kissed me quickly on the lips before hurrying into the bedroom to grab his wallet and keys.

After midnight, I woke up when the garage door opened. Minutes later, the bathroom door closed, and he crawled into bed. I rolled over. "What happened?"

"Unbelievable." His voice fired up. "His wife's psycho. Un-f-ing believable. She called the cops and said he hit her and caused the accident. But it turns out, he was defending himself. She was hitting him when he was driving, and he lost control.

She's got a freaking black belt in karate. She'd been beating the shit out of him for years. He showed me the bruises. No one had a clue."

I sat up in bed. "Wow. Is the baby okay?"

"That's another thing. She's not pregnant. She's bat-shit crazy. She thought he'd get out of deploying if she was pregnant." He wrapped his arms around me and pulled me back down under the comforter, kissing me on my shoulder, then neck. "I know the guy and I've met his wife. I never saw that coming."

"Things aren't always what they seem," I mumbled.

Since he'd left the house, I'd been thinking about only one thing: what he'd wanted to talk about before he got the call. I had to know. I pulled a few inches away from him, putting a momentary pause on his hands, which were in my pajama shorts. "You were going to ask me something. Or tell me something? Before you left for the ER?"

His body shivered slightly before he pulled me on top of him. His heart beat steadily under me and he kissed my neck. "Oh, that." He nibbled on the bottom of my ear. "I just wanted to make sure you knew how much I loved you."

I wasn't sure if that's what he was going to say on the patio, but, at that moment, with his touch on my skin, and knowing that he'd be gone in a few days, I ran my fingers down his body and focused only on the present. Sometimes that happens. Sometimes you live in the present. Matt was really good at that.

●　　　●　　　●

I figured it would be easier to have an emotional breakdown in my own home, so I told Matt I'd say goodbye to him at the house and not when I dropped him off at the barracks. We embraced in the kitchen, my shoulders convulsing, and my tears dampening his uniform. I wiped my nose with my sleeve and was surprised to see tears in Matt's eyes. He needed a half of a Kleenex, and I needed a roll of Brawny paper towels, but still.

Brushing the palm of his hand against his face, he exhaled. "We gotta go, Kel."

I turned to the sink and splashed cold water on my face, hanging my head low, taking deep breaths, determined to keep my emotions in check and not make this any more difficult than it already was.

"We'll go on a vacation wherever you want when I get back," he told me as we drove out of the neighborhood. My eyes were wet; my throat was thick. I bit the inside of my cheek, trying to hold back tears until he left me. I wanted him to think that I'd be fine; he shouldn't worry about me. He should worry about himself and get home safely.

"It'll fly by," he said quietly, as if trying to convince himself. He'd parked outside the building. "Plan something fun. For when I get back. I love you."

His eyes watered as he turned back to me one more time. We'd agreed not to hug there, but I got out, ran over to him, and embraced him hard.

"It's okay," I mumbled, my words breaking. "We'll be okay."

He broke from the hug, and he looked at me with an expression that made me hold my breath. Matt was afraid. It made me tremble. As quickly as the fear overwhelmed him and made itself visible in his eyes, it left him. Once again, he was intense Matt, but for that one moment, I saw vulnerable Matt, a version of Matt I'd never met.

He took my hands and held them between us, his eyes still wet, but once again focused. "I love you." He threw his ruck over his shoulder, turned, and walked away, leaving me so alone.

I drove away from the families dropping their soldiers off, the hugs, the long kisses, the tearful separations, and goodbyes. Pulling into an empty parking lot down the street, I leaned over the wheel and cried, blowing snot bubbles on my shirt. When I stopped choking on sobs and could see again, I drove home and sat in front of the TV. I was glad I'd taken the day off from work until I finished a box of Hostess cupcakes before noon. Then I thought, *I should have gone to work.*

Allison stopped by to sit with me, while Erin crunched Cheerios into the carpet. She talked about Jim's departure the following Wednesday and her travel plans for when he was gone. "I'll stay here until November. But we'll go home to New York, early November through Christmas. I'm not sure about January. It's cold here then, but it's miserable at my parents' house and they keep the heat at sixty degrees and tell me to put on a sweater. What about you? Will you stay here the whole time?"

"I'm not sure. I'll stay for the CPA exam. That's October. Then I'll see."

She looked at her watch. Her life was ruled by Erin's nap schedule. Her face softened, oozing sympathy. "Why don't you come over and eat with us tonight?"

"No worries. I'm good," I said, lying through my teeth.

I didn't have to tell her I'd prefer to mope alone today. She understood.

"Let's run tomorrow," she said as I walked her and Erin to the front door.

I nodded. I'd allow myself one day to mope. When she left, I downed two Tums (those cupcakes landed hard), then took a shower, crying as the water beat down on me. I changed into shorts and one of Matt's T-shirts.

I worried about Matt returning safely. And I worried about us. I was happy with Matt. I loved him. But it still wasn't perfect. He could be so intense. He zoned out. Was he sharing everything with me? Why didn't his parents like me? Should I move to Seabury after the CPA exam? Or Boston? I was treading water in Tennessee, not sure where and when I'd dock.

My father called. My mother called. My aunt called. Sara called. I didn't pick up for any of them.

When the skies darkened, I called my father. I was afraid if I didn't, he'd drive through the night and show up on my doorstep the next morning. "I'll call you over the weekend, Dad. I'm fine!"

"Are you sure, honey? I hate that you're alone down there."

I insisted I was all right. "Dad, I know we said you'd come Labor Day, but do you think we could change that to October? After my CPA exam? I feel like by October, I'll really need a visit."

"If you're sure. Of course. Whatever helps make this deployment easier for you."

I swallowed. *Why did kindness make me cry?*

Then I called my mother, and she offered to drive down, which I appreciated, because if I'd said yes, it would have been like me asking her to give up a kidney. "I'm fine," I told her.

I called my aunt. I called Sara. I lied to both of them. "I can't talk long, so much to do, but I'm fine!"

If I kept saying "I'm fine," maybe it would happen. I watched reruns of a crime show and late-night TV, and I waited for sleep, which never came. Instead, I second-guessed my life, from going to the Bahamas and meeting Matt to moving with him to Georgia and Tennessee. I was alone. I missed my father. I missed Sara. I missed Tess. I lay in bed and tried to find positives. I loved my job. I liked Allison. It was a short list that needed to grow, or I wouldn't be able to stay in Clarksville.

chapter 19

September 2004
Clarksville, Tennessee

Three nights later, I turned off the light on my nightstand and the second the room darkened, something crashed. In the kitchen? One leg still hanging out from under the comforter, I froze. I'd never lived alone. Noises in the night made my heart stop.

I pulled my leg back under the comforter and sat up in bed. Crash! Then another crash! My heart, which had stopped beating, jumped out of my chest and into my throat. I crept out of bed in the dark and tiptoed to the dresser, where I'd left a flashlight. We rented this house because it backed up to trees and gave us some privacy. The noises could be only one thing: an axe murderer, dressed in black, had crept through the woods, hopped the fence, and broke into our house.

Or was the crash outside? I wasn't sure. I couldn't turn the lights on. I didn't want to be seen. So I snuck around in the dark and bumped into furniture. I edged up along the wall to the window in the kitchen that looked out into the backyard and peered into a coal-black sky—no moon, no stars. There was no intruder with a flashlight in the yard. I waited. If I leaned forward, my ears worked better above the hum of the refrigerator.

My eyes adjusted to the dark, and I tip-toed across the kitchen to check the door to the garage. A thunderous rumble crashed near me. I leaped three feet in the air and flipped on the kitchen light, shaking.

The ice maker.

I sighed and looked at the clock: 1:17 a.m. I had to stop this craziness.

After the FRG meeting, Matt had told me some guys had security systems installed in their homes before they left, and I'd told him no; we didn't need one. It was a safe neighborhood.

I called the alarm company the next morning.

I was exhausted. After at least eight hours at work, I either ran with Allison or spent two hours at the gym before I showered, made a sandwich (I'd eaten all the cupcakes and decided I shouldn't buy more), and vegetated on the couch in front of mindless TV. When I turned out the light and my head hit my pillow, my physically drained body screamed for sleep, but my mind raced. *What if he's injured? What if he dies?*

I thought about drinking, but figured that would be worse than the cupcakes.

On the fourth day, when I got back from running with Allison, the light on the answering machine flashed. I pressed the button.

"Kelly, this is Vicky, the lady with the desserts at the FRG meeting. Checking in to see how you're doing. The first week's the worst. It'll get easier. Call me. Let's get together for lunch or coffee."

I immediately dialed her number when the machine beeped off. I felt like a wimp—pitiful—but I told myself that she seemed like a nice lady and might be a good friend or resource. I didn't need to tell her I hated being alone and wondered what I was still doing here. I was simply returning her call. Being polite.

•   •   •

The next Saturday, we sat at an outside table downtown sipping iced coffee. Vicky told me she was a second-grade teacher staying home with their fourth and sixth graders. She'd taken a year off from teaching to get the kids settled when they moved to Fort Campbell, and that year had turned into two years because of the deployment. She'd dropped both kids at soccer practice before meeting me.

"I probably should have gone back to work this year. For me, to keep me busy. But I thought it'd be less stress, less change for the kids, if I waited until Chuck got back." She shrugged as if to say who knew what the right answer was.

She asked about my routine, and I told her: work, gym or running with a friend, home, shower, a sandwich for dinner, bed. I admitted I couldn't sleep. I raised my shoulders, before dropping them. "It's crazy, but I think, 'What if he's injured?' What if —" I stared at my coffee. "What if, even worse."

"We all think that." She nodded slowly. She moved the conversation to the other wives, who was who and where they lived.

"Friday night, Diane's having everyone over. Wine and whining."

I smiled.

"Yeah, she's a character. There's a new wife — Amy Wicks — who lives over near you. They moved in a week before he left. I offered to pick her up."

"That's nice of you." I lowered my eyes and stared into my coffee. I hadn't thought about doing anything nice for anyone since Matt left. I hadn't thought about anyone except myself.

"I didn't always do this social stuff with the other wives," Vicky confessed. "When Chuck was a lieutenant and captain, the last thing I wanted to do was go out at night and meet other women. I worked, and I saw so little of Chuck. I wanted to be home at night if he was home."

I nodded, understanding. "What changed?"

"It's sad, but there was a terrible training accident on post. The officer — he was a lieutenant colonel — died, and his wife had never gone to any spouse events and didn't know any of the other spouses. A good friend of mine — I'd taught with her years ago at Fort Benning — her husband worked with the lieutenant colonel. My friend told me no one knew the wife — the widow — no one knew how to comfort her; they didn't know how to help her."

That was not where I was expecting this story to go. I pulled my head back and covered my mouth with my hand.

Vicky saw my reaction. "It was tragic. But that's when I thought there's more to this social stuff than gossiping and drinking wine. Especially now, during these deployments, it's good to know each other."

She took a sip of her coffee and looked at me from behind the straw. "Honestly though, since I started getting more involved and meeting more wives, I realized how much I missed before. I've met some really cool ladies. So strong."

I wasn't sure what to say.

"Okay, enough of that." She sipped her drink. "What about next Friday night? You in?"

It's not as if I had a lot going on. "Sure, thanks."

•　　•　　•

Sunday morning, I was in the shower when the phone rang. I turned off the water and yanked the curtain aside, shampoo still in my hair, dripping water over the floor. My heart raced when I saw the long number on the screen. I picked up the phone as I reached for a towel.

I heard Matt's voice and sighed with relief. He sounded confident, tinged with quiet excitement, as if trying to subdue it for me, or for whoever was listening to him on the other end. I asked him where he was, what it was like, who was with him.

He brushed me off. "Let's talk about you."

At the FRG meeting, they told us not to ask about locations, deployments, or dates. The chaplain warned us they wouldn't want to talk about being over there. They'd want to listen to stories about home, anything to keep their minds off where they are. I didn't want to worry him, to guilt him, so I didn't tell him about the noises I'd heard at night. I didn't mention not being able to sleep or eat; about missing him so much, my body ached like I had the flu. I didn't tell him his parents hadn't called me, or about having alarms installed on the windows and doors.

I told him about meeting Vicky for coffee and my plans to go to Diane's house with the spouses. I told him about work, how Barbara and Nancy, both middle-aged accountants with kids my age, had invited me to dinner. I told him about studying for the CPA exam. I told him about asking my father to reschedule his Labor Day trip until October, thinking that I'd need a visit then more.

"I probably shouldn't have told him not to come Labor Day." A lump clogged my throat. "I haven't seen him in so long and I could use the company. But I thought by October, I'd really need a visit. He can't do both."

After I said that, I worried Matt might worry about me, that I needed company, but he seemed distracted, or maybe he didn't hear me with the skip in the line. I rambled on about the weather, about the gym, about how I planned on getting the oil changed in the car the next week. It seemed so shallow, like we were living in a pretend world, where everything was mundane.

Suddenly, clattering and banging and commotion skipped through the line. Matt said abruptly, "I gotta go."

"Is everything okay?" I asked, worried.

"Oh yeah, no problem," he said sarcastically.

More yelling, loud noises.

"I love you," he said.

"I love you, too. Be careful," I begged.

"Will do. Out here."

Click.

I'd learn later the commotion was rocket fire. And it happened a lot.

•   •   •

Friday night, Vicky picked me up, and we drove down 41A, past the strip mall where I taught yoga, past a gas station, past the sprawling mega-church complex, and into a newer neighborhood of townhouses. She peered over the dashboard. "Look for 115A, will you?"

I pointed when I saw it, and Vicky pulled up to the curb out front. "Great. Thanks. I've never met her. I'll run up and get her."

"No need." I laughed as a small, compact woman, about my age, speed-walked down the pathway toward us. "She must have been sitting by the window waiting!"

She opened the back door tentatively and slid into the seat.

"Hi, thanks for the ride." She spoke so softly I had to turn around in my seat and lean toward her. She wore her short brown hair in a bob, and her wide, dark eyes peered out from behind black-framed glasses. Her attire screeched computer geek: navy-blue collared shirt tucked into her jeans, with a skinny belt, and penny loafers. Penny loafers! I hadn't seen them in years.

"It's great to meet you, Amy! I'm glad you came." Vicky broke the ice.

Amy nodded.

"Are you looking for a job?" Vicky asked her.

"Yes." Her head didn't stop nodding.

"What do you do?" Vicky asked.

"I'm a management information systems analyst."

She redefined the word "mumble".

"Umm," I asked. "A what?"

Finally, a half-smile. "Computer stuff," she said a little louder. "I've had no luck finding a job though."

I asked where she was from. Ohio. I asked where her husband was from. Ohio. I gave up trying to make conversation.

The Mudds lived on Fort Campbell, on a street lined with duplexes and single split-levels for majors and lieutenant colonels. Amy and I followed Vicky up the walkway toward the front door, decorated with a red, white, and blue wreath. Diane, in full Diane-mode—an aqua blouse, tight yellow pants, and a bangle of bracelets on her arm—let us in, waving a bottle of wine in her hand. Vicky laughed out loud. I grinned. Amy looked like the lion meeting the Wizard of Oz.

Diane bounced, energy darting off every tight, bright ounce of her, as she hustled us into the kitchen, the gathering spot, where four women sat in chairs around the oak table, and others stood leaning against the counter. Diane took a spoon off the counter and clanged it against the wine bottle in her hand until all eyes were on her.

"Hey! Everyone! We have two new ladies to welcome tonight! Kelly"—she pointed to me, and I smiled and stuck my hand up in a small wave—"and Amy!" She pointed to Amy, who blushed from her hairline to the top of her collared shirt.

Noting Amy's feet glued to the floor, Diane stayed by our side as Vicky wandered off to mingle. Diane asked Amy the same questions we'd asked her in the car and got the same one-word answers, before pausing mid-sentence and turning to the group of women in the living room.

"Cindy, Pam!" she yelled to two other women about our age. "Where are you two from again?"

The two women stopped their conversation and walked over toward us.

"Ohio," Cindy said. "Near Cincinnati."

"I'm from farther north," Pam said. "Near Lake Erie."

Amy's face lit up at the connection, and Diane drifted off to replenish the chips. Both Cindy and Pam were stay-at-home mothers, they told us, and our conversation soon moved from their hometowns to the daycare center on post and the preschool programs in the area. Other than their birth certificates all saying Ohio, they had little in common. When Cindy and Pam launched into a discussion of the merits of paper versus cloth diapers, I interjected as sweetly as I could. "So nice to meet you both. I think we'll get something to drink." I nudged Amy away, backing up into three women who stood in the corner.

One lady turned and looked at me, then shuffled back a step, surprised. Probably ten years older than Amy and me, she had thick brown shoulder-length hair with bangs and wore a shapeless plaid blouse under a red crocheted vest, a maxi-length denim skirt, blue tights, and clogs. I wondered if her horse and buggy were parked outside.

"Hi," I said, wondering when I got so sociable. "I'm Kelly McGowan. I'm new. This is Amy."

"Oh." The dowdy woman fumbled for words. The two women with her stared at Amy and me like we were from Mars.

I looked at Amy. She blinked her eyes and rubbed her hands on her pant legs nervously.

"I'm Donna Jones," the frumpish woman said, smiling. "It's so nice to meet you."

The tall woman piped in, "I'm Ellen Miller. My husband's the battalion S-4." She looked above our heads. No one stood behind us, so I'm not sure what her squinty hazel eyes were doing. I wondered if she had some sort of eye disorder. She wore jeans and a turtleneck tucked in with a wide belt and short ankle boots with heels. "Major Miller. Have you heard of him?"

"Oh," I replied. "Umm . . ." I had the feeling she assumed I'd heard of her husband. She probably even thought I knew what a battalion S-4 was.

To my surprise, Amy responded, with total sincerity, "No, I haven't. I'm sure he's a nice man."

I tried not to laugh out loud.

"I'm Alexa Brown," the third woman chimed in. She had curly hair tied back so tight, her forehead had to hurt. At least she smiled, though, and it was almost pleasant.

"My husband's the HHC Company Commander," Alexa said. "Is your husband in Bravo Company?"

She was looking at me. *Damn. Why didn't she ask Amy?* I took a long swig of wine, trying to remember. Bravo Company sounded familiar, but I wouldn't put my life on it. For some reason, in front of these women, I felt uncomfortable acknowledging my total ignorance concerning all things Army. I swallowed, not sure how to respond, when an arm draped over my shoulder.

"Yes, Matt's in B Company," Vicky said.

God love Saint Vicky.

"Amy's husband, Leo, is in C Company," Vicky added. "Kelly's an accountant and works downtown. Amy and Leo moved in right before the unit left. She's looking for the right job. They'll both keep busy during the deployment. I'm going to steal them and introduce them to the rest of the group. Thanks for welcoming them, ladies." Vicky smiled again before guiding Amy and me away from the three women.

When we were out of earshot, she whispered to me, "How'd you end up over there?"

We followed her back to Diane, who stood with an open box of crackers near the counter in the kitchen.

"Saved these young damsels from a couple of wife-eating dragons in the corner," Vicky said spreading the crackers on the platter as Diane emptied the box.

Diane shook her head. "Thanks."

Vicky laughed. "They mean well?"

Diane smiled. "Hmm."

On the drive home, I asked Vicky about the three ladies in the corner.

"We have a great group of ladies in the battalion," she explained. "Diane's the best. She's wild and crazy, but she's genuine and really wants to help. Some wives forget we don't get an LES."

"A what?"

"Oh, I'm sorry. LES is short for Leave and Earnings Statement. That's the pay statement soldiers get."

"Oh," I said. The list of Army acronyms was endless.

"What I meant was, we don't get paid. We're not in the Army. We just married them. My husband's a major, but I'm not a major. Wives have no rank. Sometimes wives forget that and act like, since their husband outranks your husband, they outrank you. They don't."

I nodded, thinking about it.

"Donna Jones is a sweetheart. She gets overshadowed by those other two sometimes, but she's got a heart of gold. Alexa's not bad, either. She'll do anything to help if we ask her."

I noticed she chose not to say anything about Ellen, the tall one who never made eye contact.

Vicky parked in front of Amy's town house, and as I turned in my seat to say goodbye, she surprised me by leaning forward and putting one hand on each of our shoulders.

"Thank you so much, both of you. It's been a little lonely not knowing anyone. I appreciate you going out of your way for me." She drew her hands away from us.

Vicky wiped her eyes with her shirtsleeve. "Hey, you have our numbers. Call anytime. I mean it."

We drove past the mega-church, the gas station, the strip mall, and when we pulled into my neighborhood, I said, "Hey, Amy's right. Thank you for everything."

"I'm not doing anything that you won't do in another few years. Call me if you need anything."

I nodded, grateful, and walked into my dark house.

chapter 20

September into October 2004
Clarksville, Tennessee
Couples were everywhere. In Target, holding hands. At Starbucks, sipping lattes. In every front seat, of every car, at every red light. It made me nauseous seeing them, and it was only week five. I had thirty-one weeks to go. At a red light on my way home from work, I glanced at the car passing me, and saw a couple in the front seat, so I did what anyone in my shoes would have done at that point. I moped.

When the light turned green, I decided to skip the gym and go home. Except for those panicky nights at the beginning, I'd been relatively strong since he left. I deserved a night on the couch watching *Gilmore Girls* eating peanut butter out of a jar.

Up ahead, between a Jiffy Lube and a Dollar Store, I saw a massive sign, blinking feverishly in front of a new smoothie shop. Impulsively, I flicked on my blinker. Dinner. It was healthier than super chunky with a spoon.

Standing in line, reading the menu above the counter, someone tapped my shoulder. I turned around and laughed. Amy. I hadn't seen or talked to her in the two weeks since we'd met.

"Hey! Dinner?"

She nodded. "You too?"

"Yep. Nice shirt. New job?"

She tugged the collar of her Best Buy polo. "If I play my cards right, I might get a Geek Squad car." She said it with enough faux sincerity to make me wonder whether she was serious.

"I'm kidding. It's a job. I'm still applying for real jobs."

"It stinks, doesn't it? I waitressed at a Mexican restaurant at Fort Benning." I shrugged.

"Effie's?"

I nodded.

"Best chicken nachos."

I laughed. "They were a plus."

"Want to sit and eat here?" She jerked her head to an empty booth by the window.

"Sure. I've got nothing tonight except *Gilmore Girls*," I confessed, surprised by her show of extroversion. Loneliness made even the most introverted peek out of their shells.

When we sat with our smoothies, I confessed. "All I see is couples everywhere. It's starting to make me sick."

She nodded. "I started noticing that, too. I need to plan things to look forward to, or I'll never make it."

"That's a good idea. Like what sort of things?"

"I don't know." She put her smoothie down. "A trip to Nashville to do sightseeing stuff? I haven't even been there."

"Me neither. I tried to go before they deployed, but Matt— that's my fiancé—always had an excuse."

Her eyes narrowed, and I sensed her wondering how we couldn't have visited Nashville in the month we were here before he deployed. I wanted to explain how busy he was, how tired he was, but it would sound lame, so I said nothing. Instead, I asked, "What about your family? Will they visit?"

"I doubt it. What about yours?"

"I don't know. My father was supposed to come Labor Day, but it was so soon after Matt left, I told him to wait until I really needed a visit. He's supposed to come in October. I'll be okay if my mother doesn't visit. We get along, but she makes everything hard."

I surprised myself by talking so openly. I must have been lonely, but she made it easy by acting nonplussed, so I rambled on. "My best friend — my college roommate — is married to a guy at Fort Rucker. But he's at flight school and they're still in the honeymoon stage — she won't get it until he goes to a unit."

"That's the truth," she agreed. "It's too much to explain. I don't think anyone gets it unless they've gone through it."

I was talking too much, so I asked her again, "You don't think anyone will come?"

"Nah." Her voice hesitated.

I waited.

She looked out the window. "My stepmother sounds like your mother. My mother died when I was thirteen."

"Oh, I'm so sorry." My shoulders fell with sympathy.

"Thanks. Cancer sucks. I have one brother. He's older. He was a senior in high school when she died, and he took off for Colorado right after graduation. He's not great at keeping up with me. My father remarried when I was a sophomore in high school. He didn't waste any time — not that I blame him. He'd never been alone and didn't know how to be a single parent. He's got two kids now with his wife. I'm glad he's happy . . . but his new family is his life now."

I put my drink down and leaned forward, listening.

She shrugged. "It's okay. Leo's mother's great and she's offered to come to visit, but I keep telling her I'm fine."

"I keep telling everyone that, too."

"Are you an only child?"

I shook my head. "No. I've got a sister. She's two years younger, but we're not close."

I left it there, afraid I'd scare her away. Her story made me think about the years I'd spent wondering why my parents stayed together for so long. I'd never thought about them divorcing and remarrying and leaving Megan and me to rotate between houses. I'd never thought about the unintended consequences.

Amy moved to neutral ground and told me she applied for a government job on post in the contracting office. "It'd be good to get a GS job." She explained the ratings and benefits of a government scale job and how it would allow her to move from post to post.

"I was hoping you could drive me to the next FRG meeting in your Geek Squad car!"

She laughed. "We need to do this more often. I haven't laughed in too long."

In the parking lot, we planned to meet Saturday for lunch, and we talked about going to Nashville the following weekend. When I got in my car and drove home, I thought about the atypical friendships I'd forged since I left home for college. A redheaded English major. A pierced and tatted dietician from California. A computer geek from Ohio.

Friendship is a funny thing. You don't always see it coming, but when it does, it can make you feel whole again.

•   •   •

Mid-September, one Friday night in my living room, a few glasses into a few bottles of Cabernet, I opened up to Amy and Vicky about my mother. She'd been bugging me to move away from Clarksville, and I wasn't sure why.

"She resents me. I'm sure of it," I said. "I don't get why she wants me to go back home."

"Why do you say she resents you?" Vicky pulled a Garden Salsa chip out of the bag on her lap.

"She was pregnant with me before she married my father," I said. Amy leaned toward me, and Vicky stopped munching. "She doesn't know I know. They only got married because of me.

They lived together for almost twenty years before they finally split up. Twenty years in a loveless marriage. It was all my fault." I tried to sound like it wasn't a big deal.

Amy shook her head. "No. You can't blame yourself for that. For any of that."

"I'm okay with all of it. Really. I spent years worrying about it, feeling guilty about it. It's out of my control. It is what it is." I put my glass down on the coffee table.

Vicky moved the bag of chips from her lap to the table. "Do you think your mother is worried about you and Matt? Could she be afraid you're making the same mistake she made?"

"I never thought of that," I admitted. "But I think she likes Matt."

"She might. But maybe she thinks that if you really loved him, you'd be married by now?"

The refrigerator hummed. The clothes in my dryer tumbled.

A minute passed before Amy asked, "Why do you think you guys haven't married yet? I mean, you couldn't select a date because of ranger school. But now we know they'll be back by May. So you could have picked a date in July, and you could plan it while he's deployed?"

I picked up my glass and looked down at it. "Yeah. If he'd said what you just said—'Hey, let's plan a date in July, because I know I'll be back by then'—I would have said, 'Yeah, let's do it.' But he never said that. It's as if he's holding back. And that makes me hold back."

It was as if a light bulb went off in my brain and my heart at the same time. "I've never said that out loud. If he doesn't bring it up between now and when he gets home, I guess we need to have a heart-to-heart in May. Whenever they get back."

"I'm sorry, Kelly," Amy whispered.

"You're smart," Vicky said. "And independent. You'll do the right thing, at the right time."

•   •   •

I'd spent endless hours studying for the CPA exam, but when I opened the results and learned that I'd passed every section, I wanted to shout from the roof. Instead, I called my father and told him. Then I called Amy and asked if she wanted to go out with me and celebrate. Dinner. My treat.

When I dropped her off at her town house after dinner, she leaned over in the front seat and hugged me, telling me how proud she was of me. It surprised me, her show of affection, and I slumped in my seat, taken aback. Too many emotions battled for control. I was grateful for Amy, relieved and proud I passed the exam, and sad about Matt being gone. I wanted to tell him. I wanted him to tell me how proud he was of me.

I walked into my dark house alone, flipped on the kitchen light, and the phone rang. I ran to get it, tossing my doggy bag on the counter. *Maybe it's Matt!* It wasn't. But I saw the number and picked up the phone quickly. "How'd you know to call?"

"Oh, you sound like you're happy. You got your results?"

"I found out today. Got it in the mail. I passed! Every section! But how'd you know to call tonight?"

"I didn't. It was a good guess. I was driving home from flying and remembered this was the week you thought you'd hear."

"Thanks, Alex," I said, still smiling. I turned to the photos stuck on the fridge, taking down the one of Sara, Jake, Matt, Alex, Heather, Tyler, and me on the beach in the Bahamas. I held it in my hands; blond and blue-eyed Alex grinned into the camera.

"I hope you celebrated?"

"I took Amy to dinner. Well, I tried to. She insisted on taking me to congratulate me. You'll have to meet her. She's great. I'm lucky she's here."

"I'm glad. I'm sorry Matt's not there, though. I'm proud of you!"

I put the photo back on the fridge and asked him about flight school, and he asked me what I'd heard from Matt.

"Not much. He has no time. He's always in a hurry."

"It's chaos over there, Kel," he explained. "I mean, don't worry, Matt's good at what he does. But he isn't calling because he doesn't want to. He's not calling because he can't."

"I guess. The wives I've talked to haven't heard from their husbands. I get they're not near phones and are busy. But that doesn't make it any easier."

Neither of us said what we were thinking. *Chaos in a war zone isn't comforting to those who wait.*

•　　　•　　　•

Three days after the phone call with Alex, the FedEx man left a box on the doorstep with fudge inside and a note: *I didn't think boiled peanuts would travel well. Proud of you!*

I put the fudge in the fridge and stuck the note on the door with a magnet. It was selfish of me, but I hoped Alex got orders to Fort Campbell after flight school. Germany was too far away.

•　　　•　　　•

The following weekend, as I was putting groceries away, the phone rang. I dropped the bananas on the floor and grabbed it.

"It's been pretty crazy." Matt's voice sounded weak, even farther away. "We've been in and out on patrols. Not a lot of access to phones. Sorry, Kel."

I remembered what the chaplain had said about listening and not prying, but I couldn't help myself. I paced the kitchen, firing questions off at him. "Where do you sleep? Are you getting enough sleep?" The line skipped a beat, and before he could answer, I kept pressing, "How often do you go out on the patrols? Do you drive or fly?"

He shut me down. "Kel, please. Talk about you. What's going on there?"

Vicky had recommended I keep a pad of paper on the counter and, during the week, jot down stories or things that I wanted to share with him when he called. I looked at the list and saw: *Dad's visit next week, the new girl at work, Halloween in the neighborhood, CPA exam.*

I'd planned to end the call with the good news about my exam. Instead, I blurted, "I'm a CPA! I passed! All four sections!"

The line skipped. "What? Kel? What did you say? Passed what?"

Seriously? "Passed what?" Where has he been? Oh, a war zone. "The CPA exam!"

"That's great. Awesome. When did you find out?"

"Last week. Monday. I went out to dinner with Amy to celebrate. I wish you were here." *Damn that filter. I'm sure he wished he were here, too.*

"I'm proud of you, Kel."

"Thanks." My voice caught. I was afraid I'd cry, so I stopped talking.

"You weren't sure if you'd move after the exam. What are you thinking?"

"I don't know. I thought about moving in with Sharon and Kim, trying to find a job in Boston, but now, there's only six months left until you get back. It wouldn't be worth the hassle. I love my job, and almost everyone I work with. And Amy and Vicky are great." I thought he'd be happy, but he seemed distracted. I guessed there were other things going on in his life. "Hey, what can I send you? What do you need?"

"Protein bars would be good. Lemon-flavored water packets. Wool socks. The same ones I bought before I left. More of those would be great."

I took a pen out and started a list. "No problem. Anything else?"

The line skipped, and he said something to someone else.

"I gotta go. Hey, congrats on the exam. I'm proud of you. I love you."

My knees gave out, and I leaned against the counter. "I love you, too. Be careful."

I'd been so excited to share my news with him, but I didn't feel happy. The energy had been zapped out of me, as if my enthusiasm had been vacuumed into a hole so many thousands of miles away.

War sucked.

chapter 21

October 2004
Clarksville, Tennessee
My father called as I walked in the door after yoga. He got right to the point. "I'm sorry, Kel. I've got to reschedule my visit."

"Oh, why?" I whined. When I realized how I sounded, I tried to take it back. "I mean, it's okay. I was looking forward to seeing you — that's all. No big deal. Sure. We'll reschedule."

I'd been counting down the days until his visit. After Matt left mid-August, the summer dragged on until the humidity lifted. Once the leaves turned and fell and formed a rug of crunchy faded colors on the dead grass, I'd circled on the kitchen calendar the date my father was coming. My body went limp when he said he had to cancel.

"I'm sorry, Kelly. I'll get down. What about Thanksgiving? Or Christmas? Or are you planning to come home?"

"I don't know, Dad. I don't know what I'm doing. Why do you have to cancel?" *What's more important than your oldest daughter, who has been alone in Tennessee since August?* Not saying that out loud took levels of maturity I didn't know I had.

"It's Gram." His voice cracked.

Oh, no! My heart dropped and my guilt multiplied. "What's wrong?"

"She's healthy physically, but she needs more care."

I stood perfectly still. "Dad? Is she okay?"

He paused before replying, "She's okay. But it's hard on Brendan. He and Teresa can't leave her alone. Someone needs to be with her around the clock, and they're both working."

My grandmother was a five-foot dynamo, who had been married to a drunk. My grandfather died of a heart attack when my dad was twenty-one, and according to the McGowans, even when my grandfather was around, he wasn't around, so Gram raised six kids by herself, instilling the fear of God in them, but with a nurturing heart. My father, his three brothers, and two sisters adored her. We all did.

"She needs to go into a nursing home. The move-in date is the Saturday I'm supposed to fly to Nashville. I'm sorry, Kelly."

"I understand. That's so sad. Should I take a long weekend and fly up and see her?"

"That's nice of you to offer, hon, but I don't think she'd recognize you. Sometimes she knows me, sometimes she doesn't." He spoke with sadness and resignation.

My heart sank thinking about how much I'd looked forward to seeing my father, but I was glad he was going to help with Gram. Since my parents split up, my father visited his mother and brothers in Dorchester on most weekends, and that made me happy. My mother hadn't been a fan of the McGowan family. When we grew up, we saw them once a year, on Christmas Eve, and my mother never came.

"You know what? Sara talked about visiting sometime. Maybe they'll be able to come up. It'll all work out."

We talked about Cousin Richard, who had recently come out of the closet. His parents, Uncle Gerard and Aunt Rita, who lived on the top floor in the same double-decker as Uncle Brendan and Aunt Teresa, were accepting, according to my father, but not sure what to do.

"This is new to them. They're not sure what parenting a homosexual young adult looks like. Gerard asked if he should tell our mother, and I told him, 'Sure, it's not as if she'd remember five minutes later, anyway.'"

The McGowans relied on dry humor to get through hard times. I had to smile. We said goodbye and hung up, and I turned on the TV and flicked through the channels. On a whim, I muted the TV and called Sara. We caught up briefly about work and life, and then I said, in the most casual voice I could muster, "Hey, no pressure, but this weekend is open if you guys have no plans. My father can't make it."

She didn't respond.

"Don't worry about it, though. It's late notice." Like everyone else, she'd talked about coming to visit me when Matt was gone, but, like everyone else, she got tied up in her own life. I wanted to understand. But I was too consumed with my loneliness.

"Let me talk to Jake. I'll call you."

•　　•　　•

Midnight Friday night, Jake's pickup truck pulled into the driveway, and I ran out the door barefoot in my pajamas. As soon as my three best friends from college—Sara, Jake, and Alex—got out of the truck, I hugged their innards out.

•　　•　　•

"No date?" Sara speared her fork into the bowl of fresh fruit on the table. I carried our cups of coffee to the table and sat down next to her. It was the two of us. Jake and Alex had gone for a run. I was amazed at their energy after staying up late the night before catching up.

"What?" I asked, puzzled.

"What are you thinking? Do you think the deployment has made him more committed to marrying you?"

I picked my mug up slowly, holding it in front of me with both hands.

Sara stood and walked over to the counter, returning to the table with a coffee cake they'd brought and a knife. "I mean, I figured you'd have a date by now. You're here, alone, supporting him, waiting for him."

She paused, then looked at me, and I could sense her hesitation. She cut a slice of coffee cake and slid it on a plate toward me. "I know we talked. On your way to the ranger graduation. But I guess I thought everything was resolved." She inhaled, filling her cheeks with air, before blowing out slowly. "Do you want to marry him?"

I put my mug down and stared out the window into the backyard. A squirrel ran along the top of the fence. Most of the brown leaves still clung to the branches of the trees beyond the fence, waiting for one good breeze to set them free.

"I don't know." I'd opened up to Amy and Vicky, but that had been wine induced. Plus, they didn't know me, like Sara did. They listened and nodded. Sara would play hardball. I wasn't sure I was ready for her line of questioning.

She waited, sadness seeping from her blue eyes. "Can I give you advice you haven't asked for?"

I nodded, staring into my coffee. "Like you wouldn't if I said no?"

She grinned and poked me in the arm with her pointer finger. "Roommates for four years. Friends for life. I'm allowed. So . . . if you have to make it work, it's not right. Maybe, *maybe*, you make it work if you're married, if you have kids. But if you have to make it work when you're engaged, and you know this—it's not right. It's not supposed to be this hard. You might love him, but that isn't the marriage kind of love."

Months ago, I would have tensed up and rebutted her frankness. But, that Saturday morning in October, I was too tired of it all. "You're right."

"So, why are you still here?"

"I love him. I do. I've been waiting for him to say, 'Hey, let's get married in July,' and he hasn't. And that makes me hold back. Like, he was the one who was holding up the date—with all his schools and then the deployment—and so now we could get married, and he hasn't said anything, and I wonder if he really wants to and that makes me hold back."

"Can you talk to him about it?"

I scoffed. "I wish. We can barely talk about anything for five minutes before he has to go, or there's some commotion. The connections are awful."

"What about writing him a letter?"

I thought about that. "That's a good idea." I didn't want to upset him, but I wanted to let him know what I was thinking. "I'll do that. If he doesn't want to set a date, I'll move on."

She looked at me skeptically.

"I sound so tough, right? But I have to be honest with myself. I won't desert him the day he gets back, but if nothing changes, I move on. Honest to God."

My eyes swelled when I thought about moving on. "That's the hardest part. Where would I go? What will I do? I've wasted these years. When he gets back, I'll have wasted two years of my life if we break up."

Sara shook her head slowly and held her chin high. "Are you kidding? Look at all you've done in two years. You moved away from home. Twice. Two different states. Made friends in both of them. You got job experience. You got your CPA, Kel. That's a lot. Oh, and you got the recipe for killer chicken nachos."

The front door opened, and Jake and Alex walked in, peeling off their gloves and outer jackets, laughing. Sara put her hand on my arm on the table. "You never know. He may respond to the letter with a date. He may have been so focused on this deployment, he never thought about it."

Maybe. I shrugged, punctuating the end of the conversation. I stood up to show Alex and Jake where the towels were.

•　　•　　•

The trees on the hills surrounding Nashville were tinged with faded orange as we walked and shopped on Music Row. We wandered in and out of a few stores before Alex and I fell behind Sara and Jake, who walked ahead of us holding hands. Sara wasn't one to keep secrets from Jake, so I was sure she'd shared our conversation at breakfast. I wasn't sure how much Alex knew.

He looked at me, his eyebrows drawn tight. "We haven't really talked."

He was right. I'd backed off, shied away from my friendship with him. When he called, I was quick on the phone, and I never called him—even though, at least five nights a week, I wanted to.

He swung his arm out in front of me, stopping me in place. "What's going on with you? Since I saw you in Seabury last March?"

I bit the inside of my cheek.

He tilted his head to one side. "Something's off with you. Something more than Matt stuff. Am I wrong?"

I'd always been honest with Alex. "No, you're not wrong."

He dropped his arm and tilted his head, waiting.

"People think I act like we're more than friends." I looked down at the toes of my leather boots. "Mary Ann said something to me. My aunt said something. I don't know. You're one of my best friends and I look forward to talking to you every night. But I guess it's weird to have a good friend who's a guy."

The sidewalk was packed with people enjoying the crisp fall day, and I lost sight of Sara and Jake. Alex pulled my arm calmly, urging me over to the side to let people pass.

"I like talking to you, too. You're like the sister I never had. I've had friends who are girls, but, yeah, you're different. You're more than just a friend." He looked into my eyes, forcing me to make eye contact with him.

I stared back at him, flustered. "What?"

"Yeah, you're engaged to my best friend. My brother. Nothing's going to happen between us. I'm friends with Sara. With Kate. With Heather. You're special. You always have been. Since that first night on the beach. I'm okay with that if you are."

My eyes widened, not sure what to think or say.

We walked again, when he turned to me and elbowed me faintly in the side. "You didn't ask me what post I got."

I wanted to say, *"Hold up, let's go back to what more than friends means"*; but fear or uncertainty or something else, I wasn't sure what, stopped me from saying anything. I froze in place on the sidewalk, and a large woman, carrying two oversized shopping bags, walked smack into me. Turning quickly to apologize to her, I moved off to the side, closer to the street. "What? You guys know where you're going, and you didn't tell me? Sara didn't tell me?"

"Let me clue you in on something," he teased. "If you only think about yourself and how miserable you are, and you never ask anyone about their lives, you don't find out stuff."

He was sort of kidding, but it hit me hard. He was right. I'd been so immersed in my own world; I hadn't come up for air to think about anyone else. Embarrassed, I focused on the cars stopped in traffic on the street.

"Too much? Too direct?"

"No, you're right," I told him sheepishly turning to look at him. "You're the only one who had the guts to say it to me, though."

"More than friends," he said breezily, lifting his hands, palms upward. "I'm allowed."

I grinned. I guess that's what he meant by "more than friends." He had permission to tell me when I was being a bitch.

"So we're good?" His blue eyes studied me carefully.

"Yeah, sure. I mean, I'm embarrassed for being such a bitch, but, yeah, we're okay."

"You're not a bitch, Kelly." He dropped his arm behind my neck and over my shoulder. It felt so good, having him touch me, but he pulled it away quickly.

I elbowed him back. "Did you get Germany? Is that where you'll go after flight school?"

He stood tall and pulled his shoulders back, surprised. "Oh, we really haven't talked, have we? No, that wasn't my number one choice."

"Oh, I thought Kate asked you . . ."

"Yeah, no, we spent a lot of time talking, and we spent Labor Day weekend together, when she came back to the States for a wedding. Kate's great. But we decided — again — we're better as friends."

"I didn't know." I tried not to sound as relieved as I was.

His cheeks were drawn in, as if holding something back.

"Are you okay?"

"Oh, yeah, I'm good. We dated as cadets and figured it out then, too."

"So, where're you going?" I was afraid to hear his answer.

"Air Assault!" He laughed.

"Huh?"

He shook his head, grinning. "McGowan, you have to know that's what everyone in the 101st says. Air Assault!"

"Here? You're moving here?" I threw my arms up in the air and hugged him, feeling like I won the lottery. When I released him from my tight hug, I covered my mouth with my hand, my eyes wide. "I'm so happy. Such good news!"

He laughed, and I didn't stop beaming as we walked through the crowds on the sidewalk to where Sara and Jake stood outside a restaurant waiting for us. I nudged Sara. "You didn't tell me you guys knew where you were going after flight school!"

Sara winked at Alex, then said to me, "Well, you haven't been calling your friends to check in on us."

"Okay, okay." I sighed. "You're right. I'm sorry. Message received." I slumped in place. "You guys are right. God, I stink. I've been so self-absorbed." With my hands on my hips, I asked, "Well? Where? Where are you going?"

"Fort Stewart." Her eyes danced. "Georgia."

I raised my hands over my head, then dropped them to hug her. "Oh, I'm sorry. I know you guys wanted Fort Drum, to be close to family in New York, but Stewart's in Georgia! It's drivable! I'm not sure if it's closer to Clarksville or Seabury. We can meet at the beach!"

Sara smiled. "Yeah, it's good. I'm glad. Drum's too cold. Plus, if he went to Drum," — she looked at Jake — "he'd deploy right away. Hopefully, we'll have a year at Stewart before he goes over."

Her timeline prediction made me think. "Wait," I said, suddenly realizing I'd never asked, "when do you move? When do you guys graduate from flight school?"

Jake answered for them. "Not sure exactly, but probably April or May. Depends on the weather. They never give us a good graduation date until we're closer to the end of the course."

"Oh," I sighed, disappointed. "I'd hoped it was earlier." My voice trembled. That was so far away! Matt had been gone two long months. I was relieved and happy to learn that my best friends would be close, but the reality was: I'd be alone for at least six more months.

Jake checked in with the hostess and led us to the bar to wait for a table. Following a few feet behind them, Alex touched my arm to get my attention. "I'm trying to read you. You looked so happy, but then you got sad. Is it because we ganged up on you to tell you to quit whining?"

"Nah. I'm glad you guys said something. I needed to hear it. I haven't been myself—for the past year or so . . . and I've been blaming the world, instead of looking within."

He waited for me to explain the sudden sadness. I leaned closer to him so I didn't have to yell in the crowded restaurant. "I'm happy you're moving to Campbell, and Sara and Jake are going to be in Georgia. But . . ."

He stepped closer to me, so we were merely inches apart, and put his hand on my forearm. "What?"

"I guess I hoped it would be sooner," I said. "And another thing. Sara and I talked this morning. She asked me if Matt and I had a date. A wedding date. I told her no. She asked me why not. Why hadn't we set a date for the summer when he gets back?"

This close to his face, I could have traced his lips with my finger. He tilted his head toward me, his hand still on my forearm.

"I told her the truth," I said, looking into his soothing blue eyes. "Matt never brought it up. I guess I feel like he's holding back. But she asked me—she asked if he might have been too focused on the deployment to think about anything else?"

He let go of my arm and turned his head, averting his glance from me. I wasn't sure what response I was looking for from him, but that was not it.

"Hey. What's going on?"

"Nothing." He glanced at me briefly, before turning away, as if expecting someone.

"You sure? I wondered what you thought. I'm going to write him a letter and ask him about setting a date. Do you think that's it? How he gets so focused on something, so intense about it? There's no room in his head for anything else. Maybe that's what happened before he left—when the unit was getting ready to go. He was focused on the deployment."

"Makes sense," he said as Sara and Jake moved toward us with their drinks. He looked at me, his lips opening slightly, before he said, "Yeah. He gets intense. Let me know how he responds to the letter." He looked at me and smiled. His face softened. "Hey, I'm glad I'll be moving here."

"Me too," I said. "May can't get here fast enough."

chapter 22

November 2004
Clarksville, Tennessee

I emptied the carafe of coffee into my father's cup, then rinsed the empty pot in the sink, before joining him at the kitchen table.

"Thanks, Kel." He folded the newspaper and put it aside. In his faded Celtics sweatshirt and jeans, he looked stronger and healthier than the last time I'd seen him. The skin on his face pulled tight over his bones.

"I'm worried about you." He rested his face in his palms, his elbows on the table.

That's why he flew down to spend Thanksgiving with me. Plus, he felt bad he'd canceled the October visit to settle Gram into the nursing home. When he asked if I had plans for Thanksgiving, I practically jumped through the phone.

"I'm good, Dad, really," I assured him. "I love my job. I have good friends. I'm supporting Matt." *I was freaking amazing. Making the most of this and thriving. Most of the time.* I looked out the window at the bare trees under the blue sky. "I'm sorry I backed out of going home for Thanksgiving."

"I get it." He frowned. "It's hard for you. Where to stay, all that."

"Nah, it's okay. I can split where I stay, between you and Mom. Not a big deal. I really didn't want to take time off from work."

That wasn't entirely true. It was never easy seeing my mother. She wasn't capable of uttering a noncritical word, and that got old. And I was hesitant to see Sharon and Kim, knowing they'd be selling Boston to me, encouraging me to move in with them and enjoy my early twenties. But I was stuck. I couldn't move out of this house. If I did, I'd be quitting on Matt, giving up on our relationship. The truth was: I couldn't leave him during a deployment. I couldn't do that to him.

"I'm glad Gram's okay. I sent her a card. What else can I do?"

"Nothing. It's a tough situation. I appreciate you sending the card. Brendan puts them on her TV, and she's not sure who they're from, but she likes to look at them. She's content. She's just not all there."

"I'm sorry, Dad. She's a good lady."

"The best," he agreed. "She put up with a lot over the years. Your grandfather wasn't an easy man to live with. She shielded us from a lot." He looked out the window and smiled, remembering. "We were a wild bunch, and those cousins of yours are carrying on the tradition. They always ask for you."

"I haven't seen them in so long. I guess it was Christmas Eve, junior year. I'm glad you're seeing more of them now."

We sipped our coffee quietly, before I asked, "Why didn't we spend more time with them over the years? More than Christmas Eve?"

He hesitated.

"It's all right to talk bad about Mom. It's not as if I'd say anything to her. I won't be damaged for life if you say something bad about her."

He choked back a laugh. "Your mother never fit in with the McGowans. And the McGowans never cut her any slack. When my brothers don't like someone, they let them know it. I don't blame her for not wanting to spend time with them. But you should know, it wasn't all your mother's fault. Gram didn't try to hide her feelings toward your mother."

"Why?"

I knew why. But he didn't know I knew. I wondered if he'd tell me.

My father stared into his coffee mug. He lifted his eyes and began tentatively, as if unsure how much to reveal. "Your mother and I didn't date very long. We didn't know each other well when we got married. When Gram met your mother, we'd already been to the justice of the peace. I still feel bad about that. It nearly killed my mother."

"Not being married in a Catholic church? Or being married without Gram there?"

He laughed. "Both. Also, another thing."

It was painful watching his facial expression change. One minute, he looked like he was going to tell me. The next, he stared away, thinking. I couldn't hold it in. "I know, Dad. That she was pregnant."

He blinked, confused, his body motionless.

I should have kept quiet, but I figured it was time. I'd always struggled with keeping that from him. "It's not a big deal, Dad. It happens."

"How'd you know?" His initial shock had dissipated. Middle school teachers were probably used to being shocked.

"I heard you and Aunt Patty talking at the beach. I was under the deck listening. You guys didn't know I was there. It was dark. I was supposed to be at the DelGreco's playing Monopoly or something."

He shook his head, put his hand to his mouth, and tried not to laugh. "Oh, my God. How old were you?"

"Twelve?"

"And you never told me you knew? You haven't told your mother? All this time?"

"No. I only told Sara. And Matt and Alex. Oh, and Amy and Vicky one night after drinking too much wine. But I told Sara after Jake proposed to her and we were talking about marriage. I told her how bad I felt—that you married Mom and were miserable all those years with her, and it was my fault. I'm the only reason you were together in the first place—"

"No, Kelly, no." He shook his head forcefully. "That's not true. I loved your mother. I wanted to marry her. I was *happy* when she told me she was pregnant. I insisted we get married. That was my idea. Yeah, I was surprised. We hadn't dated long—and she didn't seem like someone who'd accidentally get pregnant, but she did—and I was so happy when you were born. The proudest and happiest days of my life have been as your dad. Don't ever think that you made us unhappy."

I didn't respond.

"You've got to believe me. Kelly, you're the best thing that could have happened to me."

I nodded doubtfully. "But you stayed together for so long. You couldn't have been happy all those years with Mom."

He shrugged. "I wasn't unhappy enough to leave, Kel. I'd have been more unhappy if I had to wake up in a house without you there."

He hadn't mentioned my sister, and I assumed that was because she'd become such a pain in the ass. Placing his mug on the table, he cleared his throat. "That's why I was okay when you told me you and Matt were going to be engaged for a while. That's a good thing. Marriage is a long time." He paused, then asked, "Are you happy, Kel?"

I sighed, a long, tired sigh. "I am. But . . ."

He waited patiently as I thought about what to say and how to say it.

"When Matt proposed, he said we wouldn't plan a wedding because of the Army schools and this deployment. I understood. We couldn't have picked a date, because we didn't know when he'd graduate from ranger school. If he recycled, he'd have to do a phase over." I picked at the napkin under the spoon I'd used for my cream. "Then we moved here and knew he was deploying, but we didn't know when. So we couldn't pick a date then, either." I looked back at my father. "But once he knew he was going in the middle of August, we could have picked a date next summer." I picked up the spoon and flipped it over, back and forth, a few times.

"But you didn't," he said.

"No, we didn't. Matt didn't. He had the opportunity to say, 'I'll be back by May, so let's get married in July.' He didn't."

"But why didn't you ask him? You don't usually hold back." He squinted curiously.

"Yeah. I've thought a lot about that. I think I held back because I felt like he was holding back. I'm not going to beg for this, Dad."

He nodded. "Has everything been okay between you two?"

"That's the thing. It has been. It's been great. I think. I mean, Matt gets introspective, like something's on his mind, but I think that's the way he is, his personality. We've been together for 2 ½ years, but we've only lived together for 9 ½ months, so it's kind of hard to maintain a relationship—especially when we can barely talk. It's not his fault. It's the Army."

"So, what's your plan?"

"I wrote him a letter two weeks ago. He should have it by now, but I haven't talked to him. In the letter, I asked why he didn't pick a date to get married when he got back. The ball's in his court. We'll see what he says."

My father's lips pursed, as if he wanted to say something, but he didn't.

"Sound like a plan?" I asked, partially grinning, trying to lighten the mood and somewhat erase anything I'd said that would make him worry more about me.

He shifted in his chair. "It does. But I'll be honest with you. I don't get it. You two seemed so happy dating."

"I don't get it, either, Dad. At first, I blamed myself. I must be so hard to live with."

He shook his head. "No. Don't you go there."

"That's easy to say, but we were happy dating, and then when we moved in together, something changed. Or else, Matt was always like this, and I never noticed it when we were dating."

"Okay, Kel. Here's what I've figured out about happiness. You can't find it in your job. Or in other people. Or where you live, or how much money you make, or any of that. It's our own choice — whether we want to be happy or not."

I nodded, eager to change the subject. "Tess, my Fort Benning friend, says the same thing." Redirecting the conversation, I asked him, "Hey, I was thinking. Do you think Aunt Patty would be ok with Amy and I spending Christmas in Seabury?"

His face lit up. "She'd love it. You know that. Can I come?"

"Sure! That'd be great." I stood and brought my coffee cup to the sink.

"Oh, let's call Patty now. She'll be thrilled." He pushed himself away from the table, but before he made the call, he did something very peculiar for a McGowan. He walked over to me at the sink and hugged me.

"I'm proud of you, Kelly." His voice trembled. "You're a good kid. You're stronger than anyone I know."

My eyes watered as I fell into his embrace, but I was too surprised to say a peep. I don't think he expected a response, anyway. He walked to the phone to call his sister.

•　　•　　•

Matt called the week after Thanksgiving. I asked if he got my letter, and he told me he did and that he'd sent me a letter back because it was so hard to talk on the phone.

"It might take some time to reach you," he said. Vehicles or engines or something roared in the background. "But I love you, Kelly. I really appreciate you."

I hung up and tears welled behind my eyelids.

His letter arrived in the mail two weeks later.

chapter 23

December 2004 into January 2005
Clarksville, Tennessee
Seabury, Florida
I ripped the envelope open before the front door closed behind me.

Kelly,

First, I love you. A lot. I'm sorry I didn't set a date before I left. I promise we will talk and resolve everything when I get home. I can't wait.

I appreciate all you do for me, the letters, the boxes, being so supportive. I don't deserve you and I never have. Meeting you on that spring break trip saved my life. I mean it.

I love you.

Matt

What the hell? I called Amy and asked her to come over to help me decipher it. She sat on the couch, leaned forward, and read it a few times before she glanced between the letter and my eyes.

"Okay, I've never met Matt. But my analysis, after watching many Hallmark movies, is he loves you. But he's an idiot. He's consumed with work and not thinking about getting married.

What's his incentive to get married? You live with him. In his mind, he loves you, and you love him. So, what's the big deal?"

"Yeah, I get that. But, honestly, even if he doesn't want to marry me, it's not as if I could leave, right? I can't break up with him now. He's right. We'll talk when he gets home. If we don't pick a date, I'm out of here."

"You'll pick a date, Kel. He didn't think about it before he left. He was too busy getting his soldiers and equipment and all that crap ready to deploy."

I wasn't sure if she was right. I'd find out in May.

•   •   •

"This is exactly what I needed." Amy exhaled and lifted her arms above her head, the waves lapping at her feet. The sun was shining in the bright blue sky. "It's weird being barefoot at the beach in a sweatshirt in December, but I think I could get used to it."

"Now you know why I love it here." I bent down and picked up a jingle shell to add to the jar on my dresser. Or bring back with me to Clarksville.

"Are you sure you won't miss your mother and sister?" Amy stooped to dig out a sand dollar wedged in the wet sand. "I hope they didn't stay home because I was coming."

"Oh, those are fragile—be careful. No. Don't worry about them. Their decision had nothing to do with you. My mom always has to work. And my sister seems to be happy with this guy. She's staying in Maine with him, according to my dad. I don't remember the last time I talked to her. Maybe she'll pick up this week. You know, the Christmas spirit and all that." I tried to laugh it off, but I sensed Amy realized how much it bothered me that Megan never picked up when I called.

She listened, her lips sealed, as we walked along the water's edge.

"We just have to get through January," I continued. "Then we have February—it's a short month—and March. And April. The final stretch . . ."

The FRG made it clear they had no specific return date, but, for our sanity, we clung to a late April/early May timeframe.

"God, I can't wait for them to get home." As soon as it came out of her mouth, she looked away, her eyes cast down, her cheeks turned red.

"Hey, don't worry about it. You're allowed to miss Leo. I'm okay, really. I don't know him and I miss him. I still can't believe he sent me flowers for Thanksgiving. Who does that?"

Amy's teeth were perfectly straight and whiter than white and her smile took up her entire face. "He knows you've been so good to me."

"Pshaw." I waved her away. "The feeling is mutual."

Farther down the beach, Kyle tossed the football to Mary Ann. I'd been surprised to see her car in the driveway when Amy and I drove up, and even more surprised to see her parents arrive later with Joey and Mary Martha. When I walked across the street to see them and introduce Amy, Mary Ann told me Johnny was spending Christmas with his girlfriend's family in Georgia.

The precocious four-year-old Mary Martha I remembered had transformed into a pouty, miserable high school sophomore slathered in makeup, wearing tight jeans and a sequined top. Mary Ann told us she whined nonstop about having to spend Christmas with her family at the beach.

"I get it," Amy said, commiserating with Mary Ann. "I have a stepsister that age."

"My last summer here, Joey was six! How can he be going to Georgia Tech next year?"

The four of us—my father, aunt, Amy, and I—carried platters of sugar cookies and bottles of wine across the street to join the DelGrecos for their traditional Christmas Eve feast. This was a family that didn't miss many meals. Near midnight, stuffed and tired from laughing, we made our way back to my aunt's house, falling exhausted into bed.

I hadn't dozed off yet when a distant buzzing woke me. Amy sprang out of bed and fumbled around on the nightstand in the dark.

"Turn the light on," I mumbled before I crawled back under my blanket. I hoped Matt would call sometime, too.

When she crept back into the room later, she tried to muffle her soft sobs under the blanket, but I sat up and turned the light back on.

"Hey, is everything okay?"

"Yeah, I just really miss him. Sorry I woke you."

I shot her a sympathetic look. "I'm glad he called. Once Christmas is over, we're on the final stretch." I talked a good game, but after I turned the light out, I couldn't get back to sleep. I wanted Matt to call. I wanted him to miss me. I wanted assurance he was safe.

•   •   •

Late morning, the day after Christmas, the DelGrecos piled into their two cars and drove away. I waved goodbye from Aunt Patty's deck and walked into the house to find Amy and Aunt Patty reading on the couch, sharing a fuzzy sheepskin blanket. They both looked up at me, smiled, and returned to their books.

"Nerds." I smiled and walked down the hall past my father's room. Moving piles of clothes off one twin bed and onto the floor, he turned and saw me, a look of guilt written all over him.

Poking my head in, I asked, "What're you doing?"

"Oh." He hemmed and hawed a bit. "Not much. Getting organized."

"Hmm." Squeezing my brows together, I wondered what that was about and continued down the hall to my room. A loud knock on the sliding glass door stopped me in my tracks. No one ever knocked on the sliding glass door. Voices and laughter erupted in the living room. Aunt Patty and Amy. *Alex?*

I turned and raced back down the hall to see Alex wearing a fleece jacket and jeans, carrying two large Christmas gift bags.

"What the. . . ?" I took a step back.

"I keep up with your aunt." He looked at me, nervously smiling. "I told her I'd be driving back to Rucker tomorrow, and she insisted I stop on the way to surprise you and Amy."

"I'm surprised!" I laughed as I approached him. "I've talked to the two of you about each other for months. I'm glad you're finally meeting!"

Amy smiled shyly, and Alex grinned and extended his hand to shake hers, before opting to go in for a hug instead. My father walked up behind me. "Oh, thank God. More testosterone in this house."

·   ·   ·

"I hope I can meet Leo. It looks like the unit I report to after flight school will deploy as soon as Matt and Leo get back." Alex poked the fire with a long stick. We'd moved from the dinner table to the fire pit in my aunt's yard.

"I didn't know you were deploying right away." My voice shook, and I coughed to hide it. "That sucks."

"It's all rumor right now. I shouldn't report until May, and everything might change by then. Who knows?"

"I hope it changes, Alex," my father said. In the dark across the fire, my aunt nodded slowly.

We stared at the fire in silence, soaking in its warmth, listening to the waves beat against the shore. Amy broke the silence. "This is perfect. Thanks so much for having me, Mrs. McGowan. I really needed this. This deployment's been hard. I never realized how much I depended on Leo- for companionship."

Amy always came across as so independent. I was surprised to hear her be so open and vulnerable.

"I don't know Leo. But I've seen a lot of marriages and your independence combined with your desire to be with him- that's the best kind of marriage," Aunt Patty said softly. "And please. Call me Aunt Patty. I'm glad to have you. The same goes for you, Alex. You're both always welcome here. You made my Christmas."

"Umm, hello?" my father piped in. "What about your favorite little brother?"

"I'm waiting for you to move down here," my aunt answered.

The orange flames and the rhythmic crashing of waves mesmerized us. My eyelids fluttered until suddenly I woke with a start and the fire was out. *Oh no, this again!* I looked around and was relieved to see both Amy and Alex asleep in their chairs. I stood and tapped Amy, who woke up startled enough to yell "What?" and woke Alex.

"Sorry, Ame." I tried not to laugh. Alex wiped his mouth automatically, assuming he was drooling, which he was, and the three of us plodded up the steps into the house. We nodded good night to each other and went to our rooms for the night.

•   •   •

The next day, on our drive back to Tennessee, Amy sighed. "I was dreading Christmas without Leo. That was my first Christmas in four years without him. The holidays are so hard. I wanted to fast-forward past them."

She looked out the window at the pine trees, trying to hide her watery eyes from me. We passed a tiny town, run-down storefronts, a wooden stand selling honey. "Thanks for inviting me with you. I love your aunt and father. I love the DelGrecos. I love Alex." Pausing, she looked at me. "He's a good friend. Right?"

I began to respond, but she interrupted.

"I mean, you've talked about him, and yeah, I know, he's a friend, but after seeing you both together, it made me wonder if you were ever interested?" My long pause caused her to say, "Okay, none of my business—and he might only be a very good friend—but I feel like he thinks more of you than that."

"Nah." I brushed it off, but her eyes stayed on me, waiting for more. "All right, that trip to Nashville when he came up with Sara and Jake? He told me we *were* more than just friends."

She hit me on the shoulder. "What?"

"He just said that he had friends who were girls, but I was more special than them. So that's why we're more than friends. Which made no sense to me. He said I'm engaged to his best friend, who's like his brother, and so I guess that's why we're more than just friends. I don't know."

"Um. I'm not sure what to say."

"Nothing to say. I'm engaged to Matt. We'll see how that ends up. Alex is a catch, and someone will scoop him up soon, I'm sure."

"Oh my God, yeah. Maybe I've been away from Leo too long, but he's the best-looking guy I've seen in a long time."

I laughed.

"Those eyes. That smile. God, I miss Leo so much."

We both sighed together. She said it first, "Do we have to go back?"

"I think I could live in Seabury forever," I said.

•   •   •

I waited for a call from Matt over Christmas. It never came, but he called two days before New Year's Eve. "We weren't near a phone on Christmas. I'm sorry, Kelly. It was just another day over here. Another day closer to getting out of here."

I sat at the kitchen table and my entire body sagged with sadness for him and everyone he was with, so far away from their families. "I worry about you." I tore a paper napkin into tiny strips. I'd torn up a lot of napkins over the past year. "When I don't hear from you, I worry."

"I'm sorry I couldn't call. I don't think we'll be near a phone for the next month. I'll call you as soon as I can. Don't worry. I'm fine. Honest . . ." His voice trailed off, distracted. "Hey, Kel, I gotta go. I love you."

"I love you, too," I said. After we hung up, I sat at the table, immobile, and stared into space.

chapter 24

February 2005
Clarksville, Tennessee

I opened the blinds and groaned. The gray sky reflected a dull, dreary dimness over the backyard. Even the skeletal tree branches looked gray. We were supposed to get two inches of snow. Who knew it snowed in Tennessee?

When my bare feet hit the freezing bathroom floor, I scooted into the shower, huddled up against the wall, waiting for the water to warm. If heaven existed, it was a hot shower. Afraid I'd be late for work, I forced myself out, pulled a turtleneck, sweater, and slacks from my closet, and turned on the news as I changed.

"Oh, puh-leeze," I said out loud when a Valentine's Day commercial selling teddy bears followed a Valentine's Day commercial selling jewelry. I switched channels, but the lovey-dovey commercials were everywhere. I'd sent Matt a box with cookies, magazines, protein, and gum, but I wasn't sure if he got it. The last time I'd heard from him was a quick call mid-January. He'd told me he wasn't sure when he'd be near a phone again.

The FRG told us not to watch the news because it would only make us worry. They were right, but I watched it, anyway. I wanted to know what was going on. Every morning when I dressed for work, I tuned in to the liberal national news station;

every night when I ate dinner, I tuned in to the conservative news station. I figured the truth was somewhere in between.

That morning, I sat on the edge of the bed, put on my socks, and read the ticker across the bottom of the screen. An IED. Five soldiers dead. I stared at the TV. Matt never told me where he was located, but I had a general idea. When they flashed the map on the TV, and I saw where this attack occurred, I froze. My heart raced. I rubbed my hands back and forth on my thighs. I waited for more information, but the newscaster had moved on to a carjacking in Chicago.

I turned to the other news stations to see if they had more information. The phone on my nightstand rang, and I jumped. I looked at the number. My father.

"Just checking on you, honey." His voice wavered. He'd seen the news.

"I'm watching it now, Dad. I'll let you know if I hear anything."

"Oh, Kelly. I'm sorry you have to go through this worrying."

"Dad, I'm fine. I'm headed to work now. I'm sure Matt's fine. There are a lot of people over there. What are the chances?"

"Call me if you learn anything, honey. I love you."

"I will, Dad. Love you," I said, hanging up.

Since Matt deployed, whenever anything happened anywhere in the world to a soldier, sailor, airman, or marine, my father called. Once, he called when someone was killed in Somalia. He knew Matt wasn't there; he told me, but he still wanted to check on me. He cared, and I was grateful. But it was hard enough to worry, without having to worry about my father worrying.

I'd barely hung up the phone when it rang again. My heart raced quicker, more intensely this time. *Oh no! This is it.* Then I remembered. They wouldn't call. They'd come to the door.

I picked it up, my hand shaking. It was Vicky.

"Matt is okay." Her voice broke, crying. "Can I come over? With Captain Keller? Matt is okay. I want to tell you that. Before we show up at your door. I talked to my husband. I can confirm: Matt is fine."

"Yeah, sure," I said, confused. My heart kept racing. Despite the cold, my underarms perspired. Vicky hung up, and I put the phone down, focused on the TV. *What's going on?* I rubbed my eyes and held my chin in the nook of my hands between my thumb and pointer. It made no sense for her to come see me if Matt was okay.

I couldn't take my eyes off the TV, now talking about a fire in California. The doorbell rang fifteen minutes later, and in those fifteen minutes, I'd gone over every possible scenario. Matt must have been wounded. I pictured the worst scenarios, amputated limbs, blindness, tubes hanging out of his body in a field hospital somewhere.

I opened the door. Vicky stood on the porch with Captain Keller, the rear detachment commander. Their eyes were bloodshot and watery. Vicky wore jeans and a sweatshirt; her hair was disheveled. Captain Keller's uniform was wrinkled, her boots scuffed, her hair dirty, tied back loosely in a bun. She'd had her baby a month earlier, and it looked as if she hadn't slept since.

My heart stopped. It was Matt. It had to be. I stepped back, shaking my head. "You said he was okay!"

"Oh, he is. He is. I'm so sorry we showed up like this. We're trying to make it easier on—" Vicky stopped. She put her hand to her mouth and looked down at her running shoes.

I stared at Captain Keller. She was in uniform. She was in charge.

Trembling, Vicky said, "Kelly, you remember Dawn."

I nodded, dazed.

Dawn Keller's tired eyes blinked. "I'm sorry to show up like this. Can we come inside?"

The minute the door shut behind them, I demanded, "What's going on?"

Dawn exhaled slowly, as if trying to breathe purposefully. She held her hands together in front of her. "I'm sorry, Kelly. We need to hurry. I'm sorry to be the one to tell you this. There was an incident."

"What? But you said — You said Matt's okay?" I shuffled back and forth, shifting my weight from hip to hip, my hands by my side, my head shaking.

She nodded, her face blank. "Yes, Matt's okay."

"I saw the news," I rushed. "Is he hurt?"

"No, Matt's not hurt. He wasn't involved in the attack."

I didn't understand. I should have felt relief, but it was as if I'd been thrown in a dark place, confused, lost.

"There's no easy way to say this," she said, her tone apologetic. She paused, then looked directly at me, her face softening. Tears formed in her eyes, and she brushed them away. She looked down at her hands and her voice quivered. "Leo Wicks."

I gasped. My hands went to my face. "No."

Dawn stepped closer to me. "Lieutenant Wicks is one of the fatalities."

I crumbled in place and faded away, as if someone pulled the pin and let all the air out of me. "No, not Leo." I moaned. Tears streamed down my face.

Dawn took a Kleenex out of her uniform pocket and wiped her eyes, then pulled another one out and handed it to me. She looked at her watch. "We haven't told Amy yet."

I couldn't breathe. I couldn't stop crying. I couldn't believe this was happening.

"The chaplain's meeting us at Amy's in ten minutes." She tried to gain back some control over her emotions. "We'll tell her then. We wanted to see if you could come with us."

I leaned back against the counter, my head in my hands, rocking back and forth, sobbing. *It's a mistake. No. It couldn't be Leo.*

Vicky hugged me, folding me into her, and whispered softly through her tears, "I'm so sorry."

"We need to get to Amy's," Dawn pleaded urgently, "before she hears it from someone else. Mrs. Mudd's out of town, so Vicky's our acting FRG leader. Chaplain Moore and I will go to the door. If you and Vicky are there- in your car? She may not want to see anyone. But if she does, we'd like you to be close, ready to support her."

I nodded. My throat was raw. My body felt hollow.

"There's nothing I can say. It's. . ." Dawn's voice faded off.

Tears ran down Vicky's face.

Amy. Suddenly I thought about her watching this on the news; and my shock, my sadness, became secondary to how she might learn this tragic news.

"We have to go," I blurted. Frantically, I pulled a handful of napkins out of the basket on the counter and tossed my crumpled Kleenex into the trash. I grabbed my purse and car keys, and Vicky and I got in my car.

Neither of us spoke. We cried silently and followed Captain Keller's car out of the neighborhood to Amy's townhouse.

It was 7:30 a.m. when Vicky and I pulled up behind Captain Keller's car. The chaplain's dark sedan was parked on the other side of the street. I watched him step slowly out of his car and walk with Dawn up the walkway to Amy's front door. I sat with Vicky, suddenly sore, my chest heavy, shaking my head and crying. Vicky held her eyelids up with her fingers, willing the endless flow of tears to stop.

And then Amy opened the door. She immediately backed up, raising both hands to her face.

My stomach turned queasy. My whole body ached for Amy. Without thinking, I opened my door and ran to her. Later, I wouldn't remember how I got there. I wouldn't remember pushing the chaplain and Dawn aside. I'd only remember holding her, convulsing with sobs, her face still in her hands. Gently, I took her hands from her face and pulled her into me tight. Together, inside her doorway, we rocked, shaking and sobbing, deeper and deeper into despondency.

•   •   •

It was the worst day of my life.

Hours later, Amy's sobs interfered with her breathing, and Dawn ran to the kitchen, returned with a brown paper lunch bag, held it to Amy's mouth, and calmly instructed her to take deep breaths into the bag. Finally, by nightfall, she collapsed in my arms on the couch, overwhelmed with exhaustion.

The chaplain told me he'd send a doctor over to check on her, but no one ever came. Vicky and Dawn left that evening, both telling me to call them anytime if they could do anything. Amy fell into depression, sleeping and crying, then sleeping and crying. I called work and asked for another sick day. I was afraid to leave Amy alone until Leo's mother and father arrived the following afternoon.

•   •   •

"It's so hard," I mumbled into the phone to Alex the next night. My body was tired of crying. Leo's parents had arrived, and I'd returned to my house alone. "She loved him so much. Hell, I never met him, and I loved him. They were so in love."

"I'm so sorry, Kelly. I can't imagine. Did you hear from Matt?"

My eyes watered. Survivor's guilt. I still had Matt, but Amy didn't have Leo. "Yeah. Last night. He wanted to tell me he was okay. He had to go. I heard noise in the background again. He said he wanted to make sure I was all right."

"I'm sorry. I'm glad he called. I can understand him separating himself from this. Trying to get through the rest of this deployment safe. Not letting anything personal affect him," Alex explained. "I'm sorry for Amy. I'm sorry for you."

"Thanks." I took a deep breath.

Alex told me he was supposed to get to Fort Campbell in late May.

"It'll be like old times," I said wistfully.

He laughed. "Yeah, right, but with real jobs now. Man, I never realized what a good deal West Point was. Until I got in the real Army."

"Are you happy? Do you like it?"

"I love flying. I'm nervous about getting to an actual unit, but I'm looking forward to it, too. I'm hoping I don't deploy right away. There's still that rumor out there, though."

We talked about his timeline; when he'd arrive, what apartments he was looking at. I told him he'd better stay with us when he looked for a place, and he told me he planned on it.

Before we hung up, he said, "Kelly, I mean it. I can drive up this weekend. To give you someone to talk to. You and Amy are so close. This can't be easy for you."

And then, like I always do when someone's nice to me, I teared up.

He waited, and when my breathing became less jagged, he said, "I'm coming."

"No," I told him. "I'm leaving Friday to drive to Ohio with Amy for the funeral next week. But thanks, Alex. I really appreciate your offer." My voice trembled, filled with gratitude for his kindness.

He brushed off my sentimentality. "If you opened up to Sara, she'd be up there in a minute. Has she called you yet?"

"Yeah, but I told her I'd call her back. I can't tell her how awful it is. God knows when Jake deploys, she'll find out herself."

When we hung up, I burrowed under a blanket on the couch watching mindless TV until I fell asleep. I dreamed: Leo drove a Geek Squad car over a cliff, but Amy was in the car with him. I ran to the edge of the cliff, but then I woke up startled, worried about Amy. I texted her at 12:30 a.m. She texted back immediately, telling me she was going to take a sleeping pill, and we'd talk in the morning.

•   •   •

The day after the funeral, Amy held me and didn't let me go as we said goodbye in Ohio.

She'd decided to stay with her father and his family for a week, to put off returning to their house in Clarksville. Releasing me, she asked, "How could I do this without you?"

"You're stronger than you think." I tried to convince both of us. "I'll pick you up when you get into Nashville. I love you, Ame."

I didn't run out of tears until I was a hundred miles away from Leo's grave.

chapter 25

February into May 2005
Fort Campbell, Kentucky

How could she possibly recover? Leo's family's grief was overwhelming; it spared no room for them to think about their daughter-in-law. Amy's father was consumed with his family. After the burial, he scurried his wife away, barely hugging Amy goodbye on his way to their car. When she got in my car the next week at the airport in Nashville, she looked thinner and more tired than she did when I left her.

"If I wasn't depressed before," she confessed, "I was after spending a day with my half-sisters. I forgot how awful teenagers are. The mattress on my sofa bed was about a half-inch thick. And the cats slept with me. All three of them. I'm allergic to cats."

She only wanted to sleep. She barely ate, picking at the casseroles that were delivered daily by FRG members, neighbors, the local church. She couldn't touch Leo's stuff. His clothes and coats remained in the closets. His rucksacks and duffel bags and spare combat boots lined the wall of the guest room.

I was so worried about her I couldn't eat, either. Heavy with guilt, weighed down with helplessness, I called the chaplain.

He told me to let her grieve. "Keep checking in on her. Does she have family?"

"Not really. They're a mess."

"Thank God she has you," he said, throwing more responsibility on my shoulders.

That dream where they drove the car off the cliff together worried me enough to call Vicky and Diane, and the three of us rotated visits and phone calls. I was most surprised by Donna Jones, wearing her trademark denim skirt, who delivered food, helped with laundry, and sat with Amy when I was at work. The strength of these women humbled me.

•　　•　　•

Mid-April, two months after Leo's funeral, trying to keep myself occupied, I kneeled on my kitchen floor on a Saturday morning and cleaned out the produce shelf in the refrigerator. The phone rang.

"I stayed up last night going through his stuff," Amy told me. "I kept a few T-shirts. I'll wear them to bed. I kept a hideous leather jacket that he loved so much. But everything else went to the thrift shop. I dumped it in the donation shed before the sun came up. I called work and asked if I could come in next week. They've been so good, waiting for me to figure out what I was going to do." She paused. "I'm going to stay here, at least for a while. At first, every time I saw soldiers marching or heard a helicopter, I thought of Leo. Every time I talked to one of you, I thought of Leo."

I listened, disturbed. I never thought about what my presence might mean to Amy. I never thought about how hard it might be for her to have a friend whose loved one was still alive over there.

"But I've got nothing in Ohio. I have friends here. People who care about me. My boss has been so understanding. People get it here."

I felt relieved, grateful. It was selfish of me, but I didn't want to lose her. "You're so strong." I'd never met anyone stronger.

"Not even a little bit. Nights are the worst. I'm taking pills to sleep. I hate to, but I have to. The chaplain and the doc both tell me it's to be expected, and I won't be on them forever, but I don't know. How can anything be normal again?"

There was nothing I could say. I bit my lip and stared at the lettuce on my counter.

"A day at a time," she finally said.

After we hung up, I went back to the fridge and tossed expired salad dressings and mustards, and thought about how unfair it all was. Amy didn't deserve this. In what kind of world, can someone so sweet and kind be a widow at twenty-four? It was too much to think about. It was too hard. I closed the refrigerator door, sat down on a kitchen chair, put my head in my hands, too tired to cry.

•　　　•　　　•

"You have to go." Vicky's voice insisted on the answering machine. She paused for effect, her dog barking in the background, before she continued. "You've gone to every FRG meeting with Amy. It feels . . . disloyal . . . to go to this last one without her . . . but you *have* to go because Dawn's going to give us all the updated information about the redeployment, and, yeah, I could call you with it, but I'd really like to see you. So come. Please. Friday night. At Donna's house on post. I wish I could pick you up, but I've got to drop Addy off at volleyball and won't have time." She paused again. "Okay, well, see you there? Okay. Bye."

The next day when I ran with Allison, I told her I didn't want to go to the final FRG meeting.

"You should go." She stopped and handed Erin a juice box. "Does Amy know you aren't going?" She didn't wait for me to answer. Pushing the stroller again, she said, "She'd make you go, and you know it."

She was right; so after work on the last Friday in April, I drove through the streets of Fort Campbell looking for Donna Jones's house. Part of the reason I wanted to go was because Donna was hosting it. When I'd first met her at the beginning of the deployment, I'd judged her on her denim skirt, blue tights, and meek disposition. I thought she was odd as a duck. It turned out she was. But she was such a nice, odd duck, and had been an angel to Amy after Leo died.

I smiled when she opened the door in her skirt and tights.

"Kelly. Welcome. Please come in." Her voice exuded warmth and sincerity, a combination of the nicest preschool teacher and grandmother ever. I followed her down the hall.

Vicky stood up when she saw me and pulled me over to sit next to her. I smiled and nodded at the women sitting on folding chairs, on the carpet covered with dog hair, waiting for Captain Keller to begin.

I remembered thinking at that first FRG meeting that Dawn Keller had the best deal ever. She didn't have to deploy! But, that night at Donna's house, standing alone near the fireplace wearing loose slacks and a blouse stained with leaking breast milk, her roots glaring from hair that needed highlights, heavy bags sagging beneath her eyes, I realized I may have misread that one. That night at Donna's house, all I saw was a new mom adjusting to life with a four-month-old while trying to keep a few hundred spouses happy.

"It's important to go into redeployment with lower expectations," she started. "Expectations are usually too high. I have some handouts that might help explain what they'll be going through. We have a tentative date—it's three weeks from today. Subject to change, but that's what we have for now. We'll send emails and will follow up with the phone tree to update the date/time/location when we know more."

The handouts detailed what we'd been told: Don't make plans. They may not want to do anything. Loud noises may startle them. Crowds may cause anxiety. Be there to support them and enjoy them and love them. It may not be what you expect it to be.

I didn't know what to expect. My situation with Matt differed from anyone else's. Enormously relieved and grateful that Matt was physically alive, I understood that this deployment had been harrowing and horrible and harsh. But we who hadn't experienced it would never understand the feelings of those who had. We couldn't predict how they'd react when they got home. I didn't have high expectations. I had none.

•   •   •

When I walked into the house after the meeting, my phone rang. It was my father. He'd been checking in more often since Leo died, concerned about both me and Amy.

"Hey, Dad, what's up?"

He panted, breathing irregularly, as if he'd been crying. My father didn't cry. I stopped in place. Something was wrong. Very wrong.

"Dad?"

"Hon." His voice was so soft I pressed my ear into the phone. "I hate to do this to you. I have bad news."

I planted my feet on the floor where I was in the kitchen. "Oh, no, Dad. Gram?"

Silence.

"Dad?"

"No, Kel. Not Gram. It's . . ."

I tried to swallow. "Dad. T-tell me," I stammered.

"Megan." His breath got caught before he sobbed.

I leaned my back against the kitchen counter. Dizzy. It made no sense. I whispered, "What?"

"We think it was an overdose." He paused, blowing his nose.

"What? Is she okay?"

My father breathed deeply into the phone. "I'm sorry, Kelly. Her boyfriend found her. It was too late."

My feet wanted to run, but were stuck in place. I needed to be out of the kitchen, out of the house. I couldn't breathe. I wasn't sure how much time passed. My father cried into the phone, his volume increasing with each question. "Kelly? Are you there? Kelly. Tell me you're there. Oh, God. I'll call 911 for you, hon. Oh, God."

"No," I said, emerging back into the real world. "No, I'm here, Dad," I mumbled, shaking my head.

He sighed. "Oh, honey. It's too much on you. Too much all at once."

"I don't believe it, Dad. Is he sure? The boyfriend?"

He didn't respond, as if allowing me time to process, to acknowledge. "It's unbelievable."

I wasn't ready to concede. This was my sister, the one I taught to read, the one whose hair I braided, the one with whom I shared my dolls and my bedroom. She was twenty-two. She couldn't be gone. "But how are we sure? Did he call 911?"

"Yeah, Kel," my father said, sighing. "Tommy did. The paramedics said she'd been gone for most of the night."

"Alone? No one with her?" I slid down the side of the cabinet, sitting on the floor of the kitchen, my back against the cabinet door.

"I know." His voice faltered. "Tommy was at work."

I swallowed the lump in my throat.

"The wake and funeral will be Monday and Tuesday. I don't want you to be alone now, Kel. I'll call Amy to come over and be with you."

I couldn't talk. I held the phone in my hand and stared into space.

"Kelly. Are you still there?"

"I'm here," I managed. "I'm . . . stunned. I didn't know it was this bad. I haven't talked to her in forever." Immediately, I plunged into guilt. This was my fault for not keeping up with her. I let her go. I gave up. And now she was gone.

He paused. "I don't think it *was* this bad, Kel. None of us did. I think she messed up. She had a prescription for depression, and I think she took something with it—something that was too much for her system with the prescription. She'd been happy, living with Tommy since before Christmas—he told your mother he found her prescription bottle on the nightstand with some pot. We don't understand it."

"Dad, she never called me back," I said. My throat felt thick. "I stopped calling her because she never called me back."

"Kelly," my father said in a low, sad voice. "Don't go there. You tried. You've tried your whole life with her. You can only control what you can control. You did your part."

I moved the phone away from my face, dazed.

"I think the autopsy will show that this was an accidental overdose. Not that it makes anything any easier. Kelly, I don't want you to be alone."

"It's okay." I lied. "I'll be okay. How's Mom?"

"Not good." He sighed. "You're not the only one who feels responsible. Each of us thinks we could have done more. Your mother thinks she should never have let her move in with Tommy. As if she had a choice. Megan wanted out, away from us. Your mother's been with Mike since we found out. I'm glad she's not alone."

"What?" I wiped my eyes with a kitchen towel. "Mike? Her boyfriend?"

My mother had a boyfriend who worked in the bank across from her high school, but she'd never given me any details. According to my cousin Cathy, who occasionally emailed me the family gossip, the McGowans were convinced that my mother knew Mike before college, before she met my father. I never asked my mother, and I sure didn't ask my father.

"Yeah, she's been with him for a while," he said, implying what, I wasn't sure, but didn't want to ask.

This phone call was too much to digest. It made me want to crawl into a hole, cover my head with a blanket, and never come out.

"Kelly, let me call Amy to come over and be with you."

"No, Dad. I'll be fine. I'll get a flight up on Sunday. I'll call you tomorrow with the flight info, but I can rent a car. You don't have to get me."

"Don't be foolish. I'll be there."

We hung up, and I didn't move from where I sat on the floor in the kitchen. I sat still, my arms limp by my side, holding the phone in my hand. Before I picked up the call, I'd felt like I was a glass window, barely held together. When I learned about Megan, I shattered.

·　　·　　·

I opened a bottle of wine, and was on my second glass, when Amy showed up at my front door with her overnight bag. She hugged me wordlessly, and we sat on the couch, watching *Seinfeld*. We didn't talk about Megan or Leo or how unfair life was. I told her I was sorry my father bothered her, and she shook her head and told me to stop, please. She helped me make up the bed in the guest room, and before she went to bed, she called

Vicky, who called Dawn Keller, who emailed the company commander in Iraq, who told Matt.

At 2 a.m., I was awake in my bed, unable to sleep, when my phone rang. It was Matt. He'd only met Megan once, when we were dating. She was in her grunge phase, and, to his credit, he never judged her. After he met her, he told me he'd never have thought we were sisters.

"I'm sorry, Kelly. I just heard." Chaos and commotion came from his end of the phone. "I'm sorry I'm not with you."

I sat limply, drained.

"Are you all right?"

I inhaled deeply, trying to sound strong. "Yeah, thanks, Matt."

"I gotta go, but I wanted to check on you. Love you."

I mumbled I loved him, too, before he hung up.

•　　•　　•

My father picked me up at Logan and we listened to '70s music as we drove wordlessly to Forkton. I stared out the window at the bare trees, wondering if spring would ever come.

Monday afternoon, we drove to Venuti's Funeral Home before the public viewing. I followed the funeral director and my parents through the lobby and into the room where Megan lay. I hadn't seen my sister in over two years. That distance, that absence, had allowed me to deny that she was gone — until I saw her in the casket. I froze. Her blond hair and puffy cheeks reminded me of when I braided her hair before school. She wore a sky-blue dress, which my mother must have picked out for her. Megan would have loved how it accentuated her eyes, now closed forever. Her hands, holding tiny glass rosary beads, were folded on her chest.

It hit me. Someone took a ton of cinder blocks and loaded them on my shoulders.

My mother and father knelt beside each other, in front of the casket, their heads bowed. Their shoulders shook, and I wanted to run up and hug them, but I couldn't move. When they stood up, my father approached me and took my arm. He led me toward my sister. My knees fell out from under me onto the kneeler, and with no warning, my body heaved with emotion, overwhelmed with guilt for being a terrible, uncaring sister. Kneeling and sobbing, a bony hand rested on my back. I turned to see Aunt Patty. We hugged, rocking back and forth, as she whispered in my ear, "It's all right, Kelly. This is not your fault."

My father stood next to my aunt, and the three of us huddled close together. My mother walked to the back corner and hugged Mike, a beefy guy with big everything: a big forehead, big blue eyes, and blond hair almost as blond as Megan's. His face was blotchy from crying. My mother blotted her eyes with a Kleenex. I'd never — in my entire life — seen my mother cry before. That fact alone made me cry even harder.

Megan's boyfriend, Tommy, with long brown hair and dark wet eyes, walked toward me. His face was streaked red with tears. It looked like he'd been crying for days. He pulled me aside and confessed in a low voice, "I didn't have to work that night. I wanted the overtime. If I hadn't worked that night—"

I shook my head, wondering how many of us in the room blamed ourselves for this tragedy.

·   ·   ·

The funeral, the burial, the gathering at the house catered by the cafeteria ladies at my mother's school — it all made me feel equal parts exhausted and guilty. My mother had Mike, so I slept on the sofa bed in my father's apartment. I had no words. When I hugged him goodbye at the airport on Wednesday morning, I held him tight. I promised I'd be back more often to see him. He may have cried more at the airport than he did at the funeral, which made me even sadder.

On the plane, I looked out the window as the Boston skyline faded far below and I thought about the two funerals I'd been to in the past few months. Two lives cut short. Leo, whose loss left a void in Amy's heart so big that my heart broke for her. Megan, whose loss left pity and regret for potential never to be realized. I pulled the shade down on the window next to me and closed my eyes hard, but all I could see was my sister in the casket. I opened the shade and stared at the clouds, muttering prayers I hadn't prayed in years.

•   •   •

Saturday, shortly after noon, I sat on the couch watching another rerun of *Law & Order* and a car horn beeped in the driveway. I wasn't expecting anyone and ignored the beep. The doorbell rang. I sighed, got up and opened the door to see Alex, Sara, and Jake.

"We didn't tell you, because you'd tell us not to come." Sara held me tight, an overnight bag slung over her shoulder.

"Do we have to watch this?" Jake asked, plopping on the couch. "The Yankees are on."

They didn't say anything about Megan. After she'd put her bag in the guest bedroom, Sara softly said into my ear, "If you want to talk, I'm glad to listen."

I didn't talk. We ordered pizza and played board games and drank beer; and they spent the night, and I slept for the first time since my father's phone call the week before. They packed up Sunday at noon, and when Alex hugged me goodbye, he said,

"I'll be here in a few weeks. About the same time that Matt gets back. See you soon."

I wanted to be hopeful about Matt's return, about Alex's arrival, but I couldn't shrug this nagging thought I had: Bad things happen in threes.

chapter 26

May into June 2005
Fort Campbell, Kentucky
I paced in the dark behind the bleachers. I couldn't sit with the other spouses and families. I had to keep moving. The sun had disappeared behind the trees in the distance. It was 7 p.m., and they were supposed to have arrived three hours earlier. Most of us had been waiting over four hours, foolishly arriving early.

Word spread through the crowd. They were on their way. I hustled to the side of the bleachers and stood alone near the field. The distant rumble of the buses sent shivers through the crowd before we saw the lights approach. The bus doors on the other side of the field opened and a roar of cheers erupted from the crowd. Everyone was standing, cheering, crying, holding each other, holding signs, waving American flags.

They were back, but not all. Those of us fortunate enough to be waiting that night couldn't help but think of those who weren't there. Amy. And the four other families whose soldiers had already returned home in caskets draped with American flags.

Someone in uniform spoke briefly as the soldiers stood in formation on the field, and when he stepped aside, the commander on the ground released the formation. I hurried out onto the field with the others, searching madly for Matt. Families embraced; fathers held their babies for the first time; tears flowed. I wove in and out of the crowd, but couldn't find Matt. I panicked. *Where is he?*

Finally, I saw a familiar build walk toward me. I ran into his arms. I didn't let him go.

•   •   •

Right away, I knew. Something was off. Something wasn't right. It wasn't the hug. He embraced me tight and held on. But he seemed fragile somehow. Not physically. He was thinner, but stronger from the ruck marches and activity. When he saw me, when we ran toward each other, he didn't make eye contact with me. He looked past me, emotionally disconnected. He was different.

I'd done all the reading. I talked to the experienced wives, the ones who had been in the Army forever. They hadn't gone through this real war deployment stuff that started after 9/11, but they'd gone through enough to understand the basics. Give it time, they said. They'll be back. It takes patience.

Matt had the first week off from work to stay home and reintegrate, and I'd taken vacation time, but he told me no, that I shouldn't waste it. "Take off my first day home," he said. "But don't waste all your vacation time to watch me sleep. I'll have jet lag and I'll be trying to make up for the past nine months of not sleeping."

I understood. We spent Monday together in bed, but most of the day, he was asleep, or tossing and turning, or flipping through the channels on the TV, so I took his advice and went to work the rest of the week. After that first week, he had to report to work every other day, and I told him I'd take the days off he was off, but he insisted I work until he took his vacation time.

"I need to get to the gym and get back in shape," he told me.

"I want to be home with you," I said. I'd been lonely when he was gone. I liked having a roommate, even if it meant walking on eggshells, afraid of how he'd react. He'd lost weight and hadn't worked out. He thrashed at night, talking aloud in his sleep. I wanted to be there to take care of him. I wanted to hold him, to feed him, to make everything right for him.

He held me tight and told me not to worry.

But I did. *What if he stays home all day and drinks?*

That's exactly what he did. The first week, he drank at least a six-pack a night, but I held my tongue. His mother didn't. She called one afternoon and sensed that her son was drunk. He took the phone to the other room and sat on the couch, listening more than talking. When he got off the phone, he looked so downtrodden, I almost felt bad for him. His unshaven face drooped and his shoulders slumped.

"You good?" I walked by with a basket of laundry.

His eyes filled with tears. "She's right. I'm drinking too much."

I put the basket down, sat next to him on the couch, and took his hand.

"I'm a mess, Kelly. I have stuff going on. I'm sorry."

"What do you mean?"

"I know we're supposed to go away together, but . . ."

I'd made reservations at a cabin in the Smoky Mountains. They'd told us not to make plans, but I wanted something reserved, something for the two of us to do together when he took leave. I waited for him to continue.

He said quietly, "I need to go see the guys we lost."

I didn't understand.

"Visit their graves," he said.

I wasn't sure how to respond. *How depressing. Is this selfless? Is this healthy?* I wasn't sure. And, yes, I admit, I thought, *What about me? Does it matter what I want to do?* I squeezed his hand, urging him to keep talking.

"I'll start in Ohio with Leo and then go to Arlington for Cunningham and Hand. McEvoy's in Pennsylvania."

I asked softly, "Do you want company?"

His eyes focused on the floor.

I knew then. This was something he had to do alone. Whether it was survivor's guilt or closure, he had to do this.

"Okay," I said. "I get it."

He squeezed my hand. "Thanks, Kel."

I'd never seen Matt so unsteady. It was as if his center was off balance, and he wasn't sure how to anchor himself down to life at home again. He stood, walked to the fridge, and opened it. I held my breath. He closed the door, left the six-pack in the fridge, and walked into the bedroom.

I exhaled.

•　　•　　•

He was gone a week. He called a few times from the road, but the last three days, when he was in Pennsylvania and Virginia, I didn't hear from him. I worried. When his truck pulled into the driveway close to midnight Saturday night, I got out of bed and walked into the living room to greet him. I reached for him and held him tight. We didn't say a word. I didn't think he'd want to talk about it.

I was relieved he was home.

•　　•　　•

The next morning, I walked into the kitchen to find him sitting at the table, his head in his hands. "Hey. Did you sleep last night?" I stopped at the couch and folded the quilt. I assumed he'd slept on the couch.

"We need to talk, Kel." He lifted his head slightly. His wet eyes were red, as if he'd been drinking or crying. I walked toward the coffeemaker, grateful I'd set it on automatic the night before, and leaned over to look for beer cans in the recycle bin. There were none.

I finished pouring my cup of coffee. "Okay. Want a cup?"

He shook his head no.

My heart raced as I sat next to him. He kept his eyes focused on his hands, spread in front of him on the table.

"I'm sorry, Kelly," he mumbled softly. Pathetically. On the verge of more tears.

I put my cup down and reached over to take his hand. "What's wrong?"

He slipped his hand away from mine, and that one motion told me this was going to be bad. His eyes stayed downcast, and he whispered, "I saw Eve."

chapter 27

June 2005
Clarksville, Tennessee
Someone stuffed a sock down my throat. I couldn't speak.

He shook his head, his eyes barely open. "I'm sorry."

I stared at him. *What? Eve?* The girl whose father was his father's classmate at West Point? The girl whose mother was his mother's best friend? The girl who'd been in his second-grade homeroom? The girl he dated for four years before he met me on spring break?

He lifted his shoulders up to his ears and brought his palms up off the table, as if to rationalize his next words. "I had to."

I sprang out of my chair, words erupting as I stood. "What the hell?"

His voice was so soft, I almost missed it. "She has a son."

I shook my head, confused. "WHAT?"

"He's mine," he whispered. "I didn't know."

My head hurt. *What is he talking about?* His words jumbled in my brain. I stood still, staring at him, stunned.

"Graduation. Right before you found me on the field. I saw her with a baby. I figured she was at graduation because of Eric. Her brother. He was in my class."

I couldn't move.

"Alex saw her. So did his mother. Later, back in the barracks after the ceremony, Alex asked me about it. I told him I didn't know. He asked me whose baby it was. I told him I didn't know. He asked me, 'What if the baby is yours?' We didn't know how old the baby was, but he asked me, 'What if she found out she was pregnant, and that's why she broke up with you?' She knew if she got pregnant, I would have quit and married her. She knew how much graduating from West Point meant to me. I mean, she'd known that's all I wanted to do since second grade. So, what if she just didn't tell me?" He took a deep breath and rubbed his forehead. "I said no way. I knew Eve. If she'd had my baby, she'd have told me. I told Alex to fuck off. Mind his own business. I told him there was no way." He sighed. "But it made me think. I mean, I always thought Eve and I would get married after graduation. We'd talked about it so much."

I felt like someone punched me in the gut. I'd known he loved Eve, but I'd convinced myself that he loved me more. I fell back down into the chair, my hand over my mouth.

His eyes darted from the table to the window. He stared outside at nothing. "We'd been together for so long. And then out of nowhere, with no explanation, she breaks up with me, and never tells me why. Won't talk to me. Won't answer my calls. So, when Alex gave me his theory, I thought, I guess, maybe, could it be? . . but . . . By then, I had you. I loved you. And she hurt me."

My body went limp. *I waited in Tennessee for nine months for my fiancé to come home from war, and he comes home and goes to find an old girlfriend?* I wanted to be mad as hell, but I was too stunned.

He swallowed and shifted in his chair. "What are you thinking?"

I couldn't look at him. I couldn't stop shaking my head. "I can't believe this. I can't believe you didn't tell me. Years ago."

His shoulders dropped. "I knew you'd tell me to find out the truth. I didn't want to know — if it meant losing you."

"Two years ago." I separated my fingers and pulled them into a fist, over and over again. Pushing myself away from the table, I stood up angrily. "You should have told me at graduation. When you saw her. Instead, you left me hanging, never committing to me fully, because you didn't want to lose us both."

My emotions spiraled. Anger, sadness, self-pity, disbelief. This was why he'd been so distant. And I tried so hard to make us work. It made me sick. I ran to the bathroom. I leaned over the toilet and heaved everything in my stomach, sobbing hysterically in between my convulsions.

I felt him behind me, watching. I turned between heaves and screamed hysterically, "Leave me alone! *Go!*" Turning back to the toilet, I felt him walk away, and when he left the bathroom, I slammed the door and stood up against it, crying.

After what felt like hours, I wiped my mouth. Clutching my arms to my chest, I walked out of the bathroom and saw him sitting at the table, staring out the window in the kitchen. I fumed. "Look at me." I walked closer and bent forward, putting my hands on his cheeks, forcing him to look at me. "Do you love her?"

His eyes didn't meet mine. He paused too long.

I dropped my hands and sighed. I nodded, my breath jagged, my heart skipping from the upheaval of emotions in my heart.

He put his head in his hands, hiding his face. He said quietly, "I have a son."

"Jesus Christ." I felt hot; I needed air.

Slowly, he lifted his head from his hands and stood. He walked from the kitchen into the living room and sank pitifully into the couch. "He's two and a half."

I couldn't stop the feelings of anger swelling up inside me. "I'm so fucking pissed at you. You let me follow you around for two years, move twice, go through the deployment. You're such a selfish asshole."

Mad at him and mad at me, I turned away fast. "And I'm such an idiot. Why'd I keep hoping you'd change? Why'd I keep hoping you'd go back to being the Matt I knew before graduation?"

He sighed loudly and looked me in the eye for the first time. "You're not an idiot. You're the most patient person I know." He rubbed his temples. "You put up with so much from me. I don't know what I'd have done without you."

"You'd be happily married to the woman you love. You'd be a family. I kept you from doing that sooner." My brain alternated between shocked and mad as hell.

"I started to tell you before I left. When we were out back making burgers. But I got a call and had to leave, and then . . ."

I paced the living room. "And then you couldn't do it. You coward."

He let me be angry.

"God, I'm so stupid." I paced between the living room and the front door, looking anywhere but at him. "Who else knows?"

He looked at his feet.

I pressed him. "Your family? Your mother?"

He leaned forward on the couch, keeping his eyes on the floor. "She didn't know for sure. Eve wouldn't let her mother tell anyone. When Eve found out, Christmas cow year, I was a cadet, she knew I'd quit. She didn't want me to quit for her. So she broke up with me and thought she'd tell me before graduation, so we could figure it out after I graduated and get married then. But then she heard about you. She couldn't tell me. She said I'd leave you for her because of the baby, even if I didn't love her.

She wouldn't let her mother tell anyone I was the father. My mother heard a rumor. She pulled me aside that Christmas we were home in Virginia. She wanted me to find out the truth, whatever it was, and tell you. She told me it wasn't fair to you. I couldn't do it. I didn't want to know. I didn't want to lose you."

I stopped pacing and stared at him. "Why now? Why suddenly do you have the balls?"

A tear fell from his eye. I could barely hear him. "Right after I got over there, a guy who knew me and Eric said something about Eve's kid. I asked him what he was talking about, and he acted like everyone knew Eve had a kid, but there wasn't a father in the picture." He wrung his hands in his lap. "It makes you think. Being over there. When you see people die." His voice trembled. "It puts things in perspective. I had to find out."

I was speechless. I needed to get away from him. I needed to get out of the house. "I'm pissed at Alex. I'm pissed he knew."

"He didn't know. Hell, I didn't know. I wasn't sure. Until this past week. Until I talked to Eve. Alex wanted me to tell you what we saw at graduation. That's why we got into it at Jake's wedding. He's been on me since graduation to find out, to tell you what's going on."

Slowly, he raised his red eyes to meet mine. "I know I've been a jerk, Kelly. But I love you. I proposed to you. I wanted us to work. I knew that if I found out, if Eve wasn't with anyone, and if she told me she still loved me . . ." He didn't finish.

Something in me snapped. I shouted, "I HATE YOU!" I walked into the bedroom, locked the door, threw myself on the bed, and sobbed into the pillow.

An hour later, Matt knocked on the door and I yelled again, "Leave me alone!"

He did. A few hours later, I thought I'd cried myself out. I doused my face with water, looked in the mirror, and found more tears.

By late afternoon, I'd calmed down enough to leave the bedroom. In the kitchen, Matt still sat at the table. He still stared into the backyard. He looked up when he heard me and I saw him for the first time through the lens of an outsider—not someone angry at him, not someone trying to fix him. He looked worse than he did after ranger school. I wasn't sure when he slept last. His skin hung off his cheekbones, his brown eyes were watery and bloodshot.

I stood still, and we locked eyes, and I sat down on the couch and asked him to come over and sit next to me. When he stood, I saw a beaten man, someone who had visited the graves of soldiers, of friends, and then found out he had a son he never knew about, and an old girlfriend who still loved him. And he'd never stopped loving her.

"Matt," I said as calmly as I could. "I'm mad as hell. I wasted two years waiting for you to love me the way I thought you did before graduation." I was drained. I was exhausted. I paused before adding, "You'll always have a piece of my heart."

He exhaled, glancing from his feet to my eyes.

"I want you to have a happy life. I really do." I swallowed and sat on my hands to stop them from shaking. "I'm going to take some linens, some towels, and the kitchen plates I got at Benning. You keep the rest—"

"No," he interrupted.

I held my hand up, straightening my elbow to stop it from shaking. "You don't get a choice in this. I don't want anything."

"I'll leave, Kelly. You stay."

"No, I'm going." I walked into the bathroom. He followed me, and I saw his confused face in the mirror as I turned on the water and soaped my hand. I inched the diamond off my finger and put it on his dresser.

He didn't argue. Tears ran down his cheeks and he said again, "I'm sorry."

I turned, grabbed the towel off the sink to wipe my eyes, walked to my dresser, and packed.

An hour later, he trudged down the driveway behind me. We both carried suitcases. I told him to go back into the house, and I sat in my quiet car and waited for my emotions to abate so I could drive away. They didn't. I drove away, anyway.

part three
finding my tribe

chapter 28

June into July 2005
Clarksville, Tennessee
My eyes involuntarily opened and closed like blinds someone else controlled. I pulled in the strip mall parking lot and rubbed them angrily. It didn't help. Eventually, they got too tired. I stopped blinking enough to drive again.

I drove aimlessly up and down 41A, in and out of parking lots and side streets. When I passed Amy's neighborhood, I put my blinker on and turned. I had no other options. I parked in front of her house, left my bags in the car, shuffled up the walkway, and knocked on her door. When she opened it, I leaned into her, and she wrapped me in her arms.

I told her what had happened, and she asked me if I wanted to talk and nodded when I shook my head no, not yet. I tried to sleep in her guest bedroom, but couldn't doze off. I kept rethinking my life, wracking my brain, wondering how I ignored so many signs, how I only saw what I wanted to see. Sometime after 4 a.m., I fell into a disturbed sleep, and a few hours later, when I opened my eyes and saw Amy and Leo's framed diplomas hanging on the wall, I remembered the nightmare of the night before.

I looked at the clock. It was 7 a.m. I groaned and pulled the covers up over my head, debating whether to call in sick to work.

A knock on the door forced me to peek my eyes out from under the comforter. Amy, dressed for work, poked her head in. "Are you okay?"

I pulled the comforter back over my head. "Peachy!"

She walked over, sat on the edge of my bed, and pulled it back. "Really?"

I sat up, resigned. "Yeah. Life goes on." *How can I whine after seeing what you've gone through?*

She stood, took something out of her pants pocket, and put it on the dresser. "A key to the front door. My house is your house. Stay as long as you want. I need a roommate."

I pulled the comforter back and got out of bed, mumbled my thanks, and faced her, still wearing the clothes I'd woken up in the day before.

Amy grinned. "You didn't have to wear your best pajamas for me."

I showered, dressed, and drove to work. Keep busy, Vicky always said. I'd have to call her and tell her what had happened. *Later.* I wasn't in a hurry. I had to tell my parents. I had to tell Sara. I had to tell everyone. It could wait. I needed to figure my life out first.

•   •   •

A month later, on a stifling hot Saturday afternoon, I sat plopped up with pillows on my bed in Amy's guest room, watching reruns of *Law & Order,* when my phone rang. It was on the dresser and apathy won. I decided not to get it. *What if it's Amy? What if she has a flat tire? Doubtful.* I let it ring. A commercial came on: wedding rings, adorable couple, holding hands, roses.

"Make me barf," I said out loud. I got up, saw the long number on the phone, and grabbed it fast. Sara told me that Alex had arrived at Fort Campbell about the same time that Matt and

I broke up, but he immediately got sent over to join his unit on deployment.

"Hey," he said, between the familiar skips in the line, "how are you doing?"

"I'm okay. How are *you*?"

"I'm good. I'm sorry I haven't talked to you—"

"You're lucky, you know," I interrupted. "If you weren't deployed, I'd be so mad at you. But there's no way I can be mad, because you're deployed."

There was a pause in the line. I wasn't sure if it was a skip or if he was waiting.

"I know." His voice was faint and distant. "I'd be mad at me, too. I'm sorry. I really am. I wanted to tell you—I wanted to tell you at Jake's wedding, but I promised Matt I wouldn't. In his defense, he didn't know for sure. I wanted to tell you what I thought—what he needed to do—I should have. I should have told you. But I kept telling myself it wasn't my story to tell. I almost told you in Nashville—that afternoon in the bar. Hell, I almost told you a hundred times. But I wasn't sure. I'd only be telling you rumors. And Matt had to be the one to tell you."

The line was full of static. I pressed the volume button to the highest it would go.

"I wanted to call earlier, to see how you were doing, but it's been busy. I'm really sorry about everything."

That was a lot of apologies, and every one of them sounded very sincere. And he *was* in a war zone.

"You're forgiven," I mumbled.

No response. As if he knew I had more to say.

"I get it. Believe me. I've gone over this a million times in my head since the day Matt told me. You guys go way back. Even if you weren't deployed, I couldn't be mad."

"I'm sorry, though."

I worried about being disconnected. "Okay, I accept your apology. All of them. I don't want you to be stuck in the middle."

"Thanks." He sounded relieved.

I used his thanks to end the discussion. "So, how are you doing? Really?"

"Busy. We haven't been here long. We're still figuring everything out, and I'm not sure when we're going to fly. The unit we're replacing is ready to go, but there's stuff we have to do before we can fly."

"Be careful!" Captain Obvious herself. "Didn't you want to get some peacetime flying in before you deployed?"

"That was the plan. Well, my plan. Not the Army's, I guess." He paused. "How are *you* doing? Really?"

I sighed. "Well, this sure made it easier for me to shit or get off the pot."

The line clicked a few times, and I wondered if we lost the connection, until I heard him say, "I know it's not funny, but that made me smile."

I grinned. "I cried the first three days nonstop. At work, I cried in the bathroom. I'm done crying. I was stupid. Lesson learned, moving on. Plus, when you have a bad breakup and move in with a friend who lost her husband, your bad breakup doesn't seem as bad."

"How's Amy doing?"

"She's unbelievable. So strong. I don't know how she does it."

"I'm glad. Hey, Kelly, one thing you said, about being stupid." In the background, people yelled and engines roared. "You weren't stupid. You couldn't have known."

I didn't respond. My brain was too tired to tell my mouth to move.

"All right, so wait . . . You're at Amy's? I didn't know that. You're not in the house? Is Matt?"

I stared out the window at the new town houses being built down the street. "Have you talked to Matt?"

"No. Not since I got to Campbell and called to surprise you both, and he told me he'd found out and told you. He said it wasn't a good time for me to stay with you guys. And then I learned they were sending me over to join my unit, so I put my stuff in storage, moved into the barracks on post, and here I am. I've called home to talk to my mother, who's a nervous wreck about me being over here, but I haven't talked to anyone else. You're my first nonfamily call."

I didn't know he'd tried to connect with us when he'd arrived at Campbell. "I'm sorry you couldn't stay with us. I must have already left when you called him. I'm sorry I didn't see you before you deployed."

"Did Matt move out?"

"No, I think he's still at the house." I paused, then added, "Well, I'm sure he's still there, because I drive by and look, and Allison calls me if she sees him. So, yes, he's still at the house. I took what I wanted and left. I showed up at Amy's the day he told me, and I've been here since. About a month, I guess." I kept rambling. "I'm so embarrassed, Alex. Why did I hang on so long? I waited for him *through a deployment!*" I caught my breath, to calm down.

"Don't be hard on yourself."

"Easier said than done."

"So, wait, let me understand." Even with the lousy connection, his voice hesitated. "You said you took what you wanted. Are you guys done?"

I laughed bitterly. "I think we've been done since graduation. But, yeah, we're done."

"I'm sorry. I didn't know."

"Well, that day, after he first told me, I went through all those stages of grief. Well, no. I went through only the anger stage, and I stayed there. But then I asked him some questions."

Alex waited for me to continue.

"Only one question mattered—if he loved Eve."

I heard voices and vehicles in the background, so he had to still be there, but he stayed silent. I sighed loudly. "You know the answer, right?"

"I'm sorry."

"I'm not," I said honestly. "Thank God we never married, right?"

"Yeah. So, now what?"

Outside, a woman walked by pushing a stroller. A little girl whizzed ahead on a scooter.

"Amy wants me to stay here, and I'm lucky she's here. It's been good for both of us. But I can't stay here. I'm assuming Eve and the baby will move in with Matt, and they should. That's where they should be." I could finally say that without feeling the sharp pain of a dagger being plunged into my back.

He was quiet.

"My boss said I could work remotely if I left the area. She said she'll always have a spot for me if I decide to move back here."

"That's a good deal."

"It is. I like the people here. I'll miss Amy. I'll miss Allison and some of the other friends here."

"Well, I'll be back in April, if you want to wait around."

I wasn't sure if he was serious, so I let that hang.

His voice softened. "Kelly, can I ask you something?"

"Yeah, sure. Anything."

He waited a few seconds, or it might have been the line. "Do you still love Matt?"

"No," I answered quickly. No hesitation, no doubt. "I watched my parents live together for years, not in love, and I swore I'd never do that. And then I did it. I knew deep in my heart that love wasn't supposed to be that hard, but I kept trying to make it work. That's not love." There was silence on his end of the phone. "Are you okay?" I asked him.

"I'm supposed to be asking you that."

"No," I said, "I'm on a rant complaining about a guy who's like your brother. I shouldn't be talking bad about him to you."

"Kelly. He knows what I think. He knows he'll always be my brother, no matter how bad he screws up. And he screwed up royally, not telling you about this, not learning the truth earlier. But I want you to talk to me."

I blew a large breath out of my mouth, relieved.

The line skipped and then he asked, "Are you there?"

"Yeah." I struggled to find the right words. "I guess I figured that when I lost Matt, I'd lose all his friends."

"You're stuck with me, McGowan. So send me boxes. I'll email my address."

That made me smile.

"Wait," he said. "You said you could work remote, but where are you going? Did you tell me?"

"Well, my parents want me to move back home. My high school friends keep telling me they have room in their apartment on their sleeper sofa. My mother's new boyfriend, who may not be that new, after all — different story for a different phone call — has a fraternity brother who's a cat's ass in one of the big five accounting firms up there. I sent my mother my resume, and this guy is floating it around." I paused. "If the job transpires, it might be good, but I'm not sure about sleeping on a sleeper sofa with friends I haven't been around in six years. They live a different lifestyle. Partying, all that. I've become a boring old lady."

"Wait. What's a cat's ass?"

"A high roller. Big wig," I said. "You don't say that?"

"Must be a New Hampshire expression," he laughed. "Ok. What if you don't go back home?"

"The other option is Seabury. My aunt told me to come live with her, at least until I figure it out. I can work remote there in my current job — and pick up some part-time hours at the firm I worked at when Matt was in ranger school."

No response.

I asked, "What do *you* think?"

"You really want to know?"

"Yeah, I'm pathetic." I hated sounding so weak, but I wanted his thoughts. "Tell me what to do."

"I can't do that. But I don't think there's a better place than Seabury to figure it out. It may be forever. Or not. But if it's a bookmark. . . If you're in between chapters and need to put the book down somewhere, I think Seabury's a good place to be. Of course, I love it there, so I may be biased."

I turned from the window and walked toward the empty boxes along the wall. They'd sat there for a month waiting for me to fill them with my stuff and bring them wherever I went.

"Thanks." The line was fuzzy again, and then there was quiet. I wasn't sure if he heard me. "Thanks for the nudge."

"No problem. Throw a Seabury T-shirt in the box you're sending me. With beef jerky and protein bars. Oh, and Wheat Thins."

"You got it."

"I'm sorry I missed you when I got to Campbell. Lousy timing."

"Yeah. But it's probably better. I wasn't in a good place," I said.

"That's why I should have been there. I wasn't a good friend."

"Are you kidding? I've been moping in this room all day, watching reruns. But now I'm done. You snapped me out of it." I wondered if he was in a hangar. Engines and banging and wind roared in the background.

"You've gone through a lot—Leo, your sister, now this. I'm sorry about all of it. You're a good person, Kel."

"Nah, I'm a depressed bitch right now. Hopefully, I'll grow out of it."

Alex laughed. "I think you will. I gotta run. Thanks for picking up."

"How'd you know I wasn't going to pick up?"

"Wild guess. Keep me posted on your move."

I laughed and wondered if we'd continue our friendship. Alex and Matt had been inseparable for those four years at West Point. Roommates at that place were closer than blood relatives.

When I remembered the night I met them both on the beach, and how quickly I assumed Alex was entangled with someone else, I cringed. That mistake catapulted me toward Matt. But Alex let Matt pursue me. He wasn't interested in me. I needed to accept my life for what it was. I was dumped by a fiancé in love with his old girlfriend, and I was stuck in the friend zone with the perfect guy, who was best friends with my ex-fiancé.

"Be *careful* over there," I begged.

"Always," he said before the phone clicked off.

After he hung up, I held the phone close to my chest and took deep breaths, trying to compose my thoughts. Alex couldn't choose a side. His side was chosen when he raised his right hand with a thousand classmates the day they all reported to West Point.

chapter 29

July into October 2005
Clarksville, Tennessee
Seabury, Florida

It was borderline creepy, but I drove by the house at night to look in the windows. I couldn't help myself. Not every night. Maybe once (or twice) a week. The shades were always drawn, and the garage door closed, but one night in late July, a U-Haul trailer was backed up to the garage. He was moving out, or she was moving in. Either way, it was time for me to move, too.

"You've been driving by?" Amy asked when I told her about the truck.

I'd picked up a couple of salads on the way home from work. I shrugged, embarrassed, and reached into the carryout bag. "Yeah." I opened the silverware drawer and got two forks. "I don't know what I would've done if I'd seen him. Duck like a second grader, I guess. He was pretty much my whole life for three years. And then, wham, no conversation at all after I left. I'm good moving on, but I'm nosy. I'm wondering what he'll do."

"I've been stalking him, too." She grinned as she grabbed two napkins from the basket on the counter. "You've forgiven him, but I still say he's a total jerk. I never saw him, but was afraid I would, and I wasn't sure what I'd do. I wonder if I'd have given him the finger?"

"Nah, you'd wave. You're nicer than you think you are. Plus, the more I think about it," —I sat down—"I might almost, sort of, feel bad for him."

She raised her eyebrows.

"He loved Eve. He was hurt when she dumped him. It is what it is. I've turned the page, even though I sometimes stalk him."

"Has anyone told you that you have way too much empathy?" She opened the fridge and took a bottle of salad dressing off the door. "I mean, that's a strength, but it can be a weakness, too."

"Have we both always been so deep?" I picked at my arugula. "I need to get out of here, though. At least for right now."

She sat down next to me and doused her salad with ranch dressing. It had been over six months since Leo had died. *Am I selfish to leave her alone?*

"I won't pretend I won't miss you if you go. But you have to do what you have to do." She paused. "Do me a favor. Leave what you want here in the garage, in your room. I'm not getting another roommate. That room is your room whenever you want it."

Touched, I mumbled, "Thanks."

She speared a leaf of lettuce and moved out of that discussion, clicking the TV remote to *Wheel of Fortune*. She understood. She didn't ask me questions about where I'd go or what I'd do. Instead, she shouted out "swimming with the dolphins" before Vanna could turn another letter.

•   •   •

Three months later, I sat with my aunt, our toes in the sand, watching the orange skies turn dark.

"There's a condo, two streets over. I could rent by the month." I looked at my calves. "I've been on the internet looking."

"Is your roommate bugging you? And, yes, your calves are smoking hot from all that running on the beach you're doing. Take it down a notch, Hulk Hogan."

I smiled, choosing not to respond to the comment about my obsessive running. "No, my roommate's not bugging me. But I don't want to be bugging my roommate."

"Oh, honey. You're not. I barely see you! You're keeping very busy."

After I arrived in Seabury with everything I owned in my car, and assurances from Amy that she'd visit often, I spilled the story out to Allison — whose anger at Matt, I'm embarrassed to admit, made me happy — and I called Sara and Tess and Vicky to update them. "I'm not sure what I'm doing," I'd told them. "But I'll figure it out at the beach."

The word spread. Before the end of my first week in Seabury, my friends from Fort Benning — Maria, Ginny, and the others — called. Even Lynnette called, though she dropped into the conversation that she was hiring underlings to sell those bags if I was interested. None of these women had ever met Vicky, but each of them repeated her mantra: "Keep busy." I listened.

I might have overdone it. The day after I arrived, I began remote work for my boss in Clarksville. The next week, I got a job teaching yoga three nights a week and on Saturday mornings. I worked part time at the firm in Yarmouth, the same position I held when Matt was at ranger school, and I started an online master's program in taxation.

I buried my toes farther down into the sand. "Yeah. I may have bitten off more than I can chew."

My aunt laughed. "You think?"

"Everyone's been great. No one cares why I'm here. Do people move here to live off the grid?" I passed my arm out over the sand. We were the only two people for a mile.

My aunt grinned. "I keep telling you. October's the best month. It's always empty." She put her pointer finger up to her lips. "Shh, don't tell."

"Was that your mother on the phone last night?" Most of the conversations I had with my aunt meandered in directions I never saw coming.

"Yep," I answered.

"How'd that go?"

"It was good. She talked about selling the house. She doesn't need it. Too big. If I thought my mother had an emotional bone in her body, I'd think there might be too many memories of Megan in the house. I asked her where she'd go. She was vague. I think she's been living off and on with Mike, her boyfriend. Do you think she'll move in with him permanently?"

"I don't know. But I hope she sells. Your father could use the money from the house. And, honestly, your mother deserves happiness. Whatever that looks like for her. I understand what you mean about her being unemotional, but losing a child has got to make even a rock shed a tear."

"I've never understood her." I'd never told my aunt about that conversation I heard so many years ago. "You know, um" — I saw my aunt turn her head toward me, waiting — "one summer I was here, when I was a kid, I figured out that I could hear you and my dad talking if I stood quietly under the deck at night." I rolled my eyes and lifted my hands, palms up, guilty.

She tilted her head and looked at me blankly.

"I heard you and Dad talking about me, Megan, and Mom. That's how I found out about her — "

My aunt's eyes bulged. I'd intended to complete my sentence with *"getting pregnant with me,"* but she stopped me short.

"Oh, honey," she interrupted. "Did you tell Megan?"

I shook my head no, wondering why that was the first thing she said.

"Oh. I'm glad you didn't tell her. Megan was always so fragile, anyway. I wondered if she found out at some point, and that's why she always acted out, but your father was certain she didn't know." Her voice had settled down to a relieved tone, and she leaned back in her chair again.

I sat quietly, wondering why Megan would care. I must have looked confused, because my aunt continued speaking. "She was so close to your father. It's hard to believe there's *not* a blood connection."

I dropped my water bottle in the sand. My jaw fell two feet into my lap. I stared at my aunt.

"Shit," she said, flustered. "What were you talking about?"

I nearly yelped, "Not that! What? My father's *not* Megan's father?"

"Shit," she said again. "Okay, well, this story is not my story to tell. But too late now. What were you talking about?"

"That they had to get married because of me."

"Pshaw." My aunt waved her hand. "That's nothing. Lots of folks did that back in the day. Birth control wasn't as prevalent, and naivete was."

"Did my father love my mother?"

My aunt stared at the gulf. "I think he thought he did."

"But she didn't love him?"

"Your mother's a tough nut to crack. I think she dated him to be contrary—her parents were uppity and difficult—and not happy about her dating a hockey player from Boston. But then she got pregnant—and from what I could see, she felt obligated to marry him." She looked out at the horizon. "Whenever I saw them together, they seemed like roommates. Not husband and wife. It was a loveless marriage, for sure."

"And my mother had an affair?"

My aunt nodded slowly. "She's such a straight arrow. It's hard to believe, but she apparently had a boyfriend before she met your father. I think she went out with Billy to get the ex-boyfriend jealous. You know that was Mike, right?"

"What?" *This is* General Hospital *drama. This is my family? How could I not have known all this?*

My aunt grinned. "The plot thickens. Mike was the type of guy her parents wanted her to be with. Princeton grad, finance guru. Your father, God love him, had no clue, until years later, when she innocently mentioned to him that her old boyfriend worked in the bank near her high school."

My mind raced. "Jesus. Wait. So, how did my father know Megan wasn't his?"

My aunt looked at me sadly. "Loveless marriage, Kel."

"Oh. My. God." I mumbled.

"Well, I'd ask that you keep this between us. I shouldn't have been the one to tell you."

"I'd never say anything. But why? Why'd my father stay with her?"

My aunt rubbed her eyes. "When your mother got pregnant with Megan, Mike told her to divorce your father. Mike loved her. He always has. God knows why. But, anyway, she couldn't. I've tried to figure that out over the years, but neither of your parents wanted to divorce. Your mother didn't want to have that reputation—the high school vice principal who had an affair, got pregnant, divorced and then remarried. School boards don't appreciate that sort of drama in small-town New Hampshire. She'd have to move and start over somewhere else. Your father told her he couldn't imagine not living in the same house as you girls. He told her he'd raise the baby, Megan, like she was his own, and he did. But the rest of the McGowans didn't respond as admirably. Gram figured it out right away. It was as if she had a sixth sense. No one told her, but she knew, and from Megan's birth on, your mother was not invited to Boston."

"Oh, my God. I always assumed my mother didn't like the McGowans."

"Oh, she didn't. But your grandmother never forgave your mother for stepping out on her youngest son. Your dad's amazing. I don't think I could have forgiven. But in his mind, if he forgave your mother, he still got you. If he didn't, he'd have to share you and not be in the same house with you. And he truly did love Megan."

I sat in silence.

"He has endless love for others. But even he couldn't put up with your mother fooling around with Mike after Megan was born. That was part of the deal. He'd told her she had to end it with Mike."

"She didn't?" I stared at my aunt with my eyes wide open.

My aunt inhaled long and slow, before releasing her breath. "She did. For a while. But when you were in middle school, your father found out that they were seeing each other during the summer—when you were all down here."

"That's why we stopped coming here. When I was thirteen."

"I was so angry at your mother." My aunt shook her head. "I loved having you three for the summer. She's been on my shit list ever since. Pardon the expression."

Her comment made me want to laugh, but I was still too stunned. "This is unbelievable."

"It's not always what it seems. That's for damn sure," my aunt said.

We watched the sun dip closer to the horizon. My aunt dug her feet deeper into the sand, turned to me, and asked, "What are you thinking?"

"I don't know. That was a bombshell about Megan. It sure explains a lot. We were so different. Wow!" I shook my head slowly. "Life here in Seabury? Well, I miss my friends. I miss Amy. Allison, Sara, Tess. I miss Alex and Jake and hearing the stories from Matt about all the guys. I miss my old office." As soon as the words left my mouth, I regretted them. "I don't mean to come across as unhappy here. I love it here. I do."

"After she had Kyle," my aunt told me, "Mary Ann spent a lot of time down here. She needed to get away. She was so tired of people coming up and asking her how she was doing."

"I get that."

The sun had drifted under the horizon, and we sat in the black night, waiting for the stars to join us. I stared at the dark gulf, its water rising and falling, pulsing against the wet sand. I didn't tell Aunt Patty how much I missed Matt physically, being intimate with him, being smothered in his chest, tucked into him, safe and warm. I didn't tell her how the soothing sounds of the waves reminded me of his heartbeat.

I wiped my eyes with my sweatshirt sleeve. "What made you stay here?"

"Oh, you know the story."

"I know you landed here after college, but I don't know why you stayed here."

"Probably because my father said I'd never make it on my own. He told me I'd have to move back home. I'd never survive with an art degree. You never met your grandfather, my father. He was a mean drunk. By God, if he thought I couldn't make it on my own, then I'd do everything in my power to make it on my own." She chuckled. "I was what we might term 'a stubborn, pigheaded, rebellious kid.' Sound familiar?"

I feigned ignorance, raising my eyebrows with a gesture that said *"Who, me?"*

"I told you about Aaron. I felt guilty taking the house—I didn't even take his name when we got married—but his parents were wonderful. They told me he wanted me to have the house for a reason. When I drove through Yarmouth on my way to see the house, I saw a Help Wanted sign in the art studio. I thought nothing of it, but then I saw the house. And I remembered that Help Wanted sign."

I smiled. "You stayed?"

"I sure did. Took the job at the art studio, saved everything I made, put it toward the house, and after twenty years, I bought that art studio. Roy, the owner, practically adopted me and gave me a sweet deal." She paused, reflecting. "I guess you can say pride brought me here. But that's not what made me stay."

"What did?"

"It felt like home." In the dark, I saw her silhouette next to me, her shoulders shrugging, and her arms spread out in front of her. "Dorchester wasn't home anymore. This was."

"I don't know where home is anymore," I said quietly.

She pushed herself up from her chair to stand. "I've learned home isn't a geographic location, although it's nice to be in a beautiful one like Seabury. It's more about the relationships—the people who know you and love you and accept you for who you are."

I stood and folded my chair to walk back to the house with her. "Home was Forkton, but there's nothing there anymore. They say home is where the Army sends you. Fort Benning didn't feel like home until we were leaving, and I had friends. Fort Campbell felt like home, but it took time. Amy, Allison, Vicky—they made me feel like I was home, when I was with them."

"It's hard. You don't have to know right now. You'll find it in due time."

Beyond the dunes, my aunt's porch light illuminated the deck like a beacon, and we walked toward it in silence. I found my flip-flops in the sand near the footbridge and scuffed my feet into them, following my aunt over the bridge. Dots of light sprinkled the black skies; the moon hid behind the sky's darkness.

We rested the chairs against the wall under the house, where I'd hidden years before, listening to forbidden conversations above. Walking up the stairs that led to the deck, my aunt said,

"I understand you want to have your life outlined, with *A*'s, *B*'s, and *C*'s—where you'll be, when, with whom, doing what. But you can't always outline life. Life's not a math equation. When you try to map it out, something usually gets tossed in unexpectedly and messes up the entire plan. It'll work out. You'll know where you should be. Be patient with yourself."

"I guess. Thanks for letting me sort it out here. And thanks for letting Amy come down."

"Oh, I'm so glad she's coming. She's a sweetheart. I'm not sure about the weather with that storm headed our way next week, but I've been watching it and we should have a good beach weekend before the storm is close. She's leaving Monday, right?"

I nodded as she opened the fridge and pulled out a cellophane bag of green leaves, which she'd call dinner. She turned to me before washing them and smiled. "We'll weather this storm and be just fine."

chapter 30

October 2005
Seabury, Florida
The weather was unseasonably warm for Amy's visit, and we sat on the beach in bathing suits, catching up. Vicky had moved to Germany, but Amy told me that Donna Jones still dropped by to visit, and the spouses in Leo's company invited her to dinner and called to check in. The chaplain called at least once a week, and so did Chris, a good friend of Leo's who had been in his company and with him on the deployment.

Back at my aunt's house, it was Doomsville. The minute they gave that hurricane a name, my aunt turned on the weather channel and kept it on. Sunday night at dinner, she muted the TV, but glanced repeatedly into the living room, watching the heavily made-up bleached-blond meteorologist swoop her arm across the spaghetti models on the screen. My unflappable aunt dropped the plate of grilled vegetables all over the table.

"Hey," I said, helping her collect onions and peppers, "why don't we take a break and watch a movie?"

You'd think I'd asked if we could rent porn. She stopped mid pepper, glared at me incredulously, then turned back to the TV. "Oh, that's Hank. He's the one you never want to see in your town. Let's hope he stays where he is."

Watching my aunt anticipate this storm made me feel helpless. Amy felt it, too. After dinner, we escaped to my bedroom and sat on the twin beds talking. In a hushed voice, Amy said, "She's like we were before deployment, right? So anxious. It's the fear of the unknown. I think that's what she's going through."

I hugged my pillow with the embroidered *K* close to my chest. "I hadn't thought of it like that." I'd never seen my aunt so anxious. So uncertain. "Should we go out and sit with her?"

Before I finished asking, Amy had hopped off the bed. She grabbed her book on the way out of the room.

"Oh, good. I've been thinking," my aunt announced when we walked into the living room. "Let's leave tomorrow morning with Amy. Just to be extra cautious. I'm sure we'll be fine here, but it's always best to evacuate. Better safe than sorry."

"Um. What does that mean?" I plopped on the recliner, trying to sound like I wasn't as worried as she was making me feel.

"Oh. We'll load your car and mine, Kelly. With whatever is important that you don't want to lose, worst case. We'll stop for lunch in Alabama. Amy can continue her drive to Tennessee after lunch, and we'll stay overnight at a hotel in Alabama. Probably Dothan."

"Um, I have work, Aunt Patty. Should I just stay here and hold down the fort?"

My aunt looked at me like I had two heads. "Oh, hon. Everyone will evacuate. They'll close your office. You'll be back the next day. Call Betty and ask her."

I called both Betty and my boss in Clarksville and told them I'd be back at work on Tuesday. Betty lived farther inland in Yarmouth, and wasn't planning to evacuate, but she confirmed that the office would be closed on Monday. My Clarksville boss was less understanding, but I assured her I'd get my work done later that evening in the hotel room.

"Um." Amy looked up from her book. "Will everything be okay?"

"Hope so, honey." Aunt Patty shrugged, with what looked to be forced composure. "This is the price we pay to live in paradise. Every time I've evacuated, I've come back to my house looking exactly as it does right now, and I've lived here for four decades now. Except for the worst storm in '95. That left six inches of sand under the house. We didn't have power for a week, but the only real problem was all the sand."

I stood up, leaving Amy with her book next to my aunt on the couch. "Be right back," I told them. I walked back to my room to call my father.

"I don't know, Dad. Aunt Patty's getting me nervous. She says she wants to load her car with everything she can. Then she says that we'll be back on Tuesday, and everything will be fine. I'm not sure what to believe."

"She's gone through this so many times," he assured me. "She's being careful. That's all. Her house is up on those concrete pilings. They're twelve feet above ground. I'm sure everything will be fine. Better safe than sorry."

"Ugh. You sound like your sister. She's said that about five hundred times in the past day. Hey, and don't tell her I called you," I warned him. "She's already a mess. She doesn't need to know that I'm worried about her."

He laughed. "I won't tell her. How are you doing?"

I looked at the two jars on the dresser, one filled with sand dollars, the other with jingle shells. "I'm good. Had a good weekend with Amy. She's great. I miss her."

"She's a good friend," he said. "I'm glad she's there with you. Go enjoy her company. I'll touch base with you tomorrow night when you're in Alabama."

I hung up the phone and smiled. I was twenty-five years old, but hearing my father tell me it would be okay made me feel a little better.

.   .   .

The next morning, my aunt lugged a box marked *Art Supplies* out of the hall closet. "We were lucky. I'm glad the weather held off over the weekend for Amy."

A commercial flashed on the TV, an elderly lady in a white robe walking gingerly toward a walk-in bathtub. Using the commercial as an opportunity to do a last check of the room, my aunt put the box down on an end table, and stood with her hands on her hips. Satisfied, she bent back down to pick up the box.

"I got it." I walked over and took the box from her. "One advantage of not owning anything. I don't have much to pack." I may have sounded more bitter than I intended.

Amy piped in. "Hey, don't forget about your stuff in the storage shed in Clarksville.

I frowned. Two weeks after I moved out, Matt stuck a manila envelope addressed to me in Amy's mailbox. Inside the envelope, he had stuffed some mail: a letter from my mother, my auto insurance policy, the yoga class schedule for the following month, along with a brief note wrapped around a key. The note was classic Matt.

Kelly,

I put a few things you might want in Shed #181 at AAA Storage Sheds on Robinson Avenue. Here's the key to the dead bolt on the shed. I'll pay the monthly fee until you no longer need the shed. I'm sorry, Kelly.

Matt

I'd filed that information in the same tiny, locked, dark room in my brain that I put Matt in when I drove away from Clarksville.

"Oh, right," I said to Amy. I tried to feign ambivalence about that shed. I tried not to think about the three types of people who rented storage sheds outside Army posts. There were single deployed soldiers; families who had more possessions than square footage; or losers with no place to go. I fit neatly into the third category. But even worse, I didn't even know what was in my shed. I'd been too stubborn to ask or look before I left Clarksville. I *hoped* the kitchen table was there, but I wouldn't bet money on it. Whatever Matt had put in that storage shed was proof of the time I wasted in our relationship. That made me mad and sad, but at that point, four months after we'd broken up, it mostly made me embarrassed.

I carried the box toward the door. "If Alex gets back in town before I do, I'll ask him if he wants anything. I don't think he has any furniture."

I opened the sliding glass door with one hand, resting the box on my hip with the other, and was startled by the gust of wind that pulled the long white curtains outside the house. "I'm glad we packed the cars last night!" I shouted into the house above the wind. My hair whipped across my face, and I pulled the curtain back inside the door, sliding it shut behind me.

After I put the box in the back seat of my car, I pulled my hair back with my hand to keep it from blowing. I saw the big ceramic pot outside the storage room and remembered my aunt's comments about the sand piling up in the last big storm. Opening the door to the storage room, I pulled the pot inside, against the wall where the Irish toast hung. I looked at the plaque and smiled, thinking of Alex changing the light bulb. I needed to write to him. I didn't want to lose his friendship, but I didn't want him to think I was needy. A gust of wind slammed the door shut, forcing me out of my reverie. I locked the door behind me and hurried upstairs.

"That's it," my aunt greeted me, her voice shaky. "Hopefully, this will all be in vain. Thank you both! I couldn't have done this without you."

I grinned. She'd done it without us for the past four decades.

The three of us stood together and gazed out the large windows at the gulf. It was overcast with occasional glimpses of the sun, but other than the wind and the whitecaps, you'd never know a hurricane was out there.

"I admit"—she wrung her hands out in front of her—"this is when I think it was worth every penny to install the hurricane windows. Oh, and fortify the pilings with concrete—that cost a fortune. But every time I evacuate, I feel better knowing I did it." She glanced around the living room, her hands back on her hips, then hurried to the other side of the room. Reaching up, she removed the large, detailed painting from over the couch. "Better safe than sorry."

I rubbed my hands on my thighs. If she wanted to take that painting, she was scared. I took some old sheets out of the linen closet and helped her wrap the painting.

"I'll do a final walk-through," I told my aunt. "Why don't you guys take the painting and wait in your cars? I'll be right down."

I checked all the windows and doors and turned the air conditioner down. Peering into my room, I saw the embroidered pillow on my bed. *Silly. We'll be back tomorrow. I don't need a pillow I hugged when I was a kid.* I grabbed it, anyway.

Following Aunt Patty's sky-blue Volkswagen Bug, covered with bumper stickers of peace decals and daisies, and Amy's silver Honda Accord, bare and spotless, down Sand Dollar Lane, I thought about Amy's comments comparing the hurricane to deployment. I was worried about my aunt and about this storm, but I'd been more worried about saying goodbye to Matt before he left for Iraq. *War is life or death. Hurricanes are an inconvenience. Although, if Aunt Patty loses her house, where would I go? Jesus. I'd have lost my sister, my fiancé, my life as I knew it – and now this. No way. It can't happen.*

I turned on the radio to escape from my thoughts.

•   •   •

Saying goodbye to Amy after lunch in Dothan would have been more emotional if we weren't so preoccupied with this storm. Amy insisted I call her as soon as we had news. I told her to call me when she got home, safe and sound. We tentatively planned on getting together over the holidays, possibly meeting somewhere between Tennessee and Florida. She understood I wasn't ready to be in the same zip code as Matt.

Later that afternoon, when we stepped into our hotel room, my aunt immediately went to the TV and turned on the weather channel. Outside, the sky darkened as the parking lot filled with cars with Florida plates crammed with boxes and bags.

"It'll turn." Aunt Patty's voice lacked the confidence it had twenty-four hours earlier. "They always turn. Look at Northwest Florida." She pointed to the screen from the big bend area to Pensacola. "That's a lot of land. What are the chances of this thing hitting our tiny town? It won't happen."

•   •   •

"Oh, Jesus, Mary, and Joseph. No!"

That's what woke me up the next morning. I opened my eyes and peeked over the thin hotel blanket. My aunt sat on the end of her bed in an old T-shirt and black-and-white–checkered flannel sleep pants, staring at the TV. The curtains were drawn, but gray light peeked in through the sides. The clock on the nightstand read 6:30 a.m. I remembered it was Tuesday, and I was in a hotel in Alabama with my aunt. I blinked and rubbed my eyes.

"It's Hank. He's in Seabury." Her voice was flat. When she turned to me, her face was as gray as the outside sky.

I slid back down under the blanket and pulled the pillow on top of my face. "Shit," I mumbled. Hank was the meteorologist you never wanted to see in your town.

By ten in the morning, the hurricane was twenty miles off the coast. According to Hank, who was the "King of All Meteorologists," it was aimed directly at Seabury. My aunt and I sat next to each other at the foot of the bed, staring at the screen, waiting. Storm chasers were on the main road, near the canal, but the winds were too severe. They lost coverage. A meteorologist filmed from the fourth floor of the condo unit on the other side of the main road from Sand Dollar Lane. The images were blurry, as if the photographer were driving in a rainstorm with no windshield wipers on, and the radio turned up, in between stations, loud and volatile and full of static. The rain was relentless; the winds were howling. Trees and roofs and debris flew by.

We didn't say a word, as if our silence could move the storm back out to the gulf.

My father called. My mother called. Amy called. Sara called.

"We don't know anything. We'll let you know when we do." I tried to sound stronger than I felt.

We watched footage taken from a helicopter. It looked like a war zone. A bomb had been dropped on Seabury; tornadoes followed for the final touch. We thought we saw Sand Dollar Lane flash across the footage, but the landmarks were gone. We couldn't be sure if we were looking at my aunt's house. If we were, only one other roofless house stood nearby. Every other house on the street was gone. Nothing remained. Only rubble.

My aunt immediately thought of Betty, who hadn't evacuated. She dialed her number and put the phone on speaker so I could hear. "Are you all right?"

"We're okay. We should have evacuated. It was terrible. The noise. The winds. But that's all we got here. We didn't get the surge. We've got trees down and flying debris, but we're lucky. The trees missed our house, thank God. We lost the shed out back—two big pines fell on it. We don't have power. We've got spotty cell coverage, and Fred has the generator going." Betty paused, then said slowly, "Patty, I'm sorry. Seabury . . . That surge . . . Seabury's bad."

My aunt looked like she saw a ghost. "How bad?"

We heard the soft crackling in Betty's breathing from years of smoking. She coughed, then paused longer. I imagined her wringing her arthritic hands, wrestling with the words.

Finally, she spoke so softly, I could barely hear her. "It's gone."

chapter 31

October 2005
Seabury, Florida
"There's nothing on the beach side of Main Street." Betty's words tumbled out quickly. She caught her breath before softening her voice again. "Everything's gone."

My aunt held the phone in front of her, immobile. Her house was on the beach side of Main Street.

I took the phone from her and spoke into it, my heart racing. "Are you sure?"

Betty sighed into the phone. "Fred's friend, Paul. His plane was in a hangar in Brewster, and they had minor damage out there. Paul flew over the area. He said it's all gone. Everything."

Words stuck in my throat.

"If I hear more, I'll call you," Betty told us.

"The house? My aunt's house. Did Paul say?"

She answered slowly. "He said everything is gone beachside. The surge—the gulf waves were over eighteen feet high. I'm sorry, Kelly."

I mumbled some staccato phrases, thoughtlessly thrown together. "Thanks. Be careful. We'll be in touch." My hand trembled as I hung up the phone and sat with my aunt on the hotel room bed, staring at images that confirmed what Betty had told us. Desolation and destruction flashed on every news channel.

Tears streamed down my aunt's face. I hugged her helplessly.

When she stopped crying, she wiped her eyes with a thin hotel facecloth and stood over me. "Jesus, I'm sorry, Kelly. This has been a helluva year for you."

I tried to smile, but my cheeks stuck; my lips refused to open. She was right. Leo. Megan. Matt. And a Cat 5 hurricane. "Yeah. So much for bad things happening in threes. I think I'm up to some power of three. When things can't get worse, they can."

We stared at the TV screen. Stunned, we weren't sure what to do next.

•   •   •

Since we learned the hurricane hit Seabury, our cell phones hadn't stopped ringing. My father, mother, my aunt's brothers from Dorchester, her sister from Montana. When I saw a long number on the phone, I grabbed it.

"Kelly? Are you okay?" There were skips in the line, but they didn't hide the concern in Alex's voice.

My eyes teared up as I took the phone to the bathroom and sat on the toilet, unable to respond to him.

"Are you there? I only have a few minutes. We're headed out on a mission, but I just got an email from Jake, and he told me about the hurricane. I hadn't seen the news. I wanted to check on you and your aunt."

"We're okay," I managed. "We haven't been able to get back to the house yet to see what's left."

"I'm sorry I'm not there to help, Kelly."

I stood up and took a facecloth off the sink counter, held it against my eyes, forcing myself to keep it together. "You called from a war zone, Alex. To check on us. It's not as if you've got nothing going on over there."

"I gotta go. But let me know what's going on when you find out. Hang in there, Kelly. I'm sorry you're going through this."

When I hung up, I scrubbed my face to keep from crying.

Even Matt called. I hadn't talked to him since I'd left the house in tears over three months earlier. I hadn't heard from him since I received the manila envelope in Amy's mailbox. Allison told me a moving truck had come and gone from our old rental house, but I didn't know where he'd moved to, how he was doing.

When I saw his number flash on my phone, I didn't pick up. There were way too many emotions swirling around in my head to mess with Matt. My aunt sat on the end of her bed and looked at me, wondering why I let the phone ring. I shrugged. "Matt. Not in the mood."

She almost cracked a smile.

He left a message. He sounded far away, worried, guilty. "Hey, Kelly, I wanted to check in. I hope you're doing okay. With the hurricane. I'm sorry." I took the apology to be universal, for the hurricane, for everything. I was glad I didn't pick up, but I wondered if that had been my last opportunity to have a conversation with him. I wasn't sure what I thought about that, but it was too far down on my list of things to think about.

My aunt called her neighbors, the DelGrecos, the Smiths. No one knew anything. No one could get close enough to see anything. Main Street was loaded with debris; no one could get by. There was no power, no water, no communication.

We stared at the TV for hours, and when we saw a clip of helicopter coverage, my aunt's hand went to her mouth.

"Kelly. Was that?"

"I think it was?" I asked in response.

It looked like, in all the wreckage, my aunt's house on Sand Dollar Lane stood alone among the rubble. *Maybe it isn't as bad as we thought. Maybe Betty is wrong. Maybe my aunt's house would be all right.*

•   •   •

The National Guard closed off what was left of Seabury and wouldn't let anyone in until five days after the hurricane made landfall. Allegedly, they were securing the area, but all my aunt thought about was the mold growing by the multitudes every second we waited. I was not excited to see what awaited us when we got back into town.

On that fifth day, we drove away from the hotel in my car at 6:30 a.m. We didn't check out. We'd be back. I'd slapped down my credit card, hoping my aunt was right, that insurance would reimburse the costs for our transient housing. We'd picked up supplies the night before at Walmart: water bottles, trash bags, paper towels, sunscreen, protein bars.

"I'm used to packing for evacuating," my aunt had told me at the checkout counter. "But I've never had to return to a disaster zone before. I have no packing list for this."

As we drove south, we gasped at the first signs of what lay ahead.

"No power?" my aunt asked, pointing to the McDonald's and gas station at the interstate.

We were an hour north of Seabury. I tried to make a joke, but came up short, unable to speak. No power an hour away from Seabury was not a good sign.

My aunt reached over and turned off the radio. I liked the distraction, but I knew her well. She wanted to sit in quiet and mope.

Our normal route into town, through the forest of pine trees, was impassable, and we were detoured on a circuitous loop through back roads and into Seabury from the north. The ride took two hours longer than it typically took. We approached a checkpoint manned by National Guard soldiers, their eyes droopy, their uniforms wrinkled and dirty. When I rolled down the window to show them our driver's licenses, I was immediately repulsed by the overwhelming pollution of dust and debris in the air.

They checked our licenses for addresses and told us only residents could pass through their checkpoint. I explained I was staying with my aunt, and the young soldier nodded. "No problem. We're only trying to prevent looting, ma'am."

I thanked him, and he told me to look for a large sticker on the door. If it was green, our house was salvageable. "If the house is still there." He sounded equal parts tired and matter-of-fact. "Green means the city has gone through your house and you can go back in."

Later, we'd learn that it also meant they'd found no dead bodies in the house.

I rolled up my window and drove toward town, my eyes swiveling, my mouth open. My breathing quickened; my hands trembled on the wheel. I was afraid to see my aunt's face. We said nothing. There were no words.

Debris had been shoved to one side on the main road, creating a single lane for cars to pass. Trees were snapped in half or ripped off at the stump. Cement slabs sat where houses once stood. Mangled pieces of metal and vinyl—furniture, cars, boats—twisted and tossed, were strewn everywhere. Occasional shells of homes coated with debris, missing windows and roofs, stood randomly spared. My body sank into my seat. This happened on TV, to other people, in other towns. Not here. Not to us.

When I turned onto Main Street. I pressed my foot to the brake to stare. When I'd lived with my aunt when Matt was in ranger school, I'd watched the construction of a stunning two-story home on the beach, with decks in every direction, decorative turrets, and a pool. The house had been swept across the street, as if someone had come in with a gargantuan power saw and sliced it off at the knees, tossing the two-story structure in the air a hundred yards.

There were no landmarks remaining, and I drove by Sand Dollar Lane, not sure where we were. My aunt raised her arm and pointed at a pile of wood, debris, and rubble. "That's the house that used to be on the corner. That was Danny's house," she mumbled. "Thank God they evacuated."

"Oh my God." My aunt's whole body froze as we turned down her street. There was nothing left. Piles of bricks, hunks of stucco, chunks of concrete, lay in heaps where houses once stood. The Smiths' house, overlooking the gulf, perched precariously at an angle, one strong wind from being blown over. The red wraparound porch, the deck, the stairwell, and everything under the first floor had been swept away. Half of the roof was gone, peeled back like the skin of a banana, hanging down the side of the house.

The only other house still standing on the street was my aunt's. I parked in the middle of the street and sat in the car, staring at it. My aunt covered her mouth with her palm, her body still, her eyes blinking. I felt nauseous. The house had been built on concrete pilings with the storage room on the ground level and stairs up to the deck. The only thing that remained under the first level of the house were the concrete pilings. The storage room was gone. The shed was gone. Debris, pavers, siding, and rubble littered the gravel yard. But, somehow, miraculously, the stairs and the deck outside the sliding glass doors remained intact.

My aunt shook, breathing irregularly. I reached over and put my hand on her forearm. "Breathe deep. In and out, slow. It'll be okay." I spoke slowly, trying to steady my voice.

She inhaled, then exhaled slowly, and fumbled to open her car door.

When we opened the car doors and stepped out, we were inundated with the endless high frequency beeps of smoke detectors in the rubble and the smells from the trash, rubbish, and salt water. My mouth felt like someone stuffed it with garbage. I walked away from the car and spit the overpowering disgust out of my mouth.

From where I stood near the car, I could see the green sign on the sliding glass door. I pointed it out to my aunt, who hadn't moved. She stood next to the passenger door, her hands on her hips, her mouth open. There was no one else around. Only rubble, and us.

I walked toward the stairs of her house and motioned for her to come with me. I didn't want her to walk into the house alone. The house didn't appear to be that damaged. Half of the siding and the railing to the deck were gone, but the sliding glass doors and most of the windows looked intact.

"Be careful. I'll follow you," I told my aunt. I stood below the steps and watched her cautiously creep up the middle of the stairwell, staying far from the open sides with no railings. As she reached the top step, she stopped, bent down, and picked something up off the deck. She held it close to her chest. I couldn't see what it was, but I watched her knees buckle and her back cave. She crumbled into a ball and fell in a heap on the top step, convulsing in tears.

With the railing gone, I worried she might tumble off the step. Stepping over the pile of pavers near me, I flew up the stairs, leaving the rubble below. Her head in her hands, she sobbed as I approached. I sat next to her and held her tight. She wailed with anguish, her thin body shaking in my embrace.

"Aunt Patty," I said firmly. "We have to get off these stairs. I'm not sure how safe they are." I pulled her up and onto the deck, away from the open stairwell.

With tears streaming down her drawn face, she showed me what she'd picked up off the step. Covered with sand, the tarnished words were still visible:

May the roof above you never fall in,
And the friends beneath it never fall out.

The wall on which it had hung was gone. The storage room in which Alex had changed the light bulb was gone. But the plaque that had hung in my aunt's childhood home had survived.

My whole body shouted that it wanted to cry. But I couldn't. I wiped my eyes with the bottom of my T-shirt, bit my lip, and straightened my shoulders. *I have to be strong.* Pulling my aunt into my embrace again, I held her until her convulsions settled into quiet sobs. I closed my eyes. I'd never been religious, but I'd never been this low before, either. *God, give me strength.*

chapter 32

April 2006

Seabury, Florida

Six months later, I sat with my aunt on the tiny front porch in our one-bedroom rental house and waited for a pizza delivery. The house was a mile from the beach, but Category 5 hurricanes open lines of sight, and, over the scattered rooftops and broken trees, we could see the sun setting in the sky.

"So beautiful." I stared at the massive blue dome of sky.

"As long as you look straight out to the gulf. Not that way." My aunt pointed toward the houses in ruins, ready to topple. Some had been demolished, but most still stood, bare walls of ruin and mold, waiting for insurance claims to be settled, lawsuits to be filed.

Her cheekbones protruded from her narrow face; her skin sagged over her bones; her shoulders hunched over her tiny frame. The light in her bedroom shone under the crack of her door most of the night. I saw it. My light was on, too. We divided up the tasks, although most days her list hung untouched. There were days in those early months when she sat for hours and stared into space. It was hard to watch my spunky aunt get lost in the hurricane rubble.

•   •   •

When we got back to our hotel that first night after seeing the house, I'd called my father. Though I tried to be logical and practical about what we needed to do, my sheer shock seeped through, and when he hung up, he called to update Sara. Then he called his boss, asked for a week off, and flew down the next day. Sara insisted that she and Jake drive down to help, but she was four months pregnant, and I'd told her, "No, please stay in Georgia." After much debate, she acquiesced, but told me Jake was coming. He arrived the day after my father, lugging plywood, tools, and a generator in his pickup truck. He looked at the mess and hugged me, overcome with emotion. "I get it now. Why you didn't want Sara to come. Good call. Thanks for that."

Jake and my father boarded up the windows and doorway, and we emptied the house, carrying the kitchen table, chairs, some dressers, anything we could salvage from the onset of mold, into a U-Haul truck. Later that night, my father drove the U-Haul, following Jake in his truck, and my aunt and me in my car, to the only available storage shed we could find two hours away. As we locked the shed, my aunt hugged Jake before he began his trek back to Savannah. She fell apart in his arms, and Jake looked over her tiny frame toward me, with pity in his eyes.

A week later, too tired to think, I drove my father to the airport from the hotel.

"I feel guilty, Kelly," he'd told me. "You're here with my sister dealing with all this, and I'm flying back to normalcy."

"I can't leave her, Dad."

"I'd give notice and move down here. But I'm not sure she'll stay. What do you think?"

"I don't know. Seabury's home for her. I can't imagine her picking up at this point in her life and starting anywhere else.

But recovery and getting back to normal is going to take a long time."

"Kelly, I'm so proud of you. I knew you were a tough kid, but dealing with this. This takes a different level of tough." He looked out the window as we passed a field littered with fallen trees.

I swallowed and looked straight ahead. I didn't tell my father about the first day my aunt and I returned to the house. I didn't tell him how I left his sister in the house, how I needed to be alone. I didn't tell him how I'd walked down to the beach, disgusted by the smells, the debris. I was so angry. So angry at the gulf. So angry that this happened. I didn't tell him how I stood at the shore and looked into the gulf and bellowed. I'd screamed and yelled all sorts of profanities until my throat was hoarse. My aunt had to have seen me; she had to have heard me. I was the only one on the beach. When I returned to the house, she didn't say a word. But we both knew what we didn't speak: We were changed people. I gained the strength my aunt lost. Or else I was just sick and tired of being walked on by the world.

We lived in the hotel room in Alabama for a month. When Betty called mid-November and told us she'd learned of a one-bedroom rental house in Yarmouth, we grabbed it. We couldn't afford to be fussy. When a hurricane hits, and everyone loses their home, rental properties that have water and electricity are scarce. I bought an air mattress for the living room, and when I stuck the air pump into the wall to blow up my new bed, my aunt sat on the worn brown plaid couch, disbelief written all over her face.

I bounced on the mattress. "Perfect."

She held her head in her hands, looking past me.

I leaned the air mattress against a wall and sat down next to her. "Are you okay?"

Lifting her head up slowly, she turned to me, her eyes cloudy and wet. "Kelly McGowan, listen to me. Enough is enough. You have a life to live. Go back to New Hampshire. You can get a job in Boston. Or go live with Amy and work in Clarksville. There's no reason for you to be here during this. I'll be fine."

I shook my head. "First, we should probably cover this couch with a sheet. There's a reason this cottage was available."

She didn't smile, but that didn't stop me. "I think we'll be all right if we douse the whole cottage in bleach." She still didn't smile, so I succumbed to being serious. "Don't even think about it. After all the great summers you gave me when I was a kid? Let's make a deal. We'll do what we have to do to get us back in your house. After that, we'll play it by ear."

She hunched forward again, closed her eyes, and rubbed them with her fingers. "Thank you."

I would have been happy to drive away from the war zone we were living in. It was hell. Even the gulf, once so beautiful, was filled with wood and glass and everything that the surge deposited into it. But I couldn't leave my aunt. I had to be strong for her.

•   •   •

The rusty Ford Escort with the pizza sign on the roof drove up as my phone rang. My aunt signaled for me to take my call and I walked in the house, while she got the pizza.

I saw Sara's number. "Everything okay?"

"Why do you always think something's wrong?" She laughed. "Everything's fine. Your goddaughter is asking what day you'll arrive for her christening. She can't wait to see you."

I smiled. "I can't wait to meet her and see you guys. It's weird, right? That I automatically assume whoever is calling me has bad news? I need to stop doing that."

"I think it's probably a normal reaction for someone who's had your past year. When are you coming? I wanted to call and check on that. We can't wait."

"Is it okay if I get there Thursday night? I can take Friday off and leave after work on Thursday. I'll get in late, though, close to midnight. I'll leave there Sunday afternoon after the baptism, so I can get to work on Monday. I want to stay longer, but I've missed so much work with this hurricane chaos. I didn't have as much to do with the Yarmouth job. They lost a lot of clients because of the storm. But the Clarksville job never slows down. Which is okay, because I love it, and I'm glad I have that job, but I can't afford to ask for more time off."

"I'll take you when I can get you. I can't believe it's been so long since I've seen you," she said. "You've had the worst year. I've been such a rotten friend."

"Are you kidding? Your husband saved the day. If he hadn't come down and boarded up the house when he did, we'd never be as far along as we are now with repairs."

"How's it coming? It's been six months, right?"

My aunt walked into the kitchen, put the pizza on the counter, and took out two plates. I signaled for her to use paper plates. She nodded and put the plates back.

"It's slow," I said into the phone. "It's hard to find help. But we're doing fine compared to most. At least our house was still standing. We didn't have to go through the nightmare of rebuilding from scratch. We only had to gut it. We're waiting for the cabinets to go back in, then the floors, and we're done. Mold inspections, new roof, insulation, Sheetrock, electric, HVAC, plumbing, painting—all that's done."

Sara laughed. "You sound like a general contractor."

"Not really. But it's easy to get ripped off. I've had to learn a lot."

"Are you sure your aunt doesn't want to come up here with you?"

"Nah, she's good. We can use a break from each other. This house is smaller than our dorm room was. You know how I can drive my roommates crazy."

My aunt put a slice of vegetable pizza on a paper plate in front of me. "Oh, shush. Don't you talk nonsense. I couldn't have done any of this without you."

"What'd she say?" Sara asked.

"Nothing. Hey, I'd better go before she eats this whole pizza and doesn't save me any. I'll see you late Thursday. Can't wait."

I hung up, walked to the fridge, and took out two bottles of Coors Light.

When I handed my aunt a beer, she asked, "Excited about going?"

I sat down with her. "I am. It'll be good to see Sara and Jake. It'll be good to get away. It was nice to go home for Christmas, but that was too short of a trip, right?"

My aunt stared into her bottle of beer. "I got tired of answering everyone's questions about the hurricane. And why I don't move back to Dorchester. Of course, I didn't have to say a word. I just pointed out the two feet of snow on the ground."

I laughed. "But then when they said, 'Really, this snow is worse than that hurricane?' They had us then." I picked an olive off my piece of pizza. "I can't wait to meet Emmy. I've never seen Sara's house in Savannah. I want to sit on her couch and hold that baby."

What I didn't say, and what I knew my aunt realized, was that I wanted to drive somewhere, anywhere, and not see rubble and debris.

"Kelly." My aunt put her beer down and pointed her thin, knobby finger at me. "You've been an angel, and I couldn't have gotten through this without you. But it's time now you think about living your own life."

I reached over and put my hand on her forearm. "We're close to getting back in the house. There's light at the end of this tunnel."

"There is." She gave a partial smile. "And we're close enough to the end of the tunnel for you to move on now. *Really.* I want you to go see your friends and have a good visit. Keep an open mind when you're up there."

"What do you mean?"

"Nothing." She lifted her bottle of beer to tap mine. "Just keep your options open."

I wasn't sure what she meant, but I tapped my bottle to hers and grinned.

chapter 33

April 2006
Savannah, Georgia
I stifled a yawn as I parked in front of the only house on the street with lights on. I grabbed my suitcase and the bag of gifts I brought for Emmy, Sara, and Jake.

It was close to midnight, and I'd spent the past six hours in the car, alone for the first time in what seemed like forever. I'd lived within two feet of my aunt since the day before the hurricane. The quiet in my car should have been calming, but I was nervous. I worried that Sara and I had changed. I worried about what these changes might do to our friendship. I'd been single for ten months, too busy to try to find myself. Sara was blissfully married, a new mom. I was no longer connected to the Army. Sara was in it, waist deep.

I approached the front door and knocked quietly, assuming Emmy was asleep. No one answered, so I opened the door hesitantly and walked in. Within seconds, Sara's head poked out from around the corner down the hall, and she ran toward me with her arms open, pulling me toward her closely. My stomach unknotted, my worries fading.

When she let me go, she looked me up and down. "You look tired! No, worn-out. Exhausted."

"It's good to see you, too." I laughed, before admitting, "I'm a little tired, but I'm so glad to be here."

I hugged her again and told her, "You look great."

She'd gained the pounds I'd lost since the storm, and it looked good on her. Her cheeks were filled out, brightening her eyes; her smile was real, joyful.

"Oh, please. I'm huge. But I feel good. Tired, but good. I can't wait for you to meet Emmy. No way am I waking her tonight, though. You're welcome to get up with her at four a.m.?"

I laughed again.

"I'm kidding. It's so good to see you, Kel."

I felt warm all over, being with her again.

"Come in, come in." She walked down the hall toward the stairs. "Put your bag here. We'll bring them up later. My parents and Jake's parents are at a hotel. You'll be in the guest room, which is also the office, so I hope a futon is okay."

"I've been on an air mattress for five months. You may not get me to leave." I left my bags at the foot of the stairs and followed her into the living room.

A pillow, folded sheets, and a blanket sat on the corner of the couch, and I wondered if they were for the futon. I smiled at the baby carrier on the coffee table, and the diapers in the basket next to the end table. She led me into an open area, with a dining room table and an adjoining kitchen.

I closed my eyes and opened them again, when I saw two men standing by the counter, grinning. I didn't expect to see anyone with Jake. I suddenly felt lightheaded, as if I might faint.

"Kelly! How are you?" Jake stepped toward me and enveloped me with his trademark bear hug. I felt protected in the cocoon of his embrace, not able to see or hear anything outside of his arms. But I knew what I saw when I walked into the kitchen, and my heart raced as I waited for Jake to release me.

Stepping out of his arms, I stared behind him. Alex leaned against the counter, wearing a gray T-shirt and jeans, his grin stretching slowly into a broad smile.

"Hey, Kel." He walked toward me and hugged me. I melted in his embrace as he whispered in my ear, "We're okay, right?"

"God, I suck," I said miserably, shaking my head. "I'm so sorry. I've been such a lousy friend. I didn't even know you were back." I took his hands in mine and looked into his blue eyes and said, "I. Am. So. Sorry."

He shook his head, still grinning, holding my hands. "It's not as if you've had anything going on this year. I just got back last week. I wasn't sure if I'd be able to make it this weekend, so I didn't say anything."

When our hands parted, I reached for the counter behind me and almost collapsed with the avalanche of feelings overwhelming me. Gratitude that Alex was home safe, and in Sara's kitchen, that I was at Sara's, that my friends were still my friends, even without Matt in my life. Someone swooped in and punctured a million holes in my body and let the air out. Both hands behind me, I rested on the counter, and inhaled deeply, trying to regain my composure.

Alex's eyes squinted with concern, but Sara jumped in immediately and turned to Jake. "Can you bring a beer for Kelly out to the living room? Or wine?" She turned to me. "What do you want?"

"Whatever you're having is good," I replied.

She looked down at her breasts. "Can't have anything when I'm breast feeding."

I nodded. "Beer. Thanks, Jake."

She put her arm around my waist and led me out of the kitchen. Before she sat on the couch, she stopped suddenly. "You've got to be so tired. From the drive. From everything. Do you want to go to bed?"

I dropped onto the couch, grabbed the pillow, propped it up behind me, and pulled the blanket onto my lap. "No! I'm sorry I got emotional in there. You're right. I'm tired. But I won't be able to sleep. Too much to catch up on. Plus, aren't you the one with the new baby? I'm not getting up at four o'clock."

Jake walked in with an opened bottle of beer for me, followed by Alex with a six-pack. He handed me the beer and asked, "Tired from the drive? Or tired from the past six months? I tried to explain how bad it was down there—but I couldn't. It was too bad. I can't imagine living in that disaster zone." He shook his head sympathetically.

Alex sat across from me in the recliner, his brow wrinkled. His hair looked darker; his eyes seemed bluer. His T-shirt was snug. He'd worked out during deployment and looked good.

"Wow, Alex, you look great." It popped out of my mouth with no warning. It might have been the beer and exhaustion making my body tingle when I looked at him, but my body hadn't tingled in years, and it felt good.

He grinned, Sara laughed, and Jake said, "Hello? Here I am!"

I laughed. "Oh, you do, too, Jake. Of course! But, yeah, I admit, it was nice to drive away from it all today." I sighed. "Seeing trees along the highway that weren't cut off at their knees. The griminess, the destruction, it wears on you. It's been a long year. A year ago next month, Matt got back."

No one said anything. Jake nodded before lifting his bottle to his lips.

"And a month before that, Megan died. And two months before that, Amy's husband. And, not even a year before that, I moved with Matt to Tennessee."

I leaned my head on Sara's shoulder. "I might be tired from the past three years," I said, with a pitiful attempt to chuckle.

Jake looked at Alex. "Chronic stress."

I tilted my head, confused. "What are you talking about?" He seemed so serious, and the beer tasted so good.

Alex explained. "It's a flight school term."

"What's the solution?" Sara asked. "To this chronic stress?"

"Sleep and beer." Jake smiled.

"Sounds good to me," I said, holding the bottle in front of me. I looked at Alex. "You just got back. Don't you have jet lag? And I'm the one saying how tired I am? And you've spent the past year in a war zone. God, I'm the worst. Did I already say that? How are you?"

He smiled. "Plenty of time to talk about all that later. I got back on Monday. This week has been day on/day off. I'm almost over jet lag, I think. That good?"

I nodded. "For now." I turned to Jake. "When do you go?" Before anyone could answer, I interrupted myself. "But, before all that, let's talk about the elephant in the room. I haven't talked to Matt. I purposely haven't asked any of you what's up with him, because, honestly, I've had enough to worry about. So tell me." I took the last sip from my bottle. "What's up with him?"

The three of them looked at each other before Sara said, "Hmm, Matt." She paused and looked at me with a face that seemed to ask, *"Are you sure? You really want to know?"*

"I can handle it," I told her, reading her mind.

Jake reached forward and handed me another beer from the six-pack Alex had brought out to the living room.

"They got married," she said bluntly. "They live on post."

I bit my lip and felt my fingers grasp the bottle tight. "Okay, I expected it, but what an ass," I said, with more venom than I intended. I didn't love him. But remembering everything he let me endure made me swell with anger. I saw Sara looking at me and knew she had more to say.

"What else?" I lifted my chin higher.

"She's pregnant. Due in July."

"Well, shit," I said. "They didn't waste much time." I forced my cheeks to attempt a sad smile. What else could I do? "Okay, Alex, you're up. Elaborate, please."

He raised his eyes to mine. "Deployment was all right. Got a lot of hours flying. Good to be home."

I hadn't talked to him in so long and wanted more information. The beer loosened my tongue, and the words tumbled out. "Girlfriend?" As soon as I said it, I looked away, embarrassed I'd asked, afraid of his response.

Sara snorted and Jake's eyes opened wide. Alex grinned. "No, ma'am."

"We were curious, but were giving him a few hours to settle in, so thanks for asking, Kel." Sara laughed.

"No problem. That's what I'm here for. Jake, you're up next. Have they set a deployment date yet?" Jake looked down at his feet, and I realized this was not a pleasant conversation. I interrupted before he could respond. "Never mind. Let's not talk about it."

Sara sighed, resigned. "It's okay. We think in the fall, maybe October, if we're lucky. Afghanistan, they say. By the time he goes, your house will be ready for me to visit, right?"

"Oh my God, yes. And I can drive up here and babysit my favorite goddaughter, to give you a break."

We talked about the weekend plans. Both sets of Emmy's grandparents would be at the house for breakfast. "It's not a christening party as much as a cookout," Sara explained. "Tomorrow afternoon, since the godparents—that's you two— have to leave right after the church ceremony on Sunday."

Sara looked at her watch and hit Jake on the arm. "Let's get some sleep. Alex, do you want help making up the couch?"

"I can help him," I said, getting up and reaching for the linen on the arm of the couch. Tucking the sheet under the cushions, I patted the pillow. "You can lie down. I have too many questions for you to go to sleep yet, though."

He smiled and got up from the recliner, moving toward the couch. "All right. I'm awake."

Sara hugged me good night, then followed Jake upstairs, while I sat next to Alex and began my interrogation. My eyes barely stayed open, and I rested my head on his shoulder, leaning into him, asking him about his family, his deployment, his life. I didn't know when I'd see him again. I wanted to know everything.

He hadn't seen Matt; he told me. He'd talked to him briefly. Matt seemed happy.

I finished my second bottle of beer, thinking I should have eaten dinner. I lifted my head off his shoulder and looked into his blue eyes. "Has he asked you if you'd talked to me?"

Alex's eyes scanned the room before they met my eyes. I asked, "What was that about?"

"What do you mean? I didn't say anything."

"Yeah, but something happened. I know your eyes."

"Nothing happened. He did ask me about you. He asked me how you were doing. He wants you to be happy."

Not sure what I expected, I wasn't sure that was it. I yawned, looked at my watch, and said hesitantly, "I guess I better let you sleep."

"Wait a minute. Let me ask you something," he said as I leaned forward to get up.

"How are you really doing? Are you over Matt? Honestly? And, what about you? Boyfriend?"

"Hmm. Many questions."

He shrugged. "I'm the curious type."

"I'm doing okay," I said, fully standing up. "The hurricane was worse than the breakup, believe it or not. I was only responsible for me during the breakup. Now I feel responsible for my aunt. Oh, yeah, I'm so over Matt. I'll be hurt forever—I mean, I lost. He picked someone else. But I know it wasn't meant to be. I spent a couple of years trying to fit a square in a round hole, and working so hard trying to make it fit." I shrugged. "I know now that it never would have fit. Thank God we never got married."

He looked at me, waiting for me to say more. "Oh" —I shook my head—"no boyfriend. Not sure what I'm waiting for."

I turned to walk up the stairs, and Alex stood to hug me good night. "I'm sorry I didn't tell you what I suspected after graduation."

"No." His hug felt so right, but something made me back out of it slowly. I was so lonely. I was probably a little drunk, but I wasn't drunk enough to throw myself on my friend and regret it later. "I'm the one who's sorry that I fell off the face of the earth these past six months."

"Get some sleep." He sat back down on the couch.

When I walked away, I thought he looked at me like he did that first night on the beach, sorry to be leaving me with Matt, sorry that he was walking away with the blond bimbo. But I was so tired and so emotional and so desperately lonely for physical love, I probably imagined it.

chapter 34

April 2006
Savannah, Georgia

The following afternoon, Sara's mother slid a plate smeared with dip under my arm and into the sink full of soapy water. She put her arm around my waist, and pulled me away from the sink, nodding her head toward the backyard. "Go out there and have fun. I'll do these, honey."

I took the dishtowel she handed me, dried my hands, and walked away from the solitude at the kitchen sink. Seabury wasn't bustling with people, and when I lived in Clarksville, I'd worked and spent time with Amy. Except for occasional outings with the spouses or FRG meetings, I hadn't socialized in years. Plus, I was sure all of Jake's classmates knew about Matt and me. I wondered what story they'd heard. I wondered how they'd react to me being there without Matt.

Out of the corner of my eye, I saw Alex watching me. He put down the plate of food he'd been making. "I'll make that sandwich later. Let's go out back."

Gratefully, I followed him out the door, onto the back patio, where adults stood around the picnic table and watched toddlers throw balls at each other in the yard. He led me down the deck stairs onto the grass, sidestepping a little girl with a Hula-Hoop. We made our way toward a wiry guy with that military look: short hair, tight Patagonia T-shirt, khaki shorts, and flip-flops.

"Hey, Kenny, do you know Kelly? She's Sara's roommate from college. Aren't you from Boston?"

Kenny grinned, jerked his head back, then reached out to shake my hand. "Quincy. Where ah you from?"

"I'm from Forkton, New Hampshire, but my father's from Dorchester."

"Right next door! My wife, Audrey, she's the one chasing the three-year-old who looks like he's eight." He pointed to a petite brunette grabbing the back of a little boy's T-shirt. "She's from Dorchester. Saint Brendan's parish."

I smiled. Only people from Dorchester identified their neighborhood by their parish. "Small world. My father's family still live in Saint Ann's. I'll have to meet Audrey. She looks busy right now."

Kenny laughed. "I think she'll be busy for the next fifteen years. Do you have kids?"

I shook my head. Alex, who hadn't said anything, pointed to a couple standing with Jake near the grill. "Oh, hey, Kenny, we'll catch you later. I've got to bring Kelly to see a couple of old friends."

Kenny smiled. "Sure. Good to meet you. When Audrey passes the bruiser off to me, I'll tell her to find you and say hello."

"Tyler and Heather," Alex told me as we walked toward the grill. My heart raced. I hadn't seen either of them since their wedding. The uncertainty of how people would react to me, without Matt, made my underarms sweat. As if to confirm my concerns, we passed Sean, standing next to a short woman, with pink hair braided down her back. I hadn't seen Sean since Sara's wedding, and as I smiled, he spun his head abruptly away from me.

I stopped walking and turned to Alex. "What the hell?"

Alex put his arm around my waist and leaned into my ear. "He's always been a douchebag. He heard from Matt that you guys broke up. That you left. That's all he heard, and all he knows. I tried to tell him there's more to the story, but he said he didn't care. Matt didn't deserve someone who left him right after a deployment."

I bit my lip, feeling my cheeks turn red. I feared that's what people would say. It made my skin boil.

Alex's hand was still around my waist, and he squeezed it quickly before releasing it. "People will think what they want. Ignore him, Kel."

Heather and I made eye contact, and she practically ran toward me. She pulled me in close and whispered in my ear. "I'm so sorry, Kelly, about everything you've gone through. Sara's kept me updated. I'm so glad you're here." She squeezed my hands. "I'm sorry I haven't reached out to you. Fill me in. You're at the beach—"

Tyler interrupted. "Hey, hugs for me, too." He fidgeted a bit, and I wondered if he was more uncomfortable seeing me than Heather was. His hug was awkward, and when he stepped back out of it, he almost lost his balance. I wondered if he'd been drinking.

"Let's sit over here." He pointed to a set of high-back heavy chairs on a cement pad below the deck. That's when I saw the prosthetic below his jeans. Tyler had lost a leg. *How did I not know this?*

Heather lifted her palms up, waist high, then dropped them. "He just got a new foot. He doesn't trust lawn chairs, and those low Adirondack chairs are tough to get out of. We've had some falls."

I wrung my hands in front of me, trying to find the right facial expression, one that conveyed my empathy without pity.

Tyler shrugged. "Everyone thinks I'm always hammered."

Alex laughed. "And?"

"Hey, I've only had one beer!"

"Did you decide what to do?" Alex asked as Tyler adjusted himself in the chair.

"Yeah, the Army said I could get a master's and go back to West Point to teach. But the cold weather and the leg probably aren't a good combination."

He looked at Heather, who nodded in agreement. "I can't imagine him in that ice and snow," she said.

He scooted toward the back of the chair, trying to get comfortable. "I've got an interview with the Wounded Warrior people in Jacksonville. I think it'll be a good fit. We'll see."

"What about you, Kelly? Where are you now?" Heather tilted her head, lowered her shoulders, and leaned toward me.

"I'm on the Panhandle. Seabury. Where the hurricane hit last October. I'm helping my aunt get her house back together. It should be habitable by midsummer, I hope. After that, I'm not sure. I love it there, but I don't know if I'll stay. I'm still trying to figure it out."

Heather nodded. "It takes time. It'll work itself out."

I smiled, hoping she was right.

•　　　•　　　•

Later that night, when Emmy was in bed and the grandparents had escaped to the quiet of their hotel rooms, I squeezed one more cup into the rack, found soap under the sink, and started the dishwasher. Sara wiped the counter down with a sponge. "I'm so glad you're here. Thanks for all your help."

"I didn't do anything. Your mother kicked me out of the kitchen," I confessed.

"She told me." We walked into the living room, where Alex had collapsed on the couch and Jake had plopped on the recliner. "She said you had more in common with the people at this party than she did, that you should be talking to them, not doing dishes."

I didn't respond. *Do I? Do I have things in common with these people?* I sat on the other end of the couch and Sara motioned for her husband to scoot over in the recliner so she could sit with him. He pulled her mostly onto his lap and she snuggled in.

"Well?" Sara looked at me. "How was it?"

"It was fun. You throw a nice baptism cookout party."

She grinned, waiting for more.

"I didn't know about Tyler. How could I have not known?" I asked, blaming myself for not asking about my friends.

"It happened right after Leo. You were in Ohio at the funeral with Amy when Jake found out. I couldn't tell you, Kel. I'm sorry. I should have. And then, after you got back, there was never a time I didn't worry about you."

How ironic. I hadn't shared so much with Sara, because I was trying to shield her from what I was going through in the real Army, never realizing she was trying to protect me as well.

"I get it. But tell me from now on. I need you to be honest with me. And I'll be honest with you."

She nodded. "Okay, truth, then. How did it feel for you today? Being here?"

"It didn't feel like I *didn't* belong. It wasn't awkward. Except when Sean ignored me. That was weird. I get it. I figured people would think, 'Oh, she waited until he got back and then dumped him. She couldn't handle the PTSD. She couldn't be patient with him.' Pisses me off."

Alex leaned forward, his eyes oozing sympathy. "Your friends know you and know the truth, Kel."

"Yeah. But still. Pisses me off. Did I already say that?"

He grinned, shaking his head. "Don't let the bastards get you down."

I laughed.

Sara continued asking me questions: "Except for Sean, who's always marched to his own drummer, how was everyone else?"

"Everyone was nice," I answered honestly, knowing that was exactly what Sara hoped to hear.

She smiled and poked Jake with her elbow. "I knew it. These people are your tribe, Kel."

Alex grinned at me. "Yep. You don't need to be with someone for people to want to be with you."

My cheeks flushed and my eyes turned to my lap.

Three hours later, I woke up with a start, drooling on the couch. Alex was out cold, his head awkwardly positioned off the back of the couch. Jake and Sara must have gone to bed. The recliner was empty; the lights were off. I got up and tenderly tapped Alex, moving his head under the pillow, and lifting his legs onto the couch. His eyes fluttered, and he mumbled something as I covered him with the blanket. I stared at his sleeping face for a second, and I'm sure it was the wine or sheer emotional exhaustion, but without thinking, I leaned down and kissed him tenderly, so lightly, on the forehead, before I turned to walk upstairs. I didn't hear him move as I walked away. I didn't look to see if his eyes had opened. I wanted more, but something held me back, and I was too tired to figure out what that something was.

•   •   •

Snowbirds returning to the cooler temperatures of Michigan and Maine for the summer jammed I-95 North. I drove in the opposite direction, a fish against the tide. I was a hermit, going back into my cave in the woods after a quick trip out of the lonely forest.

I thought about the christening, holding baby Emmy on the altar, smiling at Alex, who gave no indication that he'd felt my kiss the night before. I thought about conversations with Sara and Jake, Tyler and Heather. My friends comforted me; they made me feel a part of something. I thought about living off the grid in Florida—what I missed and what I didn't. I wished I knew what I wanted to do with my life.

Before I hit the disaster zone, I called Amy and told her all about the weekend. I listened to her stories about her job. She told me about Chris, Leo's friend, who'd been in the vehicle behind Leo in the convoy when Leo got hit. Amy was sure his friendship with her was due to survivor's guilt. I didn't care. I was glad he was so good to Amy.

I told her Alex was back. "I'm going to give him your number, okay? I know you've got Chris there, but if you ever needed anything, Alex would be happy to help."

"That sounds good," she said. "I'm glad he's back."

A few hours later, the terrain changed. Trailers torn in pieces, trees toppled, piles of debris, still, six months later, waiting to be picked up. As I drove over the tiny bridge into Seabury, I exhaled. We'd move back into the house on Sand Dollar Lane by midsummer, and I'd figure out what was next for me in the fall. I loved my aunt, but I needed my own space.

Up ahead on the side of the street, someone jogged on the sidewalk. I squinted at the familiar form, eased my foot on the brake, slowed down, and stared out the window. *What the hell?* Driving slowly, I pulled up next to a brown-haired man wearing a Red Sox ball cap. I rolled down my passenger-seat window. "Want a ride?"

My father stopped jogging and looked at me, laughing.

"Hey, Kel." He pulled his T-shirt up to wipe his brow.

"What are you doing? Why didn't you tell me you were coming? Do you want a ride?"

Still laughing, he opened the passenger door and hopped in. "Sure. I'll take a ride. I'm sweaty, though. But, hey, I'm here! For good!"

"What are you talking about?" I stared at him, confused and tired.

"I moved! Here!" he told me, motioning for me to pull back out onto the street.

Shaking my head, I put my blinker on to join the traffic on Main Street. "Explain?"

"I wanted to surprise you! Your mother put the house on the market and it sold in a week. I told her not to tell you or your aunt. We closed last week. I moved my stuff out of my apartment and into a U-Haul."

I turned down the street, and sure enough, an orange-and-white truck was parked in front of the rental house.

"For good? You're moving here for good?" It was starting to sink in, but still made no sense. "What about school? Where's Mom?"

"Your mother moved in with Mike. She's happy. It's good."

My eyes must have bulged, because he repeated himself. "It's all good, Kel. She said she'd call you this week with an update. I start my new job next semester at the community college in Yarmouth. I'm here for good. I've got a short-term plan for where I'm living and will figure out a long-term plan after I check out the market here."

I turned the engine off outside the rental. I didn't say a word.

"I'll admit," — he squinted his eyes at me and wrinkled his forehead — "I thought I'd get a happier reaction out of you."

"Oh, God, it's great. I'm just surprised. Or more like stunned."

He opened his door, but didn't get out of the car. "Yeah. I can't believe it, either. Hey, how's Sara? Good weekend? Tell me all about it inside. Oh, I surprised your aunt, too. She almost had a heart attack when I drove up in that truck." He jerked his head toward the U-Haul, before stepping out of the car. "Wait till she sees my RV."

I stared at him. "What? An RV is your short-term plan?"

"For now. I'm picking it up tomorrow." His grin stretched wide across his face. "You've got a roommate on the couch tonight. Come on in. Tell us about your weekend."

Tossing my bag over my shoulder, I followed my father up the steps and into the house, shaking my head and smiling.

chapter 35

July 2006
Seabury, Florida
My father followed my aunt up the newly painted steps onto her deck. He stopped on the landing and looked down the street at the empty lots where houses once sat. "Jeezus, sis. Can you believe this? You beat everyone back. Are you the only habitable house beachside?"

"There are a couple of others, but yeah, we're back faster than most. It helped to have the house still standing." My aunt held a suitcase in one hand and jerked her other thumb behind us. "The rest of Sand Dollar Lane still looks like a bomb went off." Lowering her suitcase onto the deck, she stood next to my father. "Thank your daughter. She's the reason we're back this early. She should give up the CPA gig and become a general contractor around here."

"No, thanks." I carried a box of food around her and through the sliding glass doors into the house. For the past week, we'd made trips between the rental house and my aunt's newly renovated house on Sand Dollar Lane. This was our last trip. The city had connected the house to the water line the day before, and I'd never appreciated the relief of a flush so much.

"It's hard to believe, right?" I asked no one. "Nine months since the storm. Not bad, considering six months ago, we were looking at a house that had been gutted."

"And nothing under the house," my aunt said, following me into the kitchen. "The storage room gone. I'd love to find that refrigerator. There's probably a hundred rusty appliances somewhere under the gulf."

"It's hard to fathom the power of that surge. But hey, you both did a great job," my father said. "I never thought you'd be in the house by the Fourth."

"Oh, ye of little faith," my aunt said.

I looked out the kitchen window and understood why my father had little faith. My aunt's house was the only house on Sand Dollar Lane. The DelGreco's house—and every other single-level cinder block house on the beach side—had been swept away by the surge. The Smiths' beautiful gulf-front house had been demolished months ago.

"I'm looking forward to more houses being built on this street," my father said slyly.

My aunt laughed, and I caught a glance between the two of them.

"What's going on?" I took the canned goods out of the bag on the counter.

My father winked at my aunt. She nodded her head vigorously.

"Well, although I'll miss cleaning out the black tank on my home on wheels, I'm going to move back into my room here. But guess where I'll park my RV?" He rocked back and forth on his toes and shook his shoulders like the cat who swallowed the canary.

I held a can of tomato paste mid-air. "What are you talking about? Where?"

He walked across the kitchen to the large windows next to the table that looked out at the street and gulf. Lifting his arm up, he pointed diagonally across the street at the lot littered with weeds stemming out of broken concrete and bricks. "Right there! I want to park this baby there now, but I close tomorrow."

I thought he might pee his pants. I put the tomato paste down and stared at him, then joined him at the window. "What?"

"I bought the lot! That lot next to the DelGreco's! The people who owned that house that was there before the storm decided to sell the lot, and your aunt told me it was going on the market. I grabbed it before it went to a realtor. I'll build a little place there and live in the RV while I'm building."

"Dad, that's awesome." I high-fived him, smiling.

"It'll take a while." He high-fived me back with both hands, before walking back to his suitcase. "After I close on the lot, I'll sign the contract with the builder, and next year, for the Fourth, I'll be across the street in my own place, making sure my sister isn't throwing wild parties over here."

My aunt shook her head, chuckling. My father picked his suitcase up and danced down the hall toward his bedroom, shaking his hips and doing some sort of conga steps.

I looked at my aunt. "You knew?"

"He swore me to secrecy. Like he found the Holy Grail. He's so excited. What do you think?"

I nudged my aunt into the corner of the kitchen near the stove. "I know he loves it here, but I don't want him moving here for me. Is he moving here for me? What if I don't stay?"

"Oh, honey." My aunt took the butter and cold cuts out of the bag on the counter and placed them in the empty fridge. "He's moving here for him. But that's why he didn't want to tell you. He didn't want your plans, your life, to change because of him. He wants you to do what you want to do with your life. It has taken him so long to do what he wants to do. He's wanted to move here for years. He finally did it."

Vehicles rumbled by outside; a car and a large RV barreled down the street. My father came out of his bedroom and joined us at the window. "DelGrecos? In an RV? Someone should film this."

"Mary Ann told me she and Kyle were coming down with her parents." I gazed out the window. "She wasn't sure about the others. I have a feeling her parents will find a hotel room in Yarmouth."

My aunt laughed. "Never a dull minute on Sand Dollar Lane."

•   •   •

Early the next morning, my father and I sat alone at the beach. The sun blazed; the sand was like hot coals. I sipped from my water bottle.

The day before, we'd unloaded boxes, made beds, and hung pictures on the wall. That morning, after breakfast, my aunt insisted we take a break and hit the beach. We didn't argue.

"You look good, Kel." My father lifted his sunglasses to see me, before placing them back down on his nose.

"Thanks, Dad, so do you."

He looked more relaxed, somehow, despite the darkness of Seabury's destruction and the constant thudding and banging of rebuilding all around us. His face was tanned, more content. His body belonged to him, as opposed to in Forkton, where he was always on edge. Pulling his ball cap down to shade the sun, he said, "You're more muscular. Still too thin, but you look strong. Healthy."

"That's all the green garbage your sister feeds me," I said.

"How are you, really?" He leaned toward me, pulling the visor of his baseball cap lower to block the sun. "I'm not allowed to be happy unless you are, you know. There's an old saying, 'You're only as happy as your saddest child.'"

His comment made me think of Megan and the sorrow that her life and death brought to him. I'd never told him I knew he wasn't her biological father. I didn't see any reason; it changed nothing.

"I worry about you, Kel. You're resilient, but you've had a rough few years."

The tide receded, leaving tiny bubbles in the dark, wet sand. I looked out into the gulf and wondered how many refrigerators and cars and kitchen tables were out there.

"I'm good. It's hard to believe it's been over a year since I left Clarksville. I won't lie. This hasn't been an easy year, but I think we're coming out of it now."

"Coming out of what? The Matt situation? Or the hurricane situation?" He got straight to the point.

"I'm way over Matt, Dad. I'll always be embarrassed that I hung on for so long."

My father waited, moving his beach chair closer to the umbrella pole, deeper into the shade. I waited for him to get settled, then said, "It gets me so mad when I think about how long I waited for things to be right, waited for a date, but now I think maybe I had to."

"Had to what?"

"I dunno. Maybe I had to go through all that to figure it all out."

"Hmm. That's deep."

"It's only deep if I figure it all out. I haven't done that yet. I might just be trying to rationalize the time I spent with him. I mean, if I hadn't met him, I wouldn't have met Amy, Allison, and Vicky. They'll be friends for life. I wouldn't have dealt with ranger school and the deployment. I wouldn't be who I am today, right?"

"All true." He nodded his head. "What about the hurricane?"

"That was awful, Dad. I can't explain. You saw how bad it was. But you do what you have to do. Aunt Patty needed me here. She's good now. But you saw her after the storm. She needed me."

"She did, Kel." His voice stumbled, caught in his throat. "You've been an angel. Now I'm here. And I'm staying here. She's in her house. That was always the decision point for you. You said you'd wait until she was in her house. I wanted to tell you, to make sure you understand. You don't need to stay here for her anymore."

I sat up straight. "Wait. Did you move down here so that I could leave if I wanted?"

"No." He shook his head. "I moved down here because I had the money after selling the house. Because I love it here. Even when it looks like this." He yanked his thumb back to the ruin behind us. "I don't want you to leave, unless you want to leave. I want you to be happy." He looked at the bright blue water in the gulf. The county had cleaned the beach and the clean-swept sands blinked white. "It's beautiful here. I've always loved this place. Give it time. Time heals most things."

"Okay, Confucius." I smiled.

We looked up to see my aunt approaching. I moved my chair over to give her shade under the umbrella. "It's like old times," I said. "Except no people on the beach."

"No rentals after the hurricane," my aunt said. "That's okay with me. They'll rebuild and this beach will be packed again in a few short years. They did a great job plowing the beach, though—raking it over and over for months after the storm. I'm going to enjoy the quiet while we have it."

Sounds drifted over the dunes. Talking, laughing. We turned to see what caused the ruckus and watched the older, wider, less harried DelGreco parade walk toward us. My aunt snorted. "While we *had* it."

We heard Mrs. DelGreco's booming voice yell, "Ohhh! Ohhhh! Lookee!! Look who's here!" Mrs. DelGreco waddled toward us, wearing what looked like a bright blue-and-white-striped parachute. A wide-brimmed straw hat covered her curly hair. She was genuinely, sincerely tickled to death to see us. She took her sunglasses off to dab her eyes.

Mary Ann followed her mother, a beach bag slung on her shoulder, wearing shorts and a T-shirt over her suit. Kyle, in his swim trunks and holding a Nerf football, tagged along next to her.

I gulped when I saw the guy following Mary Ann. I hadn't seen Johnny since he was twelve. *Whoa.* His curly brown hair was cut close to his head, and he wore board shorts and a T-shirt. He carried three beach chairs with a towel draped around his neck. He set the chairs up, put the towel on one of them, walked over, hugged my aunt, then shook my father's hand. "Nice to see you again, sir." He waved to me. "Hey, Kelly."

I tried to keep my eyes on his eyes as I waved back, smiling, but it was hard not to let them wander. He looked like a Greek god with a crew cut.

Joey, wearing a Georgia Tech T-shirt, followed his older brother. His hairy legs and lily-white round face hadn't seen the sun in years. Mary Martha, wearing a bikini that should have been two sizes bigger, trailed behind the family, pretending she didn't know them. Mr. DelGreco quietly parked his chair next to my father, and the two of them launched into a conversation about the Braves and the Red Sox. He looked the same, but wider, and his forehead had extended upward, causing his dark hair, speckled with gray, to cover only the back of his head.

Mrs. Del Greco shouted over to him. "Put a hat on, honey."

He nodded and smiled, then continued talking to my father, still politely ignoring his wife after decades of marriage.

Mrs. DelGreco lowered herself slowly into the chair Joey set up next to my aunt. "I'm thrilled to hear about my new neighbor. Love it. Can you believe another McGowan on Sand Dollar Lane? I'm so glad those owners—we never knew them—they always rented that little gray house that was there before the storm. It's hard to remember which houses were on what lots!

Anyway, I'm glad they sold their lot. When we heard Bill bought that lot, we were thrilled!"

No one tried to get a word in edge-wise, which only prompted her to take a big gulp of air and keep talking. "Our big news—we have a builder. We signed with a firm out of Atlanta last week. If all goes well, next year on the Fourth, we'll be in an actual house. What a year, huh, Pat?"

I smiled, listening to her ramble and ask questions, not waiting for any responses.

"And what about the Smiths' lot?" she continued. "I heard Jennifer was going to rebuild. Have you heard anything? And the lot at the end of the street sold, too. It's going to be a new street. But the best news is that Bill bought that lot next to me. Does he need floor plans to check out? I'll ask him, never mind, they can't talk baseball all day, can they?"

I was twelve again. Mary Ann and I rolled our eyes at each other as we listened to the banter, and watched Johnny and Kyle race down to the water with the football.

"Johnny, be careful!" Mrs. DelGreco looked at us apologetically. "He's all grown up and in the Army, and I still tell him to be careful whenever I see him."

After tossing the ball around, Johnny and Kyle walked toward us, and when they got close, Johnny pulled his T-shirt up over his head and tossed it at his mother's feet in the sand. He grabbed Kyle, lifted him up over his head, and ran with him toward the water. Kyle laughed and yelled, "No, Uncle Johnny! Put me down!"

I raised my eyebrows at Johnny's six-pack, his arms, his back—every muscle ripped and tanned. It was hard not to stare. I hadn't dated since Matt. Except for that light kiss I planted on Alex's forehead and the feelings I crushed around him, I'd been too tired or busy, or so I rationalized. My mind wandered to Alex. We called each other, at least every other day, but it was always platonic.

I watched Johnny and Kyle splash around in the water for a few minutes before Kyle ran up to his mother, chased half-heartedly by his uncle. Johnny grabbed a towel from the pile near his mother and dried off his torso in front of us. I gave up trying not to look.

Later that afternoon, after everyone else had packed up in search of air-conditioning, Mary Ann and I folded our beach chairs up, called Kyle away from his most recent sandcastle, and began the trek back up the hot sand toward Sand Dollar Lane.

"I hadn't expected Johnny to be all grown up." I confessed.

"Yeah, I know he's my brother, but he's not bad-looking. He was serious with the girl he was with last year. Since they broke up, he's been rebounding. I was surprised he came down. I figured he'd spend the weekend with some girl somewhere."

"Where's he stationed?" I asked.

"Fort Drum, New York." She turned to me with her eyes open wide. "Oh my God! Are you interested?"

"Nah. He'll always be a ten-year-old brat cheating at Marco Polo. But God, he's easy on the eyes."

"He was such a brat," she agreed.

We followed Kyle over the dunes. The wooden bridge that we'd known for years had washed away in the hurricane, and whenever I looked at where it used to be, my heart ached. Watching Kyle trudge through the sand between the newly planted sea oats, I was hit by a thought. That bridge didn't matter. The people did.

"Company?" Mary Ann asked as we approached our house. A small silver car with Tennessee plates sat in front of Aunt Patty's house.

I froze in place. "Huh?"

Amy dashed down the deck steps to meet me out front. "I hope it's okay," she blurted, her words fast and furious. "We just pulled up. Your aunt insisted! It was her idea to surprise you. I didn't want to intrude on your family Fourth."

I laughed. "Are you kidding? It's great! I'm so happy to see you!"

We told Mary Ann and Kyle we'd catch up with them later, and I reached over and touched Amy's arm lightly. "Are you all right?"

"Yeah, great." She chose her words slowly. "I wanted to talk to you, though. In person."

"What? What's going on?" I could sense from her contemplative tone, her hunched shoulders, that something was up.

She shook her head. "No, it's not bad. It's all good. We can talk later tonight. When things settle down. You have a lot going on here." She pointed toward the RV. "And I didn't help by adding to it."

I didn't understand what she meant, but after a day at the beach in 500 percent humidity, I needed a shower, so I let it go and turned on the outside faucet to wash my sandy feet before going inside the house.

Amy followed me through the sliding glass doors and into the house. I heard my father talking to someone in the kitchen. *Is that another male voice?* I knew that voice.

I felt my smile rip my cheeks apart. Amy had driven down with Alex.

chapter 36

July 2006
Seabury, Florida

My father and aunt claimed exhaustion and heaved themselves up from their chairs on the deck, carrying their empty beer bottles with them into the house. I settled back on the swing, under the black sky spotted with stars, listening to the waves crash, feeling lighter than I'd felt in months.

Amy said, "So I have a problem."

Alex leaned forward before getting up. "I'll be back. Y'all catch up."

I put my beer down on the deck next to the swing, and Amy edged her Adirondack chair closer to me. She rubbed her forehead. "You know I've been friends with Chris. Leo's friend."

"Yeah?"

"It's been almost a year and a half," she said. "Hard to believe."

She paused, and I waited, but I knew her well enough to sense her apprehension, to sense that she wanted my approval, my blessing, for whatever she was going to tell me—and it probably had something to do with Chris. "A long time," I affirmed, watching her face. "It's okay to move on, Ame."

"I know. But I still feel guilty about it."

"About what? Moving on?"

"Yeah. Chris has been such a good friend. Sometimes a little more."

"That's all right, Amy. You don't have to be alone forever." I bent down to pick up my beer.

"He has orders. He's moving to Colorado, to Fort Carson, in October."

I listened, waiting.

"He wants me to move out there. With him. Not in with him, unless I wanted to, but to be out there, near him." She seemed close to tears. "To keep dating. Or doing whatever we're doing. To see what happens."

The only sound was the soft crashing of the waves. Even the DelGreco's RV was quiet across the street. I tilted my head back, staring up at the stars in the sky. "I have a question. Okay, two questions." My eyes still stuck on the dark sky. "First, are you happier with him than without him?"

"With him," she said, without skipping a beat.

I leaned toward her and met her eyes; her sincerity crossing paths with my happiness for her. My lips turned upward, smiling.

She asked me, "Second question?"

"Did you ask Vicky?"

She laughed out loud. "She's our Army mom, isn't she? Yeah, I called her."

"What did she say?"

"She told me to follow my heart."

My eyes returned to the stars as I thought about Vicky, who'd moved to Germany. I hadn't talked to her in months, but if I picked up the phone and called her, she'd be there. Of course, she told Amy to follow her heart. That was Vicky.

Amy leaned forward, her eyebrows knitted together, and added in a conspiratorial voice, "Oh, she said to tell you something."

"Huh?" I tilted my upper body toward her.

"So Chris moves in October. My lease is up at the end of December, so if I go with him in October, I'll eat three months of rent."

"Oh. Not the best timing."

"Yeah." She leaned even farther forward. "So this was Vicky's idea—she told me to tell you. She said, why don't you,"—she pointed at me—"move back, work your old job in Clarksville full-time again, and live in my apartment?"

She let that sink in. "I'm not sure if you're planning to stay here or what, but you said your boss keeps hinting for you to move back, so this might be a good option? The apartment will be there for you. The job is there for you."

I thought about it. "But you'd be gone."

She nodded. "But you'll have your old work friends, Allison, your old gym and yoga friends." She paused, and then added, "Oh, and that friend." She nodded her head toward Alex in the house. "I may have mentioned that friend to Vicky a few times in conversation."

I sat up straight and listened to the waves, that calming rhythm that made everything all right. Alex. He was special to me. More than a friend, he'd told me that day over a year ago in Nashville. But his best friend was my ex-fiancé. No matter how I felt about Alex, it would always be awkward.

Amy broke the silence. "Whatever you decide, I get it. My real concern was about me, as selfish as that sounds. Am I following a guy? Should I stay put and be independent?"

Her questions applied to us both.

"I proved myself independent," she stated, answering her own question. "And now it's time for me to be happy in another relationship. No one will be Leo. But. . ."

"But you deserve to be with someone who makes you happy." I finished her thought.

She stood up and put her hand on my shoulder. "Thanks for always being there for me, Kelly. I'm going to go in and call Chris. I mean, he knew what I wanted to do, but I kept telling him I needed to bounce it off you. Think about my apartment, will you? I'll see you in the morning."

"Sure, yeah," I said. "I'll be in soon."

On cue, as Amy walked into the house, Alex walked out.

"Okay if I sit?" He pointed to the swing I was on. I nodded, and he sat next to me, and I felt that tingle that I hadn't felt in so long. I wondered if I'd ever felt this close to anyone. I never felt this close to Matt. I never had this friendship with Matt. Looking back up to the sky, lit up by thousands of white specks, the beautiful pattern of chaos suddenly made me feel so small.

"What a year, huh?" I asked softly.

"Yeah, what a year."

I felt his eyes on me, and I turned to him.

"Are you happy? What are you thinking?" His voice was so tender and kind, it made me melt.

I sighed, wishing I could lean into him and stay there forever, but holding back because he was my friend. I couldn't do anything to jeopardize this friendship. If he wanted to do something, I'd be there, but he had to initiate.

"I'm happy. I think," I said. "But. . ." I leaned my head back and stared upward at the dark sky. "There are more stars here than anywhere else in the world, I swear."

"You are amazingly talented at deflecting a conversation, you know that?"

I grinned.

"You love it here, don't you?" He leaned his head back next to mine and stared at the sky with me.

"I do, but . . ."

He turned and looked at me. "There's that but again."

"I don't know," I said honestly. "It's complicated. I love it here. But I don't know. You were in the car with Amy for nine hours today. She talked to you about me taking over her lease?"

He nodded imperceptibly, allowing me to ramble on.

"I like my jobs, both of them. But I think I'm happier going into an office, believe it or not. I miss seeing people and I miss having friends my age."

He watched me, listening.

"The first three months here, it was perfect. It was where I needed to be to heal from the breakup. Then the hurricane. I had no choice. I had to help my aunt get through it. Now she's through it, and she's got my father." I paused.

Alex said, "You don't feel needed anymore."

"I guess that's it. But I still love it here. I mean, it's hard to look at the place. It'll take years to be right again. But the beach is beautiful, and those stars. . ."

"So let's consider the pluses and minuses," Alex said.

"You're such an engineer." I smiled, remembering he majored in some sort of engineering at West Point. "All right, the pluses. I love it. My aunt and my father. My jobs. It's good when Mary Ann comes down. But she's not here full time and I haven't made any new friends my age here."

"That's a negative. Hold up," he said. "Any more pluses?"

"I think that's it. Okay, the negatives. I miss friends my age. Believe it or not, I miss my Army friends. I know they move. You'll be moving. What? In two more years? And Sara and Jake will move, but there's something about the Army friends. I can't put my finger on it, but there's something different. You don't find that out here. Whatever that is."

He nodded, thinking.

"What do you think it is? Am I imagining it?"

"No," he said. "There's something different about this life. I could get all hooah about how they volunteered to serve and die for our country, and all that, but I'm going to take the simple answer and save the hokey speech."

"What's the simple answer?"

"We're all on a team. The spouses are on the team, too. They don't get the big salaries or any of the glory, but without their support, there wouldn't be a team. When you leave the team—because you get out of the Army, or you leave, like you did—you feel like you've lost your teammates."

My shoulders slumped. He hit the nail on the head.

"But you haven't. You still have us. You know that, right?"

"Don't make me cry." I turned my face away so he couldn't see my eyes water.

He put his arm around me, and didn't move it, letting his hand hang off my shoulder. My heart raced.

I wiped my eyes and turned toward him again. *Please keep your arm there.* "While we're being philosophical, do you think you can have it all? Can we have it together, personally and professionally, and in the right location? I have the location—I like it here. I have half the professional piece. I like my jobs, but they're not perfect. But, personally, I'm a disaster."

"You're hard on yourself."

"Yeah, yeah." I looked into his blue eyes. "But what do you think? Does anyone have the job, the personal stuff, and the location?"

Alex smiled. His teeth were perfect, and those eyes were so kind. I'd never paid attention to his ears before; but sitting this close to them, with his arm around me, I saw them and thought, *Damn, even his ears are perfect.*

"What do you think?" I looked up at him, trying to calm my heart.

"I think all we can do is appreciate what we have. And keep the door open to what we don't."

I nodded, and we sat in the quiet night under the stars, his arm still draped over my shoulders.

"I can't date." I announced it out of nowhere, surprising myself and eradicating my earlier line of thinking that I shouldn't initiate anything that might ruin our friendship—so much for that idea.

He waited.

"I'm not interested." I didn't stop. "I don't want to date anyone. Except you. I know we're friends, though." Suddenly regretful, worried that I blew it, I mumbled, "I'm sorry."

He leaned back a bit. "Why are you sorry? I think I'm a catch."

"You are a catch. But we're friends. And it's weird for you. Because of Matt."

He pulled me close, and I smelled his mouthwash. He must have brushed his teeth when Amy and I were talking. I wished I'd brushed mine. "Kelly," he whispered in my ear, "I want to be your best friend. Yeah, Matt will always be my brother. But that doesn't mean you and I can't be together. I don't want to date anyone else, either. Only you."

It was hard not to straddle him and jump into his lap. With every ounce of self-control I could muster, I rested my head on his shoulder. He put his hand on my thigh and leaned his head on top of mine.

A few seconds later, tired of that self-control, I put my hand on top of his and slowly lifted my head from his shoulder. Inches from his face, I said in a voice barely above a whisper, "It seems right, doesn't it? Taking over Amy's apartment a year after the hurricane. Maybe it's happening for a reason."

"Moving back to Clarksville?"

I tapped my fingers lightly over his, and asked nervously, "What do you think?"

Turning to face me, he removed his hand gently from under mine and took my face in both his hands, his eyes inches from mine, his lips even closer. Ever so slowly, he leaned in, his soft lips meeting mine, tenderly at first, growing with passion, a slow-burning friendship that finally caught fire.

"Wow," I said when we separated minutes later.

"Yeah, wow," he agreed. "I've wanted to do that for a long time."

I put my hand on his thigh and turned to him, hugging his side, my heart full.

chapter 37

September into October 2006
Seabury, Florida
Clarksville, Tennessee

"I won't be much help with Emmy, but I can unpack boxes when she's sleeping," Sara explained.

I held the phone up to my ear in one hand, and with the other, I slid skirts and dresses one at a time along the rod in the closet, scanning to see which still fit, which I still liked. We'd been lucky to get in the house soon enough after the hurricane to salvage most of our clothes, but I hadn't worn dresses to work since I'd left Tennessee over a year ago. It was time to clean out my closet. I pulled some off their hangers, ones that I'd worn with Matt to Army functions, his graduation ball, Tyler and Heather's wedding, and tossed them on the bed. They'd go to Goodwill.

"It's too much." I argued with Sara. "Over eight hours in the car with a seven-month-old?"

"Please, Kelly," she pleaded. "Jake's been gone a week and I haven't slept at all. I'm exhausted. I can't tell my parents, or they'll worry and drive down. I need to get out of this house."

I remembered the first week Matt was gone, hearing noises, seeing shadows, lying in bed wide awake and alone. I couldn't imagine trying to survive a deployment, along with taking care of a baby.

"Yeah, I get it. Thanks, Sara. I can't wait to see you and Em."

"Oh, great! Yay! What do you need? We have an extra TV here. Do you want me to bring it?"

"No, just bring yourselves and whatever you'll need for Emmy. I asked Amy to leave the bed frame and mattress in her guest room. And the TV in the living room. It was already mounted on the wall. I sent her a check. I'll have to go to that damn storage shed and see what's in there. I'm hoping Matt left the kitchen table there. Believe it or not, I've still never asked him. You'll have to come with me to shop for a couch and stuff."

After we hung up, I called a furniture store in Clarksville and arranged to have a queen mattress and frame delivered for the master bedroom the day I arrived. Sara and Emmy could sleep in the master, and I'd sleep in the guest room, the same room I'd stayed in after Matt and I broke up.

When I stopped packing long enough to think, my head hurt. *What was I doing?* Seabury was slowly building back into the paradise it was before the hurricane. I had my aunt and my father. I had a part-time job in Yarmouth.

My last night in Seabury, sitting at the dinner table with my aunt and father, I poked at my salad. I couldn't eat a thing.

"Okay, that's why you have that bag of clothes for Goodwill." My aunt pointed to my plate full of food. "You've lost too much weight. You've got to eat something, honey."

"'Pot calling the kettle black' much?" I grinned. My aunt had never been hefty.

"Oh, pshaw. No deflecting here, missy. Have a roll."

My father shook his head. "I'm going to miss the banter between my two favorite McGowan women. What are you nervous about, Kel?"

"I don't know. I mean, what am I doing? I'm jumping from security to the unknown."

"But your boss in Clarksville told you she wasn't sure if she could keep you on remotely, right? Didn't she highly encourage you to get back to the office there? Or give notice?"

"Yeah." I forked a crouton. "She couldn't guarantee I'd still be able to work remotely in November."

"So consider this a professional move. Amy's lease is up the end of December. You give it a few months. If it doesn't work out, you move. Back here or somewhere else. You'll always have a home here. You know that."

"And he doesn't mean in his RV, Kelly," my aunt echoed. "Your room will always be your room here." She held her fork up over her plate and leaned her head toward me. "Let me ask you something. Did you make this decision based upon a budding romance that you might now be questioning?"

"Holy Moly." I put my fork down. "You guys don't pull any punches."

They grinned, waiting for me to respond.

"Okay, well, maybe," I admitted. "I don't know."

"You've talked to him every day since he was here for the Fourth, right?"

"Yeah, and our conversations are platonic. Like they were for years. He probably got back to Fort Campbell and decided we're better as friends." I shuddered to say out loud what I'd kept inside for months.

"Could be." My father nodded. "His friendship with Matt—I'm assuming he's still friends with Matt—must make things weird for him. But even so, you've got Allison and a good job you're moving for. Some people move for far less than that. And no one said you have to stay there forever."

"You're helping your friend with rent, too," my aunt reminded me.

I nodded, exhaling, and picked up my fork again.

"Eat so you don't faint on your drive in the morning. Oh, and another thing, did your father tell you we were coming up for Thanksgiving? I've always wanted to see Nashville."

"Well, then, I guess I have no choice. I've got to move, right?" I forked a piece of chicken in my mouth, certain I'd miss this place. I concentrated on the positives in Clarksville, not the fact that over a year ago, I'd run aimlessly away from the place searching for love and belonging.

•   •   •

Late afternoon the next day, after nine hours on the road, I drove past two vans parked in front of Amy's house and pulled into her driveway. Leaving my car door open, I got out and ran over to greet the two women with strollers on the sidewalk waiting for me. Sara hugged me first; then I peeked into the stroller to smile at Emmy, before I hugged Allison.

"Did you meet?" I asked.

"Yeah," Sara said, laughing. "We were both sitting in our vans waiting for you. We figured your stalkers should say hello to each other."

"I can't believe how old Emmy is." I bent down to smile at her gnawing on a set of plastic keys in the stroller. "And you," I said to Allison, "have a baby I've never met, and Erin's so big! Oh my God! Look at her!"

I knelt to hug Erin in the double stroller and asked her to introduce me to her new baby brother.

"We're so glad you're here," Allison said. "Let's get you unpacked and organized."

I ran back to my car and grabbed my bag, and then walked toward the front door, looking for the flowerpot where Amy told me she hid the key.

Sara pushed Emmy, and Allison followed her with the double stroller behind me and into the house.

"Oh my God," Allison said. "It's immaculate."

"Look at that." Sara parked the stroller in the empty living room and pointed to the bottle of wine and new set of wineglasses on the kitchen counter.

"Just like moving into Army quarters on post," Allison said sarcastically. She pulled her stroller up next to Sara's and walked down the hall toward the guest room. "She even put sheets and a comforter on the bed in your old room!" Allison yelled back to us.

A few hours later, after the queen mattress and frame for the master bedroom was delivered, we'd unpacked the box with linens, placed the towels and shower curtains in the bathrooms, and unloaded the boxes from my car. Allison looked at her watch and told me she'd be back the next day.

When I walked her, Erin, and baby Zach to her van, I said, "I might be able to keep up with you now."

She stopped loading the kids into their car seats and turned to me, confused.

I nodded at the stroller she'd folded up to put in the back of the van. "You'll be pushing that double stroller now, right?"

She laughed. "Let's start back up when Sara leaves, but you have the stroller on hills."

I waved as I watched the van drive away, a smile stuck on my face.

When I walked back into the house, Sara was taking food out of the cooler she'd brought with her, putting it into the empty fridge.

"Hey," I told her. "How about I go to the grocery store, and you unpack and get settled in?"

"Sounds like a plan." She hoisted Emmy out of the stroller and we watched her try to crawl on the living-room floor.

"Oh, first let me get that painting out of the way." I stepped past Emmy and picked up Aunt Patty's painting, encased in Bubble Wrap, from its spot on the floor.

"My aunt carried this out to me this morning when I was leaving," I explained to Sara. "It was all wrapped up. She told me she wanted me to have it. For as long as I can remember, it hung over her couch. She's had it up in her art room for the past week. She was being very sneaky."

"Let's see," Sara said as I moved the painting out of Emmy's crawling radius and placed it on the kitchen counter.

I pulled the wrapping off the painting slowly, revealing the blue skies, the umbrellas, the paddleboards, the cottages along the dunes. I searched through the figures on the painting, and there I saw three figures I'd never seen before—a man and two small girls under an umbrella. Among the hundreds of tiny bodies swimming, sitting on beach chairs, playing in the sand, and walking, the only one with a detailed face was the taller girl. She had brown hair and brown eyes. She smiled.

"I love this painting," Sara said. "I remember it over your aunt's couch."

"Yeah, me too," I said, taking a step back. My aunt's efforts to portray me happy made my heart warm. "I'll get nails and a hammer at the store. Should I pick up takeout for dinner on my way home?"

Sara handed Emmy a toy from the basket she'd unloaded from the van, then looked at me. "Sure, that works. A salad from Chick-fil-A? With waffle fries for dessert?"

I winced, thinking about driving in Clarksville, feeling eager for the first time since I arrived.

Sara put her hands on her hips, eyeing me knowingly. "Are you okay? This is a big move for you."

"Oh, yeah." I bit my lip. "I wasn't expecting my aunt to give me this painting. But, yeah, I'm good. Thanks for being here, Sara." I turned quickly to walk out to the garage. *Please don't let me see Matt out here.*

•   •   •

The next day, I woke up early, showered, did my hair, applied makeup, and slipped into a navy-blue dress and flats.

"You actually missed this?" Sara asked, standing in her pajamas, holding Emmy at the door.

I thought for a few seconds. "Yeah, I think I did. But ask me next week, after I've had to wear real clothes for a while."

"I'd be fine wearing sweats and working from home if I could. The grass is always greener."

Hurricane recovery, working remotely, living at the beach — none of those things required makeup or styled hair. I was nervous about how I looked, anxious about meeting new people, about seeing my old coworkers. At a busy intersection, at a red light, I looked in the rearview mirror and checked my makeup. My eyes traveled to the black pickup truck behind me, identical to Matt's. I held my breath and felt sweat bubble under my armpits. *Damn. Not today. Not on my first day back to work.*

It couldn't be. I leaned forward to peer closer in the rearview mirror. A uniform. A soldier. Slightly built, gaunt face, wearing glasses, not Matt.

I exhaled. *Am I going to worry about seeing him everywhere in town?* Every soldier in this town drives a black pickup truck. I needed to get him and his black pickup truck out of my mind. The light turned green, and I drove to the office.

My boss immediately called me into her office and got right to business. "So good to see you. How are you, Kelly?"

She closed the door, sat behind her desk, and didn't wait for my answer. "Please sit down." She straightened the paperwork on her desk. "You've had a lot going on this past year, Kelly."

I sat in the chair across from her. *You think?*

"You've been such an asset to me. But I've had a job offer I couldn't refuse. A promotion, near family in New Jersey. I'm leaving next week. That's why I wanted you to be here full time. I wasn't sure if my replacement would keep you on remote."

She chatted a bit, then walked me out, showed me my desk, and introduced me to her replacement, Scott, a fiftyish man, white hair on the sides, nothing on the top. He talked to me about the project he had lined up for me. I sucked my lips together, hoping to rein in my enthusiasm, so I didn't come across as desperately excited. The project, visiting clients across the state—being a real CPA—sounded ideal. When he learned that I'd only arrived in town the day before, he told me to go home, finish unpacking, and come back to work on Monday. I didn't argue. I drove home, energized and excited.

•   •   •

Later, in sweatshirts and jeans, Sara and I sat on the back porch, with Emmy in her walker.

"The job sounds perfect for you," she told me after I relayed my conversation with my new boss. "I'm jealous. I'm worried about leaving Emmy when I go back to work in January. I'm not sure what to do."

"Why don't you stay here?" I was serious.

She smiled. "That's tempting. But you need a couch. And a table. And lamps."

"Tomorrow! We'll go furniture shopping. Okay?"

"For sure. And though it's tempting, I'll go back to Savannah a week from Saturday. If you don't mind me staying here another week."

"I want you to stay here forever. You know that."

She looked at me sheepishly. "Last night was the first night I've slept since Jake left."

"I'm glad you finally slept. You've got to be exhausted. You're welcome to stay here until he gets back. I'd love the company."

"I'd love it, too. But we have a house, and before he left, I was beginning to feel settled in. Good neighbors. Nice people in the unit. My parents and Jake's parents are both coming for Thanksgiving, so that's good. But after they leave, if I decide I can't do this alone, I'll call you."

"I'm sure you can do it," I told her. "But if you choose not to, I'm here."

"Thanks." She pulled Emmy's walker closer to her.

I told her about seeing the Matt look-alike pickup at the red light on the way to work.

"I wondered if you'd always be on the lookout for him," she said. "If you'd be worried about running into him."

"I hope it passes. It doesn't help that everyone in this town drives that stupid huge black pickup. The whole Matt story makes me sick to my stomach. When I think about the time with him—" I felt the anger swell.

"I can't imagine. I'm sure there are lots of memories here, Kel. I'm sorry."

I reached over and pulled the string on the pop-up toy attached to Emmy's walker and watched her laugh. "I wish you lived here."

"I wish I did, too."

We sat in silence for a few minutes before Sara stood up. "Hey, let's go in. Emmy and I found a winery today when you were at work. We bought a couple of bottles of the good stuff. Not that you'd know the difference. Save me a bottle and I'll be back after Emmy's on real milk and I'm drinking again."

I laughed and reached down to take Emmy out of her walker and carry her inside. When I opened the back door, I heard the front doorbell ring. Puzzled, I looked at Sara. I didn't know who was at the door, but it had been years since I had a day with both real work satisfaction and genuine friendship. Handing Emmy off to her mother, I went to answer the door, and when I opened it and saw Alex standing there, I hugged him like I hadn't seen him in years.

chapter 38

October 2006
Clarksville, Tennessee

The following night, Alex borrowed a truck from a friend and picked me up after work to go to the storage shed. I sat next to him in the truck, and we talked, an extension of our conversation from the night before, about our jobs, our families, Sara. We never talked about that kiss on my aunt's deck in July. It was as if, after that one night, we reverted to being friends again. It made me sad, but stuck. I wasn't sure what to say or do, so I followed his lead. Until I couldn't hold it in any longer.

When we pulled into the storage shed place, I looked at him next to me in the front seat of the truck. "Hey, I'm glad you're here and appreciate you bringing dinner last night and helping me now. I really didn't want to see what was in this storage shed alone." I turned and looked straight ahead, at the line of orange storage shed doors. "But are we going to talk about the Fourth or what? That kiss?"

He laughed. "I didn't know. I wasn't sure what you were thinking."

My eyes widened. "I thought I made that clear after the kiss. But, yeah, I mean, I didn't want to move here for you, but, um, I'm being honest here, you're a big part of why I'm here. I mean, I don't want to scare you away or anything, but—"

"I'm glad to hear you say that," he interrupted. Then he pulled over, next to the office, put the truck in park, and turned to me. I held my breath. He took my hand.

"Now what?" I asked him, turning to put my other hand on top of his.

"Well, we get the stuff in this storage shed." He kept his hand sandwiched between mine. "And we see where this goes?"

My heart raced, and I was sorry I hadn't worn a nicer sweatshirt. Or combed my hair. I didn't say a word.

"Um," he said nervously. "Unless you don't want to?"

"Oh, no, no, I mean. Yes, yes. Yes, I do."

He flashed that smile that made my body shiver. "So, why so quiet? That's not like you."

"I was thinking I should've combed my hair."

He lifted his hands away from mine and ran them both through my hair. "Nah, it's perfect." Then he leaned into me and kissed me softly. I dissolved into his mouth. When he released his lips, I met them again, needing more. His hands moved along my back, and I held him tight. Our lips coupled, our bodies snug.

Until a truck tried to get by in the alley and beeped.

I jumped. Alex laughed. "To be continued," he said, putting the truck in drive. "I'm glad you're here, Kel."

With my left hand on his thigh, I sighed. "Me too."

•   •   •

By Friday night, I'd unpacked the five boxes that Matt had left in the storage shed. I'd found my favorite coffee mug, a blender, empty photo frames, my framed diploma, and two lamps I'd bought in Georgia. The kitchen table and chairs that I'd finished at Fort Benning fit into the eating area in Amy's kitchen and made me think fondly of Tess. The only box I had left to unpack was one my aunt had packed for me. I wasn't sure what was in it.

Curious, I carefully opened the box to find, under layers of Bubble Wrap, the jar of jingle shells that sat on my dresser at her house. After placing them in the middle of the kitchen table, I put my hand over my heart, content.

Sara lifted the box up to take it out to the recycling bin in the garage. "Oh, wait," she said. "There's something still in here." She handed me the box.

I reached down, pulling out the Bubble Wrap, to find something solidly swaddled in newspaper. I ripped the paper off. I stood still.

It was the wall plaque. The one that had hung for decades in the McGowan's house in Dorchester before the decades it hung in my aunt's house in Seabury. It was the one we'd found at the top of her stairs after the hurricane.

May the roof above you never fall in,
And the friends beneath it never fall out.

The handwritten note from my grandmother to my aunt hadn't made it through the hurricane, but, in its place, my aunt had taped a note, with her penmanship:

Hang this and let your house become your home.

I couldn't talk. My hand went up, my fingers extended over my lips, cupping my face as if trying to keep my emotions from gushing out of my mouth. I dropped my hand and walked out to the garage, returning with the hammer and nails. I looked around and walked to the wall behind the kitchen table. I turned to Sara. "What do you think?"

She smiled. "Perfect."

chapter 39

October 2006

Clarksville, Tennessee

Saturday, Alex arrived with a box of pizza for lunch. Immediately noticing the plaque on the wall, he asked me, "Are you okay?"

I nodded, then reached up to get the paper plates out of the cabinet. "My aunt hid it in a box she sent with me."

"She's the best." He walked toward me and wrapped me in his arms. "You'll let me know if you're not okay, right?"

I nodded, kissing his neck before he released me. When he reached for a paper plate on the counter, I saw him glance at the key to the storage shed that I'd left there.

"I've got to mail that to Matt." I took a piece of pizza out of the box. "I need his address."

Sara walked into the room, heard me, and looked at Alex.

"What?" I asked nervously.

"You know how you told me you're afraid you'll run into him in the grocery store? Or the mall?" Sara asked as she spooned applesauce into Emmy's mouth.

"Well, not *afraid*, but, yeah, dreading it. It would be awkward, that's all."

Alex looked at me with his gentle blue eyes. "Why don't we all return this key to him? You can say goodbye to him, a proper goodbye, and you can move on and not worry about running into him and feeling awkward?"

I answered him very maturely: "No damn way."

Sara's eyes bulged as she looked from me to Alex, who was grinning.

Sara tried. "Wouldn't you want to see him when you were with me and Alex? Rather than alone?"

She was right, and I knew it, but I wasn't happy about it. I needed this behind me. Like a root canal. I put my pizza down. I'd lost my appetite. "Yeah, but I have to tell you. This was not on my preferred list of activities for today."

We piled into Sara's van, with Alex in the front seat directing Sara through the housing area on Fort Campbell, and me in the back seat playing with Emmy, trying to think of a reason to not get out of the van. I considered throwing up.

Sara pulled up in front of a duplex, where a man played catch in the front yard with a brown-haired boy. A woman stood in the open front door, holding a baby, watching them play.

"Shit," I said. "Sorry, Emmy."

Alex laughed and opened the door, walked up to Matt, gave him a bear hug, then said something to the boy and gave him a high five. He waved to the woman in the doorway.

Sara opened her door. "Come on," she said, turning to me. "Let's get this over with."

I climbed out of the van at the same time that Alex, thankfully, returned to walk with me toward Matt. "Hey," I said, knowing Matt well enough to realize he'd stand there uncomfortably for hours before saying anything. "Thanks for the storage shed. I'm done with it now." I handed him the key, and his eyes met mine, filled with contrition.

He said it again, "I'm so—"

I cut him off. "Enough! We're done with all the apologies. Really. Done."

I looked at the boy in the yard, and I looked at Eve standing at the front door, and I said quietly to Matt, the man I'd lived with for two years, "Introduce me to your son and your wife."

Alex looked at me, his chin high. Matt, his face flushed, waved his wife toward us. Eve, tall and slender, her blond hair pulled up in a ponytail, walked timidly out of the house, a baby in her arms. Her tired eyes looked at me, and a lump grew in my throat. She didn't mean any of this. This was not a woman who intentionally hurt people. She loved Matt. She'd loved him since elementary school. She wanted him to fulfill his dream and graduate from West Point.

Her eyes filled with tears, and she spoke, "I'm sor—" and I cut her off, too. I may have understood why she did what she did, but I was feeling spunky. "No, please. I get it. It's all good. Congratulations on the baby."

She nodded and told us the infant was born in early September. (I'd already done the math. They got pregnant six months after we'd split up, but I didn't bring that up.) Gabe, who was the spitting image of the childhood photos I'd seen of Matt, went to pre-K on post and they'd move back to Fort Benning for the career course the following summer. After that, I hoped they'd get orders to report to Greenland, but I didn't say that out loud.

Eve took their baby daughter back inside the house, and I said to Matt, "I'd tell you to say hello to your parents, but I don't think they were my biggest fans."

Matt looked at me sadly. "It wasn't that. My mother talked to Eve's mother when I was at ranger school. She never told me. She didn't know what the right thing to do was. That's why she was so distant from you."

I shrugged, not fully understanding, or forgiving, but tired of it all. "It's okay. Tell her it's okay. It all worked out."

He looked at me and then looked at Alex. "Is it okay? All working out?" He raised his eyebrows, curiously studying us. I sure as hell wasn't going to respond.

Alex spoke up. "Okay, you two haven't been together for what? Almost a year and a half, right?"

We both nodded. He continued, looking at Matt. "And you're married, with two kids, right?"

"Yep," Matt said.

"You'll always be my brother, right?"

Matt looked at him, nodding. "Yeah, man, you know that."

Alex continued speaking, looking at Matt. "You remember what I said that night on the beach? When you walked up with Ashleigh, and I handed Kelly off to you?" He looked at me. "No offense. It's not as if I actually handed you off, but I introduced you to him, remember?"

We both nodded. I remembered that moment on the beach so clearly. When Ashleigh pulled Alex away from me, I thought Alex looked upset, stuck, as he leaned into Matt and whispered something to him before he walked away. I always thought he looked at me apologetically as he left, or maybe I always just hoped that.

Matt rubbed his chin. "Yeah, I do. I remember."

"It's time." Alex put his arm around my waist.

Matt bounced lightly on his toes, tossing the ball back and forth in his hands. His eyes darted from me to Alex. "Wow. Okay."

Sara and Emmy were in the van waiting for us, and I told Matt we had to go. I waved goodbye to Gabe, who was picking the flowers in the garden near the front door. I hugged Matt, a fraternal hug, a forgiving hug, a goodbye hug, and I climbed back in the van next to Emmy and exhaled slowly as we drove away.

Alex leaned back, extending his hand between the seat to put on my knee. "How're you doing?"

"Super," I mumbled, putting my hand over his. I kept what I was thinking inside. *I really want to hate both of them for everything they put me through, but she's too nice, and he's so happy now, and in my gut, I know that this is where we all should be. But I still really want to hate them both. A little.*

He winked at me, smiling, and I wondered if he could read my mind. He turned to face the front, giving directions to Sara, leading us out of the neighborhood.

Emmy fell asleep in her car seat, and the three of us drove in silence back to the house. Once inside, Sara took Emmy into the bedroom to lay her down and I stood in the living room, staring at the painting on the wall. Eventually I'd put a couch under it, the same place it hung in my aunt's house. Alex came up beside me and we looked at the blue-green gulf, the bright blue sky.

"Miss it?" he asked softly.

"I know I will," I said honestly. "But it's nice to have a real job, real friends." I turned to him. "It's nice to be here with you."

He wrapped his arm around my shoulder and pulled me in close to his side.

I could have stayed glued to his body forever. "Hey," I asked. "What were you guys talking about? What did you say to him that night on the beach when you left me for the big blonde?"

Bringing me from his side to his front, he pulled me closer, and whispered in my ear. "I told him, 'Take care of her for a while. I'm coming back.'"

"Took you long enough." I wrapped my arms around his waist.

He smiled before his lips brushed mine. In his arms, I knew. I was where I should be. Finally, I had what I'd been looking for: a roof above my head. And friends beneath it.

acknowledgements

When I arrived at our first duty station, Fort Ord, California, in 1981, Alberta, the wife of my husband's commander, showed up at our apartment with a pan of lasagna — to welcome me to the 2-32 Buccaneer By God family. I was in the Army, too, and had no time to socialize, and then, five years later, when I came off active duty, I blinked, and we had four kids, my soldier husband was always gone, and I still had no time to socialize. Somehow, no matter how hard I tried to be an independent introvert, women like Alberta snuck into my busy life. Army spouses — Audrey, Vicky, Debbie, MA, Lynnette, Jessie, Mary, Ginny, Meg, Brender, Peggy, Arlane, Alice, Janet, Syndee, Susan, and a hundred others — marked me forever. I watched them sacrifice, with no pay, no accolades; I watched them deliver countless lasagnas. THE ROOF ABOVE was inspired by each of them. This story is dedicated to those who wait, single-parenting, with broken washing machines, sick kids, and overwhelming anxiety, all because they fell in love with someone who puts their life on the line daily to serve our nation selflessly.

Getting walloped by a Cat 5 hurricane is no fun, but if it happens, going through it with friends like "the survivors" sure helps. Thanks to the Wicks and Alves for being with us every step of the way. (If it happens again, I'm outta here.)

I'm so thankful for my readers: Erica, Maria, Mom D, Brother Paul, Pattie, Patty, Sha, Kim, Jos, MA, Kiley, and my roomies and fellow Army Veterans and spouses: Linda, Liz and Teesa. My WP classmate Mal: Your in-depth feedback made all the difference. WP authors Bob, Laurel and MyLinh: Your guidance meant the world. Thanks to my editor, Stephanie Finnegan, and to Reagan Rothe of Black Rose Writing for believing in this story.

The most important thing I've done on this earth is help raise our four adult children. Steve, Chris, Timmy, and Maria: You had front-row seats to the patriotism show, which meant not having Dad at birthdays, games, and graduations. Your resilience and lives of service make me proud. I'm grateful to each of you and love you more. Thanks to Allie and Mag, who serve by supporting and loving two of the best soldiers I know.

And, finally, all my thanks and love to my husband, Steve, who has been my biggest supporter since I met him in Old South Barracks in 1979. (He was wearing gym shorts.) Over the past decade, I whined repeatedly about giving up this wanna-be writer gig and opting instead to be a professional athlete. Without his encouragement, editing, and patience, this story would be half-written in my laptop and I'd be watching Ted Lasso on the treadmill.

about the author

Gail Dwyer graduated from the United States Military Academy at West Point in 1981, the second class with women. Her memoir, *Tough as Nails*, published in 2009, chronicles her experiences. Three days after her graduation, she married Steve, West Point Class of 1980. An Army spouse for decades, she is the very proud mom of an educator, a foster parent, and two Army officers. She respects and admires those who serve, and the spouses and family members who serve as well. Originally from Braintree, Massachusetts, she now lives in Mexico Beach, Florida, where she's the only old lady building sandcastles with her grandkids wearing a Red Sox hat.

note from gail dwyer

Word-of-mouth is crucial for any author to succeed. If you enjoyed *The Roof Above*, please leave a review online — anywhere you are able. Even if it's just a sentence or two. It would make all the difference and would be very much appreciated.

Thanks!
Gail Dwyer

We hope you enjoyed reading this title from:

www.blackrosewriting.com

Subscribe to our mailing list – *The Rosevine* – and receive **FREE** books, daily deals, and stay current with news about upcoming
releases and our hottest authors.
Scan the QR code below to sign up.

Already a subscriber? Please accept a sincere thank you for being a fan of
Black Rose Writing authors.

View other Black Rose Writing titles at
www.blackrosewriting.com/books and use promo code
PRINT to receive a **20% discount** when purchasing.